NINE DAYS

BY

TIMOTHY J. BLACKMAN

Bloomington, IN Milton Keynes, UK

authorHOUSE®

AuthorHouse™
1663 Liberty Drive, Suite 200
Bloomington, IN 47403
www.authorhouse.com
Phone: 1-800-839-8640

AuthorHouse™ UK Ltd.
500 Avebury Boulevard
Central Milton Keynes, MK9 2BE
www.authorhouse.co.uk
Phone: 08001974150

First published by AuthorHouse   2/1/2007

ISBN: 978-1-4259-9153-1 (sc)

Library of Congress Control Number: 2007900321

Printed in the United States of America
Bloomington, Indiana

This book is printed on acid-free paper.

To my Mom and Dad, who kept me safe for so many years.

TABLE OF CONTENTS

ONE

THE TEST

THE PACIFIC OCEAN WAS AN INCREDIBLE blue as it rolled by the starboard side elevator. This was Nathan's most favorite spot on the ship. It was peaceful and serene and he could watch the ocean and reflect on the events of the day. He had a letter from his wife and began to open it. He flipped it over and read the postmark. It said San Diego FPO, August 09, 2008. Only three days ago, not bad. This was his third such deployment on the aircraft carrier *USS Ronald Reagan,* CV-76. The first two were mainly training cruises with overnight stops in Tokyo and Okinawa. But this was the first deployment that he recalled that the *Reagan* may be going into harm's way. Nathan was just promoted a few months earlier and recently was offered a new assignment as the Air Wing Commander for the *Reagan.* He was responsible for the ships entire complement of deployed aircraft from helicopters to the newly deployed F-35 Joint Strike Fighters. The F-35, or "JSF's" as they were called by their pilots, were a favorite of Nathan's. The F-35's were a welcome replacement for the aging A-6E intruder and S-3B Vikings. The F-35's were a lot faster and even more stealthier. The F-35's were

1

newly deployed on the *Reagan* last year and this cruise would be the first time that the JSF's were sent into harm's way. Nathan thought about his life in the Navy, and the people he met along the way. He never once looked back when he joined the Navy. He had a vision that was, unseemingly to him, about to come true.

Commander Nathan "Bull" Buckman was a native of Austin, Texas. On his own since he was seventeen, he worked his way through college doing odd jobs and before college even tried a short "career" as a bull rider. After a month of riding he was thrown by a bull, which resulted in a broken leg. He had graduated with honors from the University of Texas at Austin with a degree in aeronautical engineering and was hired right out of college by Lockheed-Martin in Los Angeles to begin work on a top secret government project. After a few months of working for Lockheed-Martin he met a Navy Officer named Steven Alexander. Lieutenant Steven Alexander was the project manager for a top secret navy project at the San Diego Submarine Base. Steven was a Navy brat from Providence, Rhode Island who had followed in his dad's footsteps and joined the Navy. Nathan had met Steven at a security briefing at Lockheed-Martin, one of the many weekly briefings that Lockheed Martin was required to give as a result of the Navy contracts. In the next few weeks, after talking to Steven, Nathan was seriously considering a career in the Navy. Even since he was a kid he loved airplanes or for that matter anything that flew. The next time Nathan saw Steven he talked about his dream of becoming a Navy Pilot. "So Steven, how can I become a Navy pilot, I mean where do I start?" Nathan asked. "Well, for starters you can stop calling them Navy pilots, in the Navy there are referred to as Naval Aviators. I can give you an address where to go to get more information. You might as well know that a lot of people want to fly for the Navy. A lot of them don't make it. We only take the best" Steven explained. "I guess that's as it should be. What happens to the rest of them?" Nathan asked. "Well, the ones that don't make it go to Southwest or the Air Force" said Steven with a big grin. Nathan laughed, he could use some laughter right now. This was a big undertaking. It could change the rest of his life. "Nathan, since you have Monday off, go to the Human Resource Office on base. Get there after noontime and before they close at four. If you have any problems tell them that you were referred to them by me" Nathan thought for a minute, wondering what problems he might encounter. Did Steven think he couldn't handle himself? Nathan thanked him as he left to go to his office. Steven was fast becoming a friend. A friend who wanted him to succeed.

A normal day for Nathan Buckman was a quick breakfast and then off to the gym for a quick workout. He liked lifting weights. He was six feet two inches tall and weighed in at two hundred and eight pounds. He could easily bench-press his own weight, even on a bad day. A good one hour work out and then a shower and he was on his way to the base. Pulling up to the gate, a Navy guard asked his destination. "I need to go to the Human Resource office?" Nathan explained. "Very well sir, take your first right here and they will process you as a visitor and give you further directions" the guard explained. "Thank you" said Nathan as he pulled away.

Nathan pulled up to the small building to the right, which served as a welcoming center. After a few forms and ID checks Nathan was given a pass and directed to the Human Resource office. Nathan walked in and at the information desk was directed down the hall to an office marked "Human Resources". Nathan entered to find four enlisted personnel and a Navy Officer, an Ensign. The Ensign was on the phone and the other personnel were all busily involved in typing or some other type of paper shuffling. After a second or two of being unnoticed Nathan spoke. "Excuse me ma'am, I ..." Nathan was cut off by the person at the desk. "I'll be with you in just a second, sir". Nathan paused for a second. After all they were busy. After a few more minutes Nathan was becoming frustrated with waiting. He thought he'd try again. "Excuse me ma'am, I like to apply for Officer Training School" Nathan said. "OK sir, I'll need your ID, your Social Security card and any copies of diplomas, do you have that" asked the Seaman from behind the desk without looking up. "Yes ma'am, I do and I also have a resume with...". Again, the Seaman cut him off. "No, we don't need your resume right now. Just the items I asked for" the Seaman replied. Nathan's patients were wearing thin. He didn't want to step on any toes. This was frustrating. If he could only... No, he had to do this on his own merits. "Do you have the documents I asked for, Sir? If you don't have the documents now you can come back tomorrow when..." This time Nathan interrupted the Seaman. "Ma'am, I was sent here by Lieutenant Alexander and he said I should include my resume, I work for Lockheed Martin" Nathan announced. Nathan noticed the room went silent. The papers stopped shuffling, the Seaman stopped typing and the Ensign on the phone stopped talking. If that was not bad enough all eyes were now on Nathan. The Ensign on the phone spoke and said "Sir, I have a situation here, may I call you back? The Ensign hung up the phone and approached the front desk. "Hello Sir, my name is Ensign Brown and I'm the Officer-in-Charge, may I help you?" asked the Ensign. "Yes, I was sent here by Lieutenant Alexander and he told me to include my resume with this request" explained Nathan. "OK, you want to apply for OTS?" asked the Ensign. "Yes Sir, I do" said Nathan. "And you were referred to us by Lieutenant Alexander? " asked the Ensign. "Yes Sir, I was" said Nathan. "And how do you know Lieutenant Alexander?" asked the Ensign. Nathan explained that he works for Lockheed-Martin Space Systems and met Lieutenant Alexander during a security briefing about two months ago. "He is a project manager for a program I am not at liberty to discuss" said Nathan. "Very well, Mr. ... Buckman, the Ensign said looking down at the resume, we can continue this in my office, if you could come around the desk, I can help expedite your request. Can I get you something to drink? A water or cola?" asked the Ensign. "A water would be fine" Nathan said. The Ensign looked at a female Seaman First Class which had been typing at her desk. She responded by standing and saying " Aye, aye, Sir". The female typist went to an adjacent room while Nathan was led to the Ensign's office. "You have a very impressive resume" remarked the Ensign. "and it doesn't hurt to have a Top Secret government clearance either" the Ensign added. The female Seaman returned with a bottled water and set it down on a napkin on the desk in front of Nathan. She remained as if waiting for a tip. "That will be all, return to your duties" said the Ensign. "I see no problem with anything here, if you could just fill out the forms and sign them I can forward them to my Commander" the Ensign explained. The Ensign left the room and went to talk with the enlisted personnel in the front room and then made another phone call. Nathan filled out the forms carefully and signed them. The Ensign returned to the office a short time later. "So how are we doing?" asked the Ensign. " I think I'm done" replied Nathan. "Very good" replied the Ensign, "I have a meeting with my Commander at 3:00 p.m. so I'll walk your application over to him" added the Ensign. "I appreciate everything you have done" said Nathan. "Not at all, that's what we're here for, I apologize for my staff, sometimes we get real busy here" replied the Ensign. "No need to apologize, I understand" replied Nathan. The Ensign told Nathan that a class starts in two weeks and if he is accepted he will be contacted by mail. Nathan thanked the Ensign and walked to the front room where he entered. "Good luck to you, Sir" replied the female Seaman First Class that brought Nathan the water. "Thank you, have a good day" replied Nathan as he walked out past her desk. She was petite and very pretty and had her blonde hair done up on top of her head. Nathan thought for a second what she looked like with it down. Well, It was out of his hands now. He did his best. If he gets an appointment to OTS then it was to be. If not, then he still has a promising career ahead of him with Lockheed Martin. And with what they pay him annually and yearly bonuses he can afford to take private flight lessons. As he walked to his car he thought his dream of flight might someday become a reality.

It was four days since Nathan saw Steven Alexander. Where the hell was he. He hadn't seen him at work the past few days. He wanted to tell him how things went on Monday at the HR office. He made his usual drive home from work, past the school and into the apartment complex where he lived. Half way to his door he realized he forgot to get his mail so he walked back to the mail center to pick it up. This was a real nice complex. They put a lot of thought into the layout. Front and back entrances to the parking lots with a security camera at each entrance. There were about seven other people here from Lockheed Martin, on different shifts and schedules. No one really got to know each other though. Just as well, Nathan thought. He got his mail and returned to his door all the while shuffling through the letters and magazines. Wow, Air & Space came early, and Maxim too. The electric bill, cable bill and a large envelope from the Department of the Navy. Nathan stopped in front of his door. Well, this is it, Nathan thought. Either I go or don't go. Nathan feared that contact of any kind this soon meant a rejection letter. It had only been four days. Nathan unlocked the door and entered his apartment. Putting the magazines on the counter he headed for the sofa and sat down with the bills and the Navy letter. He tossed the bills on the sofa as he opened the Navy letter and began reading it. "Oh, my God, they want me!" Nathan exclaimed.

Nathan could not believe it so he read it again. Nathan looked at the envelope, it had yesterdays postmark date on it. The other papers with the letter said he had to report to the processing station not later than June 1st. He didn't have a lot of time. He was involved in a very big project at Lockheed-Martin. They weren't going to like this. Nathan called his friend, Steven. He got the answering machine, left a message and hung up. He had to tell someone. Nathan called for a pizza, then showered and ate and walked down to corner pub. Not really a drinker, Nathan just wanted to ease his mind and have a beer. Nathan walked in and over to the bar. The bar tender met him with a smile and asked his poison. Nathan ordered a Corona with a lime and sat down at the bar. The bar tender brought the beer and set it down on the bar in front of Nathan. Nathan payed him and told him to keep the change. The bar was empty this time of day except for the regulars. The bar tender initiated a conversation. "Where ya from young fella"the bartender asked. "I'm originally from Austin, Texas, Sir" Nathan said. The bar tender erupted in laughter " I knew you weren't from around here, not many people call me Sir" the bar tender replied. "My name is Jake Gibson. My friends call me Big Jake. This is my bar and has been for the past thirty years" the bar tender added. Nathan didn't have to think of why they called him *Big* Jake. Jake pretty much filled out the rest of the area behind the bar. "I'm originally from El Paso, son, Its nice to meet another Texan" Jake said. "So what do you do here?" asked Jake. "I work at the Lockheed-Martin plant" Nathan explained. "Really, my grandson works there too. John Price, ya know him?" Jake asked Nathan. "No, I haven't heard of him, it's a real big place" Nathan replied. "He gots a job in the custodial department, really good with his hands, can fix anything. How about you, you good with your hands?" Jake said proudly. Nathan probably saw Jake's grandson at some point there but was sure he didn't know him. "Yeah, I guess I'm good with my

7

hands" Nathan replied taking a drink of his beer. Jake reached down and brought another Corona up from the tub, quickly opened it and put a lime on top. " No, that's okay, I need to go anyway" Nathan replied. "Nonsense, this ones on the house, young fella" Jake shouted. Well, it was early, only eight o'clock, first test isn't until 10 a.m. tomorrow. What the hell. Nathan continued talking to Jake in between customers. Nathan had his ear when he talked about the OTS appointment. It was obvious Jake was envious and hung on every word. "Damn, I wish the grandson would get up off his ass and do something worthwhile. I mean he's only nineteen, but hell, there's a lot of things he could do" explained Jake.

Nathan awoke to his alarm at six the next morning. He felt fine except for a little dry mouth. He didn't remember how many Corona's he had the night before. Worse, he didn't remember when he left and what time he got home. He decided against going to the gym and just settled on a good shower and a hot breakfast. He wanted to have his wits about him for the mornings test. The test. Had he mentioned anything about the test the previous night? He hoped not. A lot of what he did was classified. If he inadvertently said anything to anyone, not only would he lose his job but he could end up in federal prison for a very long time. He remembered watching the news during the Gulf War, while he was in college. He saw how the Iraqi Scud missiles were launched and rained down on civilians in Saudi Arabia and Israel. The media made the most of the air-time showing successful intercepts by US Patriot Missile Batteries and showing some of the near misses by the Scuds. The military sort of downplayed the action but even the top brass was concerned that even one Scud with a biological or nuclear warhead would have disastrous consequences for the region.

During his junior year at college Nathan discovered a program that the defense contractor, Lockheed-Martin Space Systems, was involved in. It proposed an area defense weapon based on laser light that would be able to track and destroy theater ballistic missiles. Nathan believed that it could be developed into a global system and spent his last year in college researching and doing experiments. He so believed in his work that he passed his findings on to Lockheed-Martin Space Systems. As the world approached the twenty-first century it was clear to Nathan that third world countries would develop ballistic missiles and nuclear weapon programs, not just for defense but for political reasons also.

Nathan walked into Lockheed-Martin at 8:35 a.m. and was about to walk to his office by the lab when Steven Alexander met him at the corner. "Hey Steven, where the hell have you been?" Nathan asked. " I had to go to Washington for a few days and give some briefings. You know the brass, they want to see where the money goes" Steven replied. Nathan noticed the new bright gold oakleaf's on Steven's uniform, signifying he was now a Lieutenant Commander. "I see they must have liked your briefing" Nathan said. Not following him, Steven looked at him puzzled. "you received a promotion, congratulations" Nathan added. "Oh, thanks. I guess I was due for one. I hear congratulations are due for you also, you have an appointment to OTS" Steven said. Nathan wondered how Steven knew so quickly. "How did you find out? I mean, I didn't tell anyone" Nathan said. "I know the Ensign at the HR office. He lives down the street from me. He told me this morning. We occasionally hook up when we jog in the morning" Steven explained. Nathan acknowledged his explanation. Nathan thought a few seconds then got a bad feeling and asked Steven what was on his mind. "Steven, I want you to be straight with me, did you have anything to do with my getting an appointment to OTS?" Nathan asked. Steven stopped and looked directly at Nathan. "Nathan, I had nothing to do with your getting the appointment. You got the appointment on your own merits. I was told you had a tremendous background and would be an invaluable asset to the Navy" Steven replied. Nathan felt better. "Nathan, I want to get together this weekend and give you sort of a going away party. I have some friends I'd like you to meet also" Steven said. Nathan agreed and told Steven that Saturday would be a good day as Friday was going to be a late day. Steven told him he would have someone pick him up Saturday afternoon. Nathan thanked him and told him he would see him then.

Nathan walked into the lab with his jacket and briefcase and set it down on the technician's desk. Nathan worked with five technicians who he was in charge of. The lead technician came over and said good morning. "Good morning, Jack" said Nathan. Everyone that he worked with was laid back but was very professional. "Nathan, can I get you some coffee?" asked Jack. Nathan thought he could use some. "Yes, thank you, that would be great. No sugar" Nathan replied. Jack Nelson was the lead technician for the Lockheed-Martin project and was just as capable as Nathan and in some areas had more experience. The other technicians were busy preparing the test and were very anxious to see the fruits of their labor. Two months of computer simulation work were accomplished prior to this day just for a test that will last less than thirty seconds. Nathan walked around the lab taking notes and talking to the other technicians. He was proud to work with such a competent crew. After an hour or so all things were ready to go. Everything was set and the crew evacuated the lab area and went to the control room, which was fifteen feet above the lab. Nathan was satisfied everything was ready and began the checklist. "All personnel to their stations. All stations report status" Nathan replied into his microphone. The technician in charge of each of the stations replied "All systems go". Nathan gave the order to prepare the lab. The lab was sealed and the vacuum pumps started sucking air from the lab to achieve an atmosphere equivalent to 60,000 feet. After about ten minutes the pumps were put on automatic and only started if needed to maintain the conditions. Nathan observed the lab below through the viewing area. A pressurized aluminum cylinder was mounted on an oval "train track" forty-five feet by eighteen feet. The cylinder was fixed in a vertical position on a carriage that went around the track at a pre-determined speed. To the left of the track, below the control room were the two lasers. The first one was a Track Illuminator Laser (TILL) which would be fired and would spot and track the target, which in this case would be the pressurized aluminum cylinder. The second laser was a High Energy Laser (HEL) that would be fired at the target. The laser, hopefully, would dwell on the target, which in this case simulated a ballistic missile in flight. The laser would weaken the missiles pressurized oxidizer or propellant tank, which in theory, would rupture and destroy the weapon.

Nathan checked his watch. The test was scheduled to start at 10:00 o'clock. Everything was set except for a few Lockheed Martin and Government VIP's. The rear door to the control room opened and in walked three civilians and two military officers. Nathan recognized one civilian, the Vice President of Operations for Lockheed Martin. The other military officers, one Navy Admiral and one Air Force General stood at the viewing area to the right of the control consoles. The VP nodded to Nathan and said "you may proceed when ready". Nathan acknowledged and then spoke into his microphone. "All cameras on and rolling" Nathan said. "Copy, cameras rolling and normal" the technician responsible for video recording acknowledged. Nathan continued "Start test, automatic sequence start" Nathan ordered. The senior technician at the console flipped up the safety switch and hit a button on the control panel sending a signal to the "train track". At the same time with a few clicks of the mouse he started the computer program that controls the test. "All systems start, all systems appear normal" the senior technician announced. Nathan moved slightly to view the test through the safety glass. A six-inch thick piece of safety glass designed to contain fire and any errant projectiles. The target on the "train track" moved at an ever-increasing speed controlled by the computer. After about a minute Nathan hear the senior technician announce "TILL energized, all systems normal". This part of the test was critical. The TILL must follow and track the cylinder around the "train track" for a minimum of fifteen seconds before the HEL is engaged. "TILL track good, HEL engaged" the technician announced. Nathan observed a small white dot of light appear on the aluminum cylinder. "Target temperature at 617 Fahrenheit and increasing" said the technician at the console. "Target temperature at 1234 Fahrenheit and increasing" the technician announced again. Won't be long now, Nathan thought, things are heating up. A mere seconds later the cylinder that was pressurized to 1745 PSI erupted and blew apart with a deafening roar. A cloud of dust and aluminum particles bounced around the lab and up to the control room, while the VIP's appeared to be startled. "Target destroyed, all systems power down. Control room normal. Lab pressurizing to normal. Test concluded at 10:05.30" the technician at the control panel announced. The VP looked at Nathan and nodded as he and the Officers both broke into applause. The VP and Officers shook hands with all the technician and thanked them for their work before they left. The VP put his hand on Nathan's shoulder as he was leaving and told him to come to his office at 3:00 this afternoon, before he left for the day. Nathan acknowledged the invitation. The test was a complete success, but the program had a long way to go. He didn't look forward to telling the VP that he was leaving. At least he could give them a good two weeks notice.

Nathan was summoned to the lab below. When he arrived the technicians were taking post-test digital shots of the target for the archives. The remaining one-third of the target had an eight to ten inch long gash about four inches wide near where the lasing point was. The rest of the target was aluminum dust and pieces no bigger than a coke can. It was clear the Laser had done its job and the inherent design of the simulated missile had destroyed itself from within. It was also clear that someday this was to become a formidable weapon.

Nathan had a great day. He was just finishing the test report of the mornings activities when the phone rang. He answered it to find the VP's secretary. She was calling to confirm his appointment with the VP at three o'clock. Nathan checked his watch, saw it was 2:47 p.m. and told her that he would be there shortly. He put some papers in his brief case, locked it and went to his lavatory to wash up. Returning, he grabbed his brief case and jacket, set the alarm and locked his office door behind him. On the way to the VP's office he wondered how he would break it to him. He arrived at the office door, took a deep breath and went in. The secretary was sitting at a large mahogany desk with a black marble top. She stood and walked over to Nathan and introduced herself as Jill Jacobs, the Vice President's personal assistant. She asked if he would like a drink. Nathan politely declined as she escorted him to the VP's office. Nathan followed her down the hall. She was attractive, maybe in her late twenties. She wore her dark hair up on her head in a professional manner and was dressed in a nice floral print blouse with black skirt that showed off her shapely, tanned legs. She seemed to be very athletic and was very tall, even without her high heels.

Nathan could hear voices mixed with laughter coming down the hall. He also detected the odor of cigars. The sound of a party. I guess they had the right to celebrate. Nathan rounded the door and saw the VP sitting behind his desk with six others in the room. The two military Officers that were in the control room earlier, three women he did not know and Lieutenant Commander Steven Alexander. The VP saw Nathan and immediately jumped up and came around the desk, holding his drink. "Nathan, how are ya doing? Jill, get this boy a drink" the VP said, stumbling back to his chair. It was obvious to Nathan the VP was celebrating long before he got there. The VP continued his conversation with the two naval officers as Jill came over and took Nathan by the arm and led him to the counter, which doubled as a bar. "I can make you something you might like, not too powerful and kinda sweet, like me" she giggled. As she made him the drink she kept glancing at him and smiling. She handed him the drink and came close to him and whispered in his ear "If there is anything else I can do, don't hesitate to ask" she said before she walked away and out of the room. Steven came up to Nathan after she left. "It's okay, take a deep breath. She has this uncanny ability to take men's breath away" Steven laughed. "I'd like to introduce some people to you" Steven added. Steven started with the women since the men were involved in a huge fishing story. The women were talking together quietly and sipping champagne in the lounge area of the office. They all looked fantastic, each wearing a different cocktail dress. Steven introduced the women one at a time, all which seemed to be there at Steven's request. One, who seemed to have a sincere interest in Steven, was Amy. The others were friends of hers, Emily and Arwyn. Amy was about five-foot six with long shimmering red hair. She seemed the quieter of the three so Nathan sat with Amy while Emily stood up and handed Steven her empty champagne glass. Meanwhile, Arwyn excused herself and went to listen to the boys for a while. Nathan and Amy discussed everything from taxes to politics. Amy clearly was a woman with a good head for business. At some time later Nathan noticed Steven was filling the drink of the Admiral at the counter. As hard as it was to do, he excused himself from Amy and, taking her empty champagne glass, went to the bar. "So who is the naval officer?" Nathan asked Steven. "That is Rear Admiral Jack Grayson, he's an advisor to the Joint Chiefs in Washington. I can't tell you how proud he is of what you have done" Steven replied. "Amy seems like a real nice girl. Are you two together?" Nathan said "Well, I guess we are. I met her about six months ago on the beach in St. Petersburg. I was at Kings Bay on rotation and a buddy of mine convinced me to go there since it was well into spring break. We've been together ever since. She's out here with her friends visiting her sister. They are all staying with me and have to go back next week" explained Steven. "That's good, I'm glad you met someone, you look like a great couple" replied Nathan. "Thanks, I'm really not into long distance relationships, but she is one in a million and I knew I couldn't let her get away. I'm trying to get her to move here. She is looking for work while she is out here, excuse me Nathan" said Steven stepping away to deliver drinks.

Steven went to deliver Amy and Emily their drinks and then took the Admiral's his. He remained a while talking then returned to the counter where Nathan was. Nathan observed that the Admiral, the VP and Arwyn must have been engaged in a lively topic. Arwyn was sitting on the front of the VP's desk and showing a lot of leg in the process. Her short cocktail dress left little to the imagination and the Admiral seemed to be enjoying every minute of it. "Nathan, since I was going to have your party tomorrow, why don't you come out and have dinner with the girls and I. Since you'll be at the house already I don't have to get someone to pick you up. What do you say, I have plenty of room?" Steven said. "Well, I'd really like to but I'm not sure how my decision to leave here will go over" Nathan said quietly. "I'm sure I'll have to complete some papers on where I want the project to go in the next few years and how to bring the next engineer up to speed" Nathan added. "Well okay, you do what you think is right, but come Saturday I'll have someone pick you up around five in the afternoon" said Steven.

Nathan was looking forward to the party. He wasn't however looking forward to telling the VP that he had to leave the company. Nathan talked with the girls for sometime before excusing himself to the lavatory. When he returned to the VP's office he found it pretty much empty except for the Admiral, the VP and Jill, the VP's personal assistant. Jill was busy tiding up the counter and storing all the liquor bottles. She locked all the cabinets and asked the VP if there was anything else he needed this afternoon. He said no and told her to have a great weekend. She walked out of the room but not before giving Nathan a wink as she walked by. "Nathan, come on over here and sit down" replied the VP. Nathan did so and sat in one of the plush leather chairs in front of the VP's desk. The Admiral extended his hand to Nathan. "Hi son, my name is Jack Grayson. You have done some fine work here. You have a brilliant mind" the Admiral said. "Thank you Admiral, I appreciate that" Nathan replied. "Please son, don't call me Admiral, you a civilian for Christ sake! Call me Jack" the Admiral said laughing as he took a drink of scotch. "Nathan, you seem to have something on your mind, is it about the test?" the VP asked inquisitively. Nathan got a little embarrassed. Was it showing, his reluctance to tell him he was leaving. Nathan started "Sir, nothing is wrong with the test or the program. I'm sure everything will work as we have designed it" Nathan explained. The Admiral shifted in his chair and brought his full attention to Nathan. "Sir, maybe we should continue this another time" Nathan explained.

"Nonsense Nathan, the Admiral has five clearances above you and I, say what you're gonna say" The VP shot back angrily. Nathan started again. "Sir, it's no reflection on the company or anyone but I have recently applied and been accepted to Officer Candidate School for the US Navy. I have two weeks to report to Pensacola" The VP looked shocked and then relieved that it wasn't a problem with the program. The Admiral started laughing. "Well Jim, I guess we took another one from you!" Admiral Grayson said while taking another drink of Scotch. The VP looked at Nathan "Not so fast Nathan, this is critical time in the program" the VP replied. Before Nathan could reply the Admiral started in on the VP. "Jim, that a bunch of bullshit and you know it. You said yourself that the program is about ten or so years from being operational. We'll just go looking for another engineer. We just got very lucky with Nathan here" The Admiral said. Nathan believed that the Admiral was on his side. "Sir, I could prepare an outline in the next week and I'm sure it would help my successor ease into the program. My staff is also up on every aspect of the program. They would be an invaluable asset to the new engineer" Nathan explained. The VP looked as if he was going to say something but was silent. The Admiral asked Nathan what he wanted to do in the Navy. "I'd like to train to become a naval aviator and be assigned to carrier duty, sir" Nathan explained. "I think that's great son. Did you both know that the Gulf War produced some great combat aces. Those boys will become a great asset to us in years to come, not only for their experience but the training they will impart to the next generation of Aviators. That's you son, you're the future of American naval aviation, by God good luck to you, welcome aboard" the Admiral said extending his arm and shaking Nathan's hand. Nathan thanked the Admiral for his confidence. The VP looked at Nathan and spoke. "Nathan, we are surely going to miss you around here. I appreciate the work you have done for the company and the nation but I realize this is your dream. I wish you the best of luck. The paper you will write will be greatly appreciated. I'd like to go over it with you before you leave however" The VP said. "Good. Well that's settled. Jim, lets get the hell out of here and get some dinner. Nathan's got a paper to write and I'm starved. Nathan, I guess the next time you see me you *will* be calling me Admiral" the Admiral said standing up and shaking Nathan's hand. "Yes Sir, I will. Thank you" Nathan replied. "Nathan, we'll get together next week for lunch and discuss how the transition will go. In the meantime, have a great weekend" said the VP.

Nathan said goodbye to both the VP and the Admiral and left down the hall to the exit door. He grabbed his briefcase in the outer office and proceeded out the door to the elevator. He thought that it went very well, thanks to the Admiral. As he walked to the parking lot he was thinking what to put in his report next week. He walked past several cars on the way to his, not paying attention to any particular thing. A car attempted to start behind him but was having particular trouble. It tried again and seemed to die. Nathan stopped and made his way back to the car. The car door opened and a beautiful woman with long dark hair stepped out of the drivers seat. "Ma'am can I help you?" asked Nathan. She turned around and Nathan noticed her right away as Jill, the VP's personal assistant. "I was wondering if I would be rescued or not" Jill said coyly. She had her hair undone and loose around her shoulders with her unbuttoned blouse exposing just the right amount of cleavage. "This happens to me every once in while" she began. "I guess I should have taken my other car and got this one fixed. Would you be a dear and give me a ride home" she said with the greenest eyes he had ever seen. Nathan told her he would. She thanked him as she gathered her bag and locked the door. She had him stop at the guard gate, gave them the keys and told the guard that someone would be there to tow it tomorrow. Nathan left the gate and proceeded north. Nathan started with the usual small talk but then the conversation quickly proceeded to more personal things. She was married and divorced before she was twenty-two. She had no children. She liked being pampered. What woman didn't, Nathan thought. She was a very attractive young woman. Nathan figured she knew what to say and when to say it to get men to do what she wanted. She seemed a little older but that didn't matter to Nathan. Her perfume was very intoxicating, but not overpowering. Nathan thought he was doing her a favor giving her a lift but then remembered her innocent comment in the VP's office. Or maybe it wasn't innocent. He would just play this one out. She told him where to turn and he pulled into a long driveway alongside an older model Mustang. "Oh honey, pull over in front of the Mustang so I can get out" Jill said. Nathan looked at his watch, it was six -thirty. If things didn't work out here he would opt for a burger on the way home. "Thank you so much for giving me a ride home" she said leaning over to Nathan. She leaned forward some more as if asking for a kiss. Nathan finally committed himself and gave her a kiss. Not on the cheek but square on the lips. "Your very welcome, Jill" Nathan said as her kissed her. "That's the first time you called me Jill" she replied smiling. "Are you hungry, I can call for some Chinese food?" Jill asked, looking lovely. "Chinese food would be great" said Nathan. They both exited the car and walked up the back steps and into her house. She undid the alarm and threw her bag on the table. She kissed Nathan again asked what he would like to eat. "Anything really, why don't you surprise me?" Nathan replied. Jill excused herself to make a phone call for the food and use the lavatory in her bedroom. She told Nathan to make himself at home so he walked around a bit. It was a nice house with a big kitchen, which was spotless. Nathan figured either she was a clean freak or didn't really cook. Both were fine in his book. The living area overlooked the patio area through sliding glass doors and had a small pool with a separate Jacuzzi. He heard the sliding glass door behind him open. Jill walked out wearing a red silk kimono. "The food will be here in about forty-five minutes" she said "go ahead, I saw you eyeing the Jacuzzi" she giggled. "I'm gonna shower and wash my hair first, then I'll join you. Wine is in the refrigerator, so help yourself" Jill added. Don't mind if I do, thought Nathan. Walking into the kitchen he found the wine and two glasses. Nathan poured two glasses of Merlot and proceeded to the patio. He sat down at the patio table, put a glass of wine on the table and waited for Jill. This was nice. It was a beautiful night with a slight breeze. Nathan sipped his wine and thought about where the Navy might take him. He was really looking forward to flying for the Navy. A lot of things were happening now. New technologies and weapon systems were appearing which, until now, only seemed like science fiction. He hoped someday that the technology being developed might somehow change the world for the better.

TWO

SURPRISES

NATHAN WAS THINKING ABOUT HIS LETTER from home when he saw an Ensign come running towards his direction. He forgot his name but everyone secretly called him "Ensign Skippy". He was a young-looking kid from Oklahoma, just out of school and seemed to want to impress everyone. He joined the Navy because as he put it "he wanted to be where the action was". Nathan put away his letter as the Ensign approached. "Commander... The Captain ...wishes you to join him...in CIC as soon as possible" he said, trying to catch his breath. "Very well, return to your duties" Nathan said as he began the long trip towards CIC. The Combat Information Center, or CIC as it was called, was the heart of the ship. From here all the decisions about the ships operations were made. As Nathan walked to CIC it seemed that things were happening at a faster pace than normal. Nathan arrived at the door to CIC, which was guarded by two Marines. They both came to attention as Nathan walked toward them. "As you were" Nathan said as he slid his card in the card reader. The door beeped loudly a few times, then Nathan opened the door and entered. The Captain looked up while he was at the plot table and asking questions to his staff. Captain Bruce Winters was an Annapolis graduate with many deployments under his belt. He went on active duty in 1989 and had countless tours of duty in the Med and Persian Gulf. He knew Carriers and everything about them. He was a great leader and very fair, but once he made a decision you better jump and jump real high. The *Reagan* left San Diego six days ago and after stopping at Pearl Harbor for provisions and replacements, started out again for the Sea of Japan. Nathan loved the Orient. The culture and the people. It was likely though he wouldn't get to experience any of that on this deployment.

Nathan made his way to the operations table next to Captain Winters. "Sorry to disturb you, Commander, but this is of great importance. I have received a message that a Chinese "Oscar" class submarine has been located by one of our attack subs in the Sea of Japan" Captain Winters said with disgust. "I'd like you to add addition ASW patrols when we get in the operations area" The Captain ordered. "Very, well sir. I'll see to it personally" Nathan replied. This was not shaping up to be a pleasant deployment. Nathan remembered the "Oscar" class submarines from an article in "Proceedings" years ago. They were built by the Soviets during the Cold War and were designed for attacking US Carrier Strike Groups, specifically US aircraft carriers. At the end of the Cold War the cash-strapped Russian's sold some of them to the highest bidder. Naturally, some found their way to the Chinese Navy. They were considered large cruise missile carriers by the Russian's . Carrying no less than twenty-four SS-N-19 anti-ship cruise missiles, the missiles were about thirty-four feet long and had a range of about three hundred and forty miles. They could travel that distance in about ten minutes. The "Oscars" could launch the missiles in a bearing-only mode towards Carrier Strike Groups. Two hits on the *Reagan* by these missiles would turn the carrier into a floating parking lot and five hits may very well sink her. This was considering all the missiles had conventional warheads. One missile with a nuclear warhead would sink the *Reagan*.

Nathan and the other senior officers on the *Reagan* had been briefed at Pearl before they left. They were told that this would probably be their most important deployment of their career. Several Admiral's and civilian Defense Intelligence Agency workers briefed a group of twenty-five naval officers from the *Reagan* Strike Group. Nathan recalled what the senior civilian, who started the briefing, had said. "Gentleman, for many years since the late 1980's North Korea has been hell bent on becoming a nuclear power. Several attempts by spies to infiltrate the South Korean peninsula have been discovered. Some of the incidents have been reported by the media but the majority had been down played by the South Korean government as North Korean citizens trying to escape the tyranny of the North Korean dictator. The facts are however that some were defectors which were in the North Korean military and this led to them being detained by the South Korean government, only to be turned over to our own intelligence agencies. These defectors gave invaluable information to the US on nuclear power plants and missile sites throughout North Korea. According to one man, Chi Ju Yung, who defected from his post as a Colonel in the North Korean Army, told the US CIA and DIA that quote, "North Korea is building nuclear plants, missiles and nuclear explosive devices on an unprecedented scale", unquote. The president, Kim Lu Doc, has been obsessed with continuing his fathers work and has strived to accomplish it even at the expense of his countries health, safety and welfare. Another man, known only as "Chin Lo" had been a former engineer in the Military Construction Bureau of the North Korean Army. He has to date given us the most detailed information on the locations of nuclear weapons plants, missile facilities and the types of missiles actually deployed than any other person in North Korea. This information was confirmed not only by other US intelligence agencies but by satellite and covert Special Forces that were deployed in the area concerned" explained the DIA civilian.

Nathan knew of the defectors from TV. He watched the World News Network (WNN) frequently. He waited to hear what came next. An Admiral stood up and addressed the Officers for the rest of the briefing. "Gentleman, we are all Navy Officers and have sworn to obey the orders of those appointed above us. Let me read your orders from your President. The USS *Ronald Reagan,* it Officers and crew are hereby ordered to set sail for the Sea of Japan. The *Reagan* is to remain on station at longitude 39 - 01 N, Latitude 130 - 54 E. The Officers and crew of the *Reagan* are to protect the interests of the United States and their Allies with whatever resources are available to them. No action is to be taken against an adversary unless ordered by Higher Command Authority or it has been deemed an immediate threat to either the United States and/or one of it's Allies. President, Commander in Chief, Ronald L. Jackson. Gentleman, I don't have to remind you that this is a potentially volatile situation you will be sailing into. Every last man is expected to perform above and beyond the call of duty. This deployment may end in grave consequences for the rest of world. That is not my wish however. I expect to see everyone of you back here at the end of this deployment, and that is an order" the Admiral concluded.

From the side of the room another Officer announced "Attention on Deck". At once all Officers came to attention around the table. A door at the rear of the room opened and an Admiral followed by a Rear Admiral entered the room and made their way to the front of the conference room. The Admiral looked around. After being satisfied he said "Gentleman, please be seated". All the Officers took their seats. Nathan looked at the Admiral. He was an older man, hardened with age and the burden of command but Nathan still recognized him.

Admiral Jack Grayson, no longer an advisor to the Joint Chiefs of Staff, He *was* the Chairman of the Joint Chiefs. And as for the Rear Admiral, well, Nathan just knew him as Steven Alexander. Steven stood next to and behind Admiral Grayson. The Admiral started by saying "Gentleman, as you now know this deployment will be by far the most important in your career. The situation between North Korea, the United States and Japan have escalated to the point that military action seems inevitable. The United States and the United Nations have for years tried to negotiate with North Korea to stop producing nuclear weapons and ballistic missiles. These talks have recently failed however, with the latest test of a ballistic missile. The test missile was launched five days ago from an underground facility in the Kangwon province and impacted in the Pacific Ocean about 1000 nautical miles east of Tokyo, Japan. The North Korean government publicized the test prior to the launch so as not to start a general panic. The trajectory of the missile took it over the mainland of Japan. North Korea now has the capability, with the deployment of this latest ballistic missile, the Taepo-Dong 3, to reach every city in North America. At this time intelligence suggests that North Korea has between twenty to thirty missiles of this type and is estimated to have between seventy to eighty nuclear warheads in the twenty to fifty kiloton range. Some estimates show them to have as many as one hundred operational nuclear warheads" the Admiral paused to look around the table of Officers and to clear his throat. "I 'm sure to many of you that this is not good news. Our job is to see that no missiles leave the air space of North Korea. For the remainder of the briefing I will turn it over to Rear Admiral Alexander who is designated as the Strike Group Commander for this deployment" the Admiral explained. This was news to Nathan. He hadn't worked side by side with Steven in about three years. It would be good to work together again.

25

"Gentleman," Steven started. "It would like to at this time ask if you have any questions" Steven asked. Nathan looked around the table. Captain Winter's hand went up. "What is the perceived threat from submarines en route to and in the area of operations"the Captain asked. "Thank you, Captain. There is at this time a considerable threat of submarines operating in the Sea of Japan. Our latest satellite photos show that of the twelve submarines based at Wonsan, eight have put to sea. These are mostly all diesel subs of the Romeo class with one ex-Russian Whiskey class. As we speak, two Romeo class submarines are being shadowed by Japanese ASW aircraft and one of our attack subs. As for the threat en route to the area of operations, we have no information concerning that and conclude that the threat level is minimal" Steven explained. Nathan had a question that was plaguing him and was sure it was on the Captains mind also. Nathan raised his hand. Steven acknowledged him. "Sir, we know of the missile threat that exists but is there any threat of long-range aircraft and if so could they be configured with the nuclear weapons that were previously mentioned" Nathan asked. Steven looked at the Ensign by the video projector and nodded. The screen lit up behind Steven and showed a map of Korea, the Sea of Japan and the mainland of Japan. Steven began. "The nuclear devices the North Koreans have been able to produce to date are too large to be carried by the tactical aircraft now in their inventory. Presently the North Koreans have about eighty medium bomber aircraft, if I could have the next slide please, which are capable of carrying a nuclear weapon. Shown on the screen is the Il-28 medium-range bomber aircraft. The IL-28 "Beagle" has a range of 1,350 miles and a maximum speed of 560 mph. It is considered a direct threat to the Japanese mainland. Are there any other questions?" Steven asked. "Yes Sir" replied one of the other Officers in the briefing room. "Are there any other friendly units outside of the Strike Group we should be made aware of?" the Officer inquired. "Yes Captain, there are but there will be another briefing when we get underway" Steven replied. The Captain nodded, satisfied with his answer. "If anyone has no further questions you are all dismissed and may return to your duties" Steven concluded. Nathan stood up and gathered his papers from the briefing. Admiral Grayson caught his eye and motioned for Nathan to join him. Nathan approached the Admiral who was standing with other Admirals and Steven. "Commander Buckman, nice to see you again." said the Admiral shaking Nathan's hand. "Nice to see you as well, Admiral" Nathan replied. Nathan remained while the Admiral continued talking to the other Admirals and Steven. In a short time the Admiral excused himself from the other Officers and motioned Nathan to the side door. Nathan followed him and Steven to another private room adjacent to the briefing room. Both the Admiral's and Steven entered the room and each took a seat at the table. "I have been discussing things with Admiral Grayson and he has agreed with me to bring you up to speed on a few things that weren't covered in the briefing. Since you are the Air Wing Commander on the *Reagan* we both agreed that you should be made aware of a few things that may influence your decisions on this mission. As of now you have a "*Krypton*" security clearance which is six levels above your old "Top Secret" clearance. What I am about to tell you shall not be repeated to anyone outside of this room, including Captain Winters...Is that clear Commander?" Steven said. "Yes Sir, I understand completely" replied Nathan.

For the next hour Nathan heard things from the Admiral and Steven that he could only have dreamed about. It was clear to Nathan that this mission would be a very risky one but might have a positive outcome.

He came out of the briefing and said goodbye to the Admiral and told Steven he would join him back on the *Reagan*. Nathan found a phone and began dialing his home phone. It rang twice and a sweet voice answered. "Hi honey, it's me" Nathan said. "Hi baby, how are you? We miss you"she replied. "I'm ok, I miss all of you too. I'm at Pearl, we're getting ready to go soon. Honey, I was thinking that since this may be a long deployment that maybe you should take the kids and go down to Sao Paulo for a month" Nathan said. "Oh honey, do you really mean it, can we afford it?" she asked. "Sure we can, just get someone to check the house while your gone. Make the reservations, I have the address so I'll send your letters there" Nathan told her. "Honey, I'd rather you came with us. This should be a trip we both should be on" she said. "I know, but I can't. Besides you and the kids deserve a summer vacation. You find all the good spots and maybe we'll go back in a couple of years" explained Nathan. "It won't be the same without you. Is everything all right? Is there something you aren't telling me?" she asked. Nathan knew he couldn't tell her the truth. But then again he didn't want to lie to her. "No, everything is fine. I just thought you needed a vacation to get away from everything" Nathan said. " Honey, you're the best, and you're the best Dad any kid could have. We'll get ready and leave in a few days. I'll write you before we leave. Honey, I love you so much and I'll show you when you get back" she whispered into the phone. "I love you too, sweetheart. I have to get going. Give the kids a hug for me. Bye baby" he said. "Bye honey" she replied. Nathan hung up the phone. Good, she believed me. Take a vacation and get away from everything he thought. Yeah, get out of range of the TaepoDong-III's.

Nathan was feeling the effects of the wine. Since he had no food since noon the alcohol quickly found it's way to his bloodstream. Jill walked out in her kimono, carrying a few towels. "I thought you'd be in by now" she said looking at Nathan. Nathan stood up. "I was taught to always wait for the host" Nathan replied. Jill put the towels on table and walked to the Jacuzzi. "How are you on the subject of nudity?" Jill asked, cautiously untying her kimono. "Actually, I'm all for it as long as its in good taste" Nathan replied. "Good, I think we will get along very well then" Jill said as she turned on the jets for the Jacuzzi. The water swirled and turned a frothy white as Jill put her hair up, so as not to get it wet, and then let her kimono drop to the floor, revealing her self to Nathan for the first time. Nathan had anticipated this, but not so soon. Her body was absolutely stunning. As he noticed before, she was very athletic, but now, without her clothes on, her body shown every muscular detail. Her body was tanned from head to toe with only tan lines from a small thong. She stepped into the Jacuzzi and turned away from him. As she settled into a seat on the Jacuzzi, the frothy white water enveloped her tanned breasts. She looked at him and smiled. "Are you going to join me?" she asked. "Sure, don't mind if I do" Nathan replied. Nathan took off his shirt and dropped his trousers. "Is one of those glasses of wine for me?" she asked inquisitively. "Oh, yeah. I'm so sorry" Nathan said handing her the glass of wine. Nathan dropped his boxer shorts and climbed into the Jacuzzi. "You have big shoulders, you lift weights don't you?" Jill asked, as she took a sip of wine. "About three times a week. I go to a gym near my apartment" Nathan explained, stepping in the Jacuzzi while carefully holding his wine glass. "Nathan, I have a confession to make" Jill said. Nathan got comfortable in the seat next to her, his leg touching her soft thigh. "I know a lot more about you than you know about me" Jill confessed. This was not surprising to Nathan. Jill had access to personal records, so she probably did. "I want you to know that I don't invite strange men to my Jacuzzi every week. I haven't really dated anyone in about five months. I've been watching you for about three weeks now. You seem to be a real nice person. You always let the ladies ahead of you in the cafeteria. You sit alone with your back to the wall and you eat while reading the paper. You like ham and Swiss sandwiches with mustard and french fries with no catsup or salt. You wear Hugo Boss cologne, which I love, and dress in Armani suits" Jill said smiling at Nathan. Nathan reflected for a second then spoke. "You seem to be doing your homework" Nathan replied. She tilted her head down. "I just wanted you to know that your someone I'm attracted to who I'd really like to get to know better" she said looking down at the water. Nathan reached over to her and touched her chin. She looked up at him with a small tear in her eye. He caressed her soft cheek and she responded by putting her hand on his. He leaned over and gave her a kiss on her soft lips as the door bell rang. "Oh, That must be the food, I'll get it" she said wiping the tear from her eye. She climbed out of the Jacuzzi, quickly grabbed her kimono and a towel. "I'm starved, you?" she asked after quickly toweling off and wrapping herself in the kimono. "Yes, I am" Nathan replied. Jill quickly ran to the front door. Nathan climbed out of the Jacuzzi and dried off with the extra towels Jill brought out. He put on his boxers and trousers and grabbed both glasses of wine as he walked in to the kitchen. Jill returned to the kitchen with the food. "How much was all that?" Nathan asked. "Don't worry sweetie, it's my treat" Jill replied. "Thank you, that's very nice of you. Would you like some more wine? " asked Nathan as he poured the bottle . "Yes, please" Jill said smiling. "I guess I should have done this before I opened the door. The delivery guy got a good tip and a big peek" Jill said laughing as she cinched up the tie on her kimono. "He's a lucky guy" Nathan said as he raised his glass. "Let's drink a toast"

Nathan proposed. Jill grabbed her glass and raised it to Nathan's. "To good friends and lasting friendships" Nathan said.

During the next few hours they got to know each other very well. Jill had a great home. It was left to her, free and clear, by her aunt who passed away two years ago. It was decorated very tastefully and seemed very comfortable. It had a large family room, two full baths, small computer room and nice kitchen along with a large master bedroom with two additional bedrooms upstairs. The pool was small but adequate for several adults. The house had a detached two-car garage with an unfinished loft that she wanted made into an office hideaway but hadn't the money for yet. Jill started working for Lockheed-Martin over a year and a half ago. She had to go to work after her divorce and had about a half a dozen jobs before she landed this one. She was a server at an upscale restaurant when she met Jim Langdon, the Lockheed-Martin Vice- President of Operations. She was the first to agree that her looks got her the job but her personality and skill were the reason why she kept it. She graduated from Cal Tech with a honor degree in business administration. She had a job as a secretary when she got married. The marriage was doomed from the start and she claimed she was too young and he was too stupid. As Nathan talked with her he saw a woman that was exceptionally smart and vulnerable. She didn't want to be hurt again and was going to be very cautious. That was fine with him. Nathan thought about his upcoming career. Should he tell her? It might be the best thing right now.

Nathan awoke on the sofa in the family room were they both sat. Awakened by the cuckoo clock, Nathan saw it was two in the morning. Jill was tucked under his left arm with her kimono half-undone. Nathan had to urinate really bad. He tried to move and slip away to the bathroom without wakening her but she stirred, half asleep, and muttered something like "Don't leave us" whoever "us" was. Nathan stood and covered her up with the blanket on the back of the sofa. Nathan found the bathroom down the hall. What a relief. They must have drank two bottles of wine. Nathan finished, washed his hands and made his way back to Jill. He knelt next to her and touched her soft face. She stirred and looked at him, smiled, rubbed her eyes and asked what time it was. "It's after two in the morning" Nathan whispered to her. "It been a long night, I should go home" he added. "No, please don't go" Jill said, sitting up and losing the blanket in the process. She put her arms around his neck and pulled him close. "I need you next to me when I wake up, please don't go" she pleaded again. Her bare breasts pressed against Nathan's chest. Nathan began to weaken. She *was* terribly beautiful. Nathan agreed. "Ok, I'll stay" Nathan said. "Good, would you carry me to my room?" asked Jill running her fingers through her long black, silky hair, half asleep. Nathan said nothing but scooped her up in both arms and carried her to her room. He walked into her room and gently set her down on her pillow. She looked at him and smiled. "I hope you don't mind but I normally sleep in the nude" Jill replied as she slipped out of her kimono and beneath her satin sheets. Nathan slipped of his trousers but kept his boxers on. "No, I don't mind" Nathan said smiling. He slipped in bed on the other side as Jill slid over to meet him in the middle. "I know you're a gentleman, and I trust you" Jill said as she softly kissed Nathan and lay her head on his shoulder. Nathan thought whoever the guy was that she divorced must have been really stupid. She snuggled with him and, after some short conversation, fell off to sleep again.

Nathan awoke to the sound of the shower. He looked at her clock on the nightstand. It said six-twenty in the morning. The shower stopped and after several minutes she walked out wrapped in a large towel. Even soaking wet she was beautiful. "Good morning, sweetie. How did you sleep?" she asked. Nathan stood up and stretched. "I slept very well" Nathan answered. "I did too. You were a perfect gentleman last night. I must have been really out of it. I hope I didn't say anything to scare you away" Jill said. Nathan hesitated. He still wondered who "us" was. It didn't matter right now. "No, of course not. You were the perfect hostess" Nathan said. Nathan excused himself and went to take a shower. When he finished, he toweled off and made his way back to the bedroom. While he was dressing he smelled the aroma of coffee and something baked coming from the kitchen area. He walked to the kitchen and found two place mats with a coffee pot and danish on a small table in the breakfast nook. Jill walked in from the patio area with two yellow roses in her hand. She put them in a clear vase and set them on the table. "Sit down, sweetie. I hope you like cinnamon danish. I make them up ahead of time" Jill explained. So she does use the kitchen Nathan thought. Nathan waited for Jill to sit and then seated himself. He tried the danish and it was very good. Not bad he thought, looking at her. A body of a goddess and she can bake too. This guy must have been retarded to let her slip away. "I cut these roses from the bush in the back yard. I love roses, red ones are my favorite" Jill said smiling. Nathan took the hint. He finished his danish and was almost done with his coffee when he asked her. "I wish you would let me pay for the food last night" Nathan offered. "No, I said it was my treat. You can pay next time...that is if you want to have a next time" Jill said hesitantly. "Oh, sure I do. I'm not sure when though. I have some work to do today. I need to prepare a paper on the work yesterday. I'll probable be busy all day" Nathan explained. "That's fine, sweetie" Jill replied. "Maybe we can go to the beach on Sunday if you get your work done" she added. "That sounds like a great idea, I can call you Sunday morning" Nathan replied. She went to the island in the kitchen and scribbled her number on a piece of paper and walked over to Nathan. She put it in his shirt pocket and leaned down to place a kiss on his cheek. "Here is the number for you to call me and the kiss is so you don't forget" she giggled. He loved her giggle. "I won't forget but I have to get going" Nathan explained. Jill walked him to the door and kissed him again. Have a good day, sweetie. I'll see you soon" Jill told him. Nathan returned her kiss. Not soon enough, Nathan thought. "Jill, thank you for a wonderful night" Nathan said. "Don't mention it, I had a great time" Jill said, putting her arms around his neck. Nathan kissed her again before he walked out the door and over to his car. He got in, started it and backed carefully out to the street. While driving home he thought about Jill. She deserved the truth especially after all she has been through. He really was crazy about her but he was going to be gone the next few months. It was not fair to lead her on and make her wait.

He decided the next time he saw her that he would tell her.

THREE

CONFESSIONS

IT HAD BEEN TWELVE DAYS SINCE the briefing at Pearl. After meeting the Captain in CIC in the afternoon, Nathan returned to his quarters to finalize plans to provide protection for the Fleet and for any contingencies that might occur during the mission. He had learned during his "post-briefing" that a group of B-1B Lancer bombers from Ellsworth AFB had been deployed to Guam soon after the North Korean missile test. It was the second time that the US had done this. Five years ago, during the Iraqi invasion in 2003, the US deployed the bombers to Guam as a show of force. The B-1's were a great deterrent but they were far from the action. Nathan was more concerned with having something closer to the battle area. The Taepo-Dong missiles were in deep underground silos which required a hardened weapon to destroy them. Nathan was confident that when and if the time came that a weapon with these capabilities would be employed.

Nathan thought of the bomber threat against the fleet. Even though the Il-28 "Beagle" bombers were antiquated they could create havoc if nuclear weapons were employed on ground troops or installations in South Korea or Japan. Nathan added a note that an additional E-2C should be deployed once they arrive on-station. Nathan learned along time ago in War College that long-range detection of a threat was of the utmost importance. The E-2C's and F/A-18's worked very well together. The Il-28's should be no problem for the F/A-18's. They were scoring thirty-mile simulated kills in the last deployment exercise off California. Nathan read his notes on the ASW patrols. The pilots that flew the ASW helicopters and "Ospreys" were a dedicated group. They recently refined their craft during the last training exercise. They located and tracked every submarine contact during the exercise earning their squadron a 96 percentile rating by the independent evaluation team. This time it was for real. Nathan reached for the "Jane's" book above his bunk. He found what he was looking for. The data on the "Oscars" showed that they indeed had a dual-pressure hull. This wouldn't be a problem for the MK 48 ADCAP torpedoes that the attack subs carried but the helos and the "Ospreys" carried the older MK 46 torpedoes and the newer lightweight torpedo, the MK 50. These both had a smaller warhead and range considering that they would be carried on aircraft and launched near the point of contact. One MK-50 probably wouldn't kill an "Oscar" but it would sure as hell ruin their week. Nathan looked at the clock. 1753 hours. Dinner time in the Officers Mess. Nathan wasn't really hungry, more tired than anything else. He decided to go anyway. On the way to dinner Nathan met Steven in the passageway. "Good afternoon, Commander" Steven said. "Good Afternoon, Sir" Nathan replied. "I was on my way to my quarters, would you care to join me?" Steven asked. "The Officers mess is crowded these days so I told them to send my dinner to my quarters" Steven added. "Have you eaten, Commander?" Steven asked. "No sir, I haven't yet" Nathan replied. "Well then I'll phone to have them prepare another tray" Steven said. "Yes sir, that would be fine" Nathan replied. Nathan followed

Steven Alexander to his quarters. Steven rounded the corner of the passageway and the Marine Sergeant on guard at his door came to attention. "As you were, Sergeant" Steven ordered. "Sergeant, the Commander and I will be dining in my quarters. When the food arrives send them right in" Steven explained. The Sergeant acknowledged as he opened the door. Steven walked in followed by Nathan as the Sergeant closed the door behind them. Steven walked to his desk and picked up the phone. "How do you like your steak, Nathan" Steven asked. "Have them cook it medium, with a plain baked potato, thank you sir" Nathan replied graciously. Steven dialed the Officers mess. "Yes, this is Admiral Alexander, Commander Buckman will be joining me in my quarters for dinner. Please add another steak dinner, medium, with a plain baked potato. Yes, that will be all, thank you" Steven replied and hung up. Nathan looked around the Admirals quarters. It was very large with an office area and a separate berthing area. The chairs in front of the desk were plush leather and each had a small table next to it. Nathan sat in one while continuing to look around the room. Several pictures adorned the walls of the office. All the US naval aircraft from about 1965 to date were represented throughout the room. Along with some "Janes" books Steven's desk also had a manila envelope marked "Top Secret" on the front of it. Steven sat at the desk and picked up the envelope. "Here Nathan, we have some time before dinner arrives. Take a look at this. Let me know what you think." Steven asked. Nathan opened the envelope and took out the contents. It contained several reports from Lockheed Martin, TRW and several other contractors. The data sheets Nathan recognized. It was the preliminary test sheets he prepared sixteen years earlier. The reports went on to chronicle the progress of the project, its first flight and testing not less than five years earlier. Nathan looked at the pictures of the final product. He read the report on the airframe integration. They had used several of his ideas he had written about before he left Lockheed-Martin. By recycling chemicals, using high-strength composites and plastics and using a unique cooling process, the engineers that followed Nathan were able to make the laser lighter and more efficient while at the same time increasing it's power by over four hundred percent. Nathan was very pleased. The integration of the laser turret on to the 747-400F airframe went very well. The total weight of the turret was just under 12,000 pounds, a whole 1200 pounds under the estimated total. Still it was a lot of weight to hang on the nose of a 747. The aircraft, which were designated as AL-1A's, could remain on station for up to twenty hours with air refueling. The Airborne Laser had an effective range of about one hundred-fifty miles and carried enough power for twenty-two salvos at full strength. "Well, you seem to be pleased, Nathan" Steven inquired. "Yes, I am. It makes me feel good that the work I did went to good use" Nathan replied. "I'll save you some reading" Steven said. "The last AL-1A went on line last August. We now have a total of eight aircraft based at Groom Lake in Nevada. The unit that operates them is a joint service unit of Air Force and Navy personnel. From the start of the program we knew we had to get the very best that each service had to offer. The crews are a mix, the flight crew being Air Force and the fire-control team being Navy. The fire- control system resembled the Aegis system on our cruisers so the training went without a hitch. A flight of four aircraft will arrive at Pusan AB in twenty hours. Two will be on-station at all times, one will be located one hundred miles from Toksong-gun, a known missile base. The second will be on-station one hundred-twenty miles East of Ok'pyong-nodongjagu. This is where the last test missile was launched. Their orders are to shoot down any missile that leaves the ground. Your orders are to provide air cover for the AL-1A's on-station at these locations. We expect that the North Koreans will get really pissed and try to intercept the AL-1A's when they get on-station. They may also want to shoot one down. Last March we had a RC-135S Cobra Ball flying a mission near Mayang Is. to monitor any missile launchings. They were in international airspace about one hundred and fifty miles off the North Korean coast when they were intercepted by four MiG-29's. The reports from the Cobra Ball aircrew said that the MiG's were deliberately trying to crowd the Cobra Ball into North Korean airspace. The North Koreans even locked them up with their attack radar. Thankfully the Commander of the Cobra Ball aborted his mission and flew back to Kadena" Steven explained. Nathan was all too familiar with the MiG-29. He was on Combat Air Patrol over Basra, Iraq in March of 2003 when he and his wingman, James Aulicino, intercepted two Iranian MiG-29's over the Gulf in their F/A-18's. The MiG's climbed and banked into Nathan and his wingman at over 1000 knots and launched a pair of missiles at Nathan's wingman, both of which missed. In the brief encounter, Nathan downed one MiG-29 while the other one lit up and headed back to Iran. The whole thing lasted less than thirty seconds and didn't even make the papers. Nathan got credit for a "kill" but only unofficially. The only credit Nathan ever needed was landing safely back on-board the ship. Steven continued "The Korean President Kim Lu Doc has been saying for months that the US, Japan and South Korea are quote, "watching and waiting for a chance to mount a pre-emptive attack on the missile bases and other nuclear facilities" Steven said. "Japan's Premier Hiroko Nakamoto has been pushed to the breaking point. He had his military forces on high alert after the North Korean missile test. Being in such close proximity with the JMSDF we even have had a few close calls with our forces. Only with assurance from the US State Department two days ago has he dropped his counties alert level to yellow" Steven explained. "That's still a heightened state of readiness" Nathan replied. "Yes, it is" Steven replied. "The thing is Nathan the US doesn't *want* this to escalate to the point of nuclear war" Steven said. Nathan couldn't agree more. He had been to Hiroshima and Nagasaki. He had seen what nuclear weapons can do that were only one tenth the power of what was available today. "The South Korea government has been trying to nudge North Korea into adopting more conciliatory positions in the development of nuclear weapon for years. Last month the North Koreans expelled U.N. monitors and withdrew from a key nuclear arms-control treaty. They also restarted a nuclear reactor that had been mothballed for years under a U.N. seal. In the city of Yangdok, near Pyongyang, we have discovered a new ballistic missile base that is about eighty percent complete. It's a huge complex, about five square miles" Steven explained. Nathan thought about everything he was told. "Steven, I really don't think the North Koreans have really thought all this through. They don't really want to start something with the US" Nathan said. "You don't agree with that, do you Nathan?" Steven asked. "Well, I really don't know right now. With what happened in Iraq in 2004 and now this, Its anyone's guess" Nathan confessed. "Nathan, I'll agree that what happened in Iraq four years ago was shameless. We lost a lot of good people in that conflict and many more in the months that followed. But this is a new administration. A lot of things are different. The old administration and those that worked for them were concerned with filling their pockets. While we still have a presence in the Middle East, we are there because we still have a *major* interest in that area. Jackson is the first President since Reagan that has reaffirmed that the United States protect herself not only at home but abroad. He's not sending us to Korea because he wants to he is sending us there because he *has* to" Steven explained. "I agree with that" Nathan replied. "I thought back in 2003 that we were in the wrong place at the wrong time. It was clear after the Iraq invasion that Saddam didn't have any employable weapons of mass destruction. I remember sortie after sortie looking for signs of weapons and facilities in the H2 sectors and even in the North. I kept thinking, even back then, that we should be more concerned with North Korea and her nuclear build up, If we had then maybe we wouldn't be here now." explained Nathan. Steven paused and looked at Nathan. He let out a breath. "Nathan" Steven began, " Do you remember back in 2003 before the invasion when a North Korean freighter was stopped in the Indian Ocean. That ship was bound for Iran. Do you remember?" Steven asked. "Yes, I remember. If I recall it was loaded with short-range missile casings and machine parts. It was stopped in international waters and boarded by the Australian Navy" Nathan replied. "That's what was reported in the media" Steven said. "It also was reported that the vessel was released to continue on to Iran. The Secretary of State himself said on TV that he had contacted the Iranian government and that they assured him that the casings were for research and not to be used as offensive weapons" Steven added. "That part anyway was true. What wasn't reported and what only few people know was that ship never made it to Iran" Steven said as he looked at Nathan. "The truth was Nathan, that ship was loaded with Taepo-dong missile rocket motors. We knew for a long time, even before we went into Iraq, that the North Koreans were giving missiles and manufacturing technology to Iran and other countries in exchange for data on the missile tests. They took the data that they received and then improved their own missiles" Steven explained to Nathan. "So what happened to the vessel?" Nathan asked. "Nathan can you even imagine what could happen if every third world country in the world had ballistic missiles with nuclear warheads? The United States cannot let that possibility exist" Steven said. Nathan was getting very upset and tried not to show it. "So what happened to the vessel, Sir?" Nathan asked coldly. "It's at the bottom of the Indian Ocean where it belongs, and I know that because I was the one who was ordered to send it there." Steven said with a disgusted tone. The room was silent for a few seconds. Nathan knew Steven was serving on an attack sub somewhere in the Gulf at that time. They had kept in touch all through their careers. He didn't know however that he was in the Indian Ocean. Nathan felt sorry for Steven. Nathan himself had been given orders that he hadn't agreed with but he carried them out nonetheless. That was his job. That was what he was sworn to do and he did it. He knew people died because of his actions. The pilot of the MiG-29 he shot down in 2003 didn't or couldn't bail out of his stricken aircraft. He surely died though when Nathan saw the MiG plunge into the Gulf from twelve thousand feet. Nathan tried not to think about it. The MiG's did engage and fire first. Nathan had been told so many times before in Top Gun school and on deployments the most important rule of engagement, only fire if fired upon. He still felt sorry for Steven. What must he thinking? He had to carry out his orders but he attacked an *unarmed* vessel in international waters. "Steven, I'm sorry. I know this must be hard for you" Nathan confided. "Yes, It is," Steven shot back. "but it's the job I signed on for. If I couldn't do it I would resign my commission" Steven said. Steven settled back in his chair. "Like I said before Nathan, imagine what could happen if every third world country in the world had ballistic missiles with nuclear warheads?" Steven said holding up a picture of Amy he had on the desk. Her hair was a little shorter than the last time he saw her but she still looked stunning. "How are your wife and kids, Nathan? Is everyone out of danger?" Steven asked inquisitively. Nathan knew at that moment that Steven must already know. The phones at Pearl were probably tapped. It was standard procedure in this day and age."Yes, they are all doing fine and decided to go to Sao Paulo on an extended vacation until I get back" Nathan replied. "That's good" Steven said. Steven pushed back from the desk. Nathan watched as Steven went to a cabinet near the desk and opened a door revealing a safe. Steven opened the safe and removed a small, dark blue book. "I'm gonna show you our ace in the hole, Nathan. Tell no one else about this" Steven told Nathan sternly. Steven handed Nathan the book. Nathan noticed that the cover was blank except for the word "*Thor II*" emblazoned across the front in gold letters. Nathan opened the front cover, read the first page and turned to the next page. Nathan began to read the next page. He couldn't believe his eyes. He looked up at Steven and said in astonishment "Oh my God".

Nathan arrived at his apartment after stopping off for another coffee. He thought he could use one after the night before. Jill was a very lovely girl. He enjoyed her company very much. He pulled into his spot, parked and went to his apartment. He began thinking about how to tell Jill he was going away. Maybe he ought to come right out and tell her. She may be upset but at least he would show her he was trying to be honest. He wouldn't be gone forever, just about four months. Nathan turned on the computer and while it was "booting up" he opened his brief case and found the information on the Chemical Oxygen Iodine Laser or COIL as it was known at Lockheed-Martin. He sat down at the computer and began a short overview of the project. He wanted the engineer that would be replacing him to have as much information as possible on the project. Nathan also would include what he thought could be used to increase the efficiency of the Laser. It was going to be a very long time until the project could "fly". Nathan had hoped when he was chosen for the project that he would see the project through to it's completion. Nathan was on his twenty-third page when the phone rang. He looked at the clock and it was ten after four in the afternoon. Nathan answered. "Hey Nathan, this is Steven." Steven said. "Hi Steven, how are you doing?" asked Nathan. "I'm doing great, are you already for a party tonight?" Steven asked. "Yeah, I've been looking forward to this" Nathan said. "That's good, the girls left about ten minutes ago and will be picking you up in about twenty minutes. Will you be ready?" Steven inquired. "Sure, I'll be waiting for them out front" Nathan said. "Ok buddy, I'll see you soon. I have a lot to do so I'll talk to you later" Steven explained. "Ok, see you soon" Nathan said. Nathan hung up the phone and continued finishing his paragraph. He saved the file and shut down the computer and then went to change his clothes. The party probably would be casual so he decided to go with a pair of slacks and a white polo shirt. He put on just a hint of cologne and then brushed his teeth. He looked at the clock and saw it was four-thirty two. He put his shoes on and went to wait for the girls outside. Nathan was waiting near the front entrance to the apartment complex and looking for the girls. He saw a few cars go by. A Dodge pickup truck with a dog in the back, a white Mustang and a blue Chevy Impala. Still no sign of the girls. A few seconds later a silver Jeep Grand Cherokee careened into the parking lot with all the windows down. He saw a blonde girl driving, which he didn't recognize, and then saw Amy hanging out the back seat passenger window. "Hey sailor, need a ride?" she said laughing in her high-pitched voice. The Jeep stopped abruptly in front of Nathan. Her hair was shiny red in the afternoon sun. Nathan couldn't get over her. Steven was definitely a lucky man. "Well, I'm not a sailor yet" confessed Nathan. "That's Ok, you'll do. *Come on*, slide on in here" Amy said, opening the door for Nathan. Nathan got in and closed the door and then they were off. The driver went to the back of the parking lot, turned around then came back to the street entrance. "Are you ready to party?" Amy asked Nathan. "Yes, I am" replied Nathan. Amy spoke "This is Emily, you met her at the party at Lockheed-Martin Friday" she explained, pointing to the front seat passenger. "And this is my sister, Jen" Amy said, putting her hand on the driver's shoulder. Nathan said hello to both girls. As the Jeep slowed coming out of the parking lot to let a car pull in, he looked at Jen in the rear-view mirror. She had very long, blonde hair and seemed to be very tan. She had on dark sunglasses so he really couldn't see her face but he could still tell that she was very pretty. She had the seat pulled way up so Nathan gathered than she must not be very tall. She must have been looking at him through her dark glasses, catching his gaze, because she smiled at him in the mirror. She readjusted the mirror to see him better and then asked "Nathan, are you looking forward to going in the Navy" Jen asked. "Yes I am, I've always been fascinated with flying. I want to fly jet fighters someday" Nathan explained. "From what I've seen you have a good shot at it" Jen said. "Thank you" said Nathan. He wondered what she meant by that but readily accepted the compliment. "Nathan, Jen's in the Navy, she's been in for about four years" Amy said. "Really? Are you going to make it a career?" Nathan asked. Jen and Amy both laughed. "No, I'm just in for the college money" Jen explained. Well, at least she was in the Navy, Nathan thought.

They arrived at Steven's place and parked behind Stevens Jaguar. Nathan envied Steven. He must be getting a decent salary being an Officer in the Navy. Steven had a great house also, nestled high in the hills above Los Angeles. Four bedrooms, three baths, with a den, a pool and Jacuzzi. They got out of the Jeep and began going up the steps to the front door. Amy opened the door and announced their arrival, followed by Emily and then Jen. Nathan closed the door and walked in to the living area. It was decorated for the party with two "Go Navy" banners on each side of the room. Other ribbons and party favors adorned the room also. The dining area was also decorated with party favors and in the middle of the table was a huge, white sheet cake with an F/A-18 on it and the words "Good luck, Nathan" written in script. "Wow, this looks great" Nathan exclaimed. "The girls did all the decorating" Steven said, walking out from the kitchen. "Jennifer got the "Go Navy" banners for us at work" he added. Nathan looked at Jen, who now, without her sunglasses, looked a little familiar. She was combing her long, blonde hair in the mirror and winked at Nathan in the mirror and then smiled. Jennifer turned around and extended her hand "Hi, Seaman First Class Jennifer Kelly" she said shaking Nathan's hand. Now Nathan recognized her. She was the female typist that he saw at the base personnel office. He finally got to see her with her hair down and he was pleased. She was about five feet tall and had really blue eyes. "It's really nice to see you again" Nathan said. "It's nice to see you too" Jennifer said. "Amy told me that they were throwing a party for a guy at Lockheed-Martin who recently got accepted to OTS. I had a hunch it was you" she added. Nathan heard laughter and screams coming from the pool area. He saw Amy's other friend, Arwyn, and a man he hadn't met before. They were frolicking in the pool and seemed to be enjoying themselves. Arwyn was making her way out of the pool by the ladder as the man playfully grabbed her bikini. Arwyn screamed gleefully as she got out and then ran for the cabana bath, laughing. Jennifer asked Nathan if he would like something to drink. " Yes, I'll have a Corona" Nathan replied. Nathan walked to the kitchen with Jennifer. Jennifer walked to the refrigerator and got two Coronas and opened them. Jennifer put a Corona upon the counter and motioned to Nathan. Steven and Amy were both in the kitchen. Steven was busy preparing chicken for the grill outside and Amy was doing salads and preparing corn on the cob. While Steven was an excellent chef, Amy seemed to be in charge. "Nathan, I hope you like chicken" Amy said. "Yes, I do" Nathan replied. "That's good, we *certainly* have enough of it!" Amy said looking at Steven. "Steven, can I help you with anything?" Nathan asked. "Yes, you sure can" Steven said, taking Jennifer by the hand. "You can take this young lady out to the pool area and get to know her, don't worry we have everything under control" Steven replied. "Ok, I can certainly do that" Nathan said. He looked at Jennifer. "Shall we?" Nathan asked. "Yeah, lets do that, but I want to change first" Jennifer replied setting down her Corona. "Sure" Nathan agreed. "Did you bring your swimsuit? Jennifer asked. "No, actually I forgot to bring it. I wasn't sure what kind of party it was going to be" Nathan explained. Steven overheard Nathan and told him to go to his room and find one of his. "Amy will help you find one" Steven said. "*Come on sailor,* we'll get you dressed" Amy said laughing. Nathan followed her down the hall to Steven's bedroom. His room was fantastic and almost as big as Nathan's whole apartment. Steven had a huge bed with night stands on each side. He had two separate baths, his and hers, with a Jacuzzi bath in hers. Amy pulled open a drawer and pulled out a few swim trunks for Nathan to try. "Try any one of these Nathan and just leave the rest. I'll put them away later"Amy explained. "Thanks, Amy" Nathan replied. "Okay, I'll leave you in peace now" Amy said, closing the door as she left. Nathan looked at the swim trunks and chose the most conservative one there. It was a blue boxer style with a gold stripe down each side. He changed in Steven's bathroom and carefully folded his clothes and laid them on the sink. He made his way to the pool area where he found Jennifer already on a chaise lounge. She had two chaise lounge chairs pulled close together with a table on each side. She was lying on her back sitting up slightly. She wore a small white bikini with red diagonal stripes which showed a lot of skin but left just enough to the imagination. Jennifer put on her sunglasses and reached for the suntan lotion on the table. She poured some lotion in her hand and began slowly rubbing her arms, shoulders and tummy. Nathan surmised that she was the outdoor type. She liked the sun and her body showed it. "Do you want some?" she offered. "Yes, thank you" Nathan said. Jennifer reached for her Corona and took a drink. "I don't really drink a lot" Jennifer said.

"but, since this is your party and I don't have to work I decided to let my hair down" Jennifer explained. Nathan was glad that she decided that. Looking at her and Amy it was hard to believe they were sisters. Both looked entirely different but were beautiful in every respect. Nathan asked her what she planned to do in the future. "Well, in a few months, after I leave the Navy, I will be attending Florida State University in Tallahassee. I will be studying business administration and majoring in hospitality. I'd like to go into hotel sales" she explained. "That's very commendable" Nathan said. "It's interesting though" Nathan began, "Here you are ending your Navy career and I'm just beginning mine" Nathan said. "I'll be going to Pensacola in ten days and will be their for about four months" Nathan explained. "Yes, that is very interesting. You know that Tallahassee isn't that far from Pensacola" Jennifer said sort of matter of factly. Nathan noticed she was smiling. He wondered if she had a boyfriend somewhere. No one had mentioned it to him, but then again why would they. He figured he would just get to know her for right now. Steven came out to the barbecue located on the pool patio He had a huge tray of chicken with some barbecue sauce. "Are you two getting to know each other?" Steven asked. "Yes, we are Steven. He is the nicest one of your friends I have met yet" Jennifer said. "That's good, do you two need another Corona?" Nathan looked at Jennifer and saw her beer was half-full. "Yes, thank you Steven" Nathan replied. Steven left to get the Coronas. "I think I'm gonna go for a swim" Nathan said. "Will you join me?" Nathan added. "No, I think I'll watch and soak up some more sun" Jennifer replied. Nathan went to the pool steps and walked in. It was a heated pool and about 78 degrees. Just about perfect. It was a huge pool about forty feet by eighteen feet or so in a kidney shape with the smaller end being the deep end. Nathan plunged in and swam underwater and into the deep end. He came up for a breath and noticed that Amy was walking through the pool area over to where

Jennifer was. She was carrying a tray with three Coronas on it and set it on the table next to Jennifer. She had a pink colored bikini on with a matching sarong around her waist. She sat with Jennifer and began a conversation. Nathan couldn't hear it but decided that it probably wasn't for his ears. Nathan saw that Steven came back to check the chicken on the barbecue. The chicken smelled great as Steven opened the barbecue top. Nathan swam over to the shallow end and walked out of the pool. He grabbed a towel off the table, dried off a little and walked over to the girls. He picked up the Corona and took a long drink. He thanked Amy for bringing it out, excused himself and walked over to the barbecue to talk to Steven. Steven was busy turning the chicken and adding barbecue sauce. "Chicken smells great" Nathan said. "Thanks, I think another thirty minutes or so and we can eat" Steven said as he closed the lid and adjusted vents. "I hope you like this barbecue sauce, Nathan" Steven said. "It's an old family recipe handed down to me from my father" Steven added. Nathan didn't really know much about Steven's dad except he was in the Navy also. He knew he lived near Alexandria, Virginia and also had a house in the Hamptons. Nathan decided that this was a good as a time as any. "How is your dad, Steven?" Nathan inquired. "He is good, very busy these days" Steven explained. What does he do in the Navy, Steven" Nathan asked. He noticed that Steven sort of hesitated, maybe embarrassed by the question. "Well, I don't talk about it much but he works at the Pentagon" Steven said evasively. "Really, Is he involved in projects like we are?" Nathan asked. "Well no, but he used to be. He headed up the Defense Advanced Research Project Agency until a few years ago. He was chosen by the present administration at the beginning of this year as the Chairman of the Joint Chief's" Steven said as he looked at Nathan. Nathan stood there, holding his Corona, silent and stunned. He hadn't expected that. He thought Steven's dad was maybe a Captain or Rear Admiral with a ship command.

"That's great" Nathan said clearing his throat. "I don't really let that out because I don't want people to think that I get preferential treatment" Steven explained. "I understand" Nathan said. "I'll keep it to myself if you want" Nathan added. "It doesn't matter, just about everyone here and at the base knows. It's kind of a hard secret to keep" Steven said. Hard to keep indeed thought Nathan. Nathan saw that Jennifer got up and went to pool side as Amy went inside to the kitchen. Amy returned a few minutes later to Steven's side. She came over and put her arms around his waist. "Hey baby" Amy said as she hugged Steven. "Hey yourself" Steven said, bending over to kiss her on the lips. "Let me know about ten minutes before the chicken is done so I can put the corn in" Amy said. "Ok, figure about twenty minutes" Steven said. "Good, I can set the table then" she said reaching up for another kiss. Steven kissed her again and she left to go to the kitchen. "She a wonderful girl, Steven. You seem to be very happy together" Nathan declared. "I believe we are. She is too good to be true. I could never find anyone like her again so I'm not even gonna look" Steven said. "Do you ever see yourself getting married to one another?" Nathan asked. "Possibly. She wants to have a family someday and so do I but I don't want to be an absentee dad. The Navy has a tendency to do that" Steven said looking at Jennifer at the pool. She was sitting opposite Nathan and Steven on the far side of the pool. She was in the pool on the first step sitting in about a foot of water. Nathan looked at her. She motioned toward Nathan with her finger to come over and sit by her. "I think your neglecting your guest, Nathan" Steven said. "Your right, I'm sorry. Please excuse me" Nathan said, starting to step away from Steven. "Nathan, go easy with her, she's had a rough time these last few months" Steven told Nathan. Nathan promised Steven he would. He walked to the table finishing his beer and put the bottle on the table. He then walked over to Jennifer and sat next to her in the pool. She playfully splashed water on his back as he sat down. The water felt good on his back. He wet his hand and dripped some water on her shoulders. "Ooh" she screamed. "I guess I deserved that" she said laughing. He sat on the next seat lower, deeper in the water. She moved closer to him, her silky smooth thigh touching his arm. "When do you have to leave for Pensacola?" she asked. " I have to leave here two weeks from next Monday." Nathan said wetting his face with the water. "I see. I might be able to see you next week, I mean before you leave" she said. "I'd like that" Nathan replied. "Maybe we can go to a movie or dinner or something" Nathan added "Sure, but just as friends, I mean it won't be a date or anything like that" Jennifer said. "Oh sure, just as friends" Nathan said. Nathan could use more friends like Jennifer.

Jill pulled the Mustang on to Juniper Dr. and began looking for Nathan's address. She caught up to a pickup truck that was traveling slowly. She tried looking for the address and at the same time keep an eye on the pick up truck in front of her. The pick up truck had a very large dog in the back who was barking loudly and carrying on, making her avert her attention from the addresses. She began counting aloud. "Twelve fifty-six, Twelve fifty-nine" she said. The dog began barking at her, since she probable was following too close. She began again. "Twelve sixty-five. Oops, too far" she said. She turned around and headed back. According to his records he lived at twelve sixty-two Juniper Drive. It must have been the complex she had passed. She checked her precious cargo as she turned around. The chicken she had just taken out of the oven not less that twenty minutes ago was fine. Salads and her famous baked beans still okay also. She hoped that Nathan would enjoy the surprise. After working all day on the paper he had to write she was sure he would not think of getting something to eat. She slowed the Mustang as she approached the entrance to the complex. She saw a silver Jeep Grand Cherokee ready to pull out with a lot of women in it and, as she pulled in noticed Nathan in the back seat. She continued into the parking lot and pulled into a space. He hadn't known she was coming. Besides they weren't really dating. He didn't say he was going out. Still, she hoped he would be home. It would have been nice to see him again. She sat and looked at the basket she prepared and began to cry

It was August 15th and Nathan awoke at five-thirty in the morning. They would be close to Kadena AB by now. He expected some replacements to be flown aboard this morning. Three Officers had gotten sick with intestinal viruses about two days out of Pearl. No doubt they caught something while they were ashore. Nathan thought of what he learned the night before in Steven's quarters. He was sure the North Koreans had no idea of what lay before them if they decided to commit their forces against the US and it's allies. All Nathan could do was hope and pray. His wife and kids should have arrived in Sao Paulo by now according to her letter. They would be safe there. They were out of range of the weapons of war. Still, Nathan was concerned. The Chinese "Oscar" sub was of great concern, not only to Nathan, but Steven also. Years of diplomatic relations between the US and China would be strained if North Korea and the US began shooting at each other. The Chinese might even be drawn into a war with the United States. If things went bad, If the North Koreans committed to launching their missiles, it could mean a deadly nuclear war. If the powers that be let the action escalate to that level then the entire Korean peninsula could be destroyed. The world, and indeed life as we know it, would change forever.

Captain Su Loc peered through the glass of the periscope. He could see nothing but blue waves topped with the occasional white breaker. He had seen no vessels since he left Hong Kong harbor but the ESM detector had shown heavy activity on a few occasions. He stepped away and hit the lever to stow the periscope. "Prepare to dive" he said. His orders were repeated. "Dive the ship" he ordered. "Make your depth three hundred meters" he added. Again his orders were repeated. The ship dove at a 20 degree down angle, the twin screws of the "Oscar" pushing the ship deeper. The hull groaned and creaked under the tremendous pressure of the sea. Reaching two hundred meters the ship started to level out. When the ship reached it's ordered depth Captain Su Loc ordered "Make turns for eight knots, steady on this heading". His orders were then repeated by the second officer and then by the helmsman. He could hear the twin shafts vibrate and then settle into a monotonous rhythm. Captain Su Loc was the captain of the Chinese nuclear attack submarine S-132. Bought from the Russian government in 1994, the ex-"Oscar" cruise missile carrier *Belgorod*, though second hand, was the source of great pride in the Chinese Navy. The "ship" had twenty-two soviet SS-N-19 anti-ship cruise missiles on board, four of which had a five hundred kiloton nuclear warhead. It had cruised these waters many times before. It's mission today was one that it had been exclusively designed for. To locate and track an American aircraft carrier.

Seaman First Class William Conner sat at his console and listened. He was the second son of a West Virginia coal miner. Dad had gladly signed his son into the Navy at seventeen, anything to spare him the long lingering death that had taken William's grandfather. William was about five hundred feet below the ocean's surface on the United States attack submarine USS *Topeka*. A 688I class submarine, the *Topeka* was fitted with the most sophisticated sonar to date, the BQQ-10. It literally could detect targets at over two hundred miles distant. The *Topeka* detected a submerged contact over three days ago near the tip of the Korean peninsula. They detected an "Oscar" class submarine that was passing through the strait. According to the Captain they had orders to close and "shadow" the "Oscar". On duty since 0730 hours, it was now 1830 hours. He had established a history of this particular sub and had recorded it in the database. When the sub was detected two days ago they were about one hundred and sixty three miles away. Now, silent and stealthy, they had worked their way to within two miles of the "Oscar" and had remained undetected. Lt. JG John McConnell, the Sonar Officer, came into the room. "Do you still have a good track on the Oscar" he asked. "Yes Sir. He is about forty-two hundred yards ahead of us on course 037, speed about eight knots" reported William. "Very good, the Captain wants us to get closer. The next time he goes shallow, Advise the Conn" replied McConnell. "Aye, aye Sir" replied William. William knew that it probably wouldn't be long. The sub seemed to be "porpoising" every three hours or so. It was the mark of a real amateur. Rather than take advantage of the boats sensors the Oscar's Captain seemed to spend a lot of time near the surface. A submarine that big needed to spend as much time as possible in deep water to avoid detection. William had even been able to predict when it would go shallow. About two minutes before it went shallow it would slow to about four or five knots. William could hear the propeller shaft bearings vibrate and then settle down, indicative of a badly needed overhaul.

At 1950 hours William heard the familiar wobble of the "Oscars" propeller shaft bearings. The boat was definitely slowing. "Conn, sonar. Target has slowed to four knots" William reported over the intercom. He heard the Executive Officer order the crew to slow the *Topeka* to five knots. "Conn, sonar. Target coming shallow on course 032" William reported. Now was their chance to get closer. By approaching under the Thermocline, the "Oscar", who was approaching periscope depth, would never hear them. The Captain was in the control room. "Torpedo room, Conn, Load tube number one with Mk 48 ADCAP" the Captain ordered. Had the Captain orders to shoot. Only he would know. William continued listening to his earphones. It was definitely going to be a long night. William would be relieved in a few minutes. He could use the rest. His relief arrived and William briefed him on the current situation and standing orders. He made his way back to his berthing area, got undressed and rolled on to his bunk. The bunk was still warm, most likely from the sailor in engineering who shared it when William was on duty. Referred to as "hotbunking", it was the Navy's way of saving space. As tired as he was he didn't care. William still heard the staccato of the propeller beats from the "Oscar" in his ears as he drifted off to sleep.

Nathan reported to Captain Winters in CIC. He was told the new pilots had been delivered. They had to evacuate one of the pilots to Kadena because his illness became more severe. Nathan also learned that during the night a flotilla of two North Korean *Huangfeng* patrol boats and a *Najin* light frigate had been detected about one hundred miles west of Seoul. A flight of F-16's out of Kunsan AB on routine patrol detected unknown emissions and went to investigate. They reported it to Kunsan and the ROK Navy dispatched six patrol boats to investigate. It was reported that the North Koreans fired first, with two SS-N-2 Styx missiles, followed by numerous rounds of 100mm cannon. The two missiles were shot down but two ROK boats sustained numerous hits and had to be abandoned. The two *Huangfeng* patrol boats however, were destroyed by the ROK navy. The *Najin* light frigate withdrew at high speed to the North. "It seems pretty obvious that the North Koreans know that we are coming and where to look" said Captain Winters. "Yes, it does Captain, but I don't think their patrol boats will be much of a problem, I'm more concerned with the subs" Nathan said. "I agree Commander, speaking of which, a Japanese P-3C has detected a sub just outside their territorial limit" the Captain told Nathan as he took a sip of coffee. Nathan looked at the table plot and saw the red icon depicting the sub. It was shadowed by two "green" P-3C Orion's and a "green" ship icon about forty miles away. "What's this contact, sir?" Nathan asked. "That is the *Yubari*, a JMSDF light frigate which was ordered to investigate the contact" the Captain explained. Nathan hoped that the small frigate didn't close too fast. Even though the North Koreans had antiquated diesel subs, most were armed with the Russian SAET-60 torpedo. A large ship may have a chance but a small, light frigate would surely sink if hit by one. "I must have just missed you, I went to Admiral Alexander's quarters last night for a briefing. What are your plans for air cover for the AL-1A's, Commander?" Nathan was sure that the Captain didn't know everything he did. "I have ordered one four-ship formation for each AL-1A. I'd also like to have two F/A-18 on ready-five backing them up. All will be armed with AMRAAM and Sidewinder-X's" Nathan replied. "Sir, I also have ordered an E-2C Hawkeye to patrol the strait when we get near our station. We don't want anything coming up behind us" Nathan said pointing to the plot chart. "Very well Commander" the Captain said. "Sir, what is the latest intelligence on the "Oscar" that was detected?" Nathan inquired.

"Well, the *Topeka* has been tracking it for the last few days or so and is roughly in this area" the Captain said pointing to an area north of Japan's Honshu island. We'll keep an eye on this one. I want to stay at least four hundred nautical miles away from them if at all possible" the Captain added.

Major Bradford "Brad" Sanchez just finished his checklist when the tower called. "Bronco 1 you are cleared for take off on Runway 270."The tower operator said. "Bronco 1, tower. I copy that" Brad said. Brad advanced the throttles of the 747-400 slowly at first and then applied maximum thrust. The 747-400 started rolling down the runway and quickly picked up speed. At one hundred and forty knots the main gear lifted off the runway. Brad brought the aircraft into a gentle left bank and continued climbing to thirty-five thousand feet. Below him on the runway three other aircraft also took off and climbed to join him. When the other aircraft were at altitude they all headed due west, in single file with a five-mile separation.

FOUR

FIRST BLOOD

RON JACKSON WALKED DOWN THE WHITE House upper level stairs to the first floor below. Several people were at the foot of the stairs, waiting, ready to brief him on the events that occurred during the last night. As he approached the last few steps, a man closest to him addressed him. "Good Morning Mr. President, Did you sleep well?" said the aide. "As well as could be expected, I guess" Ron said. "We have coffee, Danish and fresh fruit in the situation room, Mr. President" another presidential aide reported enthusiastically.

Ronald Lawrence Jackson was sworn in as President of the United States over three years ago. He had inherited quite a few problems or "challenges" as he put it, from the previous administration. After a reorganization of the affairs in Iraq in 2006, where a new Iraqi government took control of the country, he turned his attention to the domestic issues of health care, the elderly and the dwindling job market. The Middle East was still a major concern however and as such a US military presence was still in Iraq. Continuing terrorist attacks in Europe and other countries however prompted a withdrawal of US military forces from Saudi Arabia. Since 2004 the US Central Command (CENTCOM) forward-deployed headquarters had been quietly relocated to the neighboring, more U.S. friendly country of Qatar. Two new U.S. airbases had been constructed with the approval of the Qatar government. The President of the United States had petitioned Congress for 500 million dollars in "humanitarian aid" for Qatar to help close the deal. Now, President Jackson faced the biggest challenge of his term. He was running for re-election this year and had been thrown a curve by the North Koreans. After years of talks, negotiations and treaty's on halting the proliferation of it's nuclear weapons programs, the North Korean's had launched it's most advanced ballistic missile, the Taepo Dong III, just over a week ago. This was not as much a surprise to the U.S. as it was to the rest of the world but it was of grave concern to Japan. The test was made public only twenty-four hours prior to its launch. A limited test launch, the Taepo Dong III trajectory took it over the most populated area of Japan and culminated with it's landing in the Pacific Ocean not less than one thousand miles from Tokyo. The Japanese could only look on in horror as they watched the missile track across their country. The Japanese Prime Minister had to do some thing so he ordered all his countries forces to Red Alert. The country's airspace was filled with Japanese military aircraft and the seas around Japan were teeming with Japanese Naval ships. Even some reports of friendly fire incidents surfaced in the media. Only continual prompting and assurance by President Jackson allowed the Prime Minister to lower the alert level to yellow.

President Jackson walked into the situation room, which was already bustling with activity. Several Secret Service personnel were present as were the normal collection of Army, Air Force and Naval Officers as well as their aides. Others were going about their business as the President arrived. Several of the Officers offered the President a

"Good Morning, Mr. President" and he acknowledged each one in turn, shaking their hand. He saw his Chief of Staff, Admiral Jack Grayson, across the room and walked to the end of table were his seat was. "How's the coffee today, Jack?" the President said taking his seat. "Just as good if not better than the Navy's, Mr. President" Admiral Grayson said. The Presidents National Security Advisor, Janice Lang, entered the room at a feverish pace, with notebook in hand, and made her way to the President. She bent down to the President and whispered that the Chinese President, Dao Pac Ming, was on the phone in the Oval office. The President excused himself from the room, followed by Janice. When they were out of earshot in the hallway she confided in President Jackson that the Chinese President was "considerably upset". President Jackson looked at her with a reassuring smile but said nothing.

"President Ming, this is President Jackson, How are you?" President Jackson asked, sitting at his desk in the oval office. "I am very well, Mr. President but I am greatly concerned over this business with North Korea" President Ming confessed. The President could feel the concern and anxiety in the Chinese Presidents voice. "I am concerned about it also, President Ming. The United States has for years tried every avenue available to us to deter the North Koreans from developing nuclear weapons and ballistic missiles" President Jackson said. "Yes, I am aware of your efforts with North Korea and I am sure that in the future we can establish a treaty of such a nature between *our* two countries" President Ming said. "I think that would be a good thing, *perhaps* we can do that someday" President Jackson offered. "In regards to the present situation, however, could I ask of you, Mr. President, if there are any plans that you intend to use nuclear weapons or invade North Korea?" President Ming asked cautiously. "President Ming, as you well know the United States is against the use of nuclear weapons and any weapon of mass destruction for that matter. It this age of technology it does neither friend or foe any good to wage war with these weapons. It is my sincere hope that some day in the near future that these weapons will become non existent" President Jackson explained. "As for invading North Korea, we have no plans for invading that country, regardless of what President Kim Du Loc thinks. South Korea wants nothing but peace and has no such plans either" President Jackson explained. President Jackson sensed that the Chinese President needed further assurance. He decided to try a different approach. "President Ming, The United States has no ill will against you or your country. We enjoy the trade that is set up between our countries and wish that to continue" President Jackson said. "Yes, Yes, I wish it to continue also. We very much care about the trade between our countries" President Ming shot back excitedly. So that was it. This whole conversation was about money. It was about foreign trade. To hell with North Korea, he was worried about his country's economy. A nuclear war between North Korea and the United States would adversely affect China. "Mr. President, is there any assurance I can receive from you that the United States will not use nuclear weapons in North Korea?" President Ming said. "President Ming, I can assure you that we *will not* use nuclear weapons against North Korea if the present situation escalates to that level. It is my sincere desire that it does not. If it does however, I wish to have *your* assurance that none of your military forces will interfere or engage our forces" President Jackson said. "Yes, you have my word, none of our forces will engage you. I must however advise you that we are engaged in our own naval training exercises west of the Korean peninsula" President Ming asked. "I don't think that would be a problem as long as they are in international waters" President Jackson replied. "Thank you Mr. President, I do appreciate that" the Chinese President said. "If the situation does escalate I'd like to have as few naval vessels in the Sea of Japan as possible. Do you have any vessels in that area that I should be made aware of?" asked the American President. "No Mr. President, we have no other vessels in that area. We wish not to make the situation worse" President Ming said. "As a neighbor of North Korea maybe you could reassure the North Korean president of this fact however, make no mistake, the United States remains firm in its resolve to protect itself and its allies from *any* hostile country, and that includes North Korea" President Jackson said. "Yes, I understand. I will contact President Lu Doc. I wish he would understand things as we do. Thank you, Mr. President. I appreciate your time and your candor. Good day to you, Sir" President Ming said. "Good day to you also" President Jackson said. The President hung up the phone, stood up and started walking back to the situation room. Janice joined him in the hallway, "Is he still worried?" she asked. "Worried about saving his ass maybe" the President replied.

The President returned to the situation room. He made his way to his chair, which was next to Admiral Grayson who was busy with a large, cinnamon danish. "Jack, do you realize how many calories are in one of those?" the President asked. "I try not to think about it Mr. President. Have you tried one?" Admiral Grayson asked. The President shook his head no. "Okay, good morning everyone, what have you got for me today?" the President asked. Janice, the Presidents National Security Advisor, who was sitting to his left, went first. "Mr. President, according to multiple reports yesterday, during the early morning a flotilla of two North Korean *Huangfeng* patrol boats and a *Najin* light frigate were detected about one hundred miles west of Seoul by a flight of our F-16's out of Osan AB. They reported it to Osan and the ROK Navy dispatched six patrol boats to investigate. It was reported that the North Koreans fired first, with two SS-N-2 Styx missiles, followed by numerous rounds of 100mm cannon. The two missiles were shot down but two ROK patrol boats sustained numerous hits and had to be abandoned. Several ROK personnel were killed. The two *Huangfeng* patrol boats however, were completely destroyed by the ROK navy and no survivors have been recovered. The *Najin* light frigate withdrew at high speed to the north" Janice reported. "Did the North Koreans fire on our F-16's?" the President asked. "No sir, they did not" replied Janice. "Also, early this morning a Japanese P-3C has detected an unknown sub contact just outside their territorial limit. A JMSDF Destroyer Escort, the *Yubari*, was ordered to investigate the contact" Janice added. The President looked to his right. "Where is that "Oscar" about now, Jack?" asked the President quietly, leaning over to his Chief of Staff. Admiral Grayson opened his folder and took out a paper and slid it over to the President. It was a map of Korea, the Sea of Japan and part of the Island of Japan. A point with coordinates and an red icon representing the "Oscar" was in the Sea of Japan, north of the Island of Honshu, the big island of Japan. " It's about two hundred miles off the coast, still in international waters, heading 032 at 8 - 10 knots" the Admiral said. "The *Topeka* is shadowing her, she hasn't done much since we detected her" the Admiral reported. "Well, that's good news anyway" the President said. "Mr. President, I know we all here hope that this scenario will never happen, but I think we would be remiss in our duties if we didn't plan for it. If the North Korean's do launch ballistic missiles at the United States or our allies, what can we expect our response to be?" asked the General of the Air Force, General Howard. The President sat back in his seat and wiped his eyes. He really didn't sleep all that well last night. "Well, General, I do not want to start a nuclear war, but rather, prevent one from starting. The *Reagan* Strike Group will be in position today, along with the other assets we talked about yesterday. I also understand the B-1B's and B-52's are forward-deployed to Guam, correct?" the President asked. "Yes Sir, they are on five minute alert and loaded with MK61 and MK83 nuclear weapons" the General advised. The President looked at him and then Admiral

Grayson. "Well, I know it won't be a popular decision, but no nukes General" the President ordered. Admiral Grayson looked up at the General and then the President and said "Mr. President that might be a mistake, if nuclear ballistic missiles are launched at the United States, or reach the United States…." the Admiral paused. "I understand the ramifications, Jack" the President said. "But that's *your job*. I want you to see to it that no missiles reach the United States or our allies, and that *is* an order!" the President replied adamantly. "I understand Mr. President, I will carry out the orders to the best of my ability… as I always have. If then I am to defend this country, without the use of nuclear weapons, then we must make you aware of a few programs that would contribute to such a defense" the Admiral replied. "Okay. Then lets begin" the President said. "Very well Mr. President. These programs were started covertly under previous administrations and funded in part by the DOD and the CIA. They were never made public or even talked about with the administrations that followed their development. That is until now" the Admiral explained. The President motioned for the Secret Service to leave the room as did all the Presidential aides and non-essential military personnel. The only ones that remained were the President, Janice Lang and the Joint Chiefs of Staff. For the next four hours the Joint Chiefs briefed the President on the programs that Admiral Grayson mentioned. To his amazement President Jackson never in his wildest imagination realized that the things he heard about would exist in his lifetime. Now that he knew, he wished he didn't. If a war started between North Korea and the United States, a lot of men would die. Hopefully they would not, but that was up to the North Koreans.

It was 1100 hours on the morning of August 16th. Nathan was on duty in CIC while Captain Winters was temporarily off duty getting some much needed rest. They had just finished transiting the strait between Japan and the Korean peninsula and had turned north about four hours ago. The Destroyer *USS Howard*, on the Port station about six miles from the *Reagan*, reported several fishing boats about three nautical miles distant. They were headed away so it didn't seem too important to wake the Captain. Nathan was more interested in any air threats. "Commander, Hawkeye 2 reports several unidentified contacts bearing 184 degrees from the *Reagan*, altitude 35,000 feet, speed 600 knots" reported Ensign Rockland. "How many contacts?" asked Nathan. "We show four large contacts all on the same heading. They do not answer on any frequency, Commander" Ensign Rockland reported. Nathan knew it was the AL-1A's headed to Pusan. He took out a small notebook and flipped to a few pages. Nathan motioned for the Ensign to remove his headset. He put it on and adjusted the transmitter to a pre-determined frequency. "Bronco 1 this is Big Dog, how do you read?" Nathan transmitted. No answer, Nathan tried again. "Bronco 1 this is Big Dog, how do you read?" he replied. "This is Bronco 1, we read you Big Dog" Brad said. "Welcome to the Orient Bronco 1, your cleared to your destination on flight level 35" Nathan said. "Roger, Tango Big Dog. Bronco 1 clear" Brad replied.

Nathan took off the headset and looked at a bewildered Ensign. "Sir" the Ensign began. "Don't ask" Nathan said. Nathan walked to the plot table and drew a twenty-mile corridor from the AL-1A's to Pusan. "Ensign, I need you to clear this air corridor for Bronco flight and coordinate with the JMSDF to steer clear of it, can you do that?" Nathan asked. "Aye, aye sir" the Ensign replied enthusiastically. Nathan walked to one of the controllers at the console. "Where is Sandy Flight?" Nathan asked. "They are at flight level 47, thirty-five miles out, Sir" the Seaman replied, high-lighting the flight with his "mouse". "Very well, have them escort Bronco flight to this area then return to base" Nathan ordered. Nathan circled Bronco flight on the Seaman's radar screen in grease pencil and then Pusan with a line between both of them. "Aye, aye Sir" the Seaman replied, erasing the grease pencil from the screen.

It was a really warm afternoon on Guam. Sergeant James Adams, trying to stay out of the sun, was taking tire pressures on his B-1B when the truck rolled up with the Major in it. James continued what he was doing when the Major walked towards him. "Good afternoon, Major. May I help you?" James said. "We have new orders Sergeant" the Major said. James saw the tugs with a load of two thousand pound JDAM's approaching. "Don't tell me" James said. "That's right Sergeant, download and secure all the nukes on each aircraft and then load them all with the JDAM's" the Major Ordered. "Ok, Sir. We'll get it done" James said.

Reconfiguring the war load for each bomber took less time than expected. When work had to be done on a deployment everyone pitched in and helped get the job done. The eight B-1B's and three B-52H bombers took up a lot of room on the flight line area on Guam. James had been in the Air Force for nearly fourteen years. He considered himself lucky to have been stationed near his hometown. He had been at Ellsworth AFB in South Dakota for nearly twelve years not counting the occasional deployment to Guam and Diego Garcia. He knew what he wanted to do and where he wanted to go before he signed up. Living near Ellsworth AFB he saw military aircraft on a daily basis. Since he had a mechanical aptitude, he wanted to specialize in aircraft maintenance on the B-1B bomber aircraft. When James joined the U.S. Air Force in 1994 the B-1B was just coming into it's own. The Soviet Union broke apart in 1991 so the US military went through a major reorganization after that. The B-1's were no longer destined to drop nuclear weapons over long ranges, or so it was thought. The bombers were given a new lease on life, getting major modifications allowing them to drop a multitude of conventional weapons as well as the nuclear weapons they were designed to carry. The Strategic Air Command, under which all US nuclear bombers operated, was renamed the Air Combat Command and given a new mission. Entire bomber "Wings" were broken up and dispersed around the US to different bases into "Bomb Squadrons" to take advantage of the flexibility of the B-1 bomber. The 37th Bomb Squadron was located at Ellsworth AFB and that is where James wanted to be.

Nathan awoke in the morning at about nine o'clock in one of Steven's bedrooms. He vaguely remembered the previous night, although he seemed to have had a great time. He lay awake in bed, still dressed in his boxers. Thankfully he didn't do anything to embarrass himself, or anyone else. He really enjoyed meeting Amy, Jennifer and the other girls. Jennifer was a person he would like to get to know better. Maybe they could in the next few months. They both would be near each other in Florida. Maybe they could hook up and go to an amusement park or the beach. Nathan had never been to Florida which had some great beaches. Jennifer loved to …damn, the beach! Nathan told Jill that they could go to the beach today. Nathan got up, showered and dressed quickly. He made the bed and left the door ajar as not to disturb anyone in the hallway. Nathan made his way down the hall and heard noises accompanied by the smell of coffee, eggs and toast. Amy was in the kitchen making scrambled eggs and a huge pot of coffee. "Good morning, Amy" Nathan said quietly. "Good morning, Nathan. Would you like some breakfast?" asked Amy. He didn't want to hurt her feeling, so he said "Yes please, but just coffee, I need to leave soon" Nathan explained. "Ok, well sit down. Have some eggs, they're all ready. Do you want some toast?" she asked. "Yes, thank you, that would be fine" Nathan said. "Amy, is Jennifer up yet? I'd like to say goodbye to her" Nathan asked. "No, I don't think so. I haven't heard the shower yet. I can go check if you like" Amy said. "I'd appreciate that, Amy" Nathan said. Amy poured Nathan some coffee and returned the pot to the kitchen. She walked out of the kitchen and down the hall past the bedroom where Nathan had stayed to the last bedroom. Nathan remembered that the two bedrooms shared the bathroom. He hadn't noticed any signs that someone used it in the morning so he figured she was still here. Amy returned a few moments later. "Nathan, Jennifer's not here" Amy said looking out in the driveway. "Her car is still here but her sneakers are gone. She must have gone on her run. I've been up for about an hour so she should be back soon" Amy added. Nathan finished his eggs and toast. Amy was quite the hostess. "Nathan, do you want more eggs, It won't take long? Amy asked. "No thank you, but that was very good. Actually I was going to call a cab and get going. Is there anyway I can get in contact with her" Nathan asked. "No, don't be silly. I'll drive you home if she doesn't get back soon. Here, let me give you her number. Her and I talked a bit last night after you guys passed out. She really likes you, Nathan" Amy said, writing a number on a note pad. "I think she is a wonderful girl, Amy" Nathan said. Nathan thanked Amy and told her to thank Steven again for a wonderful party. He had hoped to see Jennifer before he left but he did tell her he would call her during the week. After a few minutes Amy gathered her purse and the keys to Steven's Jaguar. They locked the door and started to walk down the steps to the car when Jennifer came running up the driveway. "Hi, Jen" Amy said. "I was gonna take Nathan home but since you're here do you want to?" she added. "Good morning, Nathan" Jennifer said. "Good morning, Jennifer" Nathan replied. "Amy I just got here. I'm all sweaty and I need a shower" Jennifer said adamantly. "I think you look lovely" Nathan said smiling. Jennifer smiled at Nathan while Amy handed him the keys to the Jaguar. "Nathan, you drive home and then Jennifer can drive back" Amy said. Nathan put Jennifer into the passenger seat and then returned to Amy to thank her. He said good bye and received a big hug and a kiss on the cheek from Amy when he left.

The Jaguar XJ6 came to life and Nathan pulled out of the drive and on to the road. "So how far do you run?" Nathan asked. "I try to do about three miles every other day" Jennifer replied. "The days I don't run I go to the gym" She added. Nathan drove home the long way, the most scenic route, so he could spend more time with Jennifer. "Boy, were you out of it last night" Jennifer told Nathan. "When you and Steven started talking Navy, us girls sort of excused ourselves to the pool area. We all drank a lot of beer last night" Jennifer giggled. "All of us girls went skinny dipping while you guys were busy talking in the living room" Jennifer laughed. "Really, Nathan said. "I'm sorry I missed that part" Nathan added. "We didn't go for long. Amy got scared that we would get caught so we just got wet and then we all put our bikinis back on" Jennifer explained with a smile. "I remember helping you to your bed, with Amy's help. I hope she doesn't think we slept together" Jennifer said. "No, she doesn't" Nathan replied. "Like I said, we all drank a lot of beer last night. Do you remember me giving you a kiss goodnight?" Jennifer asked cautiously. "No, but I wished I did. I would have returned it" Nathan said looking at her. He noticed her smiling. She had a sweet and innocent smile. "I'm sorry, I shouldn't have done that. I don't want to give you the wrong idea. I want to get to know you a lot better before…" she hesitated. "…before you go into the Navy" she finished. Nathan could tell that's not what she meant to say, but he accepted it. He also wanted to get to know her better. He pulled into the drive of his apartment complex and swung into an empty parking spot near the front. He put the Jaguar in park and set the brake. "Amy gave me your number, may I call you in a few days, Jennifer?" Nathan asked. "Yes, I'd like that" Jennifer said. "Good" Nathan replied. "I'm looking forward to seeing you again" Nathan turned to her as if he was going to kiss her. "You don't want to kiss me, I'm all sweaty" she said smiling as she looked out the passenger window. "Yeah, I know and you need a shower!" Nathan shot back. She turned around quickly and Nathan kissed her quickly on the cheek. Instead of being mad she grabbed his face in her two small hands and kissed him back. "Now go on and let me get cleaned up" she said smiling, pushing Nathan away. Nathan got out, stepped back and closed the door. Jennifer climbed over the console into the driver seat. She took off the brake, put the Jaguar in reverse and slowly backed out. Putting the car in gear she waved. "Call me"she yelled as she drove away. Oh yeah, definitely I will call you, Nathan thought.

Brad brought the 747-400 aircraft down and landed at Pusan AB with three minutes of the scheduled landing time. The flight of F/A-18 Super Hornets providing escort was a welcome sight. He knew they would be his only defense from enemy fighter aircraft during this mission. It was a long flight and he was looking forward to some rest. The ground crew would refuel and check the aircraft and it would be ready for the relief crew in about one hour. Bronco 1 had an on-station time of 1500hrs. Brad and the other crew members gathered their personal items and got ready to leave the aircraft not soon after the aircraft parked and shut off it's engines. Brad talked to the Mission Commander who was responsible for the Navy crewmembers and the Weapon System on the AL-1A. The Mission Commander said that all the diagnostics for the High Energy Laser checked out and the system was operational. He told Brad he would be leaving two personnel on board to monitor the system. As they both walked to the operations building Brad hoped that they wouldn't have to fire the laser at all. If they did it might very well mean nuclear war. Brad checked in with the operations commander who was grateful for his arriving at Pusan. Brad found the car that was parked outside which was assigned to him. He drove to the Visiting Officers Quarters, found his room and put his gear on the floor. After cleaning up, he lay on the bed resting his eyes. It was really a long flight. He thought it was such a long way from home also, as he drifted off to sleep.

Lieutenant Iso Yamuko brought his aircraft smartly around to heading 127. He hoped that the next set of sonobouys they were going to drop would re-establish contact on the submarine. The contact appeared hostile as it changed its course but always came back to it base course of 127. The subs commander must be a seasoned veteran for they had lost the contact twice when the sub went below the Thermocline and then changed course, doubled back and then changed course again. The data from the contact showed it to be a Whiskey class submarine, probably North Korean. It was eighteen miles from the three- mile international limit. If it passed this limit then Yamuko had orders to drop an active sonobouy. This would definitely tell the sub that they meant business. The Japanese P-3C Orion was loaded with four MK-50 lightweight torpedoes. One torpedo would be sufficient to send the submarine to the bottom in pieces. The radio operator informed Yamuko that the

Destroyer Escort *Yubari* was twenty miles away and closing on the submarine contact. Yamuko didn't really care for that. The P-3C's from Atsugi had matters well in hand. Sending in the Destroyer Escort was foolish. He had noticed that things had really not changed in the six years he was in the JMSDF. The P-3C had dropped two Sonobuoys and made contact with the sub directly ahead of the P-3C. Yamuko looked at his fuel gauge and determined he could stay another two hours or so before he had to leave for base.

Captain Feng knew he was playing a dangerous game, but he was up to the task. Twice he had fooled his pursuers by ordering his Whiskey class diesel submarine to evade the aircraft flying over him, trying to pinpoint his location. He knew that he would be able to accomplish his mission because his pursuers would not shoot at him unless he shot first. His mission was to deliver the four men to the Japanese shore. They would act as human intelligence for the North Korean government in case a war started. He had received word from his sonar operator that a surface ship, most likely a warship, was closing on them. It was over twenty miles away but making twenty-six knots. The aircraft above them was most likely Japanese or American. The sonar operators could hear the large turboprops of the anti-submarine aircraft reverberate through the water even at this depth. Several times the torpedo officer called and asked if he should load torpedoes. Feng told him there was no need for that now. Captain Feng realized that the entire crew must know that they are being pursued. A torpedo fired now could deter the warship that was closing on them but would definitely invite disaster. If Feng did that he would come under immediate counter attack from the aircraft above. He decided not to risk it right now. The aircraft above him had been harassing him for over ten hours. They must be low on fuel which meant they had a relief on the way also. Feng was low on fuel also, which meant battery power. He had to come to periscope depth in a few hours to charge his batteries and run on the diesel engines. They were amazing efficient but very noisy. He ordered his sub down to 400 feet to throw off his pursuers.

Captain Su Loc grew inpatient. He knew the American aircraft carrier would be close to the area he patrolled. He had been here for a few days but had no solid contacts. He decided to take the Submarine up to periscope depth once again. He ordered the vessel slowed to four knots. The submarine rose to the surface and Captain Su Loc ordered the radio antennae extended. If there were any messages they would be copied quickly and brought to the attention of the Captain. "Captain" the radio officer said. "We have an intelligence report on the American carrier!" the radio officer reported excitedly. "Very good, what is the message?" the Captain asked. "The carrier is on course 008, bearing 254 from our position. The carrier is traveling at twenty-four knots!" reported the radio officer. "What is the distance" asked the Captain angrily. "The carrier is approximately three hundred and sixty miles from our position" the radio officer replied. The Captain ordered the masts retracted and the submarine to a depth of three hundred meters. Once the "Oscar" got to its new depth he ordered an intercept course of 270, due west and increased speed to twenty-seven knots. He had to get closer to the American carrier. If he was ordered to attack the carrier he wanted to be within at least three hundred and twenty miles. The twenty-two SS-N-19 missiles he carried on board had the range and the speed to close and destroy the American aircraft carrier. If he was ordered to attack the carrier and he succeeded in sinking her, it would be a great morale builder for the crew as well as greatly contributing to his own career.

Seaman Mark Childers listened to his headphones. Nothing different that the last two times the "Oscar" went to periscope depth. He heard the rattle of her machinery and the popping of her hull as she went deep. He watched his sonar display. The sounds seemed to emanate from more off to port this time. "Conn, sonar" he said. "Possible aspect change on target. Aspect change based on bearing rate" he added. The Captain ordered the *Topeka* slowed to four knots. "Conn, sonar. Target on new course of 270. Target increasing speed!" Seaman Childers reported excitedly. "Target has increased speed to twenty-seven knots on a new heading of 270, depth approximately 950 feet" Childers reported. He is going somewhere in a hell of a hurry and doesn't care who knows, Childers thought. Childers heard the Captain change course and ordered the *Topeka* to twelve hundred feet. Once there they could be assured of going over twenty knots without cavitating. The "Oscar" wasn't losing them but he did increase his lead a bit. Better that than chase after them and possibly give away their position. They had tracked the "Oscar" this far, no sense of screwing it up now, Childers thought.

Captain Billings knew the "Oscar" had sniffed something out. A submarine doesn't travel that fast without a good reason. He looked at the plot board and drew a line on the heading of "Oscar" that extended to the coast of the Korean peninsula. He confirmed his suspicions. The "Oscar" must have information on the *Reagan* Strike Group. The "Oscar" was heading to where the *Reagan* would be on-station. He had to report this one. He ordered the *Topeka* slowed to four knots and then on up to periscope depth. Captain Billings wrote the message on a tablet and handed it to his executive officer. "Have this sent immediately, I want to get back to depth as soon as possible" the Captain said. "Aye, aye sir" the executive officer replied. The executive officer went to the communications room forward of the control room. The message was sent to the *Reagan* and returned with a personal reply from Rear Admiral Steven Alexander. It said that if the "Oscar" attempted to launch its missiles then the *Topeka* had orders to destroy it. Well, that was it then. The orders were very clear. When the "Oscar" went to fire her missiles she would have to be at periscope depth to get final targeting data. It would then have to open the cavernous missile bays, which would be heard by the *Topeka*. That was the point when the *Topeka* would have to launch her torpedoes. The radio antenna was retracted and Captain Billings ordered the *Topeka* down to twelve hundred feet. Once at depth he increased speed to thirty knots to close on the "Oscar". Captain Billings thought long and hard on his next decision. He had a Mk-48 ADCAP already loaded in tube one. The Mk-48 ADCAP carried a warhead with 650lbs of high explosive. It definitely would be capable of killing the "Oscar" but Billings wanted some back up insurance. "Torpedo room, conn. This is the Captain. Load tubes two, three and four with Mk-48 ADCAP torpedo" the Captain ordered.

Steven Alexander was in CIC when the *Topeka* radioed. He typed the orders back to the sub himself and included a personal message to Captain Billings. He had known Billings for years and he was a very competent submarine commander. He walked over to Nathan and informed him of the recent news on the location of the "Oscar". "I know its not good news, Commander" said Steven. "No it isn't, Sir" Nathan replied. "Commander, I need to have a helicopter available in about thirty minutes. I need to update the Commanders of the *Lake Champlain, Princeton* and the *Shiloh*. I should return by about 1500 hours" Steven told Nathan. "Very well Sir, I'll make the arrangements" Nathan replied.

Steven had the updated information on various targets for the Tomahawk missiles. If the North Koreans launched their missiles then the Tomahawks would be launched prior to an air attack by the *Reagan*'s aircraft. They flew at very low altitude and were used to attack "soft targets" at airfields and command centers. Additional targets were approved after the Strike Group left San Diego. Steven wanted to visit each ship and give the commanders the updated target coordinates and personally answer any questions they may have. If things went bad it was looking that the North Koreans would be on the receiving end. Nathan reviewed the flight operations for the day. Today was the first day the AL-1A aircraft would take position off the coast. The North Koreans would surely send something to intercept them. It worried Nathan that he wouldn't be able to fly the first sortie. He should be up there with his men but his duties, as Air Wing Commander, would keep him on the *Reagan* for now anyway. One of Nathan's friends, Lieutenant Commander James "Jimmy" Aulicino, would lead one of the flights of four F/A-18 Super Hornets. He was the Squadron Commander of VFA-21 nicknamed "The Wolfpack". Jimmy was a great fighter pilot and was cool under stress. He was Nathan's wingman in 2003 when Nathan shot down the MiG-29 over the Persian Gulf. Nathan and Jimmy developed a strong friendship even before that day. They went through Officer Training School and Aviation Training School together at Pensacola back in 1992 and since Nathan was an only child, Jimmy was the best man at Nathan's wedding.

The F/A-18's would take position above and behind the AL-1A at an altitude of forty-eight thousand feet. It started out to be a partly cloudy day, which was fine, for the AL-1A needed to be above the clouds for the laser to operate efficiently. The flight would be supported by an JMSDF AWACS out of Yokota AB as well as the Hawkeye's from the *Reagan*. The Hawkeye's could warn the F/A-18's of any threat headed toward the AL-1A's. Nathan went to the plot table in CIC and looked at the Korean coast. The North Koreans had several "Osa" class patrol boats that could dart out and launch their anti-ship missiles. He decided to have the JSF's do an armed recon of the coast. The F-35 Joint Strike Fighter, or JSF, was designed to carry its ordinance internally. This was very important and politicaly correct in this day and age. The F-35's could patrol up and down the coast seemingly unarmed on a "training flight" but could lash out to any threat with a mix of HARM's, Mavericks or AMRAAM's. The US Air Force was responsible for protecting the land assets of the South Korean government and the *Reagan's* responsibility extended to anything within three miles of the coast. If the JSF's encountered any surface threats that fired on them they would be dealt with.

Captain Winters entered CIC when Nathan was delivering orders to the Air Boss. "Good morning Sir, I hope you slept well" Nathan inquired. "Yes Commander, I did believe it or not. What do we have going on" the Captain inquired, rolling his cigar from one side of his mouth to the other. Nathan briefed the Captain on the "Oscar" submarine. The Captain took his unlit cigar out of his mouth and put it away. "What are we going to do about it?" the Captain asked Nathan. "Well sir, I have ordered a Combat Air Patrol from Yokosuka AB to patrol an area two hundred and fifty miles from us. The *Topeka* has orders from Admiral Alexander to sink the "Oscar" if she attempts to launch her missiles. The CAP will deal with any cruise missiles if they are launched before they get to our outer perimeter defenses" Nathan explained. "Very good Commander. Now I know why I slept so well. I can't tell you how grateful I am that you took this assignment" the Captain said. Nathan was surprised at the compliment. The Captain didn't really give compliments. "Thank you, Sir" Nathan replied graciously. "Sir, also the Admiral is off the ship. He requested a Seahawk to confer with the Commanders of the *Lake Champlain, Princeton* and the *Shiloh*. His call sign is Buster 23. He is scheduled back on the *Reagan* at 1500 hours" Nathan advised the Captain. The Captain nodded as if he already knew, which he may have. "The AL-1A flights have launched from Pusan and will be on station in about an hour. Our F/A-18's will rendezvous with them in thirty minutes" Nathan added. "Very good Commander. I'll take over for the rest of the watch. I'll call you if I need you" the Captain said. Nathan thanked the Captain and headed for his quarters. Nathan looked at his watch. It was 1430 hours. He wasn't really hungry but he could use a nap. He also needed to write a letter home. The mail run will go out by tomorrow morning. By then they will be within twenty miles of their station. He and Steven planned on having dinner in the Officer's Mess at 1800 hours. He could write his letter and still get some shut-eye.

Lieutenant Commander James "Jimmy"Aulicino had been in the Navy for sixteen years, the same amount of time as Nathan. He had been a lot of places and seen a lot of things. He had been shot at but never had fired a shot in anger. James was the third son of an Italian businessman in New York City. Rather than be involved in the family "business", he opted for college and joined the Navy soon after. This afternoon he found himself commanding a flight of four F/A-18 Super Hornets on a Combat Air Patrol mission. They were to rendezvous with an aircraft known only as "Bronco 1". James was told it was a "Special 747-400" fitted to detect North Korean ballistic missile launches. During the pre-flight briefing he was told that they needed to keep a fifteen-mile clear perimeter around the 747-400. James realized that North Korea might be planning a missile launch. There was talk a few weeks ago that they might have launched a ballistic missile over Japan into the Pacific

Ocean. James was almost to his on-station location when he saw the outline of a 747 ahead and below at about forty-three thousand feet. He called over the radio. "Bronco 1 this is Wolf 1, how do you read?" James transmitted. "Wolf 1, we read you. Thanks for your help" the pilot of the 747 radioed back. "Bronco 1 we are at Angels 47 at your six o'clock. Just relax Bronco 1, we have your back" James replied. James looked out the starboard side of his aircraft and waved to his wingman. He retarded his throttles so they kept just above and behind the lumbering 747.

The klaxon rang at 1520 hours on August 16th at Taetan AB in North Korea. It seemed to be a routine afternoon as each pilot ran to his MiG-23 fighter. The pilots had done this many times before in training. They ran to their aircraft, climbed in and pretended to start their engines. Because of fuel restrictions the pilots were forbidden to start the engines without direct orders from their Operations Commander. When Commander Choi climbed in his aircraft and established communications with the tower operator he was in a three-way conversation with two other people. Choi heard the operator yell excitedly, "This is no drill! Start your engines, launch your aircraft!" Choi started his engine, did a quick pre-flight check and taxied out of his underground shelter. Once on the runway he waited for his wingman to pull on to the runway and then advanced his throttles to military power and released his brakes. The aircraft lunged forward and quickly picked up speed as it rocketed down the runway. At three hundred feet he retracted his landing gear and pulled up into a climb to the right, towards the Sea of Japan. When Commander Choi reached five thousand feet he throttled back and looked for the rest of his flight. His wingman was with him as well as the other members of the flight, eight aircraft in all. The tower operator gave him a bearing to the threat and told them to investigate.

The contact was reported as large and slow at forty-two thousand feet. Choi ordered his flight to forty thousand feet and to maintain seven hundred and fifty knots. They would investigate all right. Just as he did many times before. The American reconnaissance aircraft that all too often would approach their shores would be taunted and played with to trying to drawing them closer to shore within the operating envelope of the shore SAM batteries. It would look better to the rest of the world if the Americans were shot down by surface-to-air missiles than aircraft.

The AWACS operator was observing Bronco 1 and Wolf Flight when eight small blips appeared on his radar screen. The standing orders were radio silence unless a credible threat was discovered. Eight aircraft in close formation at forty thousand feet was credible enough. He called for the Mission Commander. He was ordered by the Mission Commander to break radio silence and inform Wolf 1. "Wendy 23 to Wolf 1, you have company" the operator said. "You have eight bandits at angels forty on bearing 027. Bandits are closing at seven-five-zero knots" the AWACS operator added. James acknowledged the AWACS operator. "This is Wolf 1, I copy that" James replied.

Well, this was it, James thought. What they did in the next thirty minutes might determine if a war was started. "Wolf 1 to Wolf 7 and 8. Stay with Bronco 1. Wolf 4 and myself will investigate the contacts" James ordered. "Copy that Wolf 1" they replied. James turned his aircraft to intercept the contacts. He and Wolf 4 accelerated to over 800 knots. James glanced down at his scope. He detected no emissions from the contacts. Good so far, except that most of their aircraft were directed by ground intercept anyway. He did detect a lot of search radar emissions though. Somebody knew they were here and they were pissed. James looked down at his scope again. Bronco 1 was a good twenty-five miles behind them now. He looked up through his HUD and could see eight small black dots ahead in the sky. As they grew bigger James could identify the particular aircraft. "Wendy 23, Wolf 1, Visual on eight MiG two-threes" James reported. The AWACS operator replied and James heard him vector Bronco 1 away from the area.

When the American fighter aircraft appeared in front of them it startled some of the inexperienced North Korean MiG pilots. Some, who only had 100 hours of actual flight time, had never seen an actual enemy fighter in flight. Commander Choi ordered his last flight of four aircraft to evade the fighters and continue to the large contact. Sensing danger in the Commanders voice, the pilot of the third aircraft of Choi's flight, excitedly flipped his arming switch on. The infra-red sensor of the AA-11 "Archer" missile came alive and the cockpit warning sensor went off. Being inexperienced, the pilot frantically looked to shut off the sound and inadvertently hit the "hot" button. The AA-11 "Archer" missile came off the rail of the MiG's starboard wing and tracked straight past Commander Choi's aircraft, towards the American formation. Commander Choi screamed into his radio intercom as the missile went by "No, you idiot!"

James was ready for the usual cat and mouse games but was surprised when he saw the missile burst off the MiG's wing. He ordered a break right to his wingman and yelled "flares". The second flare just came off James's aircraft when the missile tracked on it and exploded, showering the "Super Hornet's" left Pratt & Whitney F414 with 7.4 kilograms of shrapnel. James never saw so many warning lights come on all at once. He called for Wolf 4 to engage at will and for assistance from the *Reagan*. He advised the *Reagan* that his aircraft was hit. James rolled and dived through the MiG formation and came around headed toward

Bronco 1. He shut down his left engine and put out the fire. He reset his master caution warning light several times but to no avail. He flipped on his attack radar, locked up two separate MiG's that were headed for Bronco 1 and pushed the hot button twice. He called "Fox One" twice as one by one two AMRAAM's came off the crippled "Super Hornet". They both tracked straight to the fleeing MiG's and exploded. James saw the two MiG's erupt in fireballs. James heard his wingman call "Fox 1". Anthony called for his wingman. "Wolf 1 to Wolf 4 where the hell are you?"James said excitedly. "I'm above you Wolf 1, stay were you are" he replied. James looked back and saw another MiG coming around on his tail. In that instant an AMRAAM came streaking down from above and blew apart the MiG. Wolf 4 told James that the remaining MiG's were heading for home in quite a hurry. James was relieved. Now he had only to get his F/A-18 home to the *Reagan*.Nathan had just finished addressing the letter to his wife when a loud, repeated knock came on the door. Nathan opened the door and a Marine sergeant told Nathan that he was needed in CIC immediately. Nathan quickly followed the Marine sergeant who ran through the passageways and yelled for other personnel to stand clear. Nathan arrived at the door to CIC, which was already open. Nathan entered and the Marines secured the door behind him. The CIC was a flurry of activity with several console operators talking at the same time and relaying orders to other units. The Captain was at the plot table as new red icons appeared near the formation of F/A-18's that were returning to the *Reagan*. "Bad News, Commander" the Captain began. "Wolf flight was intercepted by eight MIG-23's. They fired on Wolf 1 and he took major damage" the Captain added. "Is he okay?" Nathan asked. "He is for now. They downed three MiG's, but we have another problem Commander. We have two North Korean coastal patrol boats in that area and Wolf 1 may have to bail out" the Captain explained. "The two F/A-18's on ready-five alert were launched and I have two Marine HH-60 rescue helicopters on the way to that location" the Captain explained. Nathan heard the radio transmissions from Wolf 1 to the *Reagan*. Wolf 1 was steadily losing control of his aircraft as the hydraulic fluid leaked out of the hydraulic system. Wolf 1 radioed he was at four thousand feet in a descent and could not recover. He advised the *Reagan* that he was bailing out. Seconds later Wolf 4 confirmed the action and gave their location. Wolf 4 also advised that the North Korean patrol boats have changed course and speed towards Wolf 1. The Captain grabbed a mike and spoke. "Wolf 4 this is Top Dog, be advised that CSAR is on the way. You are ordered to stay with Wolf 1 and render assistance" the Captain ordered. Wolf 4 acknowledged the Captain. Nathan knew what Wolf 4 had to do. The North Koreans meant to pick up James. Wolf 4 had to prevent that.

James could see the North Korean patrol boats turn as he floated down in his parachute. The foamy white wakes turned in a half-moon as the sun glinted off them. He knew he would have a rough time of it if Wolf 4 had to leave. He reached for his right side and grimaced in pain, the result of a dislocated left shoulder. When he hit the water he struggled out of his harness but didn't inflate his raft. He could tread water for a while and there was no sense in giving away his exact position to the North Koreans. He saw Wolf 4 fly over head at about two thousand feet toward the patrol boats. The "Super Hornet" nosed over and gave the first boat a two-second burst of twenty-millimeter cannon. The boat slowed and seemed to have light, black smoke coming from it. James could hear the second boat cut loose with heavy caliber cannon. James could see the tracer's arc up and drop short of the "Super Hornet" as it pulled up and away. Wolf 4 pulled up to a safe altitude and awaited the search and rescue helicopters.

James was in the water for about a half hour when he hear the helicopters approach his position. Wolf 4 must have directed them to his exact position. The heavy Marine HH-60 flew past at about two hundred feet towards the two North Korean patrol boats which were now both within gun range. The HH-60 cut loose with its dual GAU-18 .50 caliber machine gun on the closest patrol boat. The boat that had been damaged before exploded and erupted in flames as the HH-60 flew by it, The second patrol boat continued firing it's 37mm cannon at the HH-60 as it flew by. Its tracers again fell short as the helicopter continued up in a big arc. The other HH-60 rescue helicopter came in lower at about fifty feet and hovered above James. It hovered down to about twenty feet when a Navy search and rescue crewman opened the door, jumped in and swam over to James. He asked James if he was hurt. James told him his shoulder might be dislocated. The crewman told him it was going to hurt like hell but they had to get him out of here first. James nodded and said "Let's go". The second patrol boat turned its attention to the HH-60 with the rescue crew and started firing it's 37mm cannon and 14.5mm machine guns. The cannon rounds missed, going under, but some of the 14.5mm rounds hit their target. The HH-60 pilot skidded the helicopter to the side, gave the patrol boat a short burst of .50 caliber projectiles and backed off, out of the range of the patrol boat. The situation at that point looked hopeless not only to James but also the rescue crewman with him in the water.

The Captain of the *Jang Bogo* class submarine was near the surface and peering through his periscope, having heard several loud explosions to the west earlier. The South Korean coastal submarine changed course to investigate. The Captain couldn't believe his eyes. Two US helicopters were engaged in a rescue operation while being engaged by two North

Korean SO-1 class patrol boats. The Captain of the *Jang Bogo* was enraged by what he saw. He ordered his crew to battle stations. "All hands, Battle Stations, Missile" He yelled. The crew sprung to life as they had done before. "Load tube 1 and 2 with UGM-84" he ordered. He peered through the periscope more intently. "Range to target 3800 yards, bearing 087" the Captain relayed to his crew. "Match bearings and shoot tube 1" the Captain ordered.

Wolf 4 was at four thousand feet and saw the Harpoon missile break the surface. The rocket motor fired and the missile headed down to cruise altitude, toward the North Korean missile boat. "Wolf 4 to Marine 234, take a heading of 230 and stand-by, we have a missile launch in the area" Wolf 4 radioed. The pilot of the Marine HH-60 banked the helicopter around and headed away. The North Korean gunners kept firing at the HH-60 long after it went out of range. The Harpoon missile tracked closer to the second patrol boat, close enough that the crew's attention was now diverted to it. A gunner on the dual 37mm cannon mount yelled "Missile" but it was too late. The Harpoon missile bored into the starboard quarter of the SO-1 class boat and exploded. The explosion lifted the rear of the one hundred and thirty-seven-foot vessel from the sea. The vessel quickly broke into in two and sank with the loss of all of its crew. The second HH-60 came back around to James after the explosion and hovered above him again. A second crewmember lowered the winch and began lifting James aboard. His shoulder hurt like hell but he tried to ignore it. Once James got aboard he recognized the second crewmember, Ensign Howard "Skippy" Rockland. James thought about it for a second and then realized that the Ensign got his wish, he was where the action was. The Ensign lowered the winch for the other rescue crewmember. The first patrol boat, which was previously damaged, now approached the HH-60. With most of its crew dead and its heavy weapons destroyed, the remaining crew members on the patrol boat cut loose with small arms fire. The rescue crewman just got on board when some rounds found their mark. Two rounds of 7.62mm tore into the rescue crewman's leg and sent the others to the floor of the HH-60. The HH-60 rescue pilot radioed to the other HH-60 for support. Ensign Rockland stood up, unlocked the port-side GAU-2/C mini-gun and swung it at the patrol boat. He fired a long burst at the patrol boat, which was now less that eighty yards from them. Two North Koreans were hit and fell off the patrol boat. The last gunner on the boat emptied his remaining AK-47 magazine into the HH-60 as it banked and gained speed away from the melee. The HH-60 radioed the *Reagan* that the rescue was complete and they were returning with casualties on board. Wolf 4 departed the area, leaving the first patrol boat to the same fate as another Harpoon missile streaked up from the depths.

Ensign Rockland fell back onto the injured rescue crewman as the helicopter banked and sped away. James sat up and looked at him as the helicopter leveled off. Ensign Rockland was bleeding badly from his shoulder and had a deep wound on the side of his neck. James made his way to him and tried to stop his neck from bleeding but it was too late. The kid was one hell of an officer and the first casualty of what looked to be the beginning of a long, deadly war.

FIVE

RENDEZVOUS

IT WAS AUGUST 15TH AND A beautiful, sunny day in Sao Paulo. Juan just finished serving an older couple lunch in the Grand Café and Lounge. Juan had worked for the Sao Paulo Grand Resort for about three years and truly enjoyed his work. He got to meet people from all over the world, some even celebrities. He walked to the front of the café where a woman patiently waited with two young children. "Good Morning, Mrs. Buckman, you have three for lunch, Yes?" Juan asked. "Oh yes, please" she laughed "Just something quick" she said smiling. Juan seated her in the center of the café, near the television. There were other patrons there watching the stock news and leisurely eating lunch. A World News Network (WNN) special report broke in when Juan delivered the orange juice for the children. "An update from an earlier story, WNN has just received another report that several US Navy personnel have been injured on a routine air patrol off of South Korea. It is confirmed that at least one Navy aircraft, possibly more, have crashed about seventy miles off the coast of North Korea. The aircraft is confirmed as being from the aircraft carrier *USS Ronald Reagan* which sailed from San Diego, North Island. The Defense Department has declined to comment on the incident except that the *Reagan* is on a routine patrol in the Sea of Japan" the reporter said. The children didn't really pay attention to the report but did hear the name of the *Reagan*. "Mom, that's dad's ship. Did you hear, that was daddy's ship" Nathan's daughter Nicole said excitedly. "Yes honey, I know. Please listen" The report continued telling how WNN had also received unconfirmed reports that the aircraft were intercepted by North Korean MiG's while protecting an American surveillance aircraft off the North Korean coast. The report went on to show file footage of the *Reagan* involved in air operation off of the California coast. Nicole broke her silence. "Mom, *there's* dad's ship!" Nicole said excitedly. Her mother, ignoring her, was riveted to the television. The reporter, who was obviously in Japan, reported an increase in activity of the Japanese Maritime Self Defense Force and the Air Force. "Several large aircraft, known as AWACS, have been observed taking off from several Japanese air bases. These aircraft are what the military calls their Airborne Warning And Control System aircraft. They have powerful radar's that can "see" hundreds of miles and advise the military leadership of potential hostile threats" the journalist reported. Juan returned with a chef salad for Mrs. Buckman and some sandwiches for the children. He paused to look at Mrs. Buckman, noticing a look of concern on her face. "Is everything okay, Mrs. Buckman" Juan asked. "I hope so" she said gesturing towards the television. "My husband is on the *Reagan*" she added. "I'm sure he will be fine Mrs. Buckman" he replied. She hoped he would anyway. He was a long way from home. Nathan had a way of shielding her from things. Was this his way of shielding her now? They had both talked of taking this trip together. She knew how important it was to Nathan. All she could do was hope and pray. Another reporter on the anchor desk interrupted the reporter. They said they had a special report from retired Admiral Robert S. Alexander. Good, she thought. She would feel more comfortable hearing from someone she knew. Robert, who was Steven's father, worked for WNN as a consultant in defense matters. The reporter at the anchor desk did a short history of the Admirals career before asking him what he thought of the incidents. "Well, I think at this time it's hard to tell. Given the information we now have it may be nothing more that an incident between our own aircraft. The North Koreans have intercepted our jets for years over the Sea of Japan with no incident. In fact the last time an incident took place was back in April 1969. Our own military does hundreds of intercepts each year to protect our shores from incursions, the vast majority being airliners that are off course or that have incorrect flight plans. As for the AWACS aircraft, they would normally be used on any exercise of this type and it's not uncommon to have them operate from several bases" Robert explained. "So Admiral Alexander you don't think there is any cause for alarm?" the reporter asked. Rather than hesitate the Admiral answered right away. "No, I don't think so. I know I'll sleep well tonight Tom" the Admiral said with a humorous smile. The reporter asked one more question, one that the Admiral had been waiting and rehearsed for. "Very good Admiral, one more question. Have you any information on a North Korean ballistic missile launch during the past few weeks?" the reporter asked. "No, that's a new one Tom. I hadn't heard of anything like that" the Admiral chuckled. The children were getting restless. They were finished with lunch and started their usual playful fighting which meant they were both tired. She heard the reporter go on to other events in the world. She thought about what the Admiral said about the ballistic missiles. She knew Robert well enough to know that even if he did know he wouldn't tell the world and start a panic. Something deep down troubled her though. An instinct she learned being a naval officer's wife these many years. If there was a danger then this is where Nathan would want her and his children to be.

President Jackson was awakened at 0200 hours on Aug 16th and was outraged when he was informed of the action. The surveillance recording from the AWACS was played for the President in his oval office. It clearly showed the North Koreans fired first. Whether it was intentional or not would be determined later. The President inquired into the status of the AL-1A's and the pilot of the Super Hornet. Admiral Grayson stated that the AL-1A was fine as well as the F/A-18 pilot, but a rescue crewman, a young naval officer, was killed in the rescue attempt. The President, furious from the news, tried to gather his composure before speaking. "Mr. President, there is more" Admiral Grayson said. "We have just gotten these satellite photos from Beale" The Admiral said. "Janice, lets get some air time on this one, all the networks. Make it at eight o'clock. I want to talk to the North Korean President first" The President said, looking at the photos the Admiral handed him. Janice Lang left the room and set things in motion. The President sat in his oval office contemplating the call to the North Korean President. "As you can see here, here and here Mr. President, these missile sites have shown an increase in activity during the last twelve hours. The North Koreans intercepted our F/A-18's here, which is about ninety miles from the missile base at Toksong-gun. We believe these photos show the North Koreans are preparing to launch several missiles from these sites" the Admiral said. The President did not like what he saw. "What about the other missile sites" the President asked. "We won't have updated photos on them for another six hours, Mr. President" Admiral Grayson explained. "Jack, include them in the war plan if they have missiles present" the President said. "Yes sir, we have.

We were just waiting for your order" Admiral Grayson replied. "The order is given, Jack" the President said. Admiral Grayson nodded in compliance, looking at the President across his desk. The President continued looking at the photographs, making notes on paper and looking at the clock. "Mr. President if you could excuse me I need to be going" the Admiral said. "Oh sure. Jack, as soon as you get those photos on the other bases I'd like to see them" the President said. "I'll deliver them personally, Mr. President" Admiral Grayson replied as he left his chair. Admiral Grayson said goodbye and left the oval office, holding the door for Janice. Janice approached the President and announced that the press conference was set for eight in the morning and that the North Korean President was on the line. He thanked her, picked up the phone and motioned for her to sit. "Good evening, President Lu Doc" the President started. "Yes, Mr. President, I was expecting you to call. This has been a very regretful day in our lives" the North Korean President said. "Yes, I agree and one that could have been prevented. I have been informed and seen the evidence that your Air Force has fired on our aircraft" the President explained firmly. President Lu Doc hesitated, probable collecting his thoughts and controlling his anger at the American President. "Regrettably, I have received the same report. It seems an inexperienced pilot inadvertently fired on your aircraft. He paid for it with his life as did his flight commander and another pilot. I can assure you that it was unintentional and could have been avoided if your aircraft were not that close to our shores" President Lu Doc replied coldly. The American president became enraged at President Lu Doc' nonchalant attitude. "And the rescue crewman that were shot at in our helicopters, was that unintentional also?" President Jackson shot back. "Our patrol boats were attempting to help when they were attacked by your aircraft, Mr. President. Your military deliberately fired on our patrol boats!" the North Korean President pleaded. "President

Lu Doc *you know* why we are there!" President Jackson replied angrily. "Mr. President, North Korea has the right to develop our military capability as we see fit. We know you have been poised to attack our country for years. The only thing we are doing is developing a nuclear deterrent force against our adversaries as you have with the Soviets years ago" President Lu Doc explained. The American President paused to regroup. Could the North Korean President be sincere? It was true, the United States had been in a nuclear arms race with the Soviets years ago. "Mr. President, the United States is not or ever has been interested in the conquest of North Korea. We agree that you have the right to develop your military. It is our sincere hope though that you find the wisdom to do that without the use of nuclear weapons. These weapons serve no ones interest in today's political climate" The American President explained. "These weapons are *our deterrent* against attack. We will continue to develop them and protect our shores against any incursion Mr. President" President Lu Doc said angrily. "I have talked to President Dao Pac Ming and he agrees that North Korea has this right also. The United States should consider flying no closer that fifty miles from our shores, Mr. President. Any closer and we shall consider it as an intrusion into our airspace" President Lu Doc demanded. "Mr. President, international law observes a three mile limit and so shall the United States" replied President Jackson coldly. The President's National Security Advisor listened intently, taking notes on the conversation. She looked up at her President with a somber look. She had hoped in her lifetime that another incident that approached nuclear war could be diverted. "I also have talked to President Dao Pac Ming, Mr. President, and I told him as I am telling you now that the United States will protect ourselves and our allies from any missile attack from any country including North Korea. I cannot make that any more clear, Mr. President" the American President replied. "Very well, Mr.

President, good evening to you" the North Korean president replied and then promptly hung up. President Jackson looked across his desk at Janice. "Are you a religious person, Mrs. Lang?" asked the President. Janice looked at the President inquisitively. "Yes I am, Mr. President. Why do you ask?" Janice Lang inquired. "That's good, because I would start praying" the President said.

Nathan started his usual day. He worked out at the gym and returned to his apartment to clean up. He thought about the past weekend. He had a great time with Steven and the girls. The night before with Jill was most memorable also. There was something about her that compelled him to want to get to know her better. He had tried to call her Sunday but received no answer all day. Nathan left several messages and she hadn't returned them. He wasn't worried, he got plenty of work done yesterday. Nathan knew he would see her at work today. Maybe he would surprise her and take her to lunch. Nathan got dressed and grabbed his briefcase. He drove to work, stopping off on the way for a coffee. The coffee was strong but he needed it. He had a lot to drink this past weekend, more than he had in the last three months. He wasn't usually a drinker but indulged to be sociable. He pulled into the parking lot of Lockheed-Martin and parked in an empty spot. He saw that Jill's white Ford Mustang was parked a few spots down. Good, she is at work at least. He would make a point to see her this morning.

Nathan walked to his office, greeted his secretary and picked up his messages. Nathan worked in his office for a few hours doing the second draft of his report before going up to the VP's office. He got off the elevator and met Jill coming out of her office. "Hello" Nathan said. "Hi." Jill said coldly. Nathan sensed some distress in her voice. "I called you Sunday so we could maybe go to the beach, did you get my messages? Nathan asked. "Yes, I did but I didn't, I mean I was really busy" Jill said in a hurried tone. "Oh, that's okay. If your free today I'd like to take you to lunch" Nathan inquired. "Nathan, I don't think we should be going anywhere together" Jill replied, pushing past Nathan and starting down the hallway. Nathan knew there was something wrong. "Jill, what's wrong?" Nathan said. "What's wrong?" she said, turning back to Nathan."What's wrong is that you said you would be home all day Saturday working. I was stupid and felt sorry for you so I made dinner and brought it over only to see you ride away with three other women. I don't need a man who lies Nathan, I've already been there" Jill said, finally breaking into tears. She turned to the wall to hide her face. Nathan knew that she had been hurt before, but he had done nothing intentional to hurt her. "I was wrong about you, Nathan. I'm always wrong about men" Jill said sobbing. Her makeup was running and she knew it. She made her way down the hall to the ladies room to gain her composure. Nathan called out to her but she continued to the ladies room. Nathan couldn't let things end here. He followed her to the ladies room and entered. Jill was busy washing her hands and face and reapplying her make-up. "Nathan, you can't come in her" Jill said, sobbing at the sink. "Well, I'm not leaving until I clear this up" Nathan replied. Jill straightened her blouse and tugged at her skirt. "There really isn't much more to say, Nathan" Jill replied. "Yes, there is a hell of a lot more to say" Nathan demanded. Jill turned to Nathan as if waiting for an explanation. "Jill, when I first met you Friday afternoon I never dreamed I could get hooked on someone so fast" Nathan said. Jill looked at Nathan, crossed her arms in front of her and seemed to tear up a little. "When I left you Saturday morning I went home and prepared a twenty-seven page report on the test I did Friday. During the little "cocktail party" in this office Friday, Steven Alexander invited me to a party, in my honor, on Saturday night. The women you saw me riding away with were Steven's girlfriend, her sister and her other friend. They came to pick me up at Steven's request. I stayed the night at Steven's home *alone* in my own room. It was only me and a few of my friends" Nathan explained. Just then a woman that worked in the office next to Jill walked into the ladies room. "Oh, sorry" the bewildered woman said. "Excuse me, could we have a moment here?" Nathan demanded. Jill laughed a little between the tears. The woman slowly closed the door and left. "As I was saying" Nathan said, smiling. "The only possible romantic interest I have is you. I'd like to see where this goes. I want to be honest with you though. This is not going to be easy, Jill. You see, I leave for Pensacola in a few weeks. I have been accepted into Officer Training School for the Navy" Nathan explained. Jill wiped away some tears and looked at Nathan in the mirror. "Can you promise me something?" Jill said. "I'll try" Nathan said. "If I get a little crazy like this from time to time, will you just talk sweet to me?" Jill asked, tearing up again. "Sure" Nathan said smiling at her. Nathan walked over, pulled her close and held her tight. She put her arms around his neck and held him tightly, sobbing. "By the way, what *did* you make me for dinner Saturday?" Nathan asked. "I made you my famous fried chicken and biscuits" Jill replied, looking into his eyes. "So, can we start again?" Nathan asked. "No, lets just pick up from where we left off" Jill replied, kissing Nathan on the cheek. "That's sounds good, so are we on for lunch today?" Nathan asked, looking at her pretty face. "Sure, and dinner and anything else in between" Jill replied. Nathan kissed her passionately. She had the softest lips he had ever kissed. He lingered, kissing her again and she responded. She kissed Nathan again and held him tight. She enjoyed being in his arms. She needed to be with a strong man. Jill was a woman that, above everything else, needed honesty and love.

Nathan walked Jill back to her office and said goodbye to her at the door. He had a few hours of work to do in the lab before picking Jill up for lunch. Nathan reviewed the test data with his technicians while making notes. He considered himself lucky to have gotten to work with such professional people. He had a lot of ideas he wanted to add to his final draft. He wished he could continue his work here but he already committed to a new career, a new way of life. He was looking forward to his Navy career, flying jet fighters, and hoped to be assigned to carrier duty. Nathan was more determined that ever to succeed. He decided he would do what ever it took.

Nathan met Jill at one o'clock for lunch. He took her into town to a nice Italian restaurant he saw on the way into work. It was a quaint little place with old style flair and a romantic atmosphere. Jill was all smiles and beaming when Nathan seated her. He told her of his plans for the next few months. He told her he would be away from her for a while but she would be forever in his heart. He had planned to move out of his apartment and put his things in storage. Not knowing where he would be stationed, he would gather his things when he got to his first duty assignment. Jill talked about her life growing up, her short marriage and what she wanted to do with the rest of her life. She had been alone a lot when she was married, her husband choosing to stay out with the boys, drink and not come home until the early morning hours. She said the sex was really bad but what was worse was how he treated her when he was sober, which wasn't all that often. He always either complained about the laundry, the house or the yard, not once helping her with any of it. It got so bad they slept apart the last four months. She tried to make it work but finally filed for divorce after fourteen months. Soon after her divorce was final her aunt died and she was heart broken, her mom dying just the previous year. Soon after, Jill moved into her aunt's house, which was legally hers now, and started working for Lockheed-Martin a month later. She wanted children someday but more importantly wanted a loving, caring and equal relationship with the man she chose.

Nathan knew he had found someone special. He didn't want to mess this one up. They had a leisurely lunch, laughing and sharing a kiss in a corner booth. They got back to the office at about two in the afternoon. After a few quick, passionate kisses in the car, Nathan walked her to her office door. "Good bye sweetie, have a good afternoon" Jill said. "You too, Jill" Nathan replied kissing her in the hallway, not caring who saw him. "Honey, why don't you come over for dinner tonight, is around six o'clock okay?" Jill asked. "That would be good. I'll be missing you too much past that time anyway" Nathan joked. She giggled and kissed him. "Okay, I'll see you then" Jill replied, fixing Nathan's tie. "Yes, you will" Nathan said. He kissed her as she turned away and walked in the door. She gave him a wink as she closed the door. Nathan went to his office and made a few phone calls. First he called the florist. The second call he made was to the Boeing technical representative. He had scheduled a conference call at two-thirty this afternoon. He discussed the project and future plans for system airframe integration with him and the other technicians. Nathan told the Boeing reps his ideas which could save weight and maintenance hours on the system. The representatives received them very well. He also informed them of his decision to join the Navy. They were happy he was following his dream but disappointed that he wouldn't be continuing with the program.

Nathan finished with his conference call at about four-thirty. He sat at his desk resting his eyes. His secretary called on the intercom and asked if she could leave early for a doctor's appointment with her son. He told her yes and that he had no problem with it. Nathan sat back and looked at his office. He had spent a little over fourteen months here at Lockheed-Martin. He told the VP that his last day with the company would be next Wednesday. The new project engineer would be here by this Thursday, which would be more than enough time to get him on track with the program.

Nathan left his office at about ten after five. He called Jill to see if she needed anything. She said "No, just you" but he insisted on getting a bottle of wine. He stopped by the Liquor store on the way and got a large bottle of wine for the night. He pulled into Jill's driveway and parked where he had before. He noticed her Lexus was in the garage and the Mustang was in the driveway. He went to the back of the house and knocked on the screen door. She yelled from somewhere in the house for him to come on in. Nathan entered and closed the door behind him. Nathan smelled baked ham and sweet potatoes coming from the kitchen. The breakfast nook table was clean except for the vase of red roses that Nathan had sent her. He read the card. *"To Jill, a new start, a new friendship, Love, Nathan".* Nathan was pleased that the florist got it right. The roses were fresh and smelled great. "Honey, where are you?" Nathan asked. "I'm in the dining room, sweetie" she replied. Nathan walked to the dining room, which was across from the kitchen. Jill was busy placing the linen napkins by the place settings. She lit the tall, white candles as Nathan entered the room. She looked stunning with her long, black hair was done up on her head. She had on a tight-fitting, long black evening dress that zipped up the back. It showed off her beautifully tanned shoulders and the rest of her tremendous figure. She stepped out from behind the table and walked to Nathan, showing off her long legs, accentuated by the high slits in her dress. "Does everything look okay, sweetie?" she asked, kissing Nathan on the cheek. She looked Nathan eye to eye now because of her high, strappy heels. "You look stunning and so does the table" Nathan replied smiling, returning her kiss. Nathan held her close, feeling her body through the silky dress. Nathan could detect nothing underneath her thin dress but her thong. "Thank you so much for the roses, they are so beautiful" Jill said. "If I remember right ham is a favorite of yours, correct" she asked. "Yes, it is" Nathan replied. Jill smiled. "May I pour you a glass of wine, Miss Jacobs?" Nathan asked. "Yes, please. I need to check the ham, we're just about ready to eat, sweetie" Jill replied. "That's good, I'm starved" Nathan said. Nathan poured two glasses of Cabernet and set them on the table. Jill sliced the ham and dished up the rest of dinner. At his insistence he helped her bring things to the table and then, when everything was ready, he held the chair for her and seated her. Nathan sat down and then raised his glass. "I want to propose a toast" Nathan began. Jill raised her glass to Nathan's. "To a new beginning, peace on earth and to the most beautiful woman I have ever had the fortune to dine with" Nathan said, touching his glass to hers. Jill smiled, her eyes welling up. "Please don't make me cry" she laughed. Nathan reached over with his napkin and offered it to her. She took it and smiled at him, wiping a tear from the corner of her eye. She cleared her throat and sipped her wine. Jill took a deep breath and they both began eating. They had a great dinner. He learned during dinner that her aunt taught her how to cook since Jill was there most of the time. Her mom worked as a secretary during the day and a waitress at night. Jill's aunt, her mom's sister, practically raised her. Her dad left when she was nine years old. She hadn't seen him since and didn't care to. Nathan thought back to the last time that he and Jill were together. He remembered that she exclaimed, "*Don't leave us*" as she stirred half asleep. That might explain some things. Things were really hard on them when he left, her mom having to take the second job as a waitress. Jill sometimes had to stay overnight with her aunt, since her mom worked real late during the week. "I got to see my mom more on the weekends. Saturdays were her only night off" Jill said, sipping her wine. Jill pointed to the little room off of the hallway, which was now her computer room. "That's where I stayed on many a night" she said. "I didn't complain because I loved my aunt and I felt safe here" Jill explained. "That's important to me, feeling safe. Nathan, you make me feel safe when I'm with you" she said holding Nathan's hand on the table. Jill apologized for her jumping to conclusions at work. "I should have been more adult about things" she said. "I always think the worst" she confessed. "We really aren't dating, I just met you for gods sake!" she said. Nathan looked at her. She looked beautiful as the candlelight danced off her earrings. They were diamonds, hanging low from her ears, and very elegant. Nathan was falling for her very fast. She seemed to be the one that he was looking for all his life. "I promise you that I will always make you safe no matter where I am" Nathan promised. Jill leaned over and thanked him with a wet kiss on the lips. Nathan looked at her and caressed her soft cheek. He smelled her perfume, Vera Wang, as she leaned in to kiss him. It was almost as intoxicating as the wine. "I've been thinking a lot about this, I really don't know how you feel about it but I'd like us to date each other exclusively" Nathan said, looking at Jill. Jill smiled, tilting her head and returning his gaze. "I mean, I would understand if you didn't, especially since I will be going away next week and we probably won't be able to see each other for a while" Nathan said, struggling to get the words out. Jill held her hand softly up to Nathan mouth. "It would make me very happy just dating you, no matter where you go or how long you'll be gone as long as I know we'll be together someday" Jill said, looking at Nathan with a tear in her eye. Jill leaned forward again to kiss him again. They shared a few passionate kisses and Nathan confessed that he really was falling for her. She blushed, and giggled a little, blaming it on the wine. "No, really. I have been looking for a woman like you all my life" Nathan explained. "Okay, but please, don't get down on one knee" Jill said laughing. Nathan laughed also. "Nathan, I understand what you mean" Jill said, standing up and beginning to clear the table. She walked to the kitchen with the two empty dinner plates, setting them down on the counter. "You want me to be *your* girl" Jill replied. Jill giggled at Nathan's expression. They both had a few glasses of wine and Jill seemed a little frisky. "Well, that's a another way of putting it, but yes Jill, I want you to be *my* girl" Nathan confessed holding her hand. "Nathan, I accept. I would love to be your girl. I only ask a few things in return" Jill said. "I want you to keep me safe, I want you to tell me when your hurting and I want you to love no one else but me, is that fair?" Jill asked. "Sure, that's a deal. You have my promise" Nathan said, kissing her hand.

Nathan finished clearing the table for Jill and brought the ham platter to the kitchen. Nathan was feeling good as he poured two more glasses of wine for Jill and himself. Jill rinsed the dishes and loaded the dishwasher, showing Nathan a lot of leg through the slit in her silky black dress in the process. She took off her diamond earrings and placed them on the counter. She moved closer to Nathan, taking her wineglass in her hand. She took a quick sip of wine. "I'd really like you to stay the night, sweetie" Jill said, licking her already wet lips. Nathan held her close and kissed her neck, as Jill returned his embrace. Jill took Nathan by the hand as she led him to her room.

Nathan awoke at midnight and went to the bathroom to relieve himself. He returned to Jill's bed where she lay naked on her tummy. Nathan slowly eased into bed and pulled the covers up over both of them as Jill, who stirred, moved to snuggle next to him. He pulled her close with his strong arm and kissed her. "You are awesome" Nathan whispered, rubbing her firm behind. "Thank you. You make me feel so good Nathan" she said, quietly whispering to him. "Nathan, I don't want to be hurt again. If you ever need to be apart from me please tell me. I don't want to be the last to know" she said, looking deep into Nathan's eyes. Nathan kissed her again. "Okay, but you'll never have to worry" Nathan confessed. Jill cuddled closer to Nathan and exhaled as if a great burden had been lifted off her. She confessed to Nathan that she cared for him very deeply and would always be there for him. They both lay there, in each other's arm, exhausted, but feeling like each belonged completely to one another.

Nathan awoke before Jill did the next morning. The clock said six-fifty. Jill was curled up in the fetal position facing away from Nathan, her thong tan line showing clearly. Nathan decided to go for a run before work. He dressed and went to his car to get his sneakers, running shorts and a jersey. He went back to the bedroom and quietly changed his clothes. Jill rolled over and then awoke, sensing that Nathan wasn't next to her. Nathan sat on her side of the bed and leaned down to kiss her. "I'm gonna go for a run, do you want to join me?" Nathan asked. "No thank you sweetie, you go" she replied. Jill rolled on her tummy while Nathan rubbed her shoulders and lower back. "ooh, that feels so good" Jill exclaimed. Nathan kissed her lower back when he was finished. "I'm gonna shower while you go for your run and then I'll make us a nice breakfast" Jill added. Nathan kissed her goodbye and went for a run.

He did his normal run about five miles and returned to her house. He entered the house and met Jill in the kitchen who was busy preparing some scrambled eggs and sausage. "Hi, sweetie. How was your run?" Jill asked, kissing Nathan. "Very warm" Nathan replied. "Go shower and clean up, then we can eat" she told Nathan. "Good, I'm starved" Nathan said as he went to the bathroom to shower. Nathan cleaned up, dressed and came out to the kitchen. Jill had the breakfast nook table already set for breakfast. The roses Nathan sent yesterday were just starting to open. Jill just started serving the eggs and sausage as Nathan walked in the kitchen. "Go ahead and sit down, sweetie" Jill said. "No, I'll help you" Nathan said taking the plates and taking them to the table. Jill came over to the table as Nathan held her chair and seated her. She looked lovely, wearing a short, silver kimono. "Thank you, sweetie. You take such good care of me" she said smiling at Nathan. Nathan sat and began drinking his coffee, which tasted great after his morning run. Nathan talked about the day he had planned at work, needing to probable work late with the technicians. Jill had said she had a girlfriend she usually goes to the movies with so she said they would catch an early movie and dinner after. "Did you want to stay here tonight with me?" Jill asked cautiously. "Yes I do, but I need to clean up some things at my apartment before I come here" Nathan confessed. "I was thinking too, sweetie. Instead of putting your things in storage while your gone why don't you store them here?" Jill offered. "That would be a good idea. I certainly would appreciate it" Nathan said. "When I'm in Pensacola I'd like you to come visit me" Nathan said. "So you can't be away from me for even a few months?" she giggled. "Yeah, that's it" Nathan said laughing. "I'd like to do that. I'm due for a real vacation anyway. Let's play it by ear and you can let me know" Jill said. Nathan agreed and talked to her about what movie she was going to see tonight. She had no preference, she and her girlfriend just go out to catch up with each other. They first met when Jill worked at the restaurant before she was hired by Lockheed-Martin. Both single, they went on a lot of double dates together and developed a sister-like relationship. Nathan said he would like to meet her someday, since she was an important person in her life. Nathan and Jill finished breakfast and cleaned up. Jill went to shower and since Nathan had a few minutes to spare he waited for her so they could both leave together.

Jill emerged from the shower with her towel wrapped around just her waist. She came over to her dresser and talked with Nathan while she was putting on her make up. "I don't know what to wear today" she said. "You mean you can't find anything in that big closet" Nathan said jokingly, while reading *Air & Space* on the bed. She walked into her huge closet to find something to wear to work for the day. Jill spent a lot on clothes, shoes and perfume. A short time later Jill walked out in a short white dress and carrying her shoes. She asked Nathan what he thought of her dress and he told her he loved it. He loved anything that showed off her fantastic figure. Jill finished dressing about eight-thirty and they both left together in their own cars. Jill played with Nathan on the way to work, seductively licking her lips so he could see her in the rear-view mirror. She turned a lot of heads, including the men in the pickup truck next to her at the stoplight. Nathan could imagine the view they were getting since Jill's short dresses usually rode up as she entered her Lexus. The white dress she chose today was very sexy and as she put it "was meant to be worn without a bra" which she didn't bother wearing. It was very warm when Nathan went for his run this morning. Now that the sun was higher it was heating things up a bit and both Nathan and Jill opted for some air conditioning. Nathan kept up with Jill all through town and pulled through the employee gate at work. Nathan parked next to Jill, gathered his briefcase and got out of his car. He walked around Jill's car to her door, which was already open. Her long sexy legs swung out of her car as she stood up and gave Nathan a big kiss. "How do I look?" Jill said, adjusting her dress. Since she had her air conditioning on high for a while, she shown through the white fabric of the dress. "You look good, honey" Nathan said. "I didn't think I would show through this" she confessed. "I'll be okay once I get inside and warm up" she added. Nathan walked his girlfriend up the steps of the building and to her office. The other employees were getting used to seeing them together and there was talk that Nathan had proposed to Jill. Nathan thought that it was funny. This rumor, Nathan thought, just might become reality someday.

SIX

CHESS MATCH

THE RESCUE HELICOPTERS ARRIVED BACK ON the *Reagan* at 1800 hours. Nathan ran to the flight deck and joined the medical technicians that were attending to the first rescue crewman. Nathan saw other technicians loading a litter near the HH-60 and his friend, Jimmy. Jimmy was walking, his left shoulder immobilized by a sling. Nathan approached Jimmy. "I thought you were wounded, don't think that will get you off the duty roster!" Nathan said jokingly. James looked at Nathan with a serious look. "We took a lot of fire, Commander, and we suffered some casualties" James said, gesturing to the litter on the deck, which was covered by a blue navy blanket. "We lost Ensign Rockland. He put up quite a fight as we were leaving but he caught a few" James said. Nathan didn't recognize the name but recognized the face as he knelt next to the litter and pulled back the blanket. Nathan saw Ensign "Skippy" lying on the litter with a horrendous hole in the side of his neck. "He caught some rounds from an AK-47 as we banked away from the pick point. I did all I could for him and the other rescue crewman. He was bleeding real bad...but I couldn't...god damn it, we're not at war!" James said choking on his words and throwing down his gear bag. Nathan agreed but he knew deep down they might be soon. He carefully covered up the young Ensign. "Commander, you need to report to sick bay" Nathan ordered, gesturing for the medical technician. "I will stop by later and get your initial report on what happened out there" Nathan said. Nathan already knew what happened but he wanted James to keep things in perspective. "Aye, aye Commander" James said. When Nathan arrived back in CIC the Captain was busy attending to a problem with the arresting gear on the *Reagan*. "I don't give a damn Chief just get it fixed!" the Captain yelled into the receiver as he slammed down the phone. One of the *Reagan's* arresting cables had broke during the recovery of the last aircraft. Considering the amount of air activity on the *Reagan* it was normal maintenance. The Captain's main concern was Wolf 4 who was inbound with low fuel.

The next four hours went by quickly. The arresting gear was fixed in record time and Nathan even had time to go congratulate the Chief and his crew for their expedient efforts. Nathan had dinner lone as Steven took more time on the *Princeton* than expected and returned around 1900 hours. Steven had briefed all the Commanding Officers on the *Lake Champlain*, *Princeton* and the *Shiloh* on the events so far, including the "Oscar" sub. About 2200 hours Nathan called Steven from his quarters. Steven answered. "Hello Steven, this is Nathan" Nathan said. "Nathan, I was just leaving to meet the Captain in CIC. Why don't you join me there?" Steven offered. "I certainly will Admiral, see you there" Nathan said and promptly hung up. Nathan arrived at CIC just behind Steven who had stopped to chat with the Marines. He was just delivering a punch line about a blonde and a Rabbi that all the Marines seemed to thoroughly enjoy as Nathan arrived. Steven thanked the

Marines for their service and attention and walked through the door to CIC, followed by Nathan.

The Captain was in CIC, set in front of a small TV as Steven approached. The Captain stood up and offered up his seat to Steven who graciously accepted it. Nathan approached the small television monitor, which was hooked up by satellite to most of the major networks. "The President will be on in a few minutes, Admiral" said the Captain. "These guys are just screwing around, guessing as to what the President will say" the Captain said, referring to the reporters on the television. The White House Press Secretary broke in and announced the President. "Ladies and Gentleman, The President of the United States" he said. The President was sitting in his oval office. He had a determined look on his face as he began to speak. "Good evening, my fellow Americans. I would like to talk to you this evening on some matters of great importance. During the last few hours you may have been made aware by the media of an accident in the Sea of Japan involving the military forces of the United States Navy. I am here to report to you, the American people, that the military forces of the United States were involved in an intelligence gathering mission seventy miles off the coast of North Korea. The military aircraft were well within international airspace when military aircraft of the North Korean Air Force intercepted and fired on the intelligence aircraft's fighter escort. One US Navy F/A-18E "Super Hornet" was shot down as were several North Korean Air Force MiG's. The pilot of the F/A-18 was injured as he bailed out of his stricken aircraft but was recovered some time later. During the rescue attempt by helicopters from the aircraft carrier *USS Ronald Reagan,* two North Korean patrol boats attempted to interfere with the rescue and attacked both helicopters. US Navy aircraft returned fire on both North Korean patrol boats, which were then subsequently destroyed by naval units of the South Korean Navy. During the rescue attempt, I am told that one rescue crewmember was wounded and one was killed. The crewman's names are being withheld until family members can be located and contacted. At the news of this attack I immediately placed a call to the North Korean President Kim Lu Doc. During my conversation with President Lu Doc I denounced the attack by his military forces and informed him of the United States' resolve to continue the surveillance of North Korea's nuclear weapons build-up. President Lu Doc informed me that his country will continue to develop their nuclear capability as a deterrent to other countries. As you all know the United States, South Korea and Japan have no interest in the conquest of North Korea which was made public at the United Nations in March of 2006, following North Korea's withdrawal from the 2004 Nuclear Arms-Control Treaty. The United States has renounced the use of nuclear weapons and has ceased production of all nuclear weapons as of July of 2000. Furthermore the United States and her allies have petitioned the United Nations to force other nations to follow suit. The continued proliferation of nuclear weapons programs by any nation is not in their best interest. The United States has shown that the money spent on these weapons can and should be used for other domestic programs such as health care, creating new jobs and infrastructure for our citizens. As I stated earlier, the United States will continue its reconnaissance flights in international airspace to monitor not only North Korea's nuclear weapons build-up but also other countries who pose a threat to the United States and our way of life. Thank you for your time. I wish you all a good night and god bless America." the President concluded his broadcast and the monitor returned to the WNN reporters at the White House. "Well, I think that was pretty clear" Nathan said. "Yes, but the North Korean President has a history of not understanding things" the Captain said. "He sometimes a little loco" the Captain gestured, circling his ear with his index finger. Nathan talked with the Captain for several minutes. His main concern was the "Oscar" sub. The Captain was less interested in the Oscar sub, the *Topeka* having things well in hand, and told Nathan that he received a message that confirmed that a Chinese navy was forming a task force off of Qingdao. "I'm told that they are just doing their own training exercises and evaluating some new hardware" the Captain said. Nathan went to the plot table and saw several new red icons representing the various Chinese warships. Nathan took the "mouse" and highlighted the large red icon. "The *Varyag*" Nathan exclaimed. "So they finally got that thing seaworthy" Nathan added. "Yes they did, and latest intelligence shows that it has about thirty or more SU-27 "Flanker" fighters on board along with some Russian-made ASW helicopters" Captain Winters added. "I didn't think it would even move out of its dry dock. They must have been working overtime on that one" Nathan replied. Nathan moved the "mouse" to the other contacts. "Two *Sovremennyy* class destroyers, a *Luhu* class destroyer and four *Luda* class destroyers as escorts. That's a pretty formidable training fleet" Nathan added. "Previous intelligence from two days ago had three Type 93 attack subs leaving their base at Xiangshan" the Captain explained. "You can bet your clusters that they will be out front just waiting for something to come their way" the Captain added. Nathan suddenly got a bad feeling. What if this "training" task force was a more carefully thought out plan by the Chinese *and* the North Koreans. With the "Oscar" submarine stalking the *Reagan* Strike Group it might be a coordinated effort to gain control of the sea-lanes around the Korean peninsula. With the *Reagan* out of the way, North Korea and the Chinese could blackmail South Korea and Japan into submission. If North Korea and China launched simultaneous missile strikes at Hawaii, Guam and the US West Coast, then the United States would have a hard time in reestablishing supremacy in the Pacific. "Captain, I think we should have a plan in place to deal with them if things go wrong" Nathan suggested. "I agree Commander. Better safe than sorry, even though I don't think it will go that far" the Captain said. "What do you make from all this Admiral?" the Captain asked. "I don't think it will be much of a problem. We have enough assets outside the Strike Group to take care of the Chinese if it goes that way" Steven replied. The Captain looked at Nathan and nodded. If the Admiral wasn't worried then neither was he.

It was about five o'clock in the morning when Bart awoke. Commander Bartholomew "Bart" Kennedy, the commanding officer of the *USS Michigan*, had been on patrol in the East China Sea for over forty days. The *Michigan*, which was first launched in 1982, had been given a new lease on life since being the second boat chosen for conversion to a guided missile submarine in 2003. Instead of the twenty-four Trident I D-4 nuclear ballistic missiles it was first commissioned to carry, the *Michigan* now was converted to carry one hundred fifty-four vertical launch Tomahawk cruise missiles. On this particular mission the *Michigan* carried, in addition to its twenty-four MK-48 ADCAP torpedoes, ninety-four Tomahawk TLAM missiles and sixty Tomahawk anti-ship missiles. The Tomahawk anti-ship missiles and MK-48 ADCAP's would give the *Michigan* a formidable punch if it ran into trouble on the way out of the launch area. It wasn't the standard mix but then this mission was anything but standard. Cruising at two hundred feet below the surface at five knots, the *Michigan* was, for all practical purposes undetectable. The second boat of the *Ohio* class SSBN's, the *Michigan* had never been detected or tracked since it had been launched. Thanks in part to its free-circulating S8G nuclear reactor, the *Michigan* was void from the noises that were associated with water circulating pumps that might give away its position.

Admiral Steven Alexander had briefed Bart prior to the start of this mission at Pearl. Steven told Bart that the TLAMs would be ordered to launch as part of a mission to support the *Reagan's* Strike Group. If things went bad then the *Michigan* would be given the appropriate codes over the ELF and missiles were to be launched. If nothing happened then the *Michigan* was to remain on-station undetected until its return date. That was fine with Bart. He would rather remain undetected than fight it out. At a little over eighteen thousand tons submerged and five hundred sixty feet long, the *Michigan* could only do about twenty-seven knots on a good day and wasn't very maneuverable. Its main defense was stealth. Bart looked at the instruments at the head of his bed. They were on course and about ninety minutes from their on-station location. He was fortunate to have a great crew, although the submarine service produced nothing but the best.

Bart went to the control room to get a tactical update. His executive officer, Lieutenant Commander Jeff Scott, was at the plot table. "Good morning, Captain" he said. "Good Morning, Jeff" the Captain replied. The submarine service had long a reputation of being informal when at sea, mostly in part to the very close conditions everyone had to become accustomed to. It had no effect on the professionalism of the crew and in some areas a relaxed crew performed better under times of stress. "Captain, I've been getting some indications on the BQQ-5C sonar array of an intermittent contact on bearing 263. Nothing solid, I put it at about the third convergence zone" said Commander Scott. "Very well. Have the TB-23 towed array streamed out to a thousand feet, see if we can pick up anything solid" the Captain said. "Aye, aye Sir, I was about to do that" said Scott. The Captain didn't question him. Scott knew what he was doing, which made the Captain's job easier. Having spent eight years in attack subs, Commander Scott knew how to refine sonar contacts. The Captain heard Scott order the TB-23 streamed.

The sonar officer repeated the order's, as did the enlisted personnel at their sonar consoles. After about ten minutes the TB-23 showed five distinct contacts and a few other faint ones. Bart overheard the sonar officer order the enlisted sonar technician to refine and identify one of the contacts. "Conn, sonar. We show one, correction two *Sovremennyy* class destroyers on bearings 263 and 267 from our position, at about one hundred and ninety thousand yards" the sonar officer reported. Sonar, conn. This is the Captain, can you classify the other contacts?" the Captain asked. The sonar officer hesitated and said "No sir, not at this time but we are working them" the sonar officer confessed. "Very well, keep me advised." the Captain said. The Captain was impressed. The *Michigan's* sonar technicians were some of the best in the business. They had detected and classified a contact over one hundred miles away. The Captain had some coffee sent to the control room. He didn't want to go far until he knew for sure what he was dealing with.

At about 0720 hrs the sonar officer excitedly broke in. "Conn, sonar. We have classified some other contacts. We show a *Kuznetsov* class aircraft carrier on bearing 265 from our position" The sonar officer reported. The Captain looked at Commander Scott with a raised eyebrow. "We also show no less than four *Luda I* class frigates and one *Luhu* class destroyer between bearings 263 and 268" the sonar officer added. "Sonar, this is the Captain. Classify the contacts as "hostile" and start a targeting solution for the TASM's" the Captain ordered. Bart didn't want them to be any closer and not have good data on them. If the time did come to launch he would have to act fast. He wouldn't have time to get good targeting data after the TLAM's were launched especially if there were helicopters overhead from the carrier. He assumed the vessels were Chinese. He recalled the Chinese having bought a *"Kuznetsov"* some years ago. "Jeff, do you remember the name of that old, Russian aircraft carrier that was towed to China years ago" the Captain asked. "I believe it was called the *Varyag,* Captain. Sounds like the Chinese got a good deal" Commander Scott said, jokingly. Not just an aircraft carrier, the *Kuznetsov* class carried up to twelve SS-N-19 "Shipwreck" missiles. So it seemed the Chinese had an aircraft carrier, whether or not it was operational. Being that it was at sea and accompanied by this many screening vessels, Bart was betting it was operational. Bart went to look at the plot table. In keeping with the tactical doctrine of countries that fielded carrier Strike Groups it was a sure bet that the Chinese had their attack submarines out front. "Sonar, conn. This is the Captain. Do you have any submerged contacts to the west of our position?" the Captain asked. The sonar officer replied that he had no submerged contacts. Bart knew they were out there, they just weren't hearing them. He hoped the *Ohio,* which was about two hundred miles to his south, had better luck detecting them.

At just past 0830 hours on the morning of August 17th the final preparations were made for launching the first in a series of long range missile tests by the North Korean army. Several generals from P'yongyang were flown in to witness the test first hand. It was a proud moment in the history of the North Korean army. North Korean President Lu Doc had remained undeterred by the west's demands that the North Korean government adhere to the nuclear non-proliferation treaty of the past. The technicians were busy monitoring the sensors placed on the missile to transmit telemetry back to the launch station via a Chinese satellite. The Chinese government had been more than willing to let the North Koreans use the satellites in return for the test results on the Taepo-dong missiles. The missile's planned trajectory was to take it over the Japanese mainland and reenter the atmosphere to land about one thousand miles south west of Honolulu, Hawaii. The latest variant, the Taepo-dong

III, as it is referred to by the west, was a three-stage, liquid propellant ballistic missile with an estimated range of seven thousand miles. The missile on the pad carried a dummy warhead of 815 kilograms, the exact weight of the North Korean Army's KN-725 nuclear warhead, which had a yield of 70 kilotons.

At 0857 hours the Launch Captain made the decision to replace a critical sensor on the missile, which had become defective. The sensor took mere minutes to change and the go for launch was given at 0910 hours. The missile, which was already being fueled with liquid oxygen, was nearing its launch time. When the missile was fueled the Launch Captain got a "Go" from all the launch technicians and a five-minute countdown was started. The generals took position as the countdown reached close to ten seconds. The Launch Captain counted the last five seconds himself as the missile's rocket engine fired. The missile roared to life and immediately lifted from it's pad deep inside its reinforced concrete shelter in the mountains near Ok'pyong-nodongjagu. The Generals all applauded and patted each other on the back, as if they personally were responsible for it's launch. The missile accelerated quickly, turning and heading skyward on its terminal mission. The missile technicians outside the main complex manned their cameras and followed the trajectory of the missile as it broke through the scattered clouds at thirty thousand feet. Their record would provide valuable data on the flight of the Taepo-dong III.

Jake had just finished his second cup of coffee at 0915 hours when he took the controls and started a standard right-bank at forty-seven thousand feet. He had been in the air for a little over six hours. Now on the second half of his twelve-hour shift he made started some small talk with his co-pilot. "Did you catch the Presidential press conference?"

he asked, referring to the radio. "Yeah, I caught it. I guess we are the reconnaissance aircraft that the President referred to" the co-pilot said. "That's fine with me. If all we have to do…" Jake was interrupted by the Mission Commander who called out "We have a Missile Launch" over the intercom. The Mission Commander called out the bearing, speed and altitude of the missile. Jake took the flight controls while looking down to his left from his pilot's position. Even at this range he could see the glowing white light rising and arching up to the sky above. Jake turned the 747-400 a few degrees to port so the sensors could get a better angle on the missile and then set the aircraft on autopilot. His job done, Jake remained silent as he listened to the Mission Commander as he relayed information to the "Cobra Ball" aircraft, which was about a hundred miles behind them. Jake listened as a technician on-board over the intercom. "Trajectory confirmed, its heading for the Hawaiian Islands" the technician confirmed. Jake got a sick feeling when he heard the technician. He had relatives in Hawaii. Jake overheard the Mission Commander say that the target was acquired and tracking. Moments later the Mission Commander call out "HEL energized". If it wasn't for the Mission Commander Jake wouldn't have been able to tell if the High Energy Laser was being fired or not. Jake looked out the window and could see nothing except a second later a bright flash, somewhat higher than where he saw the missile last. The Mission Commander confirmed what Jake had seen a moment earlier. "Target is destroyed at 0916 hours" reported the Mission Commander.

The Generals at the Ok'pyong-nodongjagu missile facility knew something had gone wrong. The missile technicians started scurrying around and checking data when a few technicians burst in from the other room. They conferred for a few seconds and then the Launch

Captain approached the General and informed him the test missile had blown up while in flight. The General was led to the room next door to review the data. The data all seemed to show normal until the missile reached forty-seven thousand feet. One of the sensors that measured the missiles outside skin temperature showed a "spike" just before the missile was lost. "I'd like to see the video record of the flight from all aspects" the General requested. The technicians began the preparations so the data could be viewed. After a few minutes the technicians queued up the video on the three monitors in the briefing room. The technicians reviewed the video data, which was magnified several times. The technicians first thought they saw something that wasn't quite right just before the missile exploded, so they restarted the digital video from just before that point. The General also watched as the technicians slowed the video up and zoomed in on the area in question. The technicians and the General watched the section of the missile heat up and turn white hot before the explosion took place. They all came to the exact conclusion at the same time. As if on queue both the technicians and the General exclaimed "Laser!"

After a few minutes the General exited the room and then left the missile complex. Ordering his helicopter back to P'yongyang, the General had to report what he saw to the North Korean President in person. A powerful laser had shot down the missile. The technicians had the proof that he needed to show the world. The American aircraft that orbited off the coast was most likely to blame. The General had lost a good friend when the Americans had fired on the MiG-23's that were sent to intercept it. Now the Americans would get what they deserved, he thought. This news would enrage President Lu Doc. A friend to the President for many years, the General knew he would take it as not only an attack on North Korea, but as a personal attack on his Presidency.

When the General told President Kim Lu Doc the news he reacted as the General predicted. The President ordered MiG-29s from the 57th Fighter Regiment to intercept and shoot down the American aircraft. In addition he ordered all available nuclear ballistic missiles at Toksong-gun, Mayang, Ok'pyong-nodongjagu and No-dong to be armed and ready to be launched and put on fifteen minute alert. The bombers at Taetan and Kuupri were to be armed with YJ-8K anti-shipping missiles that would be used to seek out and destroy the Carrier Strike Group that lay off the North Korean coast. The bombers were to be put on five-minute alert, the pilots already in their cockpits. The General knew that the President would follow the plan as it was set down years before. Since before the early seventies the North Korean Army had planned for the attack from South Korea and the American forces that would join them to invade North Korea. The plan called for a massive air attack on the American airfields and Seoul by the outdated MiG-17's followed by a second strike with the mainstay fighters such as the MiG-21, MiG-29 and the SU-25 close support aircraft. The plan called for a limited strike, damaging only aircraft and runways, which could be repaired and used by the North Korean Air Force at a later date. Now, years later, with the medium-range No-dong ballistic missiles, the North Korean Army had a weapon to force South Korea and Japan to their knees. The Japanese, who once suffered the horror of nuclear war, wanted no part of it and would soon back down and submit to the demands of President Kim Lu Doc. The American air base and the port of Pusan would be attacked by long range bomber aircraft escorted by front-line fighters. Once that air superiority was gained the air force would support the army and navy units and destroy any remaining units of the South Korean Navy. North Korean Navy submarines would blockade the Port of Pusan, ensuring that no reinforcements would arrive by sea. President Lu Doc was counting on an agreement signed with China back in 1992 stating that China would protect the West Coast of North Korea if the United States attacked. It was a sure bet that the Americans would attack North Korea on both coasts with their carrier aircraft. The Chinese long ago had adopted the doctrine of the Russian Navy back in the Cold War, locating the US Carrier Strike Groups and coordinating attacks with submarine and long-range cruise missile carrying bombers. Kim Lu Doc was hoping that the Chinese would be lucky enough to sink an aircraft carrier.

Janice interrupted President Jackson at 1915 hours on August 16th just as he was leaving for Andrews Air Force Base. Janice heard the Marine helicopter land early, awaiting the Presidents arrival. She walked in as three secret service agents rushed past her towards the President. Don Baker, the senior agent, told the president that the United States was under attack and they had to leave immediately. The two other agents grabbed the President by his arms and rushed him out of the oval office and to the waiting helicopter. The President ordered Janice to come along also. Once in the air the helicopter headed at top speed towards Andrews AFB. As they were arriving the President could see the E-4B Airborne Command Post on the ground. With its engines screaming the President was rushed up the stairs into the cabin and to his seat by the Secret Service. The Secret Service agents buckled him in and screamed into the intercom to "Go". The 747's engines advanced to a higher pitch and the aircraft quickly started moving. The aircraft turned onto the runway and quickly accelerated. Once airborne the aircraft pulled up into a maximum climb, which was maintained for the next fifteen minutes.

Once at cruising altitude, General Howard briefed the President. The reality of what happened hit him and Janice who sat in the seat across from him. The President looked out the window, feeling little comfort from the escort of the four F-16D's from Langley. He saw Janice turn away wiping tears from her eyes. There would probably be more attacks to follow and a response had to be made. The President ordered General Howard to forward-deploy the B-1's at Dyess AFB to Japan. "General Howard, put the boys at the *Reagan Ranch* on alert also" the President ordered. The General acknowledged the President. Known unofficially as the *"Reagan Ranch"* because of former President Ronald Reagan's support of the Strategic Defense Initiative, the base at Groom Lake, Nevada north of Las Vegas was cloaked in secrecy. Little was known about the 6553rd Aerospace Test Squadron. The aircraft it operated were far removed from the public and only a few lucky souls had seen them since they achieved operational squadron status in 1997.

The E-4B cruised at forty-seven thousand feet over the Atlantic, flying a racetrack pattern. The President made a call to the Pentagon after talking to his wife and son to make sure they were safe. The Vice-President had been in Ottawa and was now covertly being flown to Iceland. The President talked to his Chief of Staff Admiral Jack Grayson. "Jack, how are you" the President asked. "We're okay Mr. President, a little on edge though" the Admiral replied honestly. "Mr. President the AL-1's worked very well I am told. We can expect a response from the North Koreans very soon" the Admiral said. "I know Jack, I want the AL-1's protected at all costs. Do whatever you have to do" the President ordered. That was all the Admiral needed to hear. He passed the orders down the line to engage any aircraft that approached beyond visual range. The pilots need not identify the aircraft or even wait for them to fire, they could launch their AMRAAM's at long-range from a safe distance.

The Captain of the *Jang Bogo* had reason to be exuberant. The two SO-1 class North Korean patrol boats had violated international law by firing on the U.S. rescue helicopters. He had acted appropriately given the information he saw which was communicated to his home base. His crew was commended for their quick action and several of the Officers would be awarded decorations when their patrol ends the following week.. The Captain finished his report on the incident by noon and ordered his submarine to periscope depth. The *Jang Bogo* had to come to the surface to recharge her batteries, which were now at sixty percent. The North Korean Navy boats patrolled at night looking for diesel submarines near the surface so the South Koreans changed their tactics. The diesel subs could safely patrol at four knots deep beneath the sea at night and then charge their batteries during the day. The *Jang Bogo* had a top speed of twenty-one knots submerged but it could only maintain this for an hour or more. Just like other diesel-electric submarines the *Jang Bogo* relied on stealth for defense.

Originally the Captain balked about carrying the four UGM-84D "Sub"Harpoon missiles, which displaced many precious torpedoes, but the events of the previous day changed his mind. He saw how the Harpoons, much faster than his MK-48 torpedoes, could attack lightly armed vessels with success. Once launched the Harpoons could be forgotten and the submarine could retreat to the depths. Looking up the statistics on the Harpoons, the Captain decided that if the situation ever presented itself he would try a bearing-only launch. The range of the Harpoons were about seventy miles and could be launched in a bearing-only mode and set to "turn on" their seeker head at a pre-determined point. Once the seeker turned on it would search the ocean in a "wide" or "narrow" pattern, whichever was selected. The missile would fly until it detected something then home in an attack the target.

One particular "target" the Captain wished to add to his list was one of the *Najin* class light frigates that the North Korean Navy operated as a flagship on the East Coast. The flagship was operating south of the thirty-eighth parallel in May of 2003 when it encountered the *Chung Ju,* a South Korean Navy *Po Hang* class patrol corvette. In the ensuing battle the *Chung Ju* was sunk with a heavy loss of life, including the Captain's son. The radio operator gave the Captain the message as soon as it was decoded. The Captain read the message. It seems the North Koreans had launched a ballistic missile at the Hawaiian Islands, which was subsequently destroyed by the United States. All South Korean military units are to go to yellow alert and await further orders. The Captain ordered the crew to general quarters. He wanted their full attention when he delivered the news. After delivering his message the Captain secured the crew from general quarters and ordered the *Jang Bogo* to change course to 000, due north. The Captain intended to go hunting.

Nathan rounded the corner to find several Officers in line at the Officers mess. Nathan was late for breakfast and was looking forward to a Spanish omelet and some hashbrowns. He hated waiting in line. "Good morning Commander" Steven said, as he walked up behind Nathan and picked up a tray. Good morning Admiral" Nathan replied. Steven didn't have to wait in line and motioned Nathan to join him. Steven greeted some of the other Officer's in line as he walked past them. Steven grabbed some fruit, pancakes and sausage. Nathan ordered an omelet and also picked up some fruit. Navy food was some of the best. The *Reagan* served over eighteen thousand meals a day. Steven drew some black coffee from the drink machine and went to sit at the Admiral's booth to the left. Nathan's omelet was ready and he grabbed some coffee and proceeded to join Steven. He slid in across from Steven and placed his silverware on the table. "Shall we say grace, Commander?" Steven asked. "I think we have a lot to be thankful for" Steven added. "I could add a few to the list" Nathan replied. They both bowed their heads and prayed for a few minutes. When Steven was done Nathan asked him about the Chinese task force building up west of the Korean peninsula. "I heard about it when I was on the *Lake Champlain*" Steven said. "It was forming a few days ago near Qingdao. We have some good Intel on it and some great pictures, so I'm told." Steven replied. "Admiral, I was thinking that this may develop into something bigger than we expect." Nathan said. "I mean we are the only Strike Group in the Sea of Japan. The Chinese have an "Oscar" that is acting quirky like it's ready to launch and the North Koreans are pissed at us. It doesn't take a Rhode scholar to figure out that we could be between a rock and a hard place" Nathan said. Steven looked at Nathan with a serious look. He took a drink of coffee before he spoke. "Nathan, if it's any consolation I agree with you" Steven confessed. "But, thankfully, we aren't the only ones that feel this way. Admiral Grayson has had photographic reconnaissance of China and North Korean for the past five months. As we speak we have no less than six attack subs and two cruise missile subs in the East China Sea. If anything happens rest assured we'll be ready. The *Kitty Hawk* had been planned to be decommissioned in November but is being readied and will be deployed north of Guam" Steven finished his coffee and let the information he just received settle. Steven said that Admiral Grayson had photographic recon of China *and* North Korea. Nathan knew that the satellites could give good coverage but they also could be patterned as to when and what they saw. Their own Air Force did it when the Soviets and most recently China sent surveillance satellites over the United States. The satellites arrived over sensitive areas at a predetermined time and interval and the appropriate measures were taken so the satellites saw only what we wanted them to see. The SR-71's were retired years ago. There was talk back in the middle to late 90's that the US developed a super spy plane. It may even have a weapons capability. Nathan remembered an incident near Iceland back in 1994 when he and another F/A-18 pilot were on routine patrol one hundred miles south of Keflavik NAS. They were flying a loose formation at forty-five thousand feet when Nathan saw what appeared to be a high flying bomber aircraft. He informed the base of his sighting and changed course to intercept the bomber. The aircraft seemed to be at least eighty thousand feet and was traveling very fast. Nathan ordered his wingman to stay behind as he attempted a maximum climb. He had to accelerate to Mach 2 to even attempt to intercept it. At sixty-two thousand feet Nathan had a compressor stall in his number one engine. He started into a spin but recovered and slowed to subsonic speed while descending to forty thousand feet. He was forced to return to Keflavik as his fuel was running low and joined his wingman for the long flight home. The aircraft he had attempted to intercept had left him far behind. Nathan estimated the aircraft's speed at over four thousand miles per hour. He made a mental note of its configuration. It was about the length of a Backfire bomber but it had a Delta shape. The wingtips looked like they tilted down. It didn't have any engine nacelles but looked to have six engines blended into the underside of the fuselage. Nathan could see no afterburner or contrails, which didn't make any sense to him. Nathan didn't discuss what they saw until they were on the ground. His wingman thought for sure that it was a UFO. The base radar operators didn't detect it or wouldn't comment on the interception. Nathan had his own ideas, even while he and his wingman were debriefed by Air Force and Navy Officers and the Defense Department. After about three hours of questioning, the Air Force Generals told Nathan and his wingman that they had seen a B-1B bomber. The bomber was undergoing tests with advanced high altitude engines. Nathan and his wingman were sworn never to talk about the incident and had to sign several documents stating they would comply. Nathan put the incident out of his mind. That is until now.

Nathan finished his breakfast and was on his second cup of coffee. He asked Steven if the pictures of the Chinese Strike Group were available. "No Commander, I don't have them with me" Steven replied, looking over a copy of *Scientific American*. Steven looked up "Did you *need* to see them for some reason Commander?" Steven asked inquisitively. "Not really, I just wondered how a satellite could catch a Strike Group at sea" Nathan confessed. "I'm not sure that it *was* a satellite, Commander" Steven said. "Oh, I just assumed it was" Nathan replied. "Commander" Steven began "In our business it is dangerous to assume things. I think we better continue this conversation in my quarters" Steven added. They both finished their coffee and left the Officers mess. Nathan was anxious to get the answers to some questions he had for many years. Since he had a new security clearance he was sure that Steven would let him be privy to the type of information he needed to know.

President Jackson had been on the E-4B for over twelve hours. There had been no other missile launches by North Korea. He had anticipated that President Lu Doc would call and be extremely agitated with him. No such call was received. The only call that was received was from the Chinese President who had personally protested the interference of the North Korean missile *test*. President Jackson leaned back in his chair resting his eyes. The North Koreans had launched the missile as a test. The data that the United States had shown the missile's trajectory would take it to the Hawaiian Islands. In his opinion the military acted properly and in the process completed an operational test of the Airborne Laser. The Intelligence from the commanders in the field in South Korea showed that the North Korean Army and Air Force were mobilizing and on high alert. No fighter aircraft had approached the AL-1A's. The *Reagan* had increased the number of F/A-18's for the AL-1A's and the ROK Air Force had offered to fly Combat Air Patrols with their F-15K Eagles. The US accepted their offer and requested they fly sorties that were no closer that fifty miles from the AL-1A's. The AL-1A's were an expensive piece of US property and could not afford to be the victim of friendly fire.

General Howard walked in and interrupted the President. "Mr. President, we will be landing at the Groom Lake facility in about thirty minutes. We have received an intelligence update on North Korea and China and also there are some things I'd like you to see" the General said. "Very well General, thank you" the President said. The President was looking forward to seeing the facility. He had stopped here in 2005 when returning from Australia, just as a refueling stop. The President had attended a joint US-Australian Navy military exercise. The Australians had become very proficient at anti-submarine warfare. During his visit the Australian President signed an agreement to buy two new *Arleigh Burke* class Destroyers from the US government. The Australians had become the kind of allies that President Jackson could trust. The pilot of the E-4B landed at Groom Lake. It taxied to the east hanger and parked on the reinforced concrete apron. As the President looked out the window, he was surprised to see a lot of security. Since the base was remotely located he expected to see only a few security vehicles. The General came and escorted the President and the secret service agents to the vehicles below. The General explained that ever since the North Korean missile launch the *"Reagan Ranch"* was on the highest alert. The General directed the driver of the Hummer to drive to the alert entrance east of the hanger. The Hummer arrived at what seemed to be an isolated building on the eastern side of the base. An Air Force Security Policeman approached the Hummer and requested authorization. The General rolled down the window and showed the Air Force Sergeant his identification badge. The Sergeant looked at the badge, thanked him and saluted the General. The Sergeant motioned for the other guard to open the door to the building. The door rolled opened, not unlike any other garage door and the Generals Hummer proceeded inside. The building was in effect a large parking garage for the first two levels and the remaining four levels, the last of which culminated sixty feet underground, were made up of crew quarters, mess facilities, offices and operations rooms. The General showed the President most of the rooms before ordering the Electram to take the President and his Secret Service agents to the hanger bays. The Electram was an electric-powered open coach train that shuttled personnel down to the hanger and maintenance bays for the aircraft. The Electram traveled through a narrow corridor for about fifteen hundred feet before emerging into hangar bay one. The President, who sat in the second to last row of seats, saw a dark, dimly lit aircraft about the size of a B-1 Bomber. The first two Secret Service agents in the front seats remarked with a few expletives as the Electram stopped nearby, the aircraft now fully in view. As everyone stepped off and were clear, the Electram sped away to another location to service other waiting personnel. The General spoke into a hand held radio and ordered the lights brought up to eighty percent in bay one. The lights came up and seemed to get very bright. The aircraft, all black and menacing, seemed to be something out of science fiction. The General walked to the front of the group to address them. "Mr. President, gentleman of the Secret Service. Welcome to Groom Lake, home of the 6553rd Aerospace Test Squadron. The aircraft behind me is the F-57A Advanced Tactical Aerospace Vehicle or, as it is commonly referred to, at least here anyway, the ATAV" the General explained. The President had seen the designation F-57A before back in 1995 when it was included in the military's budget. He was a Senator from Iowa, then on the Senate Armed Services Committee, which had reviewed the budget before it went before the Congress. It was dropped the following year; the military citing the program was too costly. Nothing was heard about the program until late 1998 when China, North Korean and certain countries in Europe started seeing large delta-shaped objects crossing their skies at incredible speeds and altitudes. It was said, through certain defense channels, that the Chinese even attempted to bring one down by shooting an improved version of a SA-6 surface-to-air missile at it. The missile reportedly missed the aircraft by thirty-six miles and at least forty thousand feet in altitude. Subsequent sightings in 2003 and early 2004 in China and North Korea, respectively, were dismissed as meteorites in the upper atmosphere. The United States completely denied any knowledge of the phenomena.

The General seemed justifiable proud as he continued his briefing. "The aircraft measures one hundred and thirty-eight feet four inches nose to tail, has a wingspan of seventy-eight feet eight inches and is twenty- three feet six inches tall from main gear to the top of its twin tails. The ATAV has a maximum take-off weight of two hundred seventy thousand pounds. Thirty thousand pounds of that is reserved for weapons or the specially designed sensor pack for reconnaissance missions. The aircraft can fly up to altitudes of two hundred thousand feet and achieve a maximum speed of five thousand two hundred and seventy miles per hour or about Mach 7.2" the General concluded. One of the secret service members asked what type of engines it had. "The ATAV's have six Pratt and Whitney F-420-PW-2000 SCRAMJET engines each rated at fifty-seven thousand pounds static thrust below eighty thousand feet. The engines act as conventional jet engines but bypass the first stage compressor and turbine above fifty thousand feet to act as a RAMJET. The static thrust they develop then increases to eighty-nine thousand pounds" the General explained. The President was impressed. Knowing a little about metallurgy he couldn't help but ask the question. "General, the speed at which the ATAV flies, what keeps the wings from melting off?" the General smiled, acknowledging the question as a valid one. "The leading edges of the aircraft are made of a heat-resistant stainless steel known as *Inconel*. The rest of the aircraft is made up primarily of Titanium. The aircraft uses a special thermal management system, which contains a coolant known as *Syltherm* that circulates to the hot spots within the airframe to maintain skin temperatures to within specified tolerances" the General explained.

The General continued taking questions from the secret service agents. Most were about its performance and the General was enjoying explaining the questions. Some questions the General wouldn't answer such as the missions it had flown. By the end of the tour everyone knew how capable the ATAV's were and could imagine where they had been used. The General spoke into his hand-held radio and ordered that the lights be returned to normal and had the Electram return to take them back to the operations room. When the Electram stopped the General escorted the President to one of the briefing rooms the mission crews used prior to going on missions. The room had a large, half-moon shaped table with four chairs. The back of the room had a permanent white screen mounted on the wall for photographic analysis and a small projector higher over the door. The President walked in and sat down in a chair near the end of the table. The General motioned to the secret service personnel to close the door. The General picked up the phone on the table and instructed the sergeant on the other end to queue up the digital photo images from the last mission over North Korea. The images appeared on the screen in front in a few seconds. "Mr. President these photos are from a reconnaissance mission flow by Colonel Collins. I invited him to join us, I think it will give you a good idea of how the ATAV's operate" the General explained. There was knock at the door, which was promptly answered by the secret service agent at the door. The agent looked at the General, who nodded to the secret service agent. The agent admitted Colonel Collins to the room and closed the door. Colonel Collins introduced himself and sat at the seat next to the General. "Mr. President, Colonel Collins has been with the ATAV program for the last six years and has over fifteen hundred hours in the F-57's. I know that may not seem like a lot but the average mission time in the ATAV's is just over four hours" the General said. The President nodded as he looked at the image on the wall. It seemed to be of an industrial site with several tractor trailer tankers parked nearby. A small building was in the upper left of the picture with the block letters "Vent" superimposed on the photo. A small trace of what seemed like white smoke was emanating from the top of the building. "So gentleman, what do we have here?" the President said. "Mr. President, this photo is the first photo in a series that was taken above the Kamgamchan missile site" the General explained. We had thought the site was dormant for the last few years but there has been considerable activity during the last few weeks. The tractor-trailer's you see here, and here, are carrying liquid rocket propellant. The white smoke you see coming from the building is the gas venting from an underground supply storage tank. The building is nothing more than concealment for the supply valves and venting system" the General explained. In the next picture you see two missile silos open. The one silo that is occupied has a Taepo-dong III missile which was empty a few days ago. In all, this missile complex has fifteen missiles that are, we believe, being readied for launch" the

General said. The President looked at the General with a look of despair. Colonel Collins added that he had flown the three previous missions last week and had photographed two missiles being delivered and loaded into other silos. "These missiles that were delivered, can we confirm they were loaded with warheads?" the President asked. The General hit a button on the desk a few times and the digital image on the wall changed to a split screen, the same frame twice but the left side magnified about one hundred times. The frame was clearly focused on the designation number, which showed KN-530, the designation for the North Korean Army's 50-kiloton nuclear warhead. "These are the photos that were taken yesterday Mr. President." the General said. "We have several other photo's that confirm that ten other warheads in the fifty kiloton range were loaded onto Taepo-Dong missiles" the General added. The President looked at the General and then the Colonel. "Colonel Collins, have you ever dropped any ordinance from the ATAV's?" the President asked. "Yes Mr. President, I have dropped several 2000 lb. JDAM's from one hundred thousand feet and scored a kill rate of ninety-eight point seven percent on the Nellis bombing range" Colonel Collins replied. "That's good Colonel, but I need to get a weapon *inside* these silos so we can destroy them for good. These look like they are reinforced with several yards of concrete" the President said. "Mr. President, I think when the time comes, we can accommodate you" the General replied..

SEVEN

COMMITMENT

NATHAN HAD CALLED THE NAVY BASE personnel office on Friday about his Monday morning appointment. Nathan was scheduled to get the 4:30 flight from LAX to Pensacola on Monday afternoon. He was wondering if someone, specifically Jill, could accompany him to the airport also. He called the office and just by chance Jennifer Kelly answered the phone. "Hi Nathan, how are you?" Jennifer asked. "I'm fine, thank you for asking. I'm sorry I haven't called you sooner" Nathan replied. "Oh, that's Okay, I'm sure you have been very busy getting ready to leave. Two weeks isn't a lot of time" Jennifer said. "No, it isn't, have you heard from Amy?" Nathan inquired, trying to avoid the question about Jill. "Yes I did. She got home last Tuesday and she's doing fine. She asked about you also" Jennifer replied. "Again, I'm sorry for not keeping in touch, Jennifer. I'm bringing a new engineer up to date on a few things here at work, and, well I'll be completely honest with you, I have sort of met someone here at work that I have been spending my free time with" Nathan confessed. "Oh, that's good. Have you known her long?" Jennifer asked. Actually, yes, about six months but I have recently started dating her" Nathan explained. "That's wonderful, I'm happy for you. Who ever she is Nathan I think she is very lucky" Jennifer replied. "Thank you Jennifer, I didn't want you to think I blew you off" Nathan explained. "Well, I'm glad you told me. There's no reason we can't be friends right?" Jennifer asked. Nathan thought about that for a second or two before answering. He didn't want to mess things up with Jill. Jennifer was young, beautiful and smart. Jill would definitely see her as a threat. Nathan hoped that her offer of friendship was genuine. "No, I don't see why not" Nathan replied. "That's good, I'm leaving the area myself in a few months and will be going home to see my Mom in West Palm before I drive to Tallahassee and start college. Maybe we could get together some weekend and go to the beach?" Jennifer asked. "That sounds like a good idea. Hopefully I'll be in fighter pilot school by then. I might have the weekends free then" replied Nathan. "Good, I'll call you when I get settled in Tallahassee" Jennifer said. Nathan talked to Jennifer for a few more minutes before leaving his office for the last time. He thanked Jennifer for everything she did. He would most likely say nothing to Jill about Jennifer for right now. Nathan would be gone for over six months, a long time in anyone's life, especially since he was just starting a new relationship.

It was Sunday and Nathan and Jill were busy cleaning out his apartment. His landlord, Mrs. Carson, told him that if he moved out by Sunday afternoon she would prorate his rent for last week only. Nathan didn't have much in the way of furniture, just a bed and mattress, computer desk and some sofa chairs. Jill was a great help. Not only had she helped load the rental truck she had brought lunch with her. Nathan's refrigerator was empty and unplugged for the last week since he and Jill spent most of their time together. Nathan and Jill cleaned the apartment better than when Nathan had moved into it. The landlord was so happy that she paid Nathan his security deposit in full when he left. She hugged Nathan and told him to keep in touch. He was one of her favorite tenants and thought that he and Jill made a cute couple. "I think you'll have really cute kids" she replied as Nathan got into the rental truck. Nathan said goodbye to her as he put the truck in gear and started to pull away. Nathan noticed that Mrs. Carson seemed to stop Jill as she backed out to follow Nathan. She talked to Jill for a few seconds before giving her a hug that was returned by Jill. Jill followed in her Mustang as Nathan took the shortest route to her house. Nathan had to get the truck back by six o'clock. They both began to unload the truck when they arrived. The sofa furniture and computer desk fit neatly into the corner of the garage. Nathan wrestled the box spring and mattress up to the loft. Jill, sweating and breathing hard, carried the second nightstand upstairs and set it next to the bed. Nathan was exhausted and collapsed on the bed he just put together. "Mrs. Carson thinks we are a cute couple" Nathan said, wiping the sweat from his face with his T-shirt. "I know" Jill replied as she took her the pink tie out from her long black hair. "She thinks we'll have really cute kids" Jill said, catching her breath. "What do you think about kids anyway?" Nathan asked, taking off his sweaty t-shirt. " I love kids honey, but I just want to practice at it for a few years" Jill replied climbing onto the mattress and sitting next to Nathan. Jill bent down to kiss Nathan as her long black hair caressed Nathan's bare chest. Nathan had been with Jill for two weeks as of last Friday. It had been a rocky start, but both of them knew that their relationship was something special. Nathan kissed Jill again but confessed that he needed to return the rental truck. "If you hurry you can join me in the Jacuzzi when you get back" Jill said as Nathan started to get up. Jill adjusted her top and walked downstairs to the garage. Nathan followed her and kissed her goodbye as he ran for the truck. She waved to Nathan as he backed out of the driveway. Jill continued inside to her bedroom and got undressed. She was really exhausted and sweaty after moving. She smiled thinking of the day that Nathan would be her husband. She loved kids and always wanted a family. She knew she would raise polite, loving children. Nathan would make a wonderful father, not the kind that would run off when his family needed them the most. Jill began to think of her own father. He did unspeakable things to her and would often punish her for no reason at all. She was actually glad and relieved when he left. Jill began sobbing as she stood in the shower. She stood under the water spray, her arms folded in front of her, holding her breasts. She turned away from the spray as she slid down the shower wall to the floor, sobbing uncontrollable.

Nathan returned to the house about six-thirty. He entered the side door, put down his keys and went to the bedroom to look for Jill. She was not in the bedroom or the bathroom but there was sign that she took a shower. He heard a noise in the hallway and quickly made his way there to find no one. Worried about Jill, Nathan called out her name and heard a faint answer coming from the computer room. Nathan walked the short distance to the computer room door and saw her curled up on the small bed in her white bathrobe, facing the wall. "Jill, are you okay?" Nathan asked as he sat down on the edge the bed. He reached to touch her as she turned around. Nathan saw that she had obviously been crying and upset about something. She reached for Nathan and held on to him tight. Nathan caressed her gently and asked her what was wrong. "When I feel sad I come to this room. I have always felt safe when I'm in here" Jill replied. "Why do you feel sad?" Nathan asked. "I was thinking about my dad and how he treated me and my mom. Nathan, please promise you'll always treat me well" Jill replied, sobbing on Nathan's shoulder. Nathan promised he would always treat her with love and respect and keep her safe. He held her tight as Jill lay her head in his lap. Jill needed his assurance now. She had been mistreated and lied to from grade school to college. Remarkable, thanks to her mom and her aunt, Jill had grown up to be a smart beautiful woman. Her aunt had raised her to be a lady despite peer pressure. Her aunt knew that Jill might become sexually active in her teens so she had talked to her many times about protecting herself. Jill was allowed to have friends over to her aunt's house, boys and girls, but the boys have to leave before nine o'clock at night by her mom's own rule. Jill's aunt was liberal on some issues though, which allowed Jill and her friends to have some really fun parties. Jill remembered a lot of sleep overs with her girlfriends, secretly calling them "nudist parties" instead of "pajama parties" since not everyone brought pajamas. It was here that Jill learned to be comfortable with nudity and her own body.

When Jill was a freshman in high school she had a boyfriend that was a junior in the same high school. Her friends were obviously jealous and Jill took every opportunity to flaunt it. After a few months of dating, Jill, who was still innocent, found herself in a situation, which she couldn't control. After a football game, in which her boyfriend scored the winning touchdown, they both went to the local make-out place along with the other members of the football team and their girlfriends. After an hour or so of making out, her boyfriend made more serious advances towards Jill who was too scared to say no for fear of ridicule. She got home at her aunt's house way past midnight and cried most of the night. Her aunt realized that something was wrong when Jill didn't come to breakfast in the morning but continued taking showers in the hall bathroom. Jill was silent the whole time until her aunt asked if anything was wrong. Jill looked at her aunt and broke down in tears. She told her aunt the whole thing from start to finish after begging her aunt not to tell her mom. Jill's aunt had no children of her own but raised Jill as her own daughter. She was compassionate and explained the difference between sex and love and when to say no. It had helped her make the right decisions when she went to college and when she had to make the painful decisions to leave her first husband.

Nathan cuddled with Jill for an hour or more, gently wiping her tears and kissing her face. Jill nodded off occasionally, waking as Nathan stroked her long hair. Nathan asked what she wanted to do for dinner. Nathan had to leave tomorrow afternoon and this would be their last dinner together for a while. Jill had a thought, why not get Chinese food just like the first day they were together? Nathan thought it was a good idea but wanted to take her out. "No, I don't want to share you with anyone tonight. Besides its much more intimate here" Jill said. Nathan agreed and went to order the Chinese food. Jill returned to her bathroom to freshen up and change. Nathan showered and changed into his jeans and a Polo top. He liked dressing in suits but wanted to be casual tonight. Nathan watched as Jill dressed in her black skirt and donned a pretty floral print blouse. She had her hair down, loose about her shoulders and looked incredibly beautiful. Nathan gazed lovingly at Jill, knowing that he surely was going to miss her the next few months.

The day of August 18, 2008 started like any other day. Men went to work, Mothers drove their children to school, oblivious to the events unfolding half a world away. When it started it all seemed to happen at once. The North Koreans launched their IL-28 bombers first, guided by Chinese satellite intelligence towards the *Reagan* Strike Group. The thirty-eight IL-28 bombers at the *Taetan* air base launched minutes before the MiG-19 fighters stationed at *Nuchroni* and *Kuupri* launched towards Seoul. The IL-28 bombers, each loaded with four Chinese C-802K cruise missiles, were tasked with locating and attacking the American fleet and any ROK Navy units. The missile bases at *Sangwon* and *Chiha-ri* launched eight short-ranged No-Dong missiles at the American airbase near the DMZ and another ten at the command and control facilities in Seoul. Each missile carried a high-explosive warhead of over two-thousand pounds. The much- feared Taepo-Dong III nuclear missiles at *No-Dong* and *Ok'pyong-nodongjagu* were launched at Japan, Okinawa and Guam. Other nuclear missiles at the bases of *Chunggang-up*, *Kanggamchan,* and *Toksong-gun,* were to be launched at the naval base in Hawaii, Air Force bases in Alaska and major American naval installations on the West Coast. Hundreds of North Korean fighters, mostly MiG-21's, MiG-23's and Su-25's were ready for battle. Hundreds more, safe beneath the earth in hardened shelters, were fueled and loaded with missiles, bombs and rockets. The North Koreans hoped that the ballistic missiles they fired would catch the ROK Army and Air Force units by surprise and destroy them on the ground. The missiles would arrive at their targets in four minutes followed by the air strike of some sixty MiG-19 fighter-bombers two minutes later. From their airbase near Pyongyang, the Elite 56th Guards who flew the MiG-29's, would attack any fighter aircraft the American's or ROK put into the air. Four of the MiG-29's accompanied the bombers sent to attack the *Reagan* Strike Group. Each carried four PL-12 long-range air-to-air missiles. The missiles had the capability to engage and kill aircraft at over fifty miles. All NKA Navy units, including submarines, had orders to shoot at American and ROK naval units. None other than President Kim Lu Doc approved the plan. Once the plan was implemented the North Koreans knew that they could not turn back. The future of their nation, their very survival, was at stake.

The Japanese AWACS that was orbiting one hundred miles south of the *Reagan* picked up the North Korean bombers at *Taetan* as soon as they lifted off. The E-2C from the *Reagan* also picked them up and within minutes the *Reagan* was readying aircraft for launch. The F/A-18E "Super Hornets" had trained for intercept missions ever since the Navy retired the venerable F-14 Tomcats a few years ago. The "Super Hornets" each carried four AMRAAM Mod 3s, which had a range of sixty-five miles. For close in combat the "Super Hornets" carried the all-aspect AIM-9X infra-red air-to-air missile, which, through a special targeting flight helmet, could lock onto targets *behind* the pilot. Both the AWACS aircraft detected more aircraft rising from the NKA airfields. It was clear that an attack was in progress. In the next minute the AWACS detected multiple ballistic missile launches near the DMZ. The information was electronically relayed to all the Commanders of the Patriot IV air defense batteries near Seoul and the American airbase. Several ROK F-15K fighters were airborne in the first few minutes. The flight of four, F-15K's formed up and headed for the twenty MiG-19's headed for Seoul. The F-16's on alert at Kunsan AB were launched and headed north towards the North Korean aircraft. The North Koreans had drawn first blood. The launch of the No-dong missiles confirmed the attack. In less than two minutes all information acquired by the AWACS was transferred to the North American Air Defense Command at Cheyenne Mountain, Colorado. The Generals immediately contacted President Jackson on the E-4B Airborne Command Post still parked on the ramp at Groom Lake and informed him of the attack. Regretfully, he gave the Generals the code word "Drop the Hammer" which would initiate a full retaliatory response on North Korea. Within a minute all

US military forces abroad had the authority to attack and destroy any hostile North Korean military unit.

The E-4B started moving to take off position even before the President had hung up with the General at Cheyenne Mountain. The President could hear the wail of sirens as the 747 taxied to its runway. The 747 turned onto the runway and ran up all four engines to military power. The pilot released the brakes and the 747 surged forward gaining speed as it rolled down the runway on another maximum performance takeoff. The President was pushed back into his seat as the 747 accelerated upwards towards it's safe cruising altitude of fifty thousand feet. It had started now. The North Koreans had played their final hand. After years of summits, treaties and inspections President Lu Doc had taken things into his own hands and condemned his people to a life of pain and suffering. President Jackson knew that the US military would carry out their orders with extreme precision and lethality. The US military had been given the "Go" order, which had set things in motion. During the deliberations in the White House situation room a few days ago, the President, who was briefed on the new high-tech weapons, was informed the US had acquired a new "Strategic Precision Strike Capability". During the planning meeting General Howard suggested the code word the President could use for authorizing a retaliatory attack on North Korea could be the phrase "Drop the Hammer", referring to the hammer of Thor, the god of lightning in Norse mythology. The President, amused by the phrase, approved it, not once thinking of the destructive power that the *Thor II* satellite was capable of delivering.

The calm air at Whiteman AFB was shattered as the sirens went off. A dozen aircrews, twenty-four men in all, drove their alert vehicles to the waiting B-2 "Spirit" stealth bombers. Once on board the pilots did a quick pre-flight and then advanced the throttles, released the brakes and taxied to the runway. One by one, in staggered takeoff position, the B-2's took off separated by two-second intervals. Each aircraft had a pre-planned route programmed into its guidance computer, which guided it to within two miles of its Initial Point. Once there the Mission Commander would break the seal on the mission code comparing it with the code at the Mission Commanders station. If the codes matched, the Mission Commander would fly and attack his targets according to the command authority priority. Each B-2 had been loaded days earlier with eight Mark 5 Mod 2 SPECOR weapons. Each weapon was designed to penetrate deep underground before detonating its warhead, either a selectable variable-yield nuclear weapon of 2 to100 kilotons or 2,800 lbs. of conventional explosive. Because of Presidential order all warheads carried the latter. The designation SPECOR was an acronym standing for Special Core. The weapon had a total weight of 5,250lbs.,which was constructed of a special titanium core which retained the shape of the weapon while allowing it to penetrate to its designed detonation depth of up to three hundred feet, depending on the type of surface to be penetrated. During tests at White Sands Missile Range in New Mexico the MK 5 Mod 2 penetrated one hundred feet of sand and twenty feet of reinforced concrete before detonating its warhead. The concrete bunker, which was two stories tall and thirty feet by seventy feet, was completely destroyed and collapsed.

Nothing was safe from the SPECOR. The designers at Boeing had a saying "If they can build it, we can reach it". The technical representatives at Boeing were consulted prior to the loading of the B-2. The question put to them was how deep could the SPECOR penetrate through solid concrete. Some said eighty feet while some said only fifty but they all pointed out that is why it was designed with a selectable variable-yield nuclear warhead. A SPECOR could destroy anything, anywhere no matter how deep with a low-yield warhead from 2 to 100 kilotons. It was proven years ago in the Nevada desert. Underground caverns cut by small nuclear explosions still existed to this day, although they would be contaminated from radiation for the next five hundred years or so.

Major Donald Cunningham had been at Space Command for two years. Most of his duties were testing new systems and relaying confidential reconnaissance information to the National Command Authority. The United States Air Force' newest satellite, the KH-20 or *Thor II project,* had been operational for about two years. The satellite was built by a combined effort by Lockheed-Martin, Honeywell and Northrop-Grumman. The program was finished three years behind schedule, not the fault of the contractors, but by NASA, which had lost their heavy lift and repair capability when the shuttle program was canceled indefinitely in 2002. The contractors were forced to retool and machine parts and assemblies to fit in the Delta IV rockets. *Thor II* was designed from the outset as a Strategic Precision Strike Satellite. In addition to the dozen or so cameras and sensors, the satellite sported a 30 billion electron-volt particle beam weapon. The weapon was test fired at a remote island facility in the South Pacific. A simulated military complex was built in its entirety covering about fifty square miles. The facility had Command and Control facilities, a radar site, an operational airfield with support facilities, and several simulated missile silos with old Titan missiles in them. Nearby in a small harbor, several decommissioned US

Navy warships were anchored. The island facility took over ten months to build.

The first test centered on the warships in the harbor. The first targeted warship, a Spruance class Destroyer, DD 964 Paul F. Foster, exploded and broke in two, sinking, after a five-second burst from the particle beam weapon. The second warship that was targeted, a Perry class guided missile Frigate, exploded after its gas turbine engine superheated and caught fire. The Frigate was subjected to a burst of four seconds. The third warship to be destroyed, another Perry class Frigate, was loaded with four old AGM-84 Harpoon missiles and Mk 46 torpedoes. The particle beam weapon targeted the weapons specifically. Two of the Harpoon missiles detonated, after a three-second burst from the particle beam weapon. The missiles spread rocket fuel, which quickly ignited resulting in a conflagration that spread to the forward superstructure. The second burst of energy from the weapon detonated one of the torpedoes in its launcher setting off secondary explosions from other torpedoes that tore the aft third of the ship apart from the front, sinking the warship.

The airbase, which took about two months to complete, was destroyed and rendered useless in about five minutes. Several large holes were blown in the concrete runway when sections of it were subjected to the weapons beam. The concrete was superheated and the residual water that exists in all concrete exploded as if hit by a thousand pound bomb. Fuel and oil storage tanks were also targeted and blown up creating massive explosions and fires. Several old aircraft from F-4 Phantoms to B-52D's, which had been resurrected from the Arizona "Boneyard" were parked, fully fueled, on the concrete parking ramp. Ten aircraft were destroyed in less than twenty seconds; the jet fuel reaching its flashpoint in seconds as the particle beam weapon targeted each individual aircraft. The aircraft that were destroyed had no weapons aboard but continued to burn for several hours until all that was left was a smoking heap of aluminum scrap. The command and control facilities were targeted next. The concrete buildings suffered the same fate as the runway, exploding and collapsing in a pile of reinforced rubble. The missile sites, with the old unarmed Titan missiles, were the most dramatic of all the tests. A Titan II-C missile, fully fueled, weighs in at about one hundred twenty tons, several tons of that being liquid rocket fuel. The particle beam weapon targeted each individual missile, a few of which had their missile silo hatches left open. The particle beam dwelled on each missile for five seconds, superheating the Hydrazine rocket fuel and Oxidizer until it exploded. One missile whose missile silo cover was closed was destroyed in huge fireball, the explosions sending tons of earth skyward with a mushroom cloud extending up to fifteen thousand feet.

The entire firing sequence for the test took less than fifteen minutes. The power used by the particle beam weapon used less that fifteen percent of its energy reserves, only two percent more than estimated. The devastation was quick and complete. The test proved that the weapon worked and that a rapid response could be made on an adversary without warning and without endangering the lives of US military personnel. The *Thor II* project as it was called, was at the top of the "*black programs*" of National Security. The military leaders kept the project a secret even from the President for fear that the program would be compromised or worse yet, canceled. *Thor II* was designed to relay satellite imagery in real-time to the National Command Authority and have its weapon lay dormant until needed in case of a national crisis. A crisis that now seemed fast approaching.

Colonel Bill Collins was in the control tower operations room when he saw the E-4B start its engines. The explosive starter cartridges made large, black smoke clouds, which swirled around the engine nacelles as the four turbofans came to life and spooled up. Seconds later the alert horn went off signaling an attack was in progress. Colonel Collins quickly made his way to his aircraft, already dressed in his flight suit. When he arrived at the hanger bay where his aircraft was parked, The ATAV aircraft number 93-012, had most of her systems already powered up. His co-pilot and Weapon System Officer, Major Samuel P. Cox, was in the right seat and almost finished with the pre-engine start checklist. "Colonel, I have systems one through seven on-line and we can start engines in about a minute" Major Cox said. Sam was quite a jokester around the barracks but in the cockpit he was all business. With the ATAV traveling close to outer space at seven times the speed of sound there was no room for error and Sam knew it. "Very well, lets get going" Colonel Collins ordered as he sat down and strapped himself in. Colonel Collins heard the crew chief over his headset intercom say that all stations were ready for engine start. Colonel Collins acknowledged and pushed and held the switch marked "ENG 1". The engine came to life while the digital readouts in front of him relayed engine rpm, temperature and hydraulic pressure. Each of the six of the Pratt & Whitney F-120-PW-2000 engines started and all indications read normal as Colonel Collins ordered the bay doors opened. The huge blast doors rolled to the side while the bright desert sun shown in on the ATAV. From outside the hanger bay the blast doors seemed to be just part of the mountainside, carefully contoured and painted to match the desert terrain. Inside the cockpit Colonel Collins advanced the throttles slowly so the ATAV would start to taxi and not kick up too much dust. Even the concrete taxiways were camouflaged and covered with two to four inches of sand, resembling the desert floor. Colonel Collins reached the nearest "clean" taxiway and swung the ATAV north and headed for the end of runway 270. Once lined up on the runway Colonel Collins advanced the throttles to forty percent and released the brakes. The ATAV accelerated to four hundred miles per hour by the time the aircraft flew over the other end of the runway, not less than eight thousand feet away. The ATAV pitched up and banked to the right five degrees while Colonel Collins advanced the throttles to seventy percent. The ATAV broke the sound barrier as it accelerated past forty thousand feet. Below, at about twenty thousand feet, Major Cox could see the unmistakable outline of the E-4B that took off earlier. Major Cox monitored the aircraft's systems as the ATAV climbed to its cruising altitude of one hundred twenty thousand feet. The large weapons bays of the F-57A were loaded with four Mark 5 Mod 3 SPECOR weapons. It was clear to both men that this was going to be their first combat mission. The targets were the Command and Control facilities of the Third Air Combat Command located at *Hwangju*. Sam and Colonel Collins had done reconnaissance missions over this area before and were familiar with its layout.

The aircraft broke the one hundred thousand-foot mark in five minutes and started leveling off as it approached its cruise altitude. The six Pratt & Whitney F-120-PW-2000 SCRAMJETS produced a continual dull, hum-hum-hum noise in the cockpit, already having bypassed the first stage compressor and turbine. The engine was now basically a RAMJET. Colonel Collins checked his altitude and system readouts. Everything seemed normal but something didn't feel right. He dismissed it as paranoia and advanced all the throttles to eighty-five percent. The aircraft settled down to a cruise speed of 3,358 miles per hour or just above Mach 5. Major Cox kept a careful eye on the weapon and airframe thermal management system digital readouts. The skin temperature was 1158 degrees Fahrenheit, well within normal limits. The weapons bay was cooler by about 800 degrees. Unencumbered by flight plans and air controllers, the ATAV headed strait towards North

Korea. At one hundred and twenty thousand feet the earth is a beautiful sight. Basically at the edge of outer space, the continents show up clearly, except for the occasional cloud cover. Its course took the ATAV over the Rocky Mountain range of the continental US and up to Alaska and over the Bering Strait. The Kamchatka Peninsula appeared below, void of any clouds. On previous missions it took a whole seven minutes to photograph the military complexes that stretched the length of the peninsula. One thing for sure, the military was getting their moneys worth out of the ATAV's.

The Mission Commander of "Bronco 3" couldn't believe his eyes. A multiple missile launch from several North Korean missile sites. The missiles were already being tracked, since the Airborne Laser system was on automatic. The three missiles from the base at *Toksong-Gun* accelerated and turned west towards Hawaii, their intended target. Passing through the clouds at forty thousand feet the aircraft's High Energy Laser fired its first shot. The lead missile exploded after the Laser burned a hole through its outer skin. Almost as soon as the first missile exploded the second missile, acquired seconds earlier, began to heat through the second stage fuel cell. Three seconds later the second missile exploded, its warhead falling harmlessly into the Sea of Japan. The third missile was engaged last. It reached its breakaway speed as the High Energy Laser heated the missiles outer skin near the first-stage separation ring, weakening it. The resulting explosion broke the missile apart, sending the re-entry vehicle to the earth below. Since nuclear ballistic missiles were first envisioned scientists designed multiple safeguards into them to prevent premature detonation. The last and final safeguard, the accelerometer, arms the warhead after the missile reaches the speed necessary to break away from the earth's atmosphere.

The seventy-kiloton warhead, which was destined for Hickam AFB, fell on the sparsely populated North Korean coastline below. The detonation of the armed warhead scorched the North Korean countryside, destroying and searing everything within seven miles. The small fishing village, oblivious to the events unfolding, ceased to exist. The bright flash and mushroom cloud, which could be seen for several miles, was the first indication that the war had gone nuclear. It was also a chilling reminder to those unfortunate souls who didn't die immediately, of the pain and suffering to come. Bronco 3 turned a few degrees east as the missile warning went off again. The displays showed that seven more missiles were in the air, this time from the base at *No-Dong*, north of their position, about one hundred twenty miles distant. The infra-red sensor in the nose of the 747-400 detected the launch plumes as soon as the missiles came out of their silos. The first three missiles, Taepo-Dong II's, were headed for the base at Guam. The last four headed out on a different bearing towards the naval bases at *Yokosuka* and *Sasebo*.

James awoke to the wail of sirens signifying an attack. He jumped into his clothes and ran for the flight line. The flight line was bustle of activity with other crew chiefs already prepping the other B-1B's down the ramp for take-off. James arrived at his aircraft's nose gear and flipped the safety switch up and hit the "start" button for the B-1's Auxiliary Power Unit. He hear the APU wind-up and then spin up to full power as the four members of the flight crew arrived in the Hummer. By the time the crew climbed in to the cockpit and strapped themselves in the aircraft had full electric power available. James pulled the chocks on the main gear as the Aircraft Commander started engines one through four. With all engines running, the B-1B started to taxi without warning. James didn't even have time to establish communications with the crew. James ran for the cover of the Hummer as the aircraft pulled out, turned and quickly taxied to the runway. James started the Hummer while listening to the two-way radio. The operator on the other end was obviously in distress but kept relaying a message to ground personnel over and over. "All personnel this facility is under attack by inbound ballistic missiles, this is no drill, report to your assigned shelter and await further instructions!" the radio operator reported. James turned the Hummer around and accelerated towards the north end of the base. The base at Guam was reconstructed in the sixties to house up to eight Titan II ballistic missiles. The missile silos remained, their missiles removed and long retired from active service. James tried not to think of the briefings he had in the past. The missiles that could be launched from Russia and China could reach the United States in less than thirty minutes. If he was lucky he had less than six minutes to get to a shelter. James pulled up to silo shelter number two, but it seemed to be already occupied. Numerous vehicles from tanker trucks to Hummer's surrounded the entrance. James drove to silo shelter number three as other vehicles arrived behind him. He shut off the engine and ran for the missile silos open cover. The missile silos were converted so they could sustain about one hundred people for five days. Food and fresh water were stored below, as were blankets and basic medical supplies. James climbed down the entrance ladder as a Colonel ordered the silo cover sealed. It was five minutes since the bombers left. There couldn't be much time left anyway. The hydraulic operated gears slammed the silo cover shut as the emergency lights came on. James looked below, down in the depths of the silo and saw about seventy souls looking up.

James sat down next to the Officers at the top level. "What do we do now?" James asked. "Pray" replied the Colonel.

The AL-1A's were designed to have a capacity for twenty-two full power shots. "Bronco 3" had already used three and continued shooting at the other missiles shot from the facility at *No-Dong*. The missiles that were targeted at Guam were shot down in rapid succession, as were the previous ones. The missiles targeted at *Sasebo* and *Yokosuka* had a head start since all the missiles were launched within seconds of each other. Three of the last four missiles were engaged by the AL-1A and were destroyed before they could arm themselves. The last one however reached its breakaway speed and continued towards *Sasebo*. The High Energy Laser heated the skin of the Taepo-Dong II as it reached the upper limits of the atmosphere. The pressurized hydrazine fuel tank exploded as the Laser focused its ten thousand-degree beam on target. The second stage fuel tank blew up, separating the re-entry vehicle and scattering its debris over a large area. The armed re-entry vehicle continued on a ballistic course to detonate in the Sea of Japan, thousands of feet below.

The *Topeka* had been tracking the "Oscar" for days while the *Reagan* slipped up the East Coast of the Korean Peninsula. They had no other contacts but the Japanese Destroyers to the south. The Captain had a hunch that the Chinese "Oscar" was here to help the North Koreans. The SS-N-19 "Shipwreck" missiles that the "Oscar" carried made an awesome first strike weapon against a Carrier Strike Group. The "Oscar" was about two nautical miles ahead of him at a depth of nine hundred feet. It would be an easy task to dispatch the "Oscar", just match bearings and shoot. The Mark 48 ADCAP's would do the rest. The sonar officer interrupted the Captain's train of thought. "Conn, sonar. Captain, the target is coming shallow again" the sonar officer reported. Indeed the "Oscar" was going to periscope depth. The Captain ordered the *Topeka* to slow to four knots and to come to a new depth of five hundred feet. The *Topeka* slowed and angled up to its new depth. After a few minutes the sonar officer reported the "Oscar" had reached periscope depth and had raised its masts. The Captain thought that this was it. If the "Oscar" opened it's cavernous missile bays he would have to commit to shooting his torpedoes. The "Oscar" was running close to ten knots and making a lot of noise in the process. The *Topeka* reached her ordered depth of five hundred feet, deep below the Thermocline. Even if they shot now the "Oscar" probably wouldn't hear it since the Captain purposely kept the *Topeka* in the "Oscars" baffles. "Conn, sonar. The target has opened three missile bays!" the sonar officer reported excitedly. Seaman First Class William Conner, who came on duty earlier, heard the Captain order the outer doors on tubes one and two opened. He heard a muffled "thump, thump" as both the outer doors locked opened. Not a second later he also heard something large enter the water, off the bearing of the "Oscar", with a loud audible "click" that followed. William started to report the contact as a loud hum began to grow in his headset. William yelled as the hum grew beyond the tolerance of human hearing. He tore off his headset as the *Topeka* seemed to dip and then roll to port about thirty degrees, sending the sonar officer out of his chair.

Captain Su Loc had the coordinates on the *Reagan*. He also received word that the North Koreans had begun launching their missiles. Good, with any luck the Americans would be too busy to intercept all his SS-N-19 missiles. He would fire off three missiles in six volleys, the nuclear tipped missiles in the fourth volley. The *Reagan's* defenses would be sure to be overwhelmed by the first three volleys and the last missiles would surely finish it off if the nuclear missiles were intercepted by any of its escorts. He also wanted to retain some missiles in case he encountered any angry ASW Destroyers. At a depth of fifty-three feet the Captain ordered the first three missile hatches opened. The missile bay doors opened revealing the deadly SS-N-19 missiles. The sonar operators removed their headsets, deafened by the noise of rushing water over the open missile bays. Captain Su Loc looked at his launch officer and nodded as they both turned their keys to initiate the launch. The Captain ordered the first missile launched as a loud hum began to grow inside the large submarine. The Captain uttered his last order as he yelled "Emergency surface the ship!" The huge submarines starboard side seemed to implode as if it the submarine went below its test depth. Thousands of gallons of water entered the "Oscar" through cracks in its pressure hull as the submarine rolled to port about fifty degrees and then a second later tried to right itself. Personnel were thrown violently about and some fortunate ones died quickly, sparing them the long lingering death of drowning. One hundred thousand gallons of seawater under pressure washed through the hull, sweeping personnel, dead and alive, through the casing. There was no help for the crew. The interior of the submarine quickly filled up with seawater as the "Oscar" went down by the bow, diving in a counter clockwise spiral to the ocean floor below.

Captain Billings was thrown against the periscope housing and then to the floor. Others that weren't belted in were thrown to the floor. The *Topeka* had righted itself, although a little out of trim. The Executive Officer, Lt. Commander Theodore "Teddy" Brown, climbed to his feet and tried to attend to the Captain, who lay unconscious on the control room floor. Several personnel were injured, either concussions, broken arms or dislocations. Commander Brown called for a medical technician to come to the control room and a damage report from all stations. The torpedo room was the first to report minor flooding, but it was being controlled. Brown ordered the torpedo tube doors closed on tubes one and two and to emergency surface to periscope depth to assess the damage and wounded. The engine room also reported that one of the reactor coolant pumps was damaged and was being shut down. They also reported minor fires in the aft battery compartment, which were extinguished. The diving officer came over to help Commander Brown with the Captain. "Commander, what the hell happened?" asked the diving officer. "I'm not sure, I think the "Oscar's" missiles must have blown up" replied Commander Brown. The Captain regained consciousness and sat up against the periscope housing as the medical technician arrived. He had a large cut on the side of his head, which the technician attended to. "Damage report, Teddy?" the Captain asked as he rested his head against the periscope housing. "We have a few broken bones but no fatalities. One of the reactor coolant pumps was damaged and was shut down. We had minor flooding in the torpedo room and a battery fire in the engineering compartment that was extinguished. We have depth and maneuvering control and are headed to periscope depth" Commander Brown replied. "Good, what about the "Oscar"?" the Captain inquired. "I think its nuclear missiles blew up Sir" Commander Brown replied. "No, if it did we wouldn't be having this conversation. They carry five hundred kiloton warheads, which would have incinerated us. It had to be something else" the Captain explained. The Captain reached up and grabbed the 1MC microphone. "Sonar, conn. This is the Captain. Do you still have a contact on the "Oscar"?" asked the Captain. "Yes Sir. The "Oscar" is at twenty-three hundred feet, bearing 268 and breaking up. It's headed for the bottom Sir" Seaman Conner said. The Sonar Officer now fully recovered and in his seat, looked at the sonar waterfall display. He saw the contact that William had explained he heard just before the explosion took place. "Conn, sonar. Captain, sonar shows a contact on bearing 287, which entered the water just before the explosion." The sonar officer reported. The Captain replied that he received the message. "Teddy, trail the wire, see if we can pick up any radio traffic" the Captain told his Executive Officer as he stood up. The communications wire could be trailed underwater when the *Topeka* was close to the surface to pick up ELF radio transmissions. The Captain, still a little woozy from his fall, made his way to the plotting table. "Conn, radio. We have traffic on the ELF" The radio operator announced. The Captain looked at Commander Brown and motioned for him to investigate. Brown went to the radio room and received the teletype from the radio operator. He returned to the Control Room and handed the Captain the Teletype. The Captain put his reading glasses on and read the message.

FROM COMSUBPAC TO ALL UNITS. REAGAN STRIKE GROUP UNDER ATTACK BY NKA BOMBER ACFT. NKA ICBMS SHOT DOWN BY BRONCO ACFT IN SOJ. NUCLEAR EXPLOSIONS DETECTED ON NK COAST AND SOJ. IDENTIFY AND ENGAGE ALL NKA NAVY UNITS AT WILL. END OF MESSAGE.

"Well that explains the explosion" the Captain said, handing the message back to Commander Brown. "Sonar, conn. This is the Captain. Do you show any other contacts?" the Captain asked. "Conn, aye. We show just the Japanese Destroyers on bearing 178. We have classified them as the *Haruna* and the *Kongo* Sir" the sonar officer reported. "Very well" the Captain replied. "Well, we were very lucky. The North Koreans have about a fifty-kiloton warhead on their missiles.

The AL-1A's probably had no trouble shooting them down but some obviously came down armed" the Captain explained to his XO. The crew was in good shape for the most part, only five men in sick bay with three others confined to their "racks". The Captain ordered a message sent to COMSUBPAC detailing the ordeal. The returned message acknowledged his report and ordered him to remain on station at his present position. Maybe the Admiral thought they had been through enough but one thing was for certain, the *Topeka* would probably not see any more action.

The *Michigan* was at periscope depth as Bart Kennedy ordered the boat to "hover". He ordered "All hands, battle stations missile". The tempo of the crew changed as men rushed to their assigned stations. Captain Kennedy put his launch key in and turned it in unison with his Executive Officer, Lt. Commander Jeff Scott. "Open missile doors one through forty, stand-by to fire" the Captain ordered. The Tomahawk Land Attack Missiles (TLAM) were nestled in their protective capsules awaiting launch. All the coordinates had been programmed and all that remained was the launch order. "Launch missiles one through fifteen" the Captain ordered. Compressed air heaved each missile clear of its tube and then to the surface, the rocket booster igniting and separating the missile from its watertight capsule. The TLAM continued skyward until the missile's wings deployed and its tiny turbofan engine could sustain its flight, dropping it down to cruise height. The Captain ordered another group of missiles, twenty-seven in all, launched in the next volley. For the next fifteen minutes a total of one hundred and fourteen TLAM's were launched. The minute the last missile was launched the Captain ordered all tubes secured and the hatches closed. He ordered a new course of 170 and the Diving Officer to make his depth one hundred fifty feet. As soon as the *Michigan* achieved its new depth Captain Kennedy ordered maneuvering to make turns for five knots. It was really shallow on the West Coast of the Korean peninsula. Some places not more than two hundred feet deep. All the Captain could do was hug the bottom and slink out of there to the safer depths of the South China Sea. Captain Kennedy knew that the *Ohio* that was to his south would be done launching its TLAM's soon. He hoped they had success in their mission. As far as he was concerned he completed only half of his mission. The next half was getting home undetected.

EIGHT

DEATH FROM BELOW

THE *SEAWOLF* WAS THE FIRST OF her class, which numbered only two. Her sister ship, the *Connecticut*, was on duty in the Indian Ocean. The *Seawolf*, whose Homeport was changed to Pearl Harbor since 2003, was often used in clandestine missions near the Korean Peninsula. This mission was radically different. Its main mission was to protect the *Ohio* class cruise missile carrying submarines and to attack any hostile submarines. For this task the *Seawolf* carried the fastest, most powerful torpedoes of any vessel at sea. The Mark 70 EXCAP, or Extreme Capability torpedo, was 26.5 inches in diameter and weighed in at 3500lbs. It was a wire-guided, dual-purpose torpedo that had a range of over eighty-five miles at sixty-five knots and could achieve ninety-eight knots on detected targets out to fifty miles. It carried a directed-energy warhead of twelve hundred and forty-five pounds, more than enough to sink the largest submarine. The torpedo had been developed in the early nineties in response to the Russian Alfa and Akula fast attack submarines. Tests on an old decommissioned *Spruance* class Destroyer showed that the torpedo could sink a warship just by its kinetic energy alone. During SINKEX 2005 the *Seawolf* sank the Destroyer *Paul F. Foster* with an unarmed Mark 70. Guided from a range of forty-seven miles, the torpedo closed on the *Foster* at over one hundred miles per hour. It hit the Destroyer amidships and ripped through the hull, breaking the ship in two, sinking her.

Commander Arthur S. Bristol was the Commanding Officer of the *Seawolf* on that exercise and had been ever since. Commander Bristol was a good friend of Steven Alexander. They had known each other for years and had worked together on the EXCAP project when Steven was the Project Manager at Lockheed-Martin. Arthur would love to tell Steven how the EXCAP worked in combat. Judging from the latest teletype message that might come true. Commander Bristol read the message.

> FROM COMSUBPAC TO ALL UNITS. REAGAN STRIKE GROUP UNDER ATTACK BY NKA BOMBER ACFT. NKA ICBMS SHOT DOWN BY BRONCO ACFT IN SOJ. NUCLEAR EXPLOSIONS DETECTED ON NK COAST AND SOJ. ENGAGE ALL NKA NAVY UNITS AT WILL. END OF MESSAGE.

Commander Bristol checked his position on the chart. The *Ohio* and *Michigan* should be starting their egress from the launch area. He wanted to be there, covering them if they encountered any resistance. He ordered the crew to make the necessary course changes. The Seawolf dove to one hundred seventy feet and increased speed to fifteen knots, less than a third of her full speed. After cruising north for over an hour the Seawolf's sonar detected a far off contact. The Sonar technicians quickly studied the BSY-2 passive array and identified and classified the submerged contact. It was a *Romeo* class diesel submarine, possibly from the NKA Navy and it was directly in the path of the *Ohio*. Commander Bristol ordered "Battle Stations, Torpedo" and chose an

EXCAP torpedo to be loaded in tube one from his chair console in the Control Room. In the torpedo room, which was largely automated except for a few technicians, hydraulic lifts and rams moved and loaded the behemoth Mark 70 EXCAP torpedo in tube number one. The fire-control technicians matched the bearings of torpedo and "Romeo" and entered them in the fire-control computer. The red "FIRE" light began blinking on the captains chair console. In a few seconds the light stopped blinking and stayed on, signifying the torpedo was ready for launch. With the outer doors already opened the Captain flipped up the safety switch and pushed the "FIRE" button. The Mark 70 EXCAP was ejected under pressure and started its long journey to the target, its telemetry wire unspooling as it went. Once the torpedo broke twenty miles the crew on the *Seawolf* cut the wires. The Mark 70 EXCAP went active and acquired its target, increasing its speed to ninety-eight knots. The Mark 70 covered the last twenty-four and a half miles in fifteen minutes. The "Romeo" had no where to go but turned away and dived steeply while increasing its speed to a ridiculous eighteen knots. Undeterred by the fleeing submarine's countermeasures, the EXCAP bored in from behind the "Romeo" and hit it in the aft section of the hull. The directed-energy warhead exploded splitting the submarine in two and sending a geyser of water and metal boiling to the surface. Both sections of the submarine, now free of neutral buoyancy, sank to the ocean floor below.

The light frigate *Yubari* was cutting through the Sea of Japan at close to twenty-five knots, its TM3 Gas Turbine producing over 29,000 shaft horsepower. The P-3C Orion aircraft could be clearly seen now, not less than eight miles away, orbiting over the suspected submarine contact. The Captain of the *Yubari* had copied the radio broadcasts from the US Pacific Fleet and knew the US was at war. He knew the declaration for Japan couldn't be far behind. He wanted to be the first to sink an enemy submarine. The NKA "Whiskey" submarine was closing on Japans shores and posed a threat to the coastal fishing fleet as well as the international shipping lanes. The Captain of the *Yubari* had received repeated radio messages from the P-3C aircraft to stay clear but the Captain ignored them. Nothing would stop him from his task. Armed with only one Bofors ASW rocket launcher and an unseasoned crew the *Yubari* was definitely not ready for what awaited it. The Captain ordered the ship slowed to eight knots and for the sonar technicians to locate the submarine. They activated the OQS-4 active sonar and detected the "Whiskey" which was less than six miles from them on a bearing of 237. The Captain ordered the ship back up to twenty-five knots on an intercept course. The hunter had found the fox.

The active sonar pulsed loudly through the "Whiskey" sub. Captain Feng reversed his course and dove to four hundred feet as soon as the pinging stopped. His sonar technicians advised him the frigate was closing at twenty-five knots, so the Captain ordered the submarines speed to be increased to twelve knots, knowing full well the approaching frigate would not hear him. The range finally closing to four nautical miles, the Captain ordered two SAET-60 torpedoes loaded into the forward tubes and two loaded into the aft tubes. The SAET-60 torpedoes had short legs, only eight miles but had a speed of forty-two knots. The Captain ordered the bow of the submarine pointed towards the speeding frigate and the sub slowed to four knots to allow the torpedoes to "swim" out of their tubes. It was an effective tactic of the quiet diesel-electric submarines. A more quiet and discreet way of launching the torpedoes as it did not broadcast the compressed air launch noise into the water. Since the "Whiskey" was below the Thermocline the torpedoes would not be detected until it was too late. Captain Feng ordered the torpedoes launched and once the bow torpedoes were clear of the submarine he reversed course. The aircraft overhead would be sure to launch its torpedoes now. Captain Feng ordered his submarine down to nine hundred feet, its absolute depth. The pressure hull creaked and groaned, and some small leaks were reported in the engine room. The two SAET-60 torpedoes, launched five seconds apart, ran for about one nautical mile before they came above three hundred feet. The torpedoes turned slightly indicating that they had "found" something. Indeed they had as the torpedoes went active "pinging" in the *Yubari* sonar officers ears. They immediately informed the bridge and the Captain ordered a quick turn to port in an effort to evade the incoming "fish" but all it did was reduce the *Yubari* speed by six knots. The first SAET-60 hit the *Yubari* amidships as it was coming out of its turn. The explosion tore a huge hole in the hull as seawater poured into the engine room flooding the gas turbine. The cold seawater reacted with the hot turbine exploding upwards through the deck and killing some twenty-eight crewmen in the engine room. With a complete loss of power, the forward speed of the ship immediately slowed to eight knots. The second torpedo hit the *Yubari* under the 76mm gun mount, blowing the bow of the ship out of the water and breaking the keel forward of the superstructure, sealing the *Yubari's* fate. The bow of the ship settled back down in to sea, filling with water. Fires raged from below decks as personnel raced to save themselves before the munitions blew up. The stern of the *Yubari* settled low in the water as the water poured in, pulling the ship under the water. Three minutes after the second torpedo hit the P-3C Orion aircraft flew over the site where the *Yubari* went down. Less than two dozen souls remained, bobbing in the sea.

Lieutenant Yamuko decided it was time for revenge. He looked at his fuel gauges and decided he had, at the most, five minutes of reserve fuel remaining. He ordered the remaining Sonobuoys tubes loaded with active Sonobuoys. He turned the aircraft on a heading of 320 and dropped six Sonobuoys, one every three seconds. The Sonobuoys started "pinging" as soon as they entered the water. The second Sonobuoys showed a strong contact and the third one weaker but growing contact. Yamuko turned the aircraft and ordered two Mark 50 lightweight torpedoes to be dropped three seconds apart between the second and third Sonobuoys. The first Mark 50 hit the water, shedding its parachute. It continued down for one hundred and seventy feet before starting its circular search pattern. The second Mark 50 continued down to three hundred feet below the Thermocline, before starting its search. The second Mark 50 acquired the "Whiskey" and increased its speed to maximum as it nosed over to dive on the "Whiskey" another six hundred feet below. The first Mark 50 started it secondary search pattern, acquiring the "Whiskey" almost immediately. The Captain of the "whiskey" submarine looked at his crew working frantically but professionally to decoy and evade the torpedoes after them. He was proud to serve, and die, with every one of them. The second torpedo hit the "Whiskey" from above and aft of its conning tower, exploding on contact and killing everyone in the control room. The submarine began to fill with seawater while others in the forward and aft section tried to no avail to seal watertight bulkheads. The first torpedo bored into the bow of the stricken submarine, exploding while separating the submarine in two pieces, the remaining pieces settling to the ocean floor below.

The radioman on the *Chung-Hoon* copied the broadcast from the ROK Command Center in Seoul. The Teletype began to chatter again as the radioman ripped off the copy and began to read it.

TO ALL ROK UNITS. FROM ROK MILITARY COMMAND, SEOUL. NKA HAS ATTACKED ROK, US, AND JAPAN WITH BALLISTIC MISSILES. VISUAL ID AND ENGAGE ALL NK ARMY, NAVY AND AF UNITS AT WILL. LARGE PRESENCE

OF NK SSK ON EAST COAST. COORDINATE WITH US
FORCES AT EARLIEST OP. REPORT ALL CONTACTS. END
OF MESSAGE.

The radioman forwarded the message to the CIC. The
communications equipment on the *Chung-Hoon* was state of the art.
Built in 2004 and commissioned by the ROK Navy in 2006, The
Chung-Hoon was the first of three US-built Arleigh Burke class multi-
role Destroyers. A significant improvement over earlier designs, the
Flight II Destroyers added dual helicopter hangars and full aviation
support facilities. By lengthening the hull by five feet, a much larger
torpedo and missile magazine was also provided to store helicopter-
launched weapons. Since last year the *Chung-Hoon* had been assigned to
the East Coast of the Korean peninsula with Pusan being its Homeport.
The American Navy had spent considerable time training the ROK navy
personnel on the intricate systems aboard the *Chung-Hoon*. The recent
tests during the PACRIM 2007 exercises confirmed that the South
Koreans had excelled in their training, which was proven after several
US target drones were shot down by live-fire SM- 2's from the aft 64-
cell vertical launch system.

The *USS Lake Champlain,* which was responsible for coordinating
all sub-surface activity for the *Reagan* Strike Group, contacted the
Chung-Hoon. The *Lake Champlain* was on the *Reagan's* Starboard side,
about four miles away. The Officer in charge ordered the *Chung-Hoon*
to investigate sightings of several North Korean submarines by fishing
boats. The submarines were observed snorkeling, recharging their
batteries and moving south towards Pusan. The Captain acknowledged
immediately and changed course to investigate the sightings. The
Reagan, once informed of the contacts, dispatched two SH-60 ASW
helicopters to support the *Chung-Hoon*. The Captain of the *Chung-
Hoon*, a seasoned veteran, ordered the engineering officer to make

revolutions for twenty knots. The new personnel on board were taken by surprise as the LM2500 gas turbines accelerated the ship from eight to twenty knots.

After sailing for about an hour the *Chung-Hoon* received a report that a fishing fleet discovered a submarine, less than eight miles off shore. Their Captain was using the noise of the fishing fleet to mask his transit and had become entangled in one the fishing nets. The crew of the "*Romeo*" submarine was frantically trying to free the net from their twin screws as one of the SH-60 helicopters launched from the *Reagan* arrived on scene. The SH-60 reported small arms fire from the submarine so it backed off and launched its Mark 50 torpedo. The torpedo caught the "*Romeo*" submarine amidships and blew it in half, taking the fishing net with it to the bottom. The crew of the helicopter flew over the fishing boats and saw men who seemed to be cheering at them, but in reality, they were enraged with the idea of losing their fishing net, the life-blood of their village. Minutes after the "*Romeo*" submarine was sunk the radio operator copied a message from the US Military. It was forwarded to the CIC where the Captain read it.

TO ALL US AND ROK UNITS. FROM COMPACFLT. WHISKEY SUB SANK JMSDF YUBARI FF AT 1420 HRS WITH TWO TORPEDOES OFF COAST OF HONSHU. ALL ROK AND US UNITS EXERCISE CAUTION WHEN PURSUING SUB CONTACTS. WHISKEY SUB WAS DESTROYED BY P3C ORION ACFT. END OF MESSAGE.

The Captain was disgusted. The *Yubari* was lost due to ignorance. It should have been no where near the submarine contact. Outfitted mostly for surface warfare, the Captain was familiar with the *Yubari* since he spent much time in Japan. He vowed to revenge the *Yubari*, tenfold. The Captain had the ship slow to eight knots and several minutes later detected multiple submerged contacts on its SQS-53 sonar array. One was on a bearing of 283 from the *Chung-Hoon* at a little over 31,000 yards while the second was on bearing 327 at 24,600 yards. The second helicopter, SH-60 127, had just finished refueling when it was launched and directed to the location of the second sub contact. The SH-60 had no trouble finding and dispatching the *"Romeo"* which was detected after its crew dropped a series of active Sonobuoys. The first submarine contact was detected and lost, then acquired again only to be lost again. The Captain was furious, threatening to relieve the sonar officer as he gave the last known bearing of the submarine to Seahawk 127.

Captain Ming Lee had heard the explosions during the last two hours. His sonar officer had confirmed that it was a Mark 50 each time and that the target broke apart and sank. Captain Lee mourned his "brothers" of the submarine service. All crewmembers were volunteers, as was the case in other navies. The NKA Navy was particular in selecting its officer and men for their silent service. Each had to be in service for a minimum of two years and had to be extremely motivated and resourceful personnel. Captain Lee was fortunate to have all five-year veterans. They had been as far south as Pusan several times, once even attempting to land commandos and gain intelligence, but the US Navy thwarted it. Captain Lee ordered his sub to periscope depth. He refused to wait for death to come as it had to his "brothers". The six NKA commandos he had on board had a surprise for the US Navy. Through his periscope the Captain could see the Seahawk at a distance of five miles. The Seahawk showed up particularly well as it banked and headed on a new course close to but off the bearing of the submarine. The commando team at the ready, the Captain waited until the Seahawk broke the two-mile mark before ordering the submarine to the surface.

Seahawk 127 had great luck so far. It had pursued two contacts and had two "kills" to its credit. The helicopter had just recovered out of a bank, directed by the *Chung-Hoon* on a new bearing when the crewman in the rear compartment yelled "Submarine on the surface, bearing 180 true" The pilot looked to the south and saw a submarine just breaking the surface, with only its conning tower showing. The pilot put the Seahawk into a hard left bank to come around to the subs heading, not once seeing the smoke and bright flash from the conning tower. The SA-7 shoulder-launched surface-to-air missile tracked directly on the Seahawk's engine and impacted the fuselage below the main rotor. The explosive-fragmentation warhead of the SA-7 exploded as it ripped through aluminum and composite . Seahawk 127 immediately lost altitude as it nosed over and dived straight into the sea.

The radar operator on the *Chung-Hoon* advised the Captain that he lost contact with Seahawk 127. The Captain looked at the radar screen. The radar operator contacted Hawkeye 23 who was transmitting the radar images. Hawkeye 23 confirmed that Seahawk 127 had gone down. The Captain swore and returned to the plot table. The Captain ordered the radio operator to request help from Seahawk 117, the helicopter that sunk the submarine that the fishing boats had snared. Seahawk 117 acknowledged and headed at top speed towards the last known location of Seahawk 127. The crew of Seahawk 117 had more tricks than usual. At twenty thousand feet, high over head, the two stealthy F-35 Joint Strike Fighters lazily escorted Seahawk 117 on its mission. Enclosed in its weapon bays were two AMRAAM's, two HARM's and two MK-39D 250lb small-diameter laser-guided bombs. The Seahawk arrived on scene and reported debris on the surface but no survivors in the area. The crew had obviously died on impact. On a whim, the pilot dropped two Passive Sonobuoys. Both returned a contact on converging bearings about seven thousand yards from the Seahawk.

Lieutenant Frank "Spike" Lopez looked out his canopy to the deep blue ocean below. Dropping down to eight thousand feet, Frank could make out Seahawk 117 scurrying around, pursuing the contact. Frank heard his wingman, Lieutenant John "Goose" Hughes, point out a object down below. "Is that a whale or what?" John said, referring to a dark mass just under the surface of the water. Frank looked where John pointed out. "No, that's a sub" Frank replied. The submarine was coming to the surface, no doubt to deal with the new Seahawk threat. Frank contacted Seahawk 117 and gave them a safe bearing and told them to "get clear". Frank brought up his Surface Attack Display just as the submarine's conning tower broke the surface. He activated the laser, which designated the contact, and pressed the "hot" button on his control stick. The weapon bay doors opened and one of the laser-guided bombs quickly dropped away, the weapon bay doors closing immediately to retain the stealthy appearance of the F-35. The laser-guided bomb rode the beam down to the submarine, arching down from the Joint Strike Fighter who was now directly above the enemy submarine. The commando team on the "Romeo" had no idea what awaited them as they climbed through the hatch of the conning tower. The third commando, who handed up the new SA-7 missile, saw the bomb for a split second before it hit. It was the last thing he would ever see. The laser-guided bomb hit aft of the conning tower, penetrating the pressure hull before exploding, blowing a hole completely through the submarine. The submarine didn't break in two, but rather quickly filled with water from the keel up, the whole submarine acting as a ballast tank and sinking to the bottom.

The mountains outside Colorado Springs, Colorado, that once held the North American Air Defense Command, was now also home to the US Space Command. A hardened and secure facility built into the granite of Cheyenne Mountain during the 1960's, the facility was built to withstand nuclear explosions during the Cold War. The US Air Force, needing a secure place to operate its surveillance satellites, chose Cheyenne Mountain. Major Cunningham had been assigned to the Fourteenth Air Force of the Air Force Space Command (AFSPC) at Cheyenne Mountain for six years, his responsibility being the management and employment of the satellites assigned to the US Space Command. He had been with the *Thor II* Program since its inception, drawn to the idea of a strategic precision strike capability that the program promised. Once the program was operational several tests were conducted. The test firing at the mock enemy base at Kwajalein Island in the Pacific's Marshall Islands was a great success. It proved that *Thor II* could strike anywhere in the world within the hour. The launching of several unarmed minuteman missiles in mid-July of 2004 from Beale AFB had also established that *Thor II* could effectively destroy ballistic missiles in-flight.

Major Cunningham was conferring with his Senior NCO in the control room when he received word concerning the attack on the US and Japan. General Howard was with the President aboard "Looking Glass", the E-4B Airborne Command Post, which was orbiting the blue skies of the western United States. "Major, the US, South Korea and Japan are under attack by North Korean ballistic missiles. The President has authorized *Thor II* into action. You are to follow your primary war orders until further notice" General Howard ordered. "Yes sir, I understand. *Thor II* will be active in less than a minute" the Major said, punching his security code into the panel next to where the Sergeant was sitting. The Sergeant finished running the pre-operative diagnostics on the system before it was put on automatic. The targets that *Thor II* would fire on were already in its computer brain. The diagnostics confirmed the position of the satellite, its weapon status and the energy level stored on-board the satellite. On the control room floor below technicians began to move quickly as the BMEWS alert went off. The senior staff officer picked up his headset and looked up to the glass windows above the control room where the *Thor II* satellite control was located. "Major Cunningham, we show several missiles in-bound to CONUS. Launch points have been calculated and show to be in North Korea" the senior staff officer said. Major Cunningham acknowledged and turned his attention to the console. The Sergeant sitting in front of the Captain already started transferring the data from the BMEWS computer to *Thor II*. Seconds later the display in front of the Sergeant showed thirty-seven targets approaching the continental United States at fifteen thousand miles per hour. The Sergeant typed quickly on his console, re-tasking *Thor II* to intercept the missiles. "Major, the computer is transferring the info to *Thor II*" the Sergeant said. "Initiate firing sequence when ready" the Major ordered. The Sergeant flipped up the clear safety switch on the red button that was flashing. The button was marked "Initiate", which would allow *Thor II* to carry out its mission. The button stopped flashing and the Sergeant immediately pushed the button. High above the earth in a geo-synchronous orbit, *Thor II* came to life. More than two weeks had passed since it had fired its particle beam weapon, destroying space junk that was scheduled to fall on populated areas. The satellite's thrusters came on and re-positioned the satellite for firing. A hundred thousand feet below, thirty-seven ballistic missiles came arcing up into the troposphere. Each missile was armed with the smaller warhead of fifty kilotons, sufficient enough to destroy its intended target. The Naval Base's on the West Coast, North Island, San Diego and Washington were all on alert. Personnel on-duty ran to their shelters while those that weren't found shelter inside large buildings and hoped for the best. The first missile was targeted for North Island, the homeport of the *Reagan*. The "bolt" of the particle beam weapon dwelled on the missile for two seconds before it blew up in a huge explosion, consuming the nuclear material in the warhead. The particle beam weapon, which was aimed magnetically, fired at each missile with deadly accuracy. In less than a minute all the missiles were destroyed and *Thor II* was re-tasked again to attack the missile silos, airbases and surface-to-air missile sites of North Korea.

The technicians at the *Kamgamchan* missile base were exuberant that the missiles launched successfully. Unconfirmed reports in South Korea showed that some No-Dong missiles launched from other bases were intercepted by US Patriot missile batteries but several other missiles made it through to impact on the US and ROK air bases. Six No-Dong missiles with conventional warheads hit the South Korean city of Seoul. The other Taepo-Dong missiles stored nearby were transported to the empty silos and lowered while the missile technicians feverishly began to check each system. Once the missiles checked out, the technicians began the dangerous job of filling the liquid rocket propellant into the missiles. Of eight missile silos left only five could be loaded with missiles that were available. Other Taepo-Dong missiles with nuclear warheads, seventy-eight in all, were dispersed to the other the bases including *Chunggang-up*, *Toksong-Gun*, *Mayang Island*, *Paegun* and *Ok'pyong-nodongjagu*.

Technicians were busy fueling the last missile when the ground seemed to shake and then move. Large explosions rocked the walls of the underground facility, rock and concrete dust falling to the bottom of the silo. Alarms went off with technicians running for the blast doors, hoping to escape the calamity that seemed to be approaching. The Taepo-Dong missile that just was refueled began to heat beyond its boiling point. Hydrazine fuel began leaking from hoses that were left attached to the missile. A flash fire erupted and a second later the missile exploded in a thunderous explosion, sending earth and reinforced concrete skyward. The missile technicians and some nuclear scientists never made it out, being consumed in the conflagration that spread through the underground facility. Large explosions rocked the countryside around *Kamgamchan* for miles, exploding the missile silos and the deadly missiles inside.

The other missile bases suffered a similar fate as *Kamgamchan*. Deep in the mountains of North Korea large clouds of smoke and dust raised up thousands of feet showing the location of each destroyed missile base. The attacks seemed to come without warning. General Nagu, the Chief of Air Defense for the northern sector was told that no aircraft or missiles were detected on radar before the attack. General Nagu, disappointed by the news, had to inform President Kim Lu Doc in P'yongyang. The General was on his way to tell the President when he was informed of a large group of missiles approaching the First Air Combat Command Headquarters at *Kaech'n*. Air raid sirens began to sound as the General was rushed to his shelter with his staff. He knew the missiles were probably American Tomahawk Land Attack Missiles

171

(TLAM's) launched off shore from the American ships. Indeed, the missiles were Tomahawks, but they were launched from the missile submarines *Michigan* and *Ohio* on the West Coast of the Korean Peninsula. Eight missiles struck the headquarters of the General, destroying buildings and command facilities while the rest of the missiles destroyed fixed surface-to-air missile sites. Of the one hundred and fourteen Tomahawk Land Attack Missiles (TLAM) missiles fired by the *Michigan*, One hundred and three had found their targets. The missiles that didn't make it were attributed to the North Korean Army Air Defenses, which in some areas were formidable. Some of the TLAM's carried high-explosive warheads destroying buildings and hangers while others had runway-cratering munitions that destroyed runways of several North Korean Air Bases. Preceding the dozens of Tomahawk Land Attack Missiles fired from the *USS Michigan* and *USS Ohio* were other TLAM's loaded with Electro-Magnetic Pulse (EMP) warheads designed to "burn through" sensitive electronics such as those found in air defense radar's and secure communication lines. Following the first wave of missiles about eighty-seven percent of all Air Defense Radar's in and around P'yongyang were destroyed.

The TLAM's from the submarines on the west coast of the Korean peninsula were the first wave of missiles. The second wave came from the cruisers of the *Reagan* Strike Group. The cruisers *Princeton*, *Shiloh* and *Lake Champlain* and destroyers *Howard* and *Larsen* fired a total of three hundred and eleven TLAM's of various types. Major targets were the North Korean Army (NKA) surface-to-air missile sites and NKA air bases. Two hundred and ninety-seven missiles found their targets. Thousands of aircraft, some already armed and fueled, exploded setting off chain reactions in their underground shelters. Eighty-nine percent of the countries air defense capability was destroyed in the second attack. The Tomahawks performed exceptionally well in the mountainous regions of North Korean, more so than when they were employed in Iraq where they could be detected at longer ranges. The terrain-matching radar guided the TLAM's through the mountains and to their targets, their flight paths already pre-programmed to avoid the majority of the surface-to-air missile sites. While the TLAM's were some of the most technological advanced missiles on the planet, some succumbed to mobile air defense artillery and World War II type barrage balloons.

The opening shots of the war against North Korea didn't come without a price. The US Patriot missile batteries deployed near the DMZ detected the No-Dong missiles launched from the bases at *Chiha-ri*, *Sangwon* and *Sunchon*. The North Korean Army launched a total of fifty-six missiles within two minutes, hoping to overwhelm the US Army Defenses. They achieved a partial success having only twenty-four missiles intercepted by Patriot IV Air Defense Missiles. The airport at Seoul and the surrounding area suffered the most damage. The two thousand-pound high-explosive warheads of the No-Dong missiles were devastating to the buildings and facilities at Seoul airport. Destroyed military and civilian aircraft lay strewn about, burning. Communications were knocked out within the first three minutes. Personnel ran for the shelters as soon as the sirens started. Those caught out in the open were killed by blasts that were over six hundred yards away. An estimated eight missiles landed at the airport, exploding and turning the runway into rubble, effectively rendering it useless.

One of the secondary targets, the US Army's Camp Eagle near Seoul, also didn't escape damage. Two missiles struck the Camp, one destroying a half dozen AH-64 Apache helicopters. Camp's Stanton and Red Cloud received minor damage, the No-Dong missiles hitting the edge of the compounds. Camp Page received the most damage having four missiles destroy the command center, the aviation fuel storage tanks and a significant portion of the aircraft assigned to the facility. The primary targets, Kunsan Airbase and Osan Airbase, received more than their share of damage. The alert aircraft at Kunsan, four F-16's of the 35th Fighter Squadron, launched within one minute of the attack warning, escaping the ensuing destruction of the No-Dong missiles. Several ROK F-15K fighters quickly taxied out of their hardened shelters and to the runways. Two F-15K's took off from the taxiways in full afterburner, warned by the smoke trails from the Patriot IV missiles that ballistic missiles were inbound. A total of nine ROK F-15K's and eighteen US F-16 fighter aircraft got airborne before the destruction began. Two ROK F-15's on high-speed taxi collided with one another after the first No-Dong missile hit Kunsan AB, killing both pilots. Six of the high-explosive missiles targeted Kunsan with a vengeance. Runways were destroyed, as were the munition storage facilities. Large explosions rocked the base even after the last No-Dong missiles hit, the heat from the fires exploding the laser-guided and GPS bombs. Only six aircraft, F-16's from the 80th Fighter Squadron, remained intact after the attack, useless without a serviceable runway. Osan AB suffered nearly the same fate except that a fifteen hundred foot section of runway was serviceable along with most of the 25th Fighter Wing's A-10's.

The port of Pusan suffered five direct hits, mostly near the docks and maintenance facilities. After the fires were extinguished the loading and unloading of vessels continued under the renewed threat of more missile attacks. Ships that were waiting offshore were ordered in to unload their stores. Cargo ships that were empty raised anchor and left for safer ports. The aircraft at Pusan airport were spared for some unknown reason, possible inaccurate coordinates, the missiles all dropping in short of the airport terminal, destroying just a section of taxiway on the north end.

The US Patriot IV missile batteries near the DMZ did a good job under less than ideal conditions. One section, however, did receive a direct hit by a No-Dong missile, destroying the control vehicle and knocking out the phased-array radar. About a dozen US Army personnel were killed in the attack, some helping in an attempt to reload a launcher while the attack was in progress. Other missile batteries, seven remaining, showed operational statuses while waiting for a subsequent attack.

The F-16's from Kunsan climbed above eight thousand feet and could see the North Korean fighters below them. Over forty MiG-19's loaded with 500 lb "iron bombs" were flying towards Seoul to finish the job that the No-Dong missiles started. Ten of the F-16's dove to attack the closest MiG's with their AIM-9 Sidewinder air-to-air missiles, while the remainder continued to climb, detecting larger targets at longer range. The first pass by the F-16s managed to kill eighteen MiG's while the rest of them dropped to low level and increased their speed, unwavered by the pursuing F-16's. The F-16's pulled maximum gs as they turned and engaged the low flying MiG's with their AMRAAM and Sidewinder air-to-air missiles. Eight more MiG's exploded, diving into the ground in a orange fireball. The F-16's quickly caught up to the remaining MiG's, which could only make four hundred knots fully loaded. Some, while flying at only five hundred feet, tried to out-maneuver the faster and more nimble F-16's while flying through the mountains. Three MiG's, overloaded with bombs and with inexperienced pilots, crashed into the mountains. When the MiG'-19's emerged from the cover of the mountain its was the turn of the ROK HAWK surface-to-air missile batteries. The HAWK anti-aircraft missile battery at the east end of the runway downed six MiG's while the US Patriot "Echo" battery father west engaged and shot down the last five.

The nine ROK F-15K's that took off from Kunsan formed up twenty miles north and headed for the DMZ. The radar picture "beamed" from the *Reagan's* E-2C off the east coast showed a grim picture. The F-15K's radar scope shown that over ninety aircraft were in the air and closing on South Korea and the *Reagan* Strike Group. The Air Commander for the F-15's ordered them to engage all hostile targets with the AMRAAM's beyond visual range. A volley of eighteen missiles streaked out and up to high altitude before heading towards their targets, some more that sixty miles away. The F-15K's dropped down to eight thousand feet, awaiting the aircraft that were headed their way. The picture on the radar screen seemed to shift as the enemy aircraft took evasive action seeing the oncoming missiles. The first volley of missiles took out fifteen enemy aircraft, the others, probably more lucky that experienced, dove to the deck to avoid detection.

When the F-15K's came within visual range of the MiG's, they were identified as MiG-23's with MiG-21's escorting them. While the MiG-23's went for the deck the MiG-21's turned into the ROK F-15K's firing their "Archer" air-to-air missiles. The F-15K's broke away from the missiles, punching off flares as they went. One F-15K pilot inadvertently went into military power as he punched his flares. The North Korean AA-11 "Archer" missile temporarily tracking on the flare, changed direction and sped towards the F-15K's afterburner as the aircraft rolled to the right and towards the ground. The "Archer" caught the F-15K in the number one engine destroying it. The F-15K seemed to right itself and gain altitude but a second later the pilot ejected, the aircraft exploding as it dove to the ground. The MiG-21 got in a lucky shot as it climbed to ten thousand feet. The F-15K pilots, armed with AIM-9X Sidewinders, looked back at the MiG's and locked onto them for an "over the shoulder" shot. Four AIM-9K Sidewinders streaked away for about three hundred feet before turning 180 degrees and tracking on the MiG's. The four MiG's, climbing and losing speed in the process, failed to notice the missile launch, the nose of their aircraft pointing skyward. The MiG's exploded as all the Sidewinders found their targets. One MiG-21 exploded and blew in half while the rest turned over and dove into the ground, marking their final resting-place with black swirling smoke.

The remaining aircraft were engaged by the weary US and ROK anti-aircraft missile batteries. It was a testament to their skill and dedication that no enemy aircraft ever made it to within two miles of either Inch'on or Osan AB. The F-15K's roamed near the DMZ, close to Inch'on, watching and waiting for the onslaught of the North Korean army.

To the west, the F-16's from the 35th Fighter Squadron had dealt with two unorganized flights of SU-25 "Frogfoot" bombers, which seemed to be looking for ground targets. The SU-25's were easily shot down by the F-16's concentrated fire from their 20 mm cannon. To the north a few F-16's in the flight were getting SAM radar warnings so it was decided to go east, after the enemy aircraft flying towards the *Reagan* Strike Group. As the F-16's formed up at eight thousand feet the number three pilot on the flight's left wing yelled "missile" and broke away. Two Chinese PL-12 air-to-air missiles broke into view, one following the F-16 that broke away from the flight. The second flashed through the flight, narrowly missing the number two aircraft but impacting in number five. The F-16 exploded, taking its pilot with it. The PL-12 missile outmaneuvered the number three F-16 and blew off its right wing, the pilot ejecting from his stricken aircraft. The Commander of the flight ordered them to turn to the north and to descend down to five thousand feet. He and three others got a lock on four enemy aircraft at fifty-seven miles and launched their AMRAAM's. The missiles accelerated away at over two thousand miles per hour towards their targets.

Major Kunsai Chiang was the flight commander for Group 72, a flight of four MiG-29's. His primary mission was to protect the thirty-two NKA IL-28 "Beagle" bombers and fourteen SU-25 "Frogfoot" bombers that were ordered to close on the *Reagan* Strike Group. The "Beagle" bombers each carried four of the new J-82K cruise missiles, while each of the SU-25's carried two of the shorter-ranged J-8K cruise missiles. The search radar of the MiG-29 showed a large flight to his south and a large flight over one hundred miles ahead on bearing 147 degrees. The flight ahead was too far away but he had registered two "kills" on the flight to his south, with the flight apparently breaking up and scattering. Major Chiang was receiving radar emissions from ahead and identified them as coming from SPS-49 radar. He had been told the Americans would be near here. The group of aircraft ahead of him, out of range, must be coming from the *Reagan*. He knew the *Reagan* also had the SPS-49 radar set. He flipped on his attack radar and a large "blip" shown up clearly on his Radar screen. It was a single contact, which at first didn't concern the Major. He ordered six of his "Beagle" bombers to launch their missiles on a bearing-only launch. One at a time each J-82K cruise missile dropped clear of the aircraft, its rocket motor starting and accelerating the missile, while it dropped down to its cruise height of twenty meters.

The six "Beagle" bombers, now empty, turned back to the safety of their air base, the rest of the formation continuing towards the American warships. Closing on the target, Major Chiang received word from his wingman that he detected a large flight of at least twenty aircraft on a bearing of 114 degrees. He reported that he had "locked up" two of the contacts with his attack radar. Major Chiang ordered the rest of the flight to engage the targets with their remaining PL-12 missiles. In seconds all pilots indicated a positive "lock" on fourteen separate targets. The Major ordered each aircraft to launch their deadly missiles. High above the bombers, the Major launched his PL-12 missile as the four American AMRAAM's came streaking in. One exploded into the Major's wingman, blowing both wings off.. The remaining AMRAAM's found the IL-28's flying below the MiG-29's at seven thousand feet. A missile impacted the first bomber in the right wing exploding it in a brilliant explosion. The remaining missiles found their targets even after the bombers tried to evade them by diving sharply below, each aircraft falling in pieces to the Sea of Japan below.

When the attack started Nathan was more relieved than surprised. All the waiting, all the training would now pay off. He already had twelve F/A-18 "Super Hornets" in the air protecting "Bronco 1" and "Bronco 3". He knew the AL-1A's would do their job, if they were close enough. Soon after the North Korean Missiles were launched Admiral Alexander appeared in CIC. Within minutes the order from the President came through for a full retaliatory strike on North Korea's military and her command structure. Through a secure communications network Admiral Alexander ordered the cruisers *Princeton, Shiloh* and *Lake Champlain,* along with the Destroyers *Howard* and *Lassen* to launch their Tomahawk missiles. Captain Winters had been through a few wars in his time and seemed to take everything in stride. He kept his cool and acted as if this was nothing more than a training exercise, at least that's what it looked like to those around him. He ordered the *Reagan* Strike Group to increase speed from twelve to twenty knots He then ordered a standard turn to Starboard and chose a heading of 027 degrees, out into the Sea of Japan and away from any lucky NKA submarines that might make it to the inner defense perimeter. Captain was conferring with Steven Alexander as Nathan prepared the strike package the *Reagan*. Nathan had prepared for this moment his whole career. He learned long ago that the key to any war plan was inter-service cooperation. The *Reagan's* Air Group was going into battle as an advance strike force the Air Force heavy bombers that would inevitable follow. Nathan knew the small tactical aircraft that the *Reagan* carried aboard couldn't carry enough ordnance to blast through the tons of reinforced concrete to reach the hierarchy of the North Korean government. The Air Group from the *Reagan* would clear the way for the B-1's and the stealthy B-2 bombers carrying the 2000-lb JDAM's, that could penetrate and destroy the deepest command structure.

Nathan had ordered the F-35 Joint Strike Fighters loaded and ready to launch prior to the attack, saving countless hours. Some sixteen aircraft each carried two "Quick Bolt" Advanced Anti-Radiation Guided Missiles (AARGM) along with four AIM-120 AMRAAM missiles. These aircraft would deal with any air-to-air threats while they were on their way to attack the remaining "active" NKA surface-to-air missile sites. Another sixteen F-35 Joint Strike Fighters were each loaded with two AMRAAM's and two 1,000-lb JDAM's. In addition to the F-35 Joint Strike Fighters there were eight E/A-18G "Growler" aircraft. The "G" model on all previous aircraft was reserved for aircraft that were designated for the Suppression of Enemy Air Defense or SEAD mission or, as it was commonly known, the "Wild Weasel" mission. The *Reagan* was chosen in 2007 to field the new model of the F/A-18 "Super Hornet". Started years earlier, the Low Rate Initial Production (LRIP) of the E/A-18G "Growler" produced eighteen aircraft. These aircraft retained the same war load of the previous "F" models except for the 20mm gun. The E/A-18G's were each loaded with two HARM missiles and two AMRAAM air-to-air missiles. In addition to the offensive missiles, the aircraft each carried two, ALQ-99 Mod 3 jamming pods. The ALQ-99 Mod 3's were an enhanced version of the previous models allowing the crews to concentrate high-powered jamming against specific threats rather than across a broad spectrum. Most all of the F/A-18 "Super Hornets" on the *Reagan* were configured for the air-to-air role while the remainder were loaded for surface attack missions, mainly carrying AGM-84 Harpoon missiles. Nathan's aircraft was loaded with four AIM-9X Sidewinders and four AGM-84 Harpoon missiles.

The strike package on the *Reagan,* thirty-six aircraft in all, launched forty minutes after the last Tomahawk Land Attack Missile was launched. With the F/A-18's in the lead, the F-35 Joint Strike Fighters and E/A-18 "Growlers" formed up at eight thousand feet and headed for North Korea. In the air no less than twelve minutes, the E-2C from the *Reagan* warned of a large formation of aircraft, bearing 321 degrees. The Flight Leader acknowledged and flew on. Five minutes later he turned his attack radar on and saw over forty aircraft headed in his general direction. When he was about to order a turn to intercept them the controller from the E-2C come over the radio again. "Lindy Leader, Hawkeye 225. We have multiple cruise missiles launched from bandits on bearing 147 degrees" the controller reported. "Roger Hawkeye 225, we copy" Lieutenant Anthony "Genie" Nelson replied. The "bandits" were too far away, almost ninety miles. He couldn't do anything about it now. He ordered the two flights of E/A-18's to see if they could jam the missiles. The leader of Electra flight, Lieutenant Frank "Spike" Lopez, copied his request and ordered his WSO, Lieutenant JG Michael "Lars" Olsen, to try to jam the missiles. Olsen, at work in the back seat, set up the jamming sequence and pushed the "MASTER RADIATE" switch. "Lindy Leader, Hawkeye 225. We show enemy AAM's in the air towards your location, ETA seven minutes. Steer a evasive course of 193 degrees and increase to 500 knots" the controller reported. Lieutenant Nelson ordered the flight to make the necessary corrections. The Chinese PL-12 missiles flew straight towards their intended target on the bearing they were launched. When the missiles arrived at a certain point the seeker heads turned on and searched for their targets, only to find clear skies. The PL-12's, running out of fuel, crashed harmlessly into the sea. When the controller on the Hawkeye saw that the strike package was clear, it ordered them back to their base course.

The twenty-four J-82K cruise missiles launched from the IL-28 "Beagle" bombers flew on, undeterred by the jamming attempts from the E/A-18G's. "*Yang Manchun*, Hawkeye 225. We show enemy cruise missiles inbound to your location" The controller advised. The radio operator on the *Yang Manchun*, at first slow to respond, replied "Yes, we are aware, thank you" The ship turned quickly to Starboard to unmask its port 30 mm Close-In Weapon System (CIWS) and started firing its five-inch caliber gun mount at maximum elevation. The Sparrow Vertical Launch System (VLS) rippled off three missiles in rapid succession towards the incoming cruise missiles. Two Sparrows luckily scored, knocking down two of the twenty-four missiles. One more missile was burst by the five-inch gun, reducing the missiles to twenty-one. The *Yang Manchun*, a ROK Kwanggaeto class frigate, was never designed to operate alone in this environment. Firing again at the approaching missiles, the VLS spit out four more missiles and scored two more hits. The cruise missiles now within sight of the bridge, homed in on *Yang Manchun*. The Captain ordered countermeasures to be launched and seconds later chaff launchers fired their cargo. The chaff pulled two cruise missiles away, sending them away to parts unknown. The five-inch gun, firing point blank, killed its last missile as it jammed. The *Yang Manchun's* 30 mm Close-In Weapon System (CIWS) on full automatic assessed the threats and fired bursts at the closest missiles, which now were less than twelve hundred yards away. The hail of 30-mm projectiles slammed into both missiles, exploding them. The Sparrow VLS barked again, shooting out two more missiles. The Sparrows missed, the cruise missiles just being too close for the Sparrows to track on. Out of no where, four AMRAAM's exploded the four closest J-82K cruise missiles, prolonging the fate of the *Yang Manchun*.

Out of the twenty-four J-82K cruise missiles launched only ten remained. The first two did a classic pop-up maneuver and slammed down on the superstructure, penetrating through the upper deck. Three missiles, that seemed grouped together, slammed into the Port side, exploding, ripping the ship almost in two and killing most of the crew. The forward motion of the ship stopped as it took on water in the engineering section. The rest of the missiles bored in unsympathetically on the now dead ship. Two missiles did another pop-up maneuver, one on the flight deck and the other over the VLS launchers. The aft section of the stern separated from the hull leaving a large, gaping hole. The VLS launchers, no longer operational, exploded with its remaining ordnance. The last three missiles hit two fore and one amidships where no resemblance of a hull existed, only twisted, burning metal. The *Yang Manchun* listed heavily to port. Nothing could be seen on deck, except for the ROK flag, which miraculously survived on the bow of the ship. The ship rolled over on its side, its forward section twisting away, as it slid down sinking to bottom.

The younger pilots of the strike package could only look on in horror as the last missiles hit the *Yang Manchun*. Some of the pilots swore and some vowed revenge. The Flight Leader acknowledged the pilot's comments and told them to observe radio silence. Lieutenant Anthony Nelson was disgusted by what he saw. The hull of the *Yang Manchun* was sinking and seemingly void of life. Anthony choked back emotion as he called the *Reagan*. "Big Dog, this is Lindy Leader. Request CSAR at *Yang Manchun's* last location. Possible survivors in water" Anthony reported. The *Reagan* acknowledged. Now, Anthony was ready for some payback.

NINE

MCCLUSKY MELEE

PRESIDENT JACKSON AWOKE IN HIS MAKESHIFT quarters on the upper deck of the E-4B. Looking at the clock he saw it was 0300 hours on the morning of August 19th. He rolled out of his bed after three hours of sleep and sat in his chair next to the cabin window. The night sky over the Rocky Mountains was pitch black. Flying at forty-five thousand feet, he saw the occasional lights below from the sparsely populated countryside. The President knew that everyone, even those in the sparsely populated areas, knew of the events that had taken place during the last hours. Reporters in Japan and South Korea working for WNN and the other networks had broadcast the alert warnings and missile attacks to the world .The Pentagon had confirmed the reports and assured that the US had been under attack but the danger had passed. The Chairman of the Joint Chief of Staff, Admiral Jack Grayson, had assured the American people that because of the advanced weapon systems that the US possessed that there was little to be concerned about and the military action would be confined to the Asian Theater of Operations. Admiral Grayson was bombarded by questions from the media concerning what weapon systems did what. Some reporters in the know queried the Admiral on the Airborne Laser project. The Admiral confirmed only what was already available to the general public. As early as 2001 some credible information was available from Lockheed-Martin on its external website concerning the Airborne Laser project. Those intuitive persons could only surmise what the US Government had at this point.

A light knock came at the door to the Presidents cabin. President Jackson called for the person to enter. It was Don Baker, the Senior Secret Service Agent in charge of the Presidential Security Unit. "I'm sorry, Sir. Did I wake you?" Don asked. "No, I was awake, I got about three hours of sleep" the President said. " I was doing a security check and thought I heard movement. Is everything okay Sir?" Don inquired. "Oh yes, thank you for asking. Have a seat Don" the President said. "Thank you, sir" Don said as he sat in the seat across from the President. "Sir, General Howard advised me that we would be landing at Mountain Home AFB in about two hours. He said we need to land to perform periodic maintenance and take aboard supplies" Don Baker told the President. "That's fine, thank you" The President was aware that even the E-4B needed maintenance and oil for its engines about every twenty hours. He looked at his watch again. It was about twenty-three hours since they took off from Andrews AFB. It had been quite a day. "Don, I see you have a new Agent on the detail" the President inquired. "Yes, sir. Agent Calvin Welbourne. He transferred last week from the Treasury Unit. Does he meet with your approval, Sir? " Agent Baker asked. "Oh sure. Anyone who can yank me out of my chair like he did gets my vote" the President said. "Your security was our primary concern at the time, Sir. I'm sorry if we got a little rough" Agent Baker said. "You'll get no complaints from me. In fact I'm glad you did" the President said. Baker nodded his head in agreement. Don Baker had been hand picked by President Jackson almost four years ago. Don hoped he would do another four at the White House if Jackson were re-elected. After that he would be content with a desk job. Presidents liked to have the younger guys in the Presidential Security Units, besides Don would be ready for retirement in about six years anyway. "Mr. President, my family lives in Denver. I called my wife and kids yesterday and told them not to worry that I'd be home in a few days" Don Baker said as he looked at the President. President Jackson looked at Agent Baker. "I'd like to say you would but I'm not sure about that right now. Would you like to call home?" the President asked. "I would appreciate that, Sir" Don said. President Jackson picked up the phone on the table between them. He dialed the secure line at Peterson AFB and then handed the phone to Agent Baker. "Don, I'm going to see what the galley has left. Join me when you are finished" the President said as he got up from his chair. "Thank you again, Mr. President" Don replied putting the phone to his ear. "Don't mention it" the President said as he open the door and left the room.

The President walked down the stairs to the main deck in just his shirt without a tie or jacket. Agent Welbourne stood up when the President reached the last step. "Good evening Mr. President, may I get you something?" Agent Wellbourne said putting on his jacket. "Actually, yes. I'd like either a roast beef or ham sandwich if it were available. I know we are low on provisions" the President said. "I'll see to it, sir. Anything to drink with that?" Agent Wellbourne asked. "Sure, just coffee, no sugar" the President said. President Jackson made his way along the corridor to the conference room. He went in and sat at his seat. The room was empty when he went into it but was soon filled with Air Force Officers and Civilian DOD personnel. General Howard came into the room and made his way to the Presidents side. He had a few folders with him and a concerned look on his face. "Good evening, Mr. President" The General said. "Good evening, General" the President said. "I have the latest reports on the military action, Sir, if you care to hear them" the General asked. "By all means, General, proceed" The President asked pulling his chair forward. "Mr. President as of this morning the JMSDF frigate *Yubari* was sunk by the NKA submarine that was approaching the Japanese coast. The *Yubari* lost approximately eighty-four of her crew. In the subsequent action a Japanese P-3C Orion dropped two torpedoes and sunk the NKA submarine. Also, the latest report shows that a South Korean frigate of the *Kwanggaeto* class named the *Yang Manchun* was attacked and sunk by North Korean bombers with Chinese cruise missiles. They have found no survivors at this point. The *Reagan* reports that their F/A-18 fighters are repelling an attack by the same bombers on the *Reagan* Strike Group as we speak" the General said.

The President leaned back in his chair and rested his head against the plush chair back. "The first damage reports are coming in from the Korean bases. The main runway at Seoul IAP has been destroyed. The Army Corp of Engineers are working on it and will have it rebuilt in about two a week. A large percentage of the command facilities have been destroyed but the command structure has been moved to Taegu. Also the Korean President has been moved to Pusan. The North Koreans used between thirty and forty short-ranged ballistic missiles to attack the targets in South Korea. Six to eight missiles hit Kunsan Air Base destroying the majority of its aircraft" the General reported. "Thirty or forty, is that all?" the President replied. "Yes Sir. We think that was their initial first strike and that they are holding back because they plan to invade the South and need some facilities intact" the General said. "Do you have casualty figures, General" the President asked. "Yes sir. At Kunsan AB the total count was two hundred and thirty-six dead with seventy-eight wounded. Seoul airport and the surrounding area was four hundred and seven dead with one hundred twenty-three wounded." the General replied. The General looked up at the President who had his eyes closed. It may have been from lack of sleep but most likely was from the reality of the action. "I have the other figures here also, Mr. President." the General said. "That's fine, General. I can look at them later" the President said. "Sir, the Rivet Joint aircraft detected two nuclear detonations. They were both from the missiles that one of the AL-1A's shot down. One landed in the Sea of Japan and the other landed on the coast of North Korea at *P'oha-ri,* a small fishing village. The detonations both showed yields of seventy kilotons. We don't have details on the damage to the village but it probably won't be good. The detonation in the Sea of Japan seems to have sunk the Chinese "Oscar" that the *Topeka* was following. The *Topeka* suffered minor damage and is holding at her station until we can assess the contamination to her crew" the General reported. "Seventy kilotons!" the President exclaimed. "Our intelligence estimated them to only have devices of fifty kilotons or less!" the President exclaimed. "I think its clear now that their estimates were inaccurate and that the North Koreans may have nuclear devices of at least one hundred kilotons" the General said. "Okay General, they hurt us pretty good. How did we do against them" The President asked. "First of all I'd like to say the *Thor II Project* was a resounding success. *Thor II* destroyed thirty-seven ballistic missiles that would have impacted on Guam, Japan, Hawaii, Alaska and the West Coast of the United States. In retaliation *Thor II* was re-tasked to destroy the missile silos and any remaining missiles. As of now, all of the North Korean long-range missile silos have been destroyed. In addition to that most of their air bases have been rendered useless while several surface-to-air missile sites have been destroyed" the General explained. "So the direct threat to the United States is now passed, correct?" the President asked. "Yes sir. To the best of our knowledge that would be a correct assumption" the General added. "One thing however, sir. The leadership of the Korean government is still intact although our Tomahawk missiles have seriously degraded its communication ability to forward deployed units" the General said. We have put *Thor II* on stand-by until the bombers and ATAV's have completed their missions" the General reported. "When will the bombers hit *P'yongyang*, General?" the President asked. "The bombers should be at their IP in twenty minutes, the ATAV's should be there right about now Mr President" the General replied, looking at his watch. "Keep me informed General. This is the most critical point of our operation" the President said.

Colonel Collins checked the digital clock at the top of his console. He had started it just before takeoff. The total elapsed time was just over two hours. All the systems on the ATAV were operating correctly. "Commander, we're right on time. We'll be over the target in about six minutes. Targeting computer is up and running. All weapons are armed and ready" Major Cox said as he finished his pre-attack checklist. The ATAV was traveling close to Mach 5 at one hundred twenty thousand feet. "Very well, Major. Slowing to attack speed" Colonel Collins replied as he pulled the six throttles back. The ATAV seemed to continue on before the Colonel could feel the craft slow, still maintaining over three thousand miles per hour. "Bomb release in one minute ten seconds" Major Cox replied. "Roger, copy that" the Colonel replied. The ATAV flew on towards *Kaech'n*, the headquarters of the North Korean Air Force First Air Combat Command. Hundreds of military and civilian personnel worked at the command facilities, none of who were aware of the fate that awaited them. *Kaech'n* was high on the list of priority targets in North Korea. Hundreds of fighter aircraft and surface-to-air missiles protected the base against attack. The entire air defense network for the west coast of North Korea including *P'yongyang* was coordinated from *Kaech'n*. "Bomb release in ten seconds" Major Cox announced. "Roger, copy that" the Colonel replied. Thousands of feet below no one had any warning, the ATAV flying too high for conventional radar to detect them. "Bomb release in five seconds" Major Cox announced. "Roger" Colonel Collins acknowledged. "Bomb bay doors open, release in three, two, one. Bomb one away, two away, three away, four away. Bomb bay doors closed" Major Cox announced. "Roger, copy that" the Colonel replied. The Colonel took control of the yoke in front of him and put the aircraft into a slight left bank. The ATAV banked and started its wide turn towards home. Several other ATAV's in the squadron also had *Kaech'n* as their target. A total of sixteen Mark 5 Mod 3 SPECOR weapons started their deadly plunge to their target below.

General Nagu emerged from his bunker complex on the fifth level, shaken, but aware that more attacks would be coming. The American Tomahawk missiles had detonated near several locations around the base resulting in several explosions and fires. Standing in the communications center on level two the General ordered all Air Defense units in the field to report their status via two-way radio relay, the normal communications cables cut by several Tomahawk strikes. Three sites replied they were operational with others reporting several missile sites destroyed. The General ordered all sites to remain alert and await further orders.

Without warning the first SPECOR hit within one mile of the command center, setting off tremendous shock waves through the earth. At first the Staff thought it was an earthquake, but the General knew better. Shouting for personnel to get to the shelter the General made his way to the stairs, which were located near the end of the building, on the north end. The stairwell was a shelter of it's own, its walls three feet thick and twenty feet in diameter, reinforced by a roof of twelve feet of concrete. The second SPECOR drilled into the command center on its south end, penetrating to the fourth floor before exploding its 3000lb high-explosive warhead. The earth seemed to raise up and swallow that portion of the command center exposed above the ground. Hundreds of tons of earth were sent in to the air, the end of the building collapsing to the forth floor, trapping all those below. Other SPECOR's began to drop nearby, exploding and sending huge amounts of dirt and dust into the air. Several bombs destroyed the emergency power plant as well as the water and fuel supply storage tanks underground. Another SPECOR hit the command center, this time right on target. The SPECOR drilled into the center of the building punching through all five reinforced roofs before exploding. The command center ceased to function as a communication facility and a safe haven as the explosion from the warhead collapsed the shelter, burying all those below.

The other ATAV's that took off after Colonel Collins arrived at their primary targets also. The Second and Third Combat Command Centers, at *Toksan* and *Hwangju* respectively, were destroyed with heavy loss of life. Four well-placed Mark 5 Mod 3 SPECOR bombs destroyed North Korea's largest munitions and aircraft factory, near the small village of

Tokhyon. The twenty-four hour facility was destroyed in less than a minute.

Nathan rolled over against Jill's back. Her body was so warm it was like she just came out of an oven. He brought her close to him as she woke, holding his arm. "Good Morning, sweetheart" Nathan whispered. "Good Morning, sweetie" she replied reaching up and caressing his face. "How many kids *did* you want anyway?" she asked Nathan. "Wow, where did that come from?" Nathan asked surprised. "I was just thinking what your landlord said about us having really cute kids. How many would you like?" Jill asked. "I think two would be good" Nathan replied. "A boy and a girl, two boys or two girls?" Jill asked inquisitively. "I'll take whatever you give me as long as they are as sweet as you" Nathan replied. Jill smiled and held Nathan's arm tightly in front of her. She really didn't care how many children or what kind she had as long as they were Nathan's. She had spent a lot of time with Nathan the last few weeks and just knew he was the one she should be with. Nathan and Jill spent about two hours laying in bed, talking and kissing and making plans for the future.

When they finally got up, Jill made a big breakfast for the two of them. One of Nathan's favorites, a ham omelet with hash browns, was on the table when Nathan came to the breakfast table. He seated Jill and sat down to take a sip of coffee. Nathan was scheduled to get the 4:30 flight from LAX to Pensacola this afternoon. Navy representatives would meet him at the Navy Base and then escort him by bus to LAX airport. The chartered navy flight would land at Pensacola Naval Air Station. Jill would drive to LAX to see Nathan for one more time before he left for the boarding gate. The morning led to the afternoon and Nathan found himself checking his bag in the bedroom. Jill came in and quietly sat on the bed. She looked at Nathan, tears in her eyes, and said she was sorry for being a big baby. Nathan walked over to her and held her head. "I'm so sorry, I told myself I wouldn't do this" Jill said, sobbing between her words. "It's okay, babe. I'm gonna miss you too. Just realize that we'll be together soon. You'll be seeing me in a few months" Nathan explained. Nathan loved her so and told her. Kneeling in front of her he kissed her wet cheeks and wiped her tears away with the back of his hand. "Unlike the other men in your life, Jill, I *will* be coming back to you" Nathan told her. Jill smiled at Nathan and then continued sobbing on his shoulder.

Nathan consoled Jill for a while until she composed herself. He had to leave soon so after Jill fixed her makeup they loaded up Jill's Lexus and drove to the Navy Base. Once there he kissed Jill in the parking lot and told her he would see her at LAX. Jill got in her car and Nathan bent down to kiss her again. She drove away with a smile and a wave. The Ensign from the Personnel Office announced to Nathan and the other men that arrived that the bus would be there in five minutes. They were told to leave their bags at the curb and line up in a row. The enlisted person would call their names and they would be allowed to board the bus. Several moments later a grayish-colored bus arrived in the parking lot and pulled to a stop near the curb. The driver opened the door and a very beautiful, young blonde stepped off the bus dressed in a Navy blue uniform. Nathan recognized Jennifer at once and was pleased to see her. The driver shut off the engine and exited the rear of the bus helping to load the bags with one other enlisted man. "Gentleman, please have your ID ready and when I call your name please step forward" Jennifer said, taking off her sunglasses. Jennifer started with the list, in alphabetical order. She called a few people before she got to Nathan.

"Buckman, Nathan" Jennifer called out. Nathan put on his sunglasses and stepped forward to the bus. He showed Jennifer his ID, she smiled and told him to get on the bus.

The trip to the airport was rough. It was an old bus and desperately in need of new springs. Jennifer sat alone in the front seat by the door. She had her legs crossed doing some type of paperwork for half the trip then put away her pen. She took a cosmetic mirror out of her small purse and checked her make-up. Nathan, who sat two rows behind her, caught her glance in the mirror and he winked at her. She returned it and he thought he heard her giggle. The bus pulled up to the terminal and stopped. Jennifer stood up and told the men to remain seated until the bags were unloaded. The enlisted men unloaded the bags from the last two rows and then climbed back on the bus. "Gentleman, If you could all stand and follow me, we will be going to the security counter in the terminal" Jennifer announced. Once inside Nathan noticed that the Ensign from the Personnel Office was present at the security gate as were several other Navy Officers. One by one each of the Officer Candidates went through security. Nathan saw Jill near the far wall and walked over to her. He said hello and kissed her. She held him tight and saw a Navy Officer approach them. "I'm sorry to break this up, you two, but we need to move this along" The Naval Officer said. Nathan turned around to see Steven Alexander. "Hi Steven, did you come to see me off?" Nathan asked. "Well something like that" Steven replied. Jill kissed Nathan one more time as she whispered "I love you" in Nathan's ear. Nathan returned her words and hugged Jill again real tight before leaving her. Nathan went through security followed by Steven, the Ensign and then Jennifer. The Officer Candidates walked to the gate following Steven Alexander. Jennifer and the Ensign walked behind the group, talking quietly. When they all reached the gate Jennifer approached the head of the group and spoke. "Gentleman, I will give you a packet with information you need to study prior to your arrival at Pensacola. Please study the material and do not lose it. Now, Just like before, please have your ID ready and when I call your name please step forward." Jennifer said. Jennifer called the names just like before, in alphabetical order. When she called Nathan he approached and showed her his ID. She handed him his packet, a large, manila envelop, and quietly told him to read page seven *first*. "Good luck to you, sir" she said as she had told all the previous Officer Candidates, but smiled directly at him as he passed her. Nathan boarded the plane and was told he could sit anywhere he wanted to, being the plane only had eighteen men on it. Nathan sat on the left side over the wing. He sat down and put on his seat belt and without hesitation opened his packet. He flipped through to the seventh page as Jennifer instructed him but instead of printed text found a handwritten letter from Jennifer. He smiled and read the letter.

"Very good, I like a man that does what I say, when I say it! I saw your girlfriend at the base before we left on the bus. She is very beautiful and you're a lucky man. I hope that won't affect our friendship. I knew I liked you when I first met you. You and I are a lot alike. We're young, single and we're both flirts! I saw you wink at me on the bus, you are so bad!

I hope you do well in training and flight school and think of me often. I will be in Tallahassee by June 26th. I'd like to get together around July 4th if you can swing it. I'll call you around the 28th and see if we can get together. Take care of yourself and I'll be talking to you.

Love, Jennifer

Wow, Nathan thought. She saw Jill and that didn't deter her. Jennifer was a smart headstrong woman. When she saw something she liked she went for it and, more often than not Nathan thought, got it. Still, he didn't want it to affect his relationship with Jill. He had promised Jill he would return to her and Nathan kept his promises.

Nathan was in CIC on the *Reagan* when the F/A-18's began to engage the NKA bombers. The three formations of F/A-18's, Lindy, Wolf and Hoosier Flights, accelerated towards the formation of IL-28's and locked onto the bombers. The group of twelve F/A-18 "Super Hornets" launched twenty of their AMRAAM's missiles at over twenty-three miles. Nathan heard the pilots call "Fox 1" as they each launched. The electronic radar screen in the *Reagan's* CIC showed the volley of missiles streaking towards the bomber formation, now only ninety miles from the *Reagan*. Each AMRAAM closed on the bombers at a speed of nineteen hundred knots.

Major Chiang couldn't believe it that the PL-12's didn't track on the F/A-18's. Every missile missed and crashed into the sea. The bomber formation flew on for another ten minutes. Moments later, Major Chiang detected another ship on his surface search radar at eighty-seven miles and then another on a different bearing. Other ships came onto the screen as he flew towards the contacts, much larger than the ships he usually saw off the Korean coast. He was elated. He had found the American fleet. He radioed the information to the bomber fleet. Each aircraft picked several targets and then when everything was set they planned to launch all the missiles simultaneously, hoping to overwhelm the American defenses.

As if all at once several of the bomber aircraft's radar warning receivers went off. The formation was under attack by the American F/A-18's which were approaching. Major Chiang, flying his MiG-29 at ten thousand feet, could make out several missiles at a distance diving and closing on the IL-28 bombers. The bombers tried to take evasive action but it was to no avail. Seventeen of the aging IL-28 "Beagle" bombers were hit by the American AMRAAM's and blew apart, pieces of wreckage and missiles falling to the sea seven thousand feet below. Major Chiang ordered all the remaining bombers to launch their missiles on the four different headings in which the large ships were detected before the next volley of American air-to-air missiles came in. During the next fifteen seconds a total of fifty-two J-82K cruise missiles were launched towards the *Reagan* Strike Group from the remaining NKA Air Force bombers. After launch the bombers executed a one hundred eighty-degree turn and headed back to Taetan, or, unknown to them at the time, what was left of it.

Major Chiang ordered his flight of MiG-29s, now only three aircraft, to fly towards the last position of the reconnaissance aircraft suspected of shooting down the ballistic missiles headed for Japan. The MiG's accelerated to nine hundred knots as they leveled out, heading towards the AL-1A, known as "Bronco 1". Major Chiang ordered the flight to remain on this heading until they intercepted the target. He had planned to avenge the death of his friend, Commander Choi, who was killed by the Americans only three days ago. He had noted earlier that several aircraft were in the vicinity of the AL-1A, more than likely a fighter escort. If he could get close enough he could bring down the AL-1A with his last PL-12 or, once past the fighter escort, he could launch any of his heat-seeking air-to-air PL-9 missiles. Major Chiang ordered his flight to climb to fifty thousand feet to take advantage of the clear skies and to conserve the precious fuel that the thirsty Tumansky engines where using up.

The E-2C broke the radio silence from the *Reagan*. "Wolf Leader, Hawkeye 234. You have three contacts on bearing 047. Contacts are climbing to Angels 50 at over nine hundred knots" the radar operator reported. Lieutenant Commander James Aulicino replied to the radio operator and ordered Wolf Flight to intercept the MiG's. James had two AMRAAM's left on his aircraft and four AIM-9's, more than enough to engage the MiG's. Wolf Flight accelerated to intercept the MiG's over fifty miles away.

Major Chiang detected some new contacts on his side-looking radar. Four small contacts heading on an intercept course for his flight. He decided to attack the American AL-1A on his own. He ordered his number three and four aircraft to launch their missiles at the ROK fighter escorts before turning to engage the American fighter aircraft. Two PL-12's sped away towards the two unsuspecting ROK F-15K fighters while the two MiG's changed course and altitude to fire on the approaching F/A-18 "Super Hornets". The number three MiG-29 shot first, aiming at the first aircraft in the formation. The PL-12 missile tracked straight to the lead aircraft, Lieutenant Commander James Aulicino's F/A-18. James ordered the flight to break as the missile came into view. The third and fourth aircraft split up, one going low and another pulling six G's as it climbed in full afterburner. James' wingman went left and high while James rolled over and went low as he pulled close to seven-G's trying to evade the radar-directed missile.

The PL-12 was making close to Mach 3.5 when its active-seeker acquired the lead aircraft. The airframe of the PL-12 missile was designed to withstand stresses up to 38 G's. The evasive action by the F/A-18 required only a slight course correction by the missile as it bored into the bottom of the now inverted "Super Hornet". The PL-12 warhead exploded and the F/A-18 started to come apart, the aircraft exploding as its fuel tanks ignited. The front half of the "Super Hornet" came apart from the rest of the structure, falling and spinning to the sea below. James' wingman rolled out of the top of his climb and called "Fox 1" as he locked up the third MiG and sent an angry AMRAAM after it. The MiG didn't even go evasive, it just kept coming as the AMRAAM struck under the cockpit and blew the aircraft apart. The three and four aircraft from Wolf Flight formed up at twenty thousand feet and both locked up the number two MiG. The pilot of Wolf Three called "Fox 1" as it sent an AMRAAM after the number two MiG, over ten miles away. The second MiG-29, now close enough to use it's heat-seeking PL-9's, launched two missiles after James' lone wingman. The first missile missed for some unknown reason but the second tracked onto the engine and impacted between the twin tails of the "Super Hornet" destroying the aircraft. The remaining aircraft of Wolf Flight quickly looked for signs of parachutes. Neither pilot saw any parachutes or could hear any beacon locators on their pre-arranged frequency. Reporting the action to the *Reagan*, they pursued the remaining MiG-29.

Major Chiang noticed that the ROK F-15's were destroyed by the PL-12 missiles launched earlier. He had lost contact from the rest of Officers in his Flight. If they had died then they had given their lives for a noble cause. The Major was only forty miles from the American reconnaissance aircraft flight when he launched his last PL-12. With the American aircraft out of the way the NKA would be able to resume launching ballistic missiles at Japan and the US. He tracked the PL-12, updating the computer through the missiles mid-course guidance unit. When the missile broke twelve miles the Major lost contact with it. The cockpit readout for the missile flashed and read "MALF" for a malfunction in the system. The warhead did not detonate suggesting the missile malfunctioned. Whatever happened, the Major vowed to shoot the aircraft down with his remaining PL-9 missiles. When the Major could see the target he was amazed. At a little over eight miles it seemed to be a large commercial airliner, a Boeing 747. He concentrated on the target, got good tone and pushed his "hot" button twice. The PL-9's rippled off from the MiG's wing streaking straight towards the 747. Major Chiang pulled up and slowed to four hundred knots, temporarily losing sight of the doomed 747. When he again regained visual contact the PL-9's could not be seen. The 747 however turned in front of him and was broadside at less than four miles. Swearing, the Major again tried to lock up the 747 before he flew over it. His cockpit Master Caution sensor went off. He pushed it to shut it off but it went off again with other caution lights going off on his warning panel. His fuel temperature was in the red as he noticed loss of his primary and secondary hydraulic system. As he banked hard to the left to keep a bead on the 747 his radar went out and an acrid smoke began to fill the cockpit.

"Bronco 1" had been advised that the MiG-29 was approaching by the launch of its two PL-12's that had destroyed the ROK F-15's. It was too late for them but maybe the AL-1A could save itself. The Infra-Red Track and Search (IRST) sensor proved that it could track air-to-air missiles back as early as 1981. All that was needed was a laser and computer software powerful enough to destroy the missiles which was exactly what the AL-1A's had. The PL-12 that Major Chiang launched was destroyed two seconds after the High Energy Laser (HEL) hit it. The two PL-9's also were destroyed within seconds of each other. The Infra-Red Track and Search (IRST) sensor was tracking the MiG-29 in a priority mode since it fired the PL-12. When the MiG-29 fired the two PL-9's the MiG went to the end of the "list" as the HEL engaged the air-to-air missiles first. With the missiles gone, the High Energy Laser acquired and dwelled on the fuselage of the MiG. Four seconds later the MiG's jet fuel flashed and the aircraft erupted in a horrendous explosion consuming the remaining fuel and the pilot.

The radar operators aboard the *Reagan* received the information from the remaining aircraft of Wolf Flight. Nathan grieved silently for his friend, James Aulicino. He couldn't understand what happened, more so he didn't want it to influence the decisions he knew he had to make now. The remaining aircraft of Wolf Flight had been directed by Nathan to return to the *Reagan*. Nathan was confident that "Bronco 1" could take care of itself until he could get his two other "Super Hornets" on station near it. The E-2C on station behind the *Reagan* fed the real-time data from its powerful radar to the *Reagan*'s CIC computers. Nathan's main concern was the approaching NKA cruise missiles, so he held off launching a rescue mission to look for any survivors of Wolf Flight. The radar operators confirmed fifty-two missiles inbound from about seventy miles. The entire Strike Group went to "battle stations". The cruisers *Shiloh* and *Princeton* along with the destroyer *Howard* illuminated the missiles with their Aegis SPS-62 fire-control radar. The air was soon filled with SM-2 Standard surface-to-air missiles. Seven SM-2's rippled from the USS *Howard*'s forward Vertical Launch System (VLS) and sped down range to intercept the J-82K cruise missiles, the same type of missiles that "killed" the ROK Frigate "*Yang Manchun*". Three missiles burst from the aft VLS launcher on the USS *Shiloh*, its missiles supporting the *Howard* in an effort to defeat the threat of the missiles aimed in its direction.

In the USS *Princeton*'s CIC the fire-control radar locked up twelve cruise missiles and launched an equal amount of SM-2's from the forward and aft VLS cells to deal with the threat. The missiles streaked over the *Howard* with a deafening roar as they went down range. The Hawkeye's radar confirmed knocking down ten missiles. With the help of the *Princeton*, the threat was reduced to three missiles. The *Shiloh*' Aegis radar switched on to deal with the threat before it, Eighteen more J-82K cruise missiles. This time it was the *Howard*'s time to help. Six SM-2 missiles burst from the aft VLS cell of the USS *Howard* as the cruise missiles sped forward. The 5"/62 cal gun on the forward deck began to fire, queued by the Aegis fire control system. The deck gun engaged and "killed" the remaining missiles headed for the *Howard*. The six SM-2 Standard missiles from the *Howard* knocked down four missiles, the remaining missiles missing their targets. The *Shiloh* once again fired missiles from its aft VLS launcher, adding its punch to the fight. The

Shiloh' 5"/62 cal gun, now within range, began spitting out projectiles towards the oncoming cruise missiles. The combined firepower of the *Shiloh* and the *Howard* defeated the eighteen cruise missiles on a bearing towards the *Reagan*. Eleven cruise missiles remained however, aimed off the bearing of the *Shiloh*. The guns of the *Shiloh* engaged the missiles one at time while the SM-2's kept firing from the aft VLS cell. The forward chaff launchers fired automatically, drawing two missiles off and sending them on a different bearing, which was good for the *Shiloh*. It was however, very bad for the *McClusky*.

The USS *McClusky*, a Perry class guided missile Frigate, was on the Starboard quarter of the *Shiloh*, four miles away. The bridge personnel on the *Reagan* could see the *McClusky* about two miles ahead and off her starboard bow. The remaining missiles off the *Shiloh'* bow were defeated by her defenses. Since the *McClusky* was in the "safe zone" no SM-2 missiles were fired in her direction, the risk of hitting her too great. In fact, since the *McClusky* was in the operating envelope of the *Shiloh'* deck gun, she was basically on her own. The *McClusky* turned to Starboard to unmask her 76mm gun and 20mm CIWS cannon. The 76mm gun fired twice as the two cruise missiles bored in. Once the missiles were in range the 20mm CIWS started to fire. One J-82K cruise missile was hit and exploded within two hundred yards, showering the aluminum superstructure with shrapnel. The second cruise missile pulled up three hundred yards from the *McClusky*, reminiscent of a Harpoon missile, and dived onto the forward superstructure of the *McClusky*. The 165-kilogram warhead of the Chinese-built J-82K cruise missile exploded deep in the forward hull of the *McClusky* below the bridge, destroying the MK-13 missile launcher. The ship immediately took a list of ten degrees to port and slowed from twenty to four knots. Built as a low-cost, mass-produced patrol frigate, the *Perry* class ships had many attributes but operating in a high-level threat environment was not one of them. The hot shrapnel from the first missile cut through the thin aluminum hull, causing fires in the engineering spaces and killing about eight enlisted personnel. The damage control teams managed to stop the fires as others, the remaining engineering personnel, stopped the flow of seawater into the engineering spaces.

Forward in the ship, things were worse. The J-82K's warhead had exploded in the hull below the bridge killing most, if not all, of the bridge personnel of the *McClusky*. Terrible fires raged in the compartments below decks. Six enlisted and two Officers formed a makeshift damage control party and bravely fought to extinguish the flames before they consumed the ship. Cold seawater poured in as the ranking Officer of the damage control party ordered the attempt abandoned and the last watertight door closed and secured. Several enlisted personnel, some burned and exhausted, climbed topside towards fresh air and safety. The Officers decision to abandon the attempt was a correct one. The *McClusky* seemed to settle down by the bow but retained enough buoyancy to remain afloat, it watertight doors holding back the sea. The seawater quickly extinguished the flames in the forward missile magazine, saving the *McClusky* from a worse fate.

The Officers of the *McClusky* mustered on the aft deck where it was found then that the ship's Captain had been killed. He was on the bridge when the missile hit, directing the ship as its guns fired. The ship's CIC was evacuated, as smoke partially filled the room and there was a complete loss of power. The Executive Officer ordered a message sent to the *Reagan*. It was clear they could not make headway and, with the bow close to the waterline, the watertight doors could not hold for long. The second Officer now had a responsibility to the crew, for their safety and well being. He ordered an evacuation of the *McClusky*.

The Captain of the USS *Jarrett*, Commander Jason Polk, was ordered to lend assistance to the *McClusky* as soon as it was hit. The *Jarrett*, the second Perry class frigate in the *Reagan* Strike Group, was following the *Reagan* off her port quarter. Commander Polk ordered the *Jarrett* ahead full to help the *McClusky*. The bridge personnel of the *Reagan* relayed the visual real-time data to the *Jarrett* as the behemoth carrier went by the doomed ship on its port side. Its speed now zero, the *McClusky* was not a fighting platform but a hindrance to navigation. The *Jarrett* carefully approached the *McClusky* on her starboard side. The seriously injured personnel were taken off by a SH-60 Seahawk helicopter from the *Reagan*. Injured personnel that could wait were evacuated and treated on-board the *Jarrett*. Once all the personnel were evacuated Commander Polk radioed the *Reagan* for further orders. Captain Winters and Admiral Alexander both consulted on the matter as Nathan listened in. His responsibility rested with the *Reagan's* Air Wing and not the Strike Group. "Admiral I looked at the *McClusky* as she passed to our starboard. She is down by the bow and listing to port about twelve degrees" the Captain explained. "Any chance we can salvage her, Bruce?" Steven asked. "I don't see how, sir. If we attempt a tow it might ship too much water through the hull and bust the watertight doors. We could probably make only five knots anyway, judging from the damage" the Captain added. "Have all the casualties been removed?" Steven asked. "All those that could be found, Sir. We couldn't locate the Captain and three of the bridge crew. It was just one big mess" the Captain concluded, taking his glasses off and wiping them. "I understand, Captain. Have the *Jarrett* sink the *McClusky* as a hazard to navigation and return to her station" Steven ordered. "Aye, aye Sir" Captain Winters acknowledged. The Captain turned to the operator at the console and motioned for his headset. It was understood in the Navy that only an Officer could order the sinking of another

Navy ship. Nathan heard the Captain order the *Jarrett's* commander to sink the *McClusky* and return to station at best possible speed.

Not one of the Captains favorite tasks, Commander Polk reluctantly ordered the crew to engage the *McClusky* with the *Jarrett's* 76mm cannon. The torpedo crews were also ordered to launch one Mark 50 torpedo into the side of the *McClusky*. The 76mm rounds found their target, which was only two hundred yards away. Several armor-piercing rounds ventilated the hull of the Frigate. The Mark 50 torpedo hit the *McClusky* amidships sending up a tremendous geyser of water that cascaded down over the ship. Hundreds of gallons of seawater, now free to enter the ship, flooded the engineering section of the *McClusky*. The ship settled deeper in the water as the air escaped through the holes made by the 76mm shells. Once the ships upper deck was awash the *McClusky* went down quickly by the bow, taking with her the souls of all those who fought and died on her to the ocean floor below. Commander Polk watched as the *McClusky* slipped beneath the waves. It could have easily have been his ship, the two vessels trading positions throughout the deployment. Why, he thought, had the Navy decided that the Perry class frigates should still accompany the fast Carrier Strike Groups was beyond him. This was prime example that the Perry class Frigates could not survive in this environment. It was the main reason that the Arleigh Burke Destroyers were built in the early 1990's. More than double the displacement of the Perry frigates, the Arleigh Burke's superstructure was constructed mainly of steel and carried additional armor over the engineering spaces and other vital areas. Once called "the most survivable ship in the Navy next to the Aircraft Carrier" by a retired Admiral, the class of ship went on many deployments through the years and was constantly upgraded. The survivability of the class was most evident during the USS *Cole*' visit to a refueling depot in the Middle East during the late '90's. A small suicide boat, driven by terrorists, was exploded into the port side leaving a large hole in the hull. The *Cole* survived the incident and was shipped back to the United States for repairs and was ready for deployment the following year. Even though there was no question that the Arleigh Burkes could defend themselves at sea, the incident showed the Navy that certain security measures had to be employed when the ships were operating in a confined environment. Commander Polk ordered his crew to return to their station at best possible speed. The *Reagan* Strike Group was seven miles away. The *Jarrett* came up to flank speed to return to the protective umbrella of the *Reagan*.

TEN

PAYBACK

THE REMAINDER OF THE NKA BOMBERS littered the Sea of Japan. Lieutenant Anthony "Genie" Nelson was the leader of Hoosier Flight, a group of F/A-18 "Super Hornets" which was escorting the F-35 Joint Strike Fighters to their targets. He was saddened by the loss of two of his fellow aviators and vowed it to never happen again. After the last AMRAAM downed the last SU-25, the radar picture ahead of him was clear. The E-2C radar down-link provided a clear radar picture out almost to Seoul. Oddly enough, the area to his rear was clear also, the stealthy F-35 Joint Strike Fighters not showing up on radar at all. As far as everyone was concerned, the North Koreans included, there were just sixteen aircraft, eight E/A-18's and eight F/A-18s approaching North Korea. Once the F-35's crossed the coast the aircraft would disperse to their targets, mostly surface-to-air missile sites and radar sites that needed to be destroyed before the bombers arrived an hour from now. The Joint Strike Fighters carried the new Advanced Anti-Radiation Guided Missile (AARGM). The AARGM's had a range of 90 miles and hit their targets without mercy at close to two thousand miles per hour. The AARGM's were tested in mid- 2005 at White Sands Missile Range and achieved a high success rate of 98.7 percent, although this would be its first time in combat.

The lead aircraft of Electra flight, a group of E/A-18 "Growlers", indicated that a group of "Fan Song" type Radar's were operating near the DMZ. The "Fan Song" radar was a class of Soviet radar of megawatt power and most often associated with the deadly SA-2 Surface-to-Air Missile (SAM). Made in the 1960's, the SA-2's were still a credible threat and could knock down a bomber with one hit. As the flight approached 80 miles a "Growler" launched a High-speed Anti-Radiation Missile (HARM) at the radar site. The HARM disappeared from view, but the data-link from the Hawkeye kept track of it position. The missile reached its target and exploded, sending steel fragments into the radar dish, shutting it off permanently. Immediately other radar emissions started showing up on the E/A-18 sensors, the North Koreans sensing an imminent attack. A total of six more HARM's were launched at the radar source's, some of which shut down before the missiles arrived. The electronics in the HARM's guided the missiles to the last known position of the emitter and dove to attack it. Most of the sites were destroyed except for one that was mobile, A "Flat Face" type radar mounted on a heavy truck that moved on orders from its Officer in Charge.

Flying over the T'aebaek mountains, the pilots of Hoosier Flight detected a flight of NKA SU-7B "Fitter" fighter-bombers flying south, low through the clouds, which were quickly shot down by Hoosier Flights three and four aircraft. Loaded down with bombs and rockets, the SU-7B's didn't put up too much of a fight, one even pulling up into a cloud bank to out run a AIM-9X Sidewinder. The Sidewinder tracked straight up the SU-7's tailpipe and exploded, the SU-7 turning over on it's back and diving into the mountains. The pilot of Hoosier 4 noticed a parachute coming from the cloud were the SU-7 disappeared into and radioed the E-2C. Within minutes an U.S. Army SH-60 from the 2nd Infantry Division at Camp Stanley near Uijongbu was dispatched along with two AH-64 Apache attack helicopters to search for the downed pilot.

After searching for about an hour the SH-60 found the downed NKA SU-7 crewman. He was lying down near a small group of scrub when the SH-60 came over the hill. When he saw the SH-60 he promptly stood up and fired his Makarov 9mm pistol at the SH-60 as it passed above him. The North Koreans shots missed the S-60, which gained altitude and circled down wind. One of the AH-64 Apache' came over the hill from behind and let loose a one-second burst of 30mm projectiles from its Hughes M230A-1 chain gun cannon. The rounds from the Apache missed also, mostly by luck, but it took the fight out of the pilot, who then threw down his weapon and put his hands in the air. The Apache helicopters hovered, holding the crewman while the SH-60 landed and deployed its soldiers to capture the North Korean pilot. The US soldiers put the North Korean pilot on the SH-60 and flew back to Camp Stanley.

With the mission of the Apaches completed they were ordered to patrol near the DMZ and look for signs of intrusion. The Apache helicopters flew on a northwesterly heading, advised by an OH-58 Helicopter from Camp Stanley that there was unknown activity north of the Camp. The Apache' flew closer to the ground as they approached the area in question. The pilot had flow this run hundreds of times before, dodging ROK fighter aircraft acting as the aggressors in the last

Operational Readiness Exercise. As the pilot pulled his Apache round the next mountain he spotted a pair of North Korean BTR-60 armored personnel carriers stopped on the road. Several personnel were out of the vehicles and when they saw the Apache some scattered while some started firing their assault rifles and the machine guns mounted on the BTR-60's. The pilot of the first AH-64 uncaged his 30mm cannon and fired a two-second burst across the first BTR, while the second Apache gained altitude and designated the second BTR with its laser. Seconds later an AGM-114 Hellfire anti-tank missile streaked off from beneath the Apache's stubby port wing pylon. The Hellfire missile hit the second BTR-60 head on and blew it to pieces. The soldiers nearby were thrown to the ground. The first BTR was hit by no less than one hundred and fifteen 30mm projectiles. The BTR exploded and caught fire, some of the soldiers escaping while still on fire. The Apache's circled the site and looked for any other signs of resistance. Some of the North Korean's were seen escaping into the woods but with the main threat of the BTR's dealt with, the Apaches continued on towards the location given by the OH-58.

The lead pilot of the Apache told his wingman that the BTR's were probably a scout team for an armored column and to keep his eyes peeled. The Apaches flew on through the mountain for another few miles before seeing something in the road ahead. Not immediately recognizing the vehicle he did recognize that it was firing at him by the gun's muzzle flashes. The first pilot pulled up just above the tree line while the second Apache sent a Hellfire missile into the BTR-40, silencing the guns. A command and reconnaissance vehicle, the BTR-40 mounted a dual 14.7mm anti-aircraft machine gun, a potent close-in weapon system for dealing with low flying aircraft such as helicopters.

The first Apache, now high above the trees, drew the full attention of the armored column located half a mile behind the now smoldering BTR-40. The pilot and the gunner of the first Apache saw no less than twelve T-55 medium tanks, seventeen T-62 medium tanks and about twenty-two additional BTR-60 armored personnel carriers. The gunners on the armored vehicles with heavy machine guns opened fire at the Apache's immediately. Wheeling about and diving below the tree tops, the Apaches backed off out of range and flew away to get a better firing position on the North Korean armored column. The Apache pilots radioed their exact position by GPS coordinates and called for addition support from Camp Stanley. The first Apache designated the rearmost T-55 tank in the column with its laser and let loose a Hellfire missile. The missile hit the tank and blew the turret apart as the stored 100mm main gun ammunition started to explode. The second Apache targeted the front of the column, starting with the first T-62 tank. At three miles away and out of range of the machine guns, the Apache attack helicopters fired their missiles with impunity. The two Apache's fired their full complement of Hellfire's, sixteen in all before they engaged the thinner skinned BTR-60's with their 30mm chain guns. In all the Apache's had destroyed fourteen tanks, twelve armored personnel carriers and one command vehicle. The Apaches turned around to fly back to their base as ten other Apache's arrived above the smoldering North Korean column to finish the job.

The news of the North Korean armored thrust into South Korea reached the Pentagon within the hour. With the airport at Seoul destroyed and the Airbase at Kunsan out of commission, the only aircraft available for ground support were the US Army helicopters, the USAF A-10's at Osan AB and the aircraft from the *Reagan* which was over one hundred and fifty miles off the coast. Admiral Grayson, who was concerned that the Chinese would attempt to reinforce the North Koreans, ordered the *Kitty Hawk* and her Strike Group to proceed to the Yellow Sea, off the west coast of the Korean Peninsula. The *Kitty Hawk* had been undergoing a second Service Life Extension Program (SLEP) at Yokosuka when the North Koreans launched their first missile test over the Japanese mainland. The *Kitty Hawk* was hurriedly put to sea with its Strike Group, the Pentagon anticipating more serious action by the North Koreans. The intelligence on the Chinese was not good, indicating the Chinese were at a heightened state of alert. The P-3C Orion's from Kadena AB on Okinawa kept a close watch of the Chinese Strike Group while they approached the peninsula. The first day of surveillance the Chinese seemed to tolerate the P-3C's flying around but by the third day they seemed to be outright annoyed. A flight of SU-30's from the *Varyag* intercepted each P-3C as it approached. Some P-3C pilots even reported the SU-30's crowded them off course, attempting to force them away from the Strike Group. To prevent an international incident, the Pentagon, on orders from President Jackson, withdrew the surveillance by the P-3C Orion's in favor of real-time reconnaissance by the ATAV's. The ATAV's could give Strike Group Commanders real-time imagery from a satellite down-link and through good mission planning could provide round-the-clock surveillance. The ATAV's used in conjunction with the *Thor II* Project were rapidly becoming a viable and potent military option.

The *Kitty Hawk* left Yokosuka days earlier and had been off the coast of Japan when they received their orders. Captain Jonathan Brookfield, Commanding Officer of the *Kitty Hawk,* received the message on the morning of August 17th. The message read:

TO COM USS KITTY HAWK CV-63. FROM

COMPACFLT. PROCEED AT BEST SPEED TO COORDINATES YS. CONDUCT SEA DENIAL AND STRIKE OPERATIONS AGAINST NKA, NAVY AND AF UNITS. COORDINATE WITH ROK AND USAF AT EARLIEST CONCERNING CAP MISSIONS. BE ADVISED OF CHINESE NAVY UNITS OPERATING IN YS NEAR OPS AREA. EXERCISE CAUTION AND OBSERVE RULES OF ENGAGEMENT. END OF MESSAGE.

Captain Brookfield ordered the Strike Group Southwest towards Tanega-shima, an island off the coast of Kyushu. Once passing it by, he turned Northwest and began launching combat air patrols. Receiving data from the *Reagan's* E-2C, he launched a single E-2C to cover the approaches to the west of his Strike Group.

The Captain looked out to port and could see the USS *John S. McCain* from his bridge chair. The *McCain* was one of three Arleigh Burke class destroyers in the *Kitty Hawk's* Strike Group, the others being the *Higgins* and the *Curtis Wilbur*. Along with a VLS Ticonderoga guided missile cruiser, the USS *Cowpens*, the rest of the Strike Group was made up by two Perry class guided missile frigates, the USS *Gary* and the USS *Vandegrift*. The Captain heard of the attack and subsequent sinking of the USS *McClusky*. He chose to keep to the Perry class frigates on each stern quarter of the *Kitty Hawk*, which was under the protective umbrella of the Arleigh Burke destroyers air defenses. Captain Brookfield was from the old school, which didn't question the orders that made up the Strike Group, but he was determined to protect the small Frigates trusted to his care.

The aircraft in Hoosier flight had seventeen "kills" to their credit. Mostly MiG-21's and 23's, the NKA Air Force fighters didn't do much when

Hoosier flight engaged them. Some just flew straight and level trying to dive or climb away from their pursuers, not once banking sharply to throw off the F/A-18's, which were now engaging them at close range with their 20mm cannon. Lieutenant Nelson also caught a few Su-25's at low-level looking for trouble. Not detecting his launch he downed both SU-25's with a pair of AIM-9X Sidewinder air-to-air missiles. Nelson saw he was approaching bingo fuel and ordered his flight to form up at angels twelve and head home. Other aircraft in the strike package were also headed home. The F-35 Joint Strike Fighters completed their missions with success and were returning with empty weapons bays. The majority of the targets, SA-2 and SA-3 missile sites were destroyed, as was a convoy of SA-2 missile's en route to a mobile launcher. The F-35's dropped their 500-lb. laser-guided JDAM's from six thousand feet and destroyed on all the vehicles in the column, leaving nothing but burning vehicles and bodies. The Joint Strike Fighters had proved they could attack deep, well-defended targets with impunity. Not a single F-35 was shot down or even detected on North Korean radar. The red carpet had been laid for the B-1 and B-2 bombers to carry the fight to the enemy.

The B-1B bombers attacked what was left of the North Korean Army airfields with their 2000lb JDAM's while the B-52's attacked the command and control facilities with their Joint Stand-Off Missile's in and around the capital of P'yongyang. The B-1's penetrated North Korean airspace at supersonic speed and at low-level while the B-52's launched their missiles from stand off range. All things considered the mission went without a hitch. All aircraft returned to Guam, except for one B-52, which had to make an emergency landing at Taegu for an unknown reason. With the command links to the combat forces in the field severed, the North Korean Army was cut off from all intelligence on the disposition of the ROK and US forces. The B-2 Spirit bombers that were launched from Whiteman AFB were scheduled to arrive in the Korean theatre in six more hours. Flying from Whiteman AFB to Alaska to refuel, the B-2's would fly towards Guam and await further orders. Each bomber carried eight of the Mark 5 Mod 2 SPECOR weapons which were targeted for various underground facilities in North Korea. While the main elements of the NKA Air Force were destroyed the US knew that many more aircraft were in shelters underground near the capital city of P'yongyang. In fact the SPECOR weapons were expressly designed for this type of mission. Hitting the target at over fifteen hundred feet per second, the SPECOR weapon penetrated soil and rock up to a depth of over three hundred feet. The three thousand-pound blast warhead was designed to detonate when it reached maximum penetration or when it sensed a change in ground density, as when it breaks through a concrete wall or tunnel.

The *Chang Bogo* had been cruising for hours at eight knots when the sonar technician advised the Conn that he had two "solid" contacts between bearing 347 and 349. The technician advised the Captain that both contacts were within the first convergence zone, which put them about thirty miles away. Perfect, the Captain thought, just the opportunity he was looking for to fire the other two Sub-Harpoon missiles he had on-board. The Captain quickly ordered the crew to "Battle Stations, Missile" and began to plot the trajectory the missile should take. He figured each contact was making about ten knots and heading on a course of 168 degrees, towards the American Strike Group. He ordered the seeker heads of the missiles programmed to turn on at twenty-five miles and be restricted to a narrow search pattern. He didn't want the missiles going off on another bearing lest they attack an unarmed merchant ship. With the missiles both programmed, he ordered tubes one and two each loaded with UGM-84 Sub-Harpoon and made ready in all respects. The Captain ordered the crew to have the *Chang Bogo* slow to four knots and come to periscope depth. He wanted to see the launch so it could be recorded on the video camera inside the periscope. With the *Chang Bogo* at periscope depth and the periscope fully extended, the Captain ordered the outer doors opened. The Captain peered through the periscope as the outer torpedo tube doors locked open. He started the video by pushing the button on his control yoke and ordered *"Launch tube 1"* seconds later he ordered *"Launch Tube 2"*. The Sub-Harpoons, enclosed in their watertight capsules, were ejected under high pressure from the torpedo tubes. Shooting towards the surface, the Sub-Harpoons broke the surface as their rocket motors ignited propelling them skyward. The Captain acquired the first and then the second missile in the periscope as they came out of the sea and then arced back down to cruise height. The Captain followed the missiles as long as he could before they went out of sight. He stopped the video and secured the periscope. He ordered the torpedo tube outer doors closed and had the *Chang Bogo* dive down to one hundred feet to listen for signs of the attack.

The USS *Pasadena*, A *Los Angeles* class attack submarine assigned to the *Reagan* Strike Group, had just rounded the north west corner of Mayang Island. The Commanding Officer, Commander Clayton Jones, was thinking this was going to be just another quiet patrol when the sonar supervisor advised the Conn of a submerged contact about fifty miles due south. The sonar technicians were trying to classify the contact when the sonar supervisor advised the Captain that the contact had just opened its outer doors. Seconds later a sonar technician announced that the contact had launched a pair of Sub-Harpoon missiles from an undetermined shallow depth. The Sonar supervisor confirmed the report. "Sonar, Conn. Classify the contact as friendly. Advise when you have a type and class." The Captain ordered. "Conn, aye" came the reply from the Sonar supervisor. It was obvious the contact was friendly since it fired the Harpoon. It still had to be classified but the Captain was pretty sure it was a South Korean submarine, probably the one that had been detected by the *Reagan* F/A-18's a few days ago when the first MiG intercept occurred. The *Pasadena* was cruising just below the surface at one hundred feet and making eight knots. The Captain knew the sub had detected something in order to launch the Harpoons, but what? A few minutes later the Captain found out. "Conn, Sonar. We show the friendly contact is a Type 209 Class submarine. Also we have new multiple surface contacts at bearing 347, 349, 352 and 357. Show the contact at bearing 352 as hostile, classified as a *Najin* Class patrol boat" the Sonar technician reported. The Captain went to the plot table and pulled out the *Jane's* book. The *Najin* patrol boat was about as big as a World War II Destroyer Escort and bristled with guns of several caliber types. It carried a few surface-to-surface missiles in addition to a light ASW loadout, so it was still a credible threat. No doubt the South Korean sub thought so also. The Captain ordered the Officer of the Deck to sound *"General Quarters"*. Crewman ran to their stations as the *Pasadena* prepared for war. "Conn, sonar. Captain the contact at bearing 357 is classified as a *Komar* missile boat and is at 36,245 yards" The Sonar supervisor reported. "Conn, aye. Load tubes two and three with Mark 48 ADCAP. Make tubes ready in all respects" ordered the Captain. The Officer of the Deck repeated the orders the Captain stated as the crew went into action. The *Pasadena* was getting ready to fight.

The Harpoon missiles flew towards their targets blindly at over five hundred knots, both on slightly different headings. When they broke the twenty-five mile mark the computer turned on the radar seeker head and the missiles actively began sending out radar emission pulses, hoping for a radar return. The first missile detected a target first, and corrected its course slightly to intercept. The second missile, its intended target farther away, continued on its present heading. The first target, probably detecting the emissions from the Harpoon, spun about ninety degrees and increased speed to twenty knots. The Harpoon adjusted its course and homed in on the *Sariwon* patrol boat, now only four miles away. The large caliber guns started firing at the oncoming Harpoon when it came into view but it was just too fast, the shells shooting past the missile as it came closer. When the missile reached eight hundred yards it started an evasive S-turn and then pulled up in a pop-up maneuver to attack the North Korean warship from above. The inexperienced gunners had no hope of following the missile and some leaped from their guns foolishly trying to find shelter. The Harpoon missile hit the *Sariwon* amidships, just aft of the forward superstructure, and detonated deep inside the hull. The explosion ripped the hull apart, destroying the diesel engines. Fires raged from the explosion as the hull broke apart, the stress from the seawater entering the hull too great for the fragile keel. The *Sariwon's* aft hull remained afloat for a few minutes before disappearing beneath the waves. The forward section of the hull list sharply to port by forty degrees after the aft hull separated, spilling personnel, some dead, living and dying, into the sea. Some North Korean sailors, who clung to the superstructure, died when it rolled completely over and sank, pulling them with it into the depths below.

The second Harpoon missile received a return in its radar seeker head and homed in on the *Najin*. At a range of six miles the Harpoon bored straight in on the unsuspecting North Korean patrol boat. Maybe the sailors on the *Najin* were preoccupied, the smoke from the *Sariwon* appearing in the distance, but the *Najin* failed to detect the approaching Harpoon until it was too late. The Harpoon hit the port side hull above the waterline and between the second gun turret and superstructure, burying itself before the computer detonated the warhead. The second gun turret exploded from within as personnel on the Bridge were killed immediately as the blast-fragmentation warhead sent splitters the size of sledgehammers through the superstructure shredding everything in their path. The blast blew through the starboard side of the hull rocking the ship back and forth. Large fires raged from below the weather deck as ammunition for the 100mm gun started to go off. A secondary explosion blew up the 100mm gun turret as the front of the ship started to gather seawater and sink by the bow. Personnel that weren't killed from the explosions gathered aft in an attempt to launch a lifeboat, while others jumped into the sea with their life jackets. The fires raged on and made their way aft as the ship finally came to a full stop. The others that jumped in the sea were no where to be seen as the remaining crew of twenty-six sailors launched the only serviceable lifeboat. Extremely overloaded, the sailors paddled away from the burning ship as it sank lower in the water, the crew hoping it would go under before the fires reached the CSS-N-1 surface-to-surface missiles. When the lifeboat was half a mile away the fires reached the first missile, the 1000lb warhead exploding, sealing the fate of the *Najin*. The seasoned warship, now shredded and ablaze, settled lower in the water by the bow and slipped beneath the waves.

The Sonar operator heard the explosions on a bearing close to the last position of the contact. "Captain, we have detected an explosion near the location of the first contact" the operator announced. The Captain of the *Chang Bogo* acknowledged the Sonar operator's discovery. Good, the first target was destroyed, he thought. He knew that wherever the Harpoon hit it would sink the warship. He hoped it would be the *Najin*. Whatever happened this cruise he hoped to sink the *Najin*. His beloved son, now gone and only a memory, would relish in his dad's victory. The Captain thought, at times, he felt his son's presence in the control room. Not one to back down from a fight, he knew his son would be there, to give guidance to his loving Father. "Captain, target one is breaking up and sinking" the Sonar operator reported. The Captain shook his head in the affirmative, as he walked back and forth silently. Several minutes later the excited Sonar operator reported "Captain, explosion on the bearing of the second target" he reported, listening to his headset. "Captain, I hear secondary explosions, the target is breaking up and sinking" the sonar operator added. The Captain was elated but didn't show it for there was still a possibility of more warships out there. The *Chang Bogo* could detect them but had only four torpedoes left and no Harpoon missiles.

The *Pasadena's* Sonar Officer reported the destruction of the two North Korean missile patrol boats to the Captain. Commander Jones left to go to the sonar room forward of the control room. Talking to the Sonar Officer he heard the digital replay of the explosion while the Sonar Officer showed the Captain the Sonar waterfall display where the sounds were recorded. "Damn, I guess they really got hammered, huh guys?" the Captain said to the two enlisted Sonar operators that were sitting nearby. "Yes sir, Commander. They really got it rammed up..." the enlisted man said, stopping in mid-sentence. "Good. Carry on men, and pay attention so we don't get it rammed up ours" the Captain said, handing the headset back to the enlisted man, bringing him back to reality. The Captain returned to the Control room. This was no time to relax, as there was still the two other contacts out there. The Sonar technicians classified both contacts as *Komar* class missile boats. Both probably seeking out the *Reagan* Strike Group the Captain thought. The Captain went to one of the plot tables where an enlisted crewman was keeping the position of the *Pasadena* and the *Komar* patrol boat updated. "Sonar, Conn. What course is the contact at bearing 357 on?" the Captain asked. "Conn, Sonar. The contact at Bearing 357 is on course 167 at ten knots" the Sonar supervisor reported. "Conn, aye" the Captain replied. Commander Jones did some calculations of his own and then consulted the enlisted crewman at the plot table. After refining more calculations he addressed the Officer of the Deck. "Officer of the Deck, come right to course 027. Make your depth four hundred feet and then increase speed to twelve knots" the Captain ordered. The Officer of the Deck repeated the Captains orders while the Helmsman turned the submarine and the Planesman put the sub in a shallow dive. The Officer of the Deck ordered Engineering to make turns for twelve knots. The *Pasadena* pushed ahead, closing the distance on the *Komar*.

Sometime later the Captain, standing at the plot table, asked the Sonar room the distance to the *Komar*. The Sonar technician reported that the contact was 28,200 yards from the *Pasadena*, still making ten knots. The Captain acknowledged the Sonar officer and added ""Designate the contact as Sierra 02". The sonar room received the order and acknowledged it. The Captain knew that the *Komar's* could make forty knots, at least according to the Jane's book. He now was in range with his Mark 48 ADCAP torpedoes. The *Komar* was not equipped with Sonar so it would have no warning until the ADCAP detonated underneath it. The Captain ordered "Battle Stations, Torpedo" as the *Pasadena* surged closer to its target through the East Korea Bay.

"Torpedo room, Conn. Firing point procedures. Match bearings on Tube 2 with Sierra 02" the Captain ordered. "Torpedo room, Aye. Match bearings on Tube 2 with Sierra 02" The Weapons Officer replied. "Torpedo room, Conn. Make tube 2 ready in all respects" The Captain added. "Torpedo room, aye. Make tube 2 ready in all respects" replied the Weapons Officer. A few moments later the Weapons Officer called in. "Conn, Torpedo room. Tube 2 is ready in all respects, we are ready to shoot" The Weapons Officer reported. "Conn, aye. Shoot tube two" the Captain ordered. The Captain could hear the ADCAP being fired as the compressed air heaved the torpedo out of the tube. "Conn, Torpedo room. Tube 2 fired electrically. Unit is running hot, straight and normal" the Weapons Officer reported. The Mark 48 ADCAP torpedo ran straight towards the *Komar* at over sixty-five knots, the thin guidance wires unspooling as it went. The technicians aboard the *Pasadena* kept plotting the location of the *Komar* as the ADCAP approached it. When the torpedo was within five thousand yards the Captain ordered the torpedo room to cut the wires to the torpedo and told the Officer of the Deck to come left to course 287. The ADCAP reached its programmed range and went active, searching the area ahead and on both sides of the torpedo. The ADCAP acquired the *Komar* almost immediately and adjusted course slightly to intercept it. The ADCAP went straight for the *Komar* and came up close to the surface and cruised in at a depth of eight feet, just slightly below the hull depth of the *Komar*. When the ADCAP went under the hull the 660lb warhead detonated and lifted the 80-ton missile boat out of the water. The hull shattered by the explosive, the *Komar* flipped up and sideways before it crashed back down in the water, bow first. The *Komar* missile boat filled quickly with water and sank. With most of the crew of twenty thrown into the air from the torpedo detonation, the rest of the crew died as the missile boat slammed back down in the water. The *Pasadena* had struck and made its presence known.

The *Chang Bogo'* Sonar technician detected the torpedo launch from the *Pasadena*. It was obvious from the sonar signature and subsequent active sonar frequency that the torpedo was a Mark 48 ADCAP. The Captain ordered the crew to change course and avoid the American submarine. The American's surely knew that the *Chang Bogo* was here due to the launch of its Harpoon missile. The Captain reviewed the last position of the other *Komar* missile boat. It was a little over 43,000 yards from the *Chang Bogo*, but Sonar had estimated the missile boats speed at over thirty-five knots. The Captain wouldn't have to do anything. The *Komar* would come to him. The Mark 48 torpedoes that the *Chang Bogo* carried would do the job, although they weren't as fast as the ADCAP's, the Mark 48 still could do about 43 knots.

The Captain of the *Chang Bogo* ordered the Mark 48 loaded into torpedo tube number four. With all the calculations having been updated for the last hour the Captain ordered tube number four containing the Mark 48, fired. The torpedo launched normally, according to the Weapons Officer and set off at a normal speed of twenty-eight knots. The Mark 48 torpedo followed its pre-programmed course for about ten thousand yards before the active sonar in the nose turned on. The torpedo acquired the *Komar* at 4300 yards, turned to the left and immediately increased to its attack speed of forty-three knots. As the torpedo closed on its target it came to within six feet of the surface, still maintaining its top speed of forty-three knots. The torpedo hit the starboard side of the hull near the aft quarter. The warhead detonated and blew up the aft portion of the hull, exploding the CSS-N-1 surface-to-surface missile. Liquid fuel from the missile spread over the aft portion of the ship and ignited as a fire from the engine room broke through the deck. The crewmember's that survived the explosion ran for the bow of the ship, some on fire from the flames. The missile boat, which was now off keel because of the missing missile canister, listed to starboard and capsized. Some of the crew swam away from the boat; those that couldn't died through an agonizing death by drowning.

ELEVEN

NELSON'S FOLLIES

THE PRESIDENT WAS BUSY ON THE phone conferring with the Vice-President when he saw Admiral Grayson enter the conference room. The E-4B had just finished refueling and maintenance when the Admiral's jet landed at Mountain Home AFB. He hurried with two of his staff members aboard the E-4B just as the jet received clearance for take-off. The President finished his call then stood up. "Jack, thank God. Its good to see you again" the President said as he reached out to shake the Admirals hand. "Thank you, Mr. President. It's good to be seen. It was touch and go for a while at the Pentagon, I forgot how many levels there really were" the Admiral said jokingly. "Jack, I just finished talking to Vice-President Cobb as you arrived. We are both in agreement that we need to finish this business with North Korea as soon as possible before China gets dragged into it" the President said. "I couldn't agree more, Mr. President. Let me give you an update of what has happened in the last few hours." Admiral Grayson said as he motioned to the two nearest chairs. "I assume that General Howard has briefed you on the loss of the USS *McClusky*" Admiral Grayson asked the President. The

President and the Admiral both sat down, side by side. "Yes, he did. That was tragic. Twenty-six men dead with dozens more injured. How could it have happened?" the President asked his Chief of Staff. "Mr. President, the *Reagan* and her Strike Group were sailing in what is known as "expanded formation". What this means is the ships were in a larger formation that usual considering the nuclear threat from the "Oscar" and the North Korean Air Force. If the ships were in standard formation and a nuclear missile detonated it may very well destroy other ships in the immediate area. The problem was the *McClusky* was in a position that prevented it from being defended past a certain point. The *McClusky'* Captain knew this as well as the rest of the crew, Mr. President" the Admiral explained. "That won't make any difference to the families of the dead sailors, Jack" the President replied. "No Sir. It won't. If I could change it, I would" the Admiral said. "Were the families notified, Admiral?" the President asked. "Yes Mr. President, they have been" Admiral Grayson replied. The President sat back in his chair, a boiling rage churning inside him. "Everyone of those sailors will get the Navy Cross, Admiral" President Jackson said after clearing his throat. "Mr. President, if I might…" the President interrupted the Admiral. "I *said* every one of them! Every last one of those sailors Admiral, is that clear!" President Jackson said angrily, leaning forward quickly and slamming his fist on the hardwood table, looking the Admiral squarely in the eye. "Yes Sir, I'll see to it personally" the Admiral replied. He knew not to challenge his President on such matters. The President was a firm but compassionate man. The Admiral quickly spread a map of Japan and the Korean peninsula on the table in front of the President. "Mr. President, not to make light of the *McClusky* incident but I'm sure your aware by now of the great success of the *Thor II* project. It has exceeded all our expectation and has been put on stand-by for the time being. You also may have heard of the term

"Force Multiplier" in certain military jargon." The Admiral said. "Yes Jack, I have heard the term. I'm a little more up on things than my predecessor" the President said jokingly. "That couldn't please me more, Mr. President. I'll cut to the chase, Sir. Only a large number of bombers could only have duplicated the attack missions that we accomplished with *Thor II*. We estimate that we would have needed at least two hundred B-1 bombers based two hours from the targets in question to perform the same tasks and receive the same results. Not only did *Thor II* do it more efficiently it did it with no risk to our military personnel" the Admiral explained. "That's a big one in my book" the President said. "Mine also Mr. President. With that said I'd like permission to re-call the bombers that are en-route from the bases in the US to Japan. I think it would be unwise to deploy them any closer until we can confirm, for sure, that the North Korean short-range missile threat is defeated" the Admiral explained. "I was under the impression, Admiral, that the threat *had* passed" the President said. "The long-range missile threat to the United States has passed Mr. President, but recent intelligence has surfaced showing that the North Koreans may be bringing out some mobile launchers. Some of the missiles not accounted for could reach Northern Japan or even as far south as Guam. We have Army Intelligence in cooperation with the CIA working to find the location of the launchers" the Admiral explained. "Great, now we'll never find them" the President remarked, jokingly. The Admiral was amused but tried not to show it. "You remember the Gulf War in '91 when we expended great man hours looking for the Scud launchers in the Iraqi desert?" the Admiral asked the President. "Sure, I had hoped we learned some thing after that" the President replied. "I think we did. Sir, if you want to hide something in the desert, what would you do?" asked Admiral Grayson. "Bury it in the sand?" replied the President. "Exactly, and if you wanted to hide something in the mountains of Korea you would..." the Admiral was cut off in mid-sentence. "Put it in a mountain. Oh my God. Have we been looking in the wrong place?" asked the President. "Not entirely. The North Koreans know that if we can see a target we can hit it. Back in the late eighties and early nineties the North Korean's expended many years mining for Uranium in the mountains North of the DMZ. A by-product of the mining operation was that it left huge tunnels, which they could move troops, tanks and *missiles*. The CIA, in its infinite wisdom, started a plan called "Operation Weasel". Hundreds of agents posing as geological survey students planted geological sensors in the mountains *South* of the DMZ back in July of 1995" the Admiral explained. "Did you say *South* of the DMZ?" the President asked. "Yes Mr. President, I said South. The sensors were put in place with the help of the South Korean government under the cover story that they would be used to gain significant information on seismic activity in the Korean peninsula. The sensors were built by MIT and remained dormant except for indicating a tremor in 1998. In February of 2000 however the sensors picked up considerable activity at eight locations south of the DMZ" The Admiral paused for a few seconds to help let the President digest what he had just heard. "Jack, do you mean to tell me that the North Koreans have tunneled *under* the DMZ into South Korea?" the President asked confoundedly. "Yes sir, that's precisely the information we have. A few hours ago a pair of our Apache helicopters shot up a North Korean armored column about eight miles north of Camp Stanley." the Admiral said, pointing to an area on the map of Korea. This same column was sighted thirty miles north of the DMZ by our satellite reconnaissance. The column didn't ford any rivers and they weren't airlifted but managed to show up here four hours later, unseen" the Admiral said pointing to a location on the map. "An Army OH-58 on routine patrol found them by accident and called in the Apaches" Admiral Grayson said. "The sensors that were placed years ago, if they are still active can we use them to pinpoint were the next column will come from?" the President said. "We seem to be on the same page, Mr. President" the Admiral said. "We have located three areas where we believe the North Koreans will break out of. The tunnels were built so only ten or twenty feet of rock has to be removed so the armored column can emerge from the mountain. The North Koreans probable already have charges set on six of them. The sensors detected large vibrations here and here, before a major vibration showed up here hours ago. We believe that's were our first armored column came from" Admiral Grayson explained. "It seems to me if we could catch them in the tunnels and seal it up, that would solve a lot of problems" the President said. "That's precisely why I'm here, Mr. President. I have drafted a plan to do exactly that, but we need to act fast" the Admiral said. "Well lets get going before the little rats come out of the hole" the President said.

The Admiral picked up the phone intercom and summoned General Howard to the conference room. When he arrived, the Admiral ordered the General to commence "Operation Cinder Block" on the timetable discussed earlier. The General acknowledged the order and left the room to make the arrangements while holding the door for Janice Lang. Janice entered the room and sat across from the President. "I have a message from Chinese President Ming" Janice said handing the President the message. President Jackson looked at the message, which was in small type. Squinting rather than take out his glasses the President read the message:

Dear President Jackson,

I have heard learned of the nuclear detonations on the coast of North Korea and in the Sea of Japan. This has saddened me tremendously. I hope none of your military were injured and I will contact the North Korean President to express my dismay and to see if there can be a peaceful solution to this conflict. This action is most unfortunate and should have never been allowed to escalate to this level.

Sincerely,

Dao Pac Ming

Peoples Republic of China

The President slid the message across the table to Janice. "Sounds like he's sincere anyway" the President said. "Do you think he is searching for information, I mean he didn't really say anything about the "Oscar" submarine but it seems he is looking for answers" Janice said. "Well, he's not going to get any here, not right now anyway. Things just don't feel right. I'd like to trust the Chinese but too many things add up" the President said. "Like the trade agreements?" Janice added. "No, not just that but other things like how we know the Chinese have been sending weapons to North Korea. The North Koreans have exported tons of offensive materials to several Middle Eastern countries as well as Pakistan. If you remember not many years ago that Pakistan was accused of selling nuclear weapon technology to North Korea. There is no way North Korea could be supplying the other countries without China's help. I afraid what were seeing here is the culmination of China as world power, with all the other countries siding with China" the President explained. Admiral Grayson and Janice Lang looked at each other and then to the President. "I tend to agree with you Mr. President. The data that we have compiled seems to support that conclusion. The Iranian government, long hostile to the United States, has rejected United Nation's attempts to inspect their nuclear plant near Tehran. Our satellites show that the plant is now fully functional" the Admiral said. "That explains the Israel Prime Minister's call yesterday. He was adamant that the United States take out the reactor" Janice said. "If they want it taken out let them do it. We have too much at stake in the region right now. Besides they did it back in '81 when they took out the Iraqi's reactor!" the Admiral spoke excitedly. "Jack, your right. We do have a lot on our plate right now. We have to finish this business with the North Koreans quickly" the President said. "And we have to do it without the Japanese getting anymore involved than they already are" President Jackson added. "We really don't need them any closer than they are, Mr. President" Admiral Grayson replied. "They have several of their cruisers and destroyers forming Surface Action Groups right now. One off of Hokkaido Island and another one is approaching the Korea Strait. We have good intelligence that the North Koreans are going to attempt to blockade the Port of Pusan. If the Japanese show up near there, well, it could get interesting" the Admiral added. "Jack, I trust we have the situation well in hand off Pusan then?" the President asked. "Yes sir, you can count on that. Pusan is our most important deep-water port. We have several surprises awaiting the North Koreans" the Admiral said. "Also, Sir. The *Kitty Hawk* Strike Group has rounded the tip of Kyushu and is in the East China Sea. They will be On-Station in about six hours. We're sure the Chinese are aware that we're there. The base at *Qingdao* has shown considerable activity during the last six hours. We're keeping on eye on it though" the Admiral said. "Jack, I don't want a confrontation if we can help it" President Jackson replied. "Understood Mr. President" the Admiral replied. The President stood up slowly, tucking in his shirt. "Janice, I want a press conference in about an hour. The American people should be aware of what's going on" the President ordered. "Very well Mr. President." Janice replied.

On board the USS *Sante Fe* the Executive Officer, Lieutenant Commander Cory Miller was checking the course of the ship when the Sonar Officer reported two submerged contacts bearing 345 and 358 from the *Sante Fe*. For the last three days nothing except freighters then this. "Conn, aye. Classify and designate the contacts unknown" the executive officer ordered. Commander Miller was nearing the end of his shift and, after giving control of the submarine to the Officer-of-the-Deck, went to wake the Captain. Commander Miller walked down the passageway a short distance and knocked on the thin wall separating the Captains quarters from the passageway, but heard no reply. He opened the door and entered the small room that was the Captains stateroom. Waking the Captain gently, Dennis Edwards rolled over and sat up. "What's wrong Cory, did you run us aground?" the Captain said jokingly. "No sir, you told me to wake you before your shift" Cory Miller replied. "Yeah, I know, thanks. What's going on" the Captain said. The Captain's questions were always vague, which allowed his Officers to comment on anything that they thought worthwhile. To the Captain "what" meant anything. "We have detected two submerged contacts on separate bearings, possibly hostile. Also, the Japanese tanker *Hamana* is at bearing 047 and headed into Pusan harbor" Cory said. "How is sonar doing in classifying the two contacts?" the Captain asked while tying his shoes. "They are working on it, Captain. We just discovered them" Cory replied. "Good, lets go" the Captain said as he walked into the passageway and went forward to the Control Room.

Commander Dennis Edwards thought he had the best job of anyone on earth. Dennis had become the Commanding Officer of the Sante Fe two years ago and had been lucky enough to get assigned to some interesting duty assignments. His mission during this conflict was to protect the Port of Pusan and commercial traffic from North Korean submarines that were intending to blockade the Port. He could fire on hostile contacts but had to be *sure* they were hostile. Hundreds of trawlers, cargo vessels and military vessels entered and left this area everyday and his sonar crew was working overtime to classify each contact. The success or failure of the mission rested on their shoulders but the Captain would ultimately take the blame if things went wrong. That was proved years ago when the USS *Greenville* surfaced and came up underneath a Japanese survey ship, sinking it and losing some oceanographic students. Even though an inexperienced sonar crewman on the *Greenville* misread the data, ultimately the Commanding Officer is responsible for the safety of the ship and it's crew. It had been that way for over two hundred years. Captain Edwards stepped into the Control room as the Officer-of-the-Deck announced "Captains on the Bridge". Commander Edwards went right to the plot table and observed the updated tactical map. The enlisted crewman at the plot table stepped back as both the Captain and his Executive Officer hovered over the table. We received the first detection here, about eight minutes now" explained Cory Miller. The Captain grabbed the microphone on the table. "Sonar, Conn. This is the Captain, I need the classification on those two contacts" Captain Edwards said angrily. "Sonar, aye. Captain we show another contact on bearing 048. We are attempting to classify it now" the Sonar Officer replied. "Conn, aye" the Captain replied. "Three unidentified contacts and commercial traffic all around us. That's just great" the Captain said out loud, expressing his dismay to the crew. Seconds later the Sonar Officer broke the silence. "Conn, sonar.

Contacts at bearing 345 and 358 classified as "Romeo" class diesel-electric submarines" the Sonar Officer replied. "Conn, aye. Designate the contacts at bearing 345 and 358 as Sierra 20 and 21, respectively" the Captain ordered. Well they had two enemy submarines out there looking for easy prey. Commander Edwards was going to make sure they didn't get their wish. "Officer-of-the-Deck sound Battle Stations" the Captain ordered. The Officer-of-the-Deck sounded the horn for Battle Stations while the crew ran to their stations. "Torpedo Room, Conn. This is the Captain. Load tubes two, three and four with Mark 48 ADCAP torpedo. Make weapons ready in all respects" the Captain said. The Weapons Officer received the order and repeated it as the torpedo crews began to feverishly load the torpedoes. Less than five minutes later the Weapons Officers reported tubes two through four, ready to shoot. "Conn, sonar. Contact at bearing 048 is also classified as a *"Romeo"* class diesel-electric submarine" reported the Sonar Officer. "Conn, aye. Designate the contact as Sierra 22" replied the Captain.

The Captain now had three hostile targets within range of his weapons. The *Santa Fe* was cruising at five knots and was at a depth of one hundred and seventy feet. The Captain knew when he fired his torpedoes all the targets would hear them. That's was good in a way, adding terror to the equation of the enemy submarines crew. The Mark 48 ADCAP had a range of over twenty-five miles at 65 knots. The torpedomen nicknamed them "wish me dead" torpedoes. Captain Edwards had no problem shooting an enemy who couldn't shoot back. The *"Romeo's"* were here to shoot unarmed commercial shipping anyway. The commercial ships had no way of shooting back or even detecting them until it was too late. The Captain went to the periscope housing and picked up the 1MC microphone. "Torpedo room, Conn. Match bearings on targets Sierra 20 through 22 and shoot" the Captain ordered. The crew heard the compressed air surge from the tanks as the

ADCAP's were launched one by one at the waiting North Korean subs. "Conn, Torpedo room. Units 2 through 4 fired electrically. All units running hot, straight and normal" the Weapons Officer declared.

The Captain of the NKAN *Romeo* class submarine near the Port of Pusan was at periscope depth. He saw the entrance to the Port in the distance but dared not raise the periscope up anymore unless he wanted to be detected. This was the closest he had been to Pusan since four years ago when he delivered spies to the region to the west of Pusan. The Captain lowered and secured the periscope as his sonar operator indicated a sonar target approaching at high-speed, out of the submarine's baffles. Possible a destroyer the Captain thought as he ordered the submarine to come about and pursue a course of bearing 180. The submarine started its turn and the sonar officer about came out of his seat. "Captain, incoming torpedo, bearing 023!" screamed the sonar officer. The Captain immediately ordered a turn to port and increased speed to maximum. Once at maximum speed, the Captain ordered the submarine to dive down to two hundred feet, barely thirty feet from the bottom. Running at an angle away from the torpedo was what was taught in submarine school but the *"Romeo"* was making twelve knots, barely enough to get out of its own way. The ADCAP closed the distance in a short time. It bored in on the mid-section of the submarine, it's computer brain quickly determining the middle of the target. The ADCAP hit "Sierra 20" and exploded on contact, blowing the *"Romeo"* in two halves that quickly found their way to the ocean bottom.

"Captain, I have a explosion bearing 263" the sonar operator of Sierra 22 reported. "Very well, what is the distance?" asked the North Korean Officer. " The distance is close to 22,500 yards, Captain" the sonar operator replied. The Captain thought that a commercial cargo vessel was attacked by a fellow submarine officer. It would be one of many since the North Korean Navy planned to blockade the Port of Pusan. The explosion indicated that possible ships were coming out of the port. The Captain intended to target some vessels also so he ordered a new course of 357, straight towards Pusan. Maybe it was because of inexperience, fatigue, inattention or all three on the part of the sonar crew but the first indication of the attacking torpedo came from the outside, the active sonar of the ADCAP torpedo "pinging" through the hull. The Captain couldn't even speak or issue an order, the last things he saw was his valiant crew, which were soon replaced by the vision of his wife and his three children. The fifty crew members of "Sierra 22" died within fifteen seconds of each other, the blast of the ADCAP's warhead blowing the small submarine apart, robbing it of all power and life.

The sonar crew of the *Santa Fe* heard the explosions of "Sierra 20" and "Sierra 22". It was painfully evident that the *Santa Fe* scored two quick kills. The crew remained silent, their attention focused on the last torpedo. The last submarine to be attacked was the one designated as Sierra 21, now close to 29,000 yards away from the *Sante Fe*. The two previous explosions must have alerted the "*Romeo*" submarine that torpedoes were launched because it turned and ran. "Conn, sonar. Sierra 21 has reversed course and increased speed" the sonar officer reported. "Conn, aye" the Captain replied. The Mark 48 ADCAP was making only 45 knots to increase its range but it was moving off the bearing of the *"Romeo"*. "Fire-control, conn. Steer the torpedo" the Captain ordered. The fire-control technician adjusted the course of the torpedo through the thin trailing wires that were attached to the *Sante Fe*. The torpedo gradually came back to an intercept course. Once the ADCAP was within two thousand yards the Captain ordered the wire cut to the unit. The ADCAP Torpedo immediately began "pinging" searching for its target. No one knew why but the *"Romeo"* submarine remained at its present depth as the ADCAP accelerated towards it at sixty-five knots. The Captain on the *"Romeo"* ordered a quick turn to starboard and an emergency surface as the ADCAP's active sonar filled the interior of the *"Romeo"*, a last desperate attempt to evade the torpedo. The "Romeo" started to rise quickly, the water in it's ballast tanks replaced by high pressure air as the ADCAP hit the *"Romeo"* and exploded just forward of the starboard propeller shaft, blowing off the stern section of the hull and sending the *"Romeo"* submarine rolling on her port side. The submarine righted itself and seemed to approach the surface.

On board the *"Romeo"* submarine all hell had broken loose. After the explosion the submarine had lost all electrical power. The emergency lights came on sending an eerie glow through the submarine. Crewmen were screaming while still others were more concerned with sealing off the aft portion of the hull. The sea rushed in where steel shafts and seals once were. Fifteen of the engineering crew died immediately, while seven more died when the rest of the crew sealed off the engine room. With the aft portion of the submarine now flooding, the *"Romeo"* remained at a twenty degree up angle. The submarine seemed to remain motionless after the torpedo hit but after the ballast tanks began to empty the submarine headed for the surface. The submarine came to the surface about eighteen miles south west of the Port of Pusan, its bow poking out of the sea by about eight feet, the conning tower slightly above the surface. The Captain, realizing they had to get out of the submarine, ordered all of his personnel to proceed to the control room under the conning tower for an orderly evacuation. The Executive Officer was the first to open the hatch at the conning tower. It was getting dark and very windy. He could see that the forward torpedo hatch was above the water and relayed the information to his Captain. Within seven minutes all the remaining crewmembers, twenty-eight in all, were on the forward hull of the stricken "*Romeo*". Several crewmembers had life rafts and were in the process of inflating them. The Captain conferred with his first officer as to the plan for the evacuation. On the submarine were confidential documents that, if captured could undermine the North Korean government and severely handicap the military. He ordered the Executive Officer to form a team of four personnel to destroy the documents and set charges to send the stricken submarine to the bottom of the Korea Strait. Two life rafts were launched while the last waited for the four men sent below. The Captain, his Executive Officer and two other crewmen waited as the charges were set. The men worked quickly, not knowing if another torpedo was on its way or not. No one wanted to die but to live to fight another day. One of the demolition charges were set at the aft main bulkhead watertight door, which now held back the sea. The others were set near the main induction valves for the diesel engines. The charges would blow apart the valves and start a tremendous flood in the engine room. With the rest of the submarine open it would take only minutes for it to sink. The charges were set for seven minutes and the men ran for the ladder to the conning tower and safety. The Captain ordered the life raft launched as the first crewmember emerged from the conning tower. As the last man ran towards the raft the Captain entered the lifeboat and helped the last man in. The crewmen already started paddling away as the Captain ordered the life raft to shove off. One of the crewmembers advised the Captain that the demolition charges should go off within five seconds. Seconds later an explosion could be heard deep within the casing as steam and debris shot from the open hatches on the conning tower and forward deck. The submarine remained motionless for about a minute and then began to sink. In less than four minutes the "*Romeo*" submarine slipped silently beneath the surface. The other survivors, having waited for the Captain, paddled closer so than they could brave the approaching weather and night together.

Nathan was in the CIC on the *Reagan* when the last F-35 was recovered on the aft deck. It was a busy day. The three squadrons of F/A-18's had completed seven sorties that day with the F-35 Joint Strike Fighters coming in with six sorties per Squadron. The new squadron of EA-18G "Growler" aircraft accompanied every sortie that the F-35's flew except the last. With the main surface-to-air threat diminished, the F-35's could operate on their own. The *Reagan* Strike Group had encountered two North Korean "Whiskey" class submarines on the outer perimeter, about twenty-seven miles from the *Reagan*. The Destroyer USS *Lassen* had detected the submarines, which were ahead of the Strike Group and about fourteen miles apart. The *Reagan* launched two SH-60 Seahawk helicopters which destroyed the enemy submarines. Despite the amount of sorties launched only two incidents happened. An air-to-air missile from a MiG-29, shot down and killed Lieutenant Commander Aulicino, Nathan's friend, over the Sea of Japan. Another F/A-18 was lost when it missed the third wire and flew off the *Reagan's* deck. The pilot reported an engine failure and had to eject when he couldn't gain altitude. The pilot was plucked from the sea by the waiting rescue helicopter and only suffered a concussion when he hit the water. It was getting dark and despite the Combat Air Patrols flown by the F/A-18's for the AL-1A's, the rest of the aircrews on the *Reagan* settled in for the night. Nathan looked at the digital clock on the wall. It was almost 2100 hours on the 19ᵗʰ of August. Commander Robert "Billy" Sampson, the Commanding Officer of Squadron 17, was due to relieve Nathan. The Commander had flown two sorties in his Joint Strike Fighter during the day, hitting surface-to-air missile sites around the North Korea naval base of *Wonson*. Nathan heard the door to CIC beep and saw Commander Sampson walk in. "Good evening Commander" Nathan said. "Good evening" replied Commander Sampson "The last F-35 just landed minutes ago. We have no further orders except the standing orders for Combat Air Patrols of the AL-1A's" Nathan explained. "That's good, the crews can use the rest" Billy replied. "How did you do over *Wonson?*" Nathan asked. "I guess okay, I'm still living. I ran into a lot of small caliber stuff at low level, mostly below three thousand feet. Probably single barreled 23 and 57mm guns, not very accurate and I didn't pick up any radar emissions from any fire-control" Billy explained. "That's good. I don't want you to take any chances. If you get any warnings then get out of there and hit them with the AARGM's" Nathan ordered. "I heard that" Billy mused. "How did you do on primary targets?" Nathan asked. "Well, I hit a mobile SA-2 site on the coast that was camouflaged as a building site. They were reloading a missile when I dropped a SDB in their lap. They never even knew it was coming. I saw a lot of secondary explosions so I think I used up their budget for the month!" Commander Sampson said raising his arms, as if in an explosion. "I continued over the naval base and saw some submarines tied up near a jetty. I came around again and dropped the remaining five SDB from three thousand feet. When I looked back all I could see was black smoke and the jetty on fire" Billy explained. "I'd like to have been there to see that" Nathan replied. Indeed Nathan would have loved to see it. He wanted to be in the middle of things, that is the reason he joined the Navy in the first place.

Nathan gave Commander Sampson the details on ship and weapons status before transferring control of CIC to the Commander. Nathan left and went to the galley to get a quick bite. He opted for a chef's salad instead of a burger, since he planned to retire quickly after reading his mail. After eating he returned to his quarters, removed his shoes and sat on his bunk. His mail was already delivered, waiting on his desk. His copy of *Air & Space* was there as was a letter from his wife. The letter was dated on August 14, 2008. Not bad considering the *Reagan* was in a combat situation at sea and was five hundred miles away from where they were yesterday. Nathan lay back on his pillow while opening the letter. He was tired. He hadn't slept in twenty-two hours. The loss of Jimmy Aulicino weighed heavily on his mind, more so than what his wife was about to say. At least she and the kids were safe, and so was Jimmy, now that he thought about it. Jimmy was a person who wanted no harm to come to anyone. He joined the Navy because of his love of flying and as a way to provide an "honest" living. His wife Cindy was the love of his life. Nathan and his wife knew Cindy very well. Jimmy, Cindy, Nathan and his wife spent a lot of time together when both Nathan and Jimmy were assigned to the *Nimitz* in Norfolk, VA. Nathan wished he could be there to console her tomorrow. The two Naval Officers would arrive at eight o'clock in the morning along with a Chaplain. Nathan had done the detail twice before and knew that the Officers would be walking up the front steps with knots in their stomachs. Their job was to help the widow and make arrangements for anything she needed including the upcoming services. Cindy was a strong woman but this would devastate her. Nathan prayed that her faith would guide her and give her strength to carry on as he fell asleep in his bunk.

Except for the Combat Air Patrol, taking off every four hours, the night operations on the *Reagan* had been considerable slow. The F/A-18s that were on-station above "Bronco 1" were ordered not to pursue contacts over the Korean peninsula between the hours of 2100 hours on 19 August and 0400 on 20 August. No one had been told why but it was a good bet that it came from the Pentagon. With most of the offensive missiles and their silos destroyed, the North Koreans had only a small force of mobile No-Dong surface-to-surface missiles armed with High Explosive and Chemical warheads. It was known they intended to use them also, which was why additional AL-1A's arrived from Groom Lake and patrolled behind the DMZ. The Pentagon knew that the missiles were underground and had a lot of resources looking for them. President Jackson had already discussed the other targets of opportunity to the military with his Chief of Staffs. The world had seen for itself that North Korea had launched its missiles in an attack on South Korea, Japan and the United States. The United States had retaliated forcefully and was about to put the cork on North Korea's dominant nuclear aspirations. It was decided that North Korea's Nuclear Program would be ended here and now. The North Korean's had constructed about half a dozen Nuclear Reactors around their country along with half as many separations plants manufacturing weapons grade plutonium. The largest plant near *Yongbyon*, housed between 2,500 to 3,000 scientists and researchers, many of whom studied nuclear technology in the Soviet Union, China and Pakistan. The military, the nuclear weapons program and the intelligence service were all under the close supervision of President Kim Lu Doc.

After their first sortie of the conflict, the ATAV's returned to Groom Lake for maintenance, refueling and re-arming. The pilots got to catch a few hours sleep while some ATAV's were turned around in four hours for a real-time data-link reconnaissance mission. One ATAV was scheduled to cover the Northern half of North Korea while another was to cover the southern half including the DMZ with special thermal imaging sensors. The last ATAV would take off for China and had similar sensors as the second ATAV. Colonel Bill Collins would pilot the last ATAV, serial number 93-012, while Major Samuel P. Cox would ride in the right seat. Colonel Collins and Major Cox were briefed on the mission in the late afternoon and reviewed the route they would take. After climbing out to 100,000 feet the ATAV would accelerate to Mach 6 and head straight for the Chinese Strike Group in the Yellow Sea. After downloading photos of the Strike Group to the *Kitty Hawk*, the ATAV would turn towards the Naval Base at Qingdao. It was hoped that the ATAV could photograph key facilities at the base and other naval installations nearby. Of particular interest was any shipping traffic headed for North Korea with missiles, other weapons or materials. After its mission was completed the ATAV was to turn to the north and head for the RAF Strathclyde airbase in Northern Scotland. The United States had used the base for years, with an unwritten agreement existing between the United States and the UK for shared information of the ATAV's real-time imagery.

The first ATAV took off ten minutes before the second, with Colonel Collins taking off fifteen minutes later. The first ATAV would be used to record Bomb Data Assessment from the targets in the North that the B-2 Spirit bombers attacked. The B-2's were launched from Whiteman AFB earlier in the day when the action started but were dispersed and recovered at various bases in Hokkaido, Guam and Okinawa once the Ballistic Missile threat passed. Now, with the path cleared by the *Reagan's* Joint Strike Fighters and EA-18's, the B-2's launched and were scheduled to deliver their deadly payloads to the North Korea's infrastructure.

The first B-2 bomber flew over the DMZ at 2200 hours. The crew headed straight for their target at *Yongbyon* while the crew spent much of their time concentrating on fuel consumption and missile warning threats. They encountered a few search radar's en route to the target but no fire-control radar's indicating they were being tracked by surface-to-air missiles. The eight Mark 5 Mod 2 SPECOR weapons were "warmed up" when the B-2 was ten minutes away. The facility, which was built in 1987, was a large single-story building constructed on top of the main plutonium reprocessing facility located deep underground. The facility, which was active and running 24 hours a day, 365 days a year, had been estimated by the CIA to hold up to twelve hundred personnel at any one time. The reasoning used by the Pentagon to attack the facility was twofold. The facility was the largest in the country, estimated to produce about thirty nuclear weapons annually, and it was the first such facility constructed. North Korea began nuclear research back in 1964, when Kim Sung Pac, the father of the current President, Kim Lu Doc, ordered the construction of an atomic energy research complex in *Yongbyon*, which was about sixty miles north of the capital of Pyongyang. Destroying the facility, which was thought of as his Dad's legacy by the current President, might be more than the President could bear and could some how hasten his removal from political office.

The B-2 reached its drop point and dropped four closely spaced SPECOR weapons from its cavernous bomb bay, the remaining four weapons reserved for its secondary target. The bombs fell quickly and when their radio altimeters indicated they were about five thousand feet above the ground the rocket motor in the rear of the weapon ignited and propelled it into the building at over 1200 feet per second. Each bomb hit within one second of the other and penetrated through tons of dirt and reinforced concrete. When each weapons computer had sensed it penetrated to its maximum depth, the 3,000-lb. warhead exploded, sending a massive shockwave through rock, earth and concrete. The shockwave from the other weapons met and crumbled the massive underground structure trapping hundreds of people seven stories underground. Those that weren't killed in the initial blast were pinned by falling debris and then thrown into complete darkness. Those few that survived could hear the cries and screams from others nearby. Those that would live and see the light of day again vowed that they would do everything in their power to help make North Korea a strong country, not dependent on the will of a tyrannical dictator.

Over the course of the next few hours the B-2's destroyed a total of four reprocessing plants along with six nuclear reactors and seven hydroelectric plants. The major nuclear reactors at Yongbyon, Taechon, Simpo and Sunchon were shut down by two SPECOR weapons each, along with several electrical transformer stations. The hydroelectric plants, which produced over seventy percent of North Korea's electric power, were shutdown as of 0245 on the morning of 20 August. Railroad traffic in the north came to a virtual standstill since the North Koreans operated electric locomotives for a large amount of their transportation needs. Several military trains were stopped on the way to supply points in the south. The trains, void of any other protection except the dark, moonless night, would become inviting targets for the Joint Strike Fighters during the day. A few diesel locomotives from the rail yards tried to move some 60-ton freight cars but didn't get far because the other electric locomotives blocked the lines. The ATAV sent to recon the north captured the destruction of the hydroelectric plants in real-time video.

A total of four B-2 bombers were vectored to new coordinates by the ATAV flying high over the DMZ. Several places south of the DMZ had shown up on the thermal sensors as possible armor columns, which seemed to be located inside tunnels. The sensors were a combination of thermal imaging and ground-penetrating radar that detected fissures or tunnels in the earth's crust. The thermal sensors detected and confirmed heat escaping from inside the mountain as would be common from an armored column. The B-2's dropped a total of twenty-three SPECOR weapons in eight different locations, which collapsed an entire mountainside on one armored column, starting a landslide in the vicinity of *Kumhwa*, South Korea. Other columns, which were the bulk of the North Korean advance into the south, had their vehicles trapped in the mountains. Some personnel escaped their rock tombs by digging and climbing out of fissures left by the penetrating weapons dropped by the B-2's. After attacking all their targets the B-2's returned to Guam for refueling before starting the long trip home to Whiteman AFB.

While the B-2's departed the peninsula the North Koreans were making preparations for another missile launch. A section of the North Korean Army was preparing to launch the last of its missiles at Seoul and Inch'on. Its standing orders were to launch the last salvo on the morning of August 20th no later than 0400 hours. Fourteen mobile missile launchers were moved from their camouflaged position twenty miles north of the DMZ. The crews, dressed as common North Korean civilians, went about their business in the nearby village as if nothing was wrong. They observed the American warplanes and missiles flying overhead the last few days and prayed that the No-Dong missiles would not be located. Eight of the missiles carried a deadly high explosive warhead while the remaining ones had chemical warheads. Some of the chemical warheads were destined for Osan AB and Seoul, while the rest of the missiles were to be targeted for the army military installations close to the DMZ. The Missile Squadron's Commander hoped that he could help his brothers in the armored attack columns, which were sent to capture some bases in South Korea. The crews raised and set up the missiles and took final readings of their position before programming the guidance systems. The missiles had a range of a little over eight hundred miles with its 2,500 lb. high explosive warhead. The high explosive missiles would rain down destruction, while the chemical warheads would detonate overhead and send clouds of deadly gas across the American bases to overcome the soldiers defending the base.

Once the preparations were complete, a five-minute countdown was started as the crews prepared for the launch. Once the missiles were launched and on their way to their targets the crews would move their vehicles to the railroad depot that was fifteen miles north to receive a reload for their Transporter-Erector-Launcher (TEL) vehicles. The Commander looked at his watch, five seconds to go, four, three, two, one. All at once fourteen rocket motors ignited and the missiles began to streak towards South Korea. The area was blasted with dust and rock particles as the missiles lifted off. The missile crews, safe inside their vehicles, began to leave the area as soon as they could see.

Three modified Boeing 747-400s, were flying a racetrack pattern about forty miles south of the DMZ. The 747-400's or AL-1A's as they were now called, were each designated with a "Bronco" call sign. "Bronco 5" was near the city of *Uijongbu* while "Bronco 6" and "Bronco 7" were to the east, spaced at equal intervals. "Bronco 6" was the first to make the detection of the No-Dong missile launch. The weapon system was on automatic and its High Energy Laser had tracked and "killed" three of the missiles that were bound for Seoul. The Commander of "Bronco 6" relayed the information to the *Reagan* Strike Group while "Bronco 5" began to track a missile headed in its direction. The High Energy Laser began to dwell on the missiles outer skin for a few seconds before it exploded and broke apart. The chemical warhead headed for Camp Stanley was consumed in the ensuing explosion at an altitude of 63,000 feet. "Bronco 5" continued firing at the missiles until the ones in its quadrant were destroyed. "Bronco 7", which was turning towards North Korea, fired the last five "bolts" which destroyed the remaining missiles. Debris from the No-Dong missiles fell just short of the DMZ, on the north side in an unpopulated area. After the attack the location of the launch sites were forwarded to the *Reagan*. The E-2C Hawkeye from the *Reagan* was flying at thirty thousand feet off the East Coast of South Korea. They advised the command center at Camp Stanley of the missile attack and within ten minutes four AH-64 Apache helicopters were airborne. The Flight of Apaches headed for the location of the launch site, which was less than fifty miles away.

At 0345 hours on August 20, aircraft on the *Reagan* began to move as orders from CIC came down to the hanger deck. Twenty-four F-35 Joint Strike Fighters, sixteen F/A-18E "Super Hornets" and eight E/A-18G "Growler" aircraft were readied during the night, some of the maintenance crews putting in a twenty-hour day. Eight of the "Super Hornets" were each loaded with four, GBU-31 2000 lb. Joint Direct Attack Munitions (JDAM) as well as the standard complement of AIM-9X Sidewinders. The rest of the "Super Hornets" were each loaded with two AGM-84H SLAM-ER missiles and external fuel tanks. The AGM-

84H SLAM-ER missiles were a follow-on to the successful Harpoon missile. Known as "The Slammer" to Navy pilots, it was the weapon of choice for attacking hardened targets such as command bunkers and aircraft shelters. Each "Slammer" carried an 800-lb. penetrating blast warhead and had a range of up to 93 miles. Cruising at over five hundred miles per hour, the "Slammer" was a devastating weapon. The Joint Strike Fighters were each loaded with four of the newer GBU-39D 250-lb laser-guided Small Diameter Bombs (SDB). The SDB were specifically designed for the tight internal weapons bay of the Joint Strike Fighters. Each F-35 also carried two AIM-9X Sidewinders for self-protection. The F-35's were scheduled for precision strikes this morning and would rely on their stealth and cover from the F/A-18's. One of the E/A-18's, were to accompany each flight, to provide jamming and suppression in case the strike aircraft ran in to enemy air defenses.

All the aircraft were launched in the morning an hour before daybreak and headed for their targets in North Korea. It was a testament to the training and skill of the ground handlers and launch crews that the strike aircraft launched successfully. Some have described the operation as a delicately balanced and coordinated ballet. One aircraft, and then another, left the forward catapults and while the two waist catapults launched their aircraft, other aircraft were raised from the hanger deck and positioned for launch. Lieutenant Frank "Spike" Lopez was the flight leader for his flight, which consisted of four F-35 Joint Strike Fighters. Frank was briefed that his target was the rail center near Sepori, North Korea. Several rail lines intersected there and it was important to destroy any weapons or materials that were stranded around the area. Other flights had similar targets, mostly in and around the capital city of Pyongyang. Satellite photos and real-time reconnaissance by the ATAV's had shown that the capital had been dark and silent for the last few hours, the electrical power shut off to most of

North Korea by the B-2 bombers earlier. The F-35's would arrive over the railyard at daybreak with the other strike aircraft reaching their targets about one half hour later.

Flying in at five thousand feet, Frank Lopez could see the main line from the North coming towards the railyard. Several railcars were on the line, stopped about a mile or so away and fully loaded with what appeared to be single-stage ballistic missiles. Frank ordered his wingman to follow him and set up for the attack. He activated his laser and got a good lock on the first rail car. He ordered his wingman to target the third and fourth railcars. Frank put the Joint Strike Fighter in a shallow dive as he dropped two of his GBU-39D 250-lb laser-guided bombs. The weapon bay doors opened and the bombs dropped away, the aircraft automatically shutting its weapon bay doors. Frank's wingman followed his example but dropped four bombs on the target. Both aircraft banked and screamed over the railcars at four thousand feet while the bombs hit their targets. The first bomb followed a ballistic course directly to the laser point, which was the middle of the railcar and on the top of the first No-Dong missile. The bomb detonated on impact with the unfueled missile, destroying it and the railcar. The second railcar and missile was destroyed as the first and flipped the railcar off its track. Frank's wingman had let a string of bombs go, which culminated in several explosions, which destroyed the rest of the railcars and their cargo. The missile's warheads, not yet armed, lay burning near the railway bed.

The other aircraft in Frank's flight hit the railyard while the sole E/A-18G in the flight stayed at five thousand feet, radiating confusing jamming signals for any enemy radar that turned on. The main and secondary rail lines of the railyard were destroyed and it was certain that no rail traffic would go through here for some time. Frank gathered the rest of his flight, climbed to eight thousand feet and headed back to the *Reagan*. The other F-35 flights from the *Reagan* met similar success. No enemy fighters came up to meet them and no fire-control radar's appeared indicating enemy air defenses.

The AH-64 Apaches from Camp Stanley had reached the area where the ballistic missiles were launched. It was obvious to each pilot that mobile launchers launched the missiles. The amount of scorched ground and heavy tire marks headed north indicated TEL vehicles. The Apaches headed north in search of the launch vehicles. The Apaches followed the roadway at an altitude of three hundred feet, winding through the mountains. After about fifteen minutes the lead Apache sighted a TEL vehicle kicking up a lot of road dust while it rounded a turn in the road ahead. The Apache climbed abruptly to five hundred feet to get a better view of the vehicles. The pilot and gunner saw between ten or twelve eight-wheeled TEL vehicles on the road ahead. The gunner designated the first vehicle in the column with a laser and launched his first Hellfire missile. The Hellfire streaked for the first TEL vehicle, over the heads of the other vehicles, and detonated on top of the launch vehicle. The vehicle exploded, turned to the left and overturned. The other vehicles traveling behind it, which were making close to thirty miles per hour, either stopped or slowed down to go around the destroyed vehicle. The second to the last vehicle in the column, and probably the smartest, pulled off the road and stopped as its crewmembers quickly exited the vehicle. One of the crewmen ran for the hills while others looked for a safe place to hide. The other Apaches in the flight climbed to five hundred feet and began to engage the thin-skinned TEL vehicles at will with their 30mm cannon. A mix of armor-piercing and explosive rounds hit the vehicles, shredding metal and human tissue, exploding fuel tanks and turning the vehicles into burning metal coffins. The fourteen vehicles in the column were destroyed in less than five minutes, the flight leader finishing off the last few vehicles with two Hellfire missiles. The crews of the Apaches counted about fifty or so bodies of North Korean soldiers that lay near the destroyed TEL vehicles. The Apache flight circled above the destroyed column one last time, as if paying their respects, before heading back to Camp Stanley.

Lieutenant Anthony Nelson was the third aircraft in a flight of eight, headed for the North Korean Naval base at Nampo. His flight of heavily-loaded F/A-18E "Super Hornets" had crossed the East Coast fifteen minutes after sunup and flew on towards their target. Since the start of hostilities, and even before that, the North Korean navy on the West Coast had been pretty active in the Yellow Sea. Several types of gunboats, some of Russian and Chinese origin, proliferated in the Yellow Sea off the coast of South Korea. Years of skirmishes between the ROK and North Korea had taken place over nothing more than fishing rights near the cease-fire line. The North Koreans had built up the Navy to include several missile boats and large frigate-size vessels of 1950 and 1960 vintage. The mission of Lieutenant Nelson's flight was to put an end to the North Korean naval presence on the West Coast. Anthony's flight would destroy the docks, maintenance and repair facilities and munition storage areas while a flight of eight AH-64D Longbow Apache helicopters flying from Camp Stanley would engage the missile and gunboats. Two E/A-18G "Growler" aircraft accompanied the strike aircraft to deal with any enemy air defenses. No search radar's or fire-control radar's were operating on the way to Nampo, which was good news for Anthony. He would like nothing more than to drop his load and get back out to sea and safety.

The flight was within visual range of the naval base. The tank farm, which stored all the fuel for the ship's, stood out as the largest target. Anthony looked at his watch, they were right on time. He looked to his left and below and could barely make out the rotors of the approaching Apaches. With any luck the base facilities would be burning, which would covering the approach of the Apaches. The attack group split into two flights. Anthony's flight would attack the tank farm, while the other would attack the command facility and the munition storage and loading area. Just as Anthony told his wingman to increase his speed and drop to eight thousand feet, he saw the two oil tankers sitting off shore of the tank farm. Good, that's a bonus and told his wingman to save a JDAM for the second tanker. As he approached the tank farm Anthony noticed the tracer balls streaking slowly up to his altitude. The 57mm anti-aircraft guns were getting close but were still out of range, the speed of the "Super Hornet" too fast for the gunners on the ground. Anthony called out the location of the ground fire as he nosed his aircraft over and let two 2,000 lb. JDAM's loose at the tank farm below. Banking to the left slightly he lined up the first tanker and hit the "hot" button twice, sending the last two JDAM's earthward. Pulling up and banking to the right Anthony went to military power and headed to the north away from the Naval Base. As he banked hard to the right he saw the mobile SA-2 surface-to-air missile site come to life. His radar-warning receiver went off and a second later a missile was arching upwards. Anthony went into afterburner, rolled inverted and pulled back on the yoke sending the F/A-18 hurtling towards the earth. The SA-2 missed Anthony's jet and turned, coming apart in-flight, not stressed for greater than twelve G's. Anthony leveled out and headed west away from the naval base at two thousand feet. The remaining aircraft in his flight must have took care of the tank farm because

Anthony could see several secondary explosions and thick, black clouds of smoke rising in the distance behind him.

The other pilots in the flight had indeed took care of the tank farm and also the SA-2 missile site. A second SA-2 missile streaked up to meet the last F/A-18 just as two JDAM's from the third aircraft in Anthony's flight exploded fifty feet from the launcher and fire-control radar unit, destroying them. The airborne SA-2, now with no guidance, seemed to go out of control and head for the ground. The SA-2 crashed and exploded harmlessly to the west of the base. Anthony heard the second flight call out a second SA-2 missile site that was to the east side of the base, near the munition storage and loading docks. Second later came the awful news that a F/A-18 was hit and the pilot had bailed out over the bay. Anthony knew the rescue helicopters would come in but not when it was this hot. Anthony ordered the flight to turn south west and suppress any anti-aircraft fire from the base. They screamed in at four hundred knots looking for tracer fire and found an abundance of it. All the patrol boats were alerted and every person on board that was capable of firing did so. As Anthony approached across the bay the JDAM's from the second flight began to hit. The command center took two big hits as well as another large building, probable a maintenance hanger. The second JDAM that took out the maintenance hanger also had the added benefit of destroying a 57mm anti-aircraft gun that was getting the range on some fast-flying Apache helicopters. Anthony saw the direction of the tracers change dramatically as word must have reached the gunners of the approaching Apaches. Taking advantage of this Anthony turned towards the closet 57mm gun, his wing man close behind. They both agreed to make one pass and then form up and fly home, their fuel already dangerously low. Anthony flew over several SO-1 class patrol boats, already starting to move and take evasive action. At two thousand feet Anthony nosed over slightly and began strafing two of the Taechong II class patrol boats that were tied up on the long pier. One exploded as he flew over it, which did concern him a little but he didn't dwell on it. He lined up his next target the 57mm gun emplacement and pulled the trigger. Three hundred 20mm cannon projectiles spit out of the "Super Hornet" in as many seconds and tore up the anti-aircraft gun and the North Korean soldiers that were manning it. As he pulled up Anthony could see fast tracers passing before him and from his right as he gained altitude. Seconds later he heard the agonizing sound of "Whumpf,Whumpf,Whumpf" followed by two more "Whumpf, Whumpf". His airspeed slowed by twenty knots and he thought he was okay until his Master Caution light came on and his number two engine died. If that wasn't enough a fire warning came on for his number two engine. He was at four thousand feet now so he shut down the engine and hit the fire extinguisher. He felt the controls and they seemed sluggish, not a good sign and definitely not normal. He called to his wingman and told him he received damage. Seconds passed and his wingman didn't answer. He called again and still no answer. The leader of Baker flight, the second group answered him and told him they saw a "Super Hornet" go down west of the base. No one had called out being hit so it might have been him. Anthony hoped for the best. He advised Baker flight leader he would try to make it to Osan AB as he turned his crippled "Super Hornet" south.

The first AH-64 Apache came under direct fire from the same gun that crippled Anthony's jet and killed his wingman, a ZPU-4. The ZPU-4 was a 14.7mm quad heavy machine gun with a range of 1,400 meters and a rate of fire of 600 rounds per minute per barrel. It was fired by a crew of four, two of whom mostly fed the ravenous appetite of the guns. It was sighted optically and had a mechanical lead-computing sight that gave off no energy emission's to an enemy's radar warning receiver. It was similar to the US quad .50 caliber machine gun and could fire the same type of ammunition such as Armor Piercing, Armor Piercing-Incendiary and High Explosive-Incendiary. It was a potent weapon to helicopters and low-flying aircraft.

Passing through the smoke cloud from the maintenance hanger the Apache gunner designated his first target, a Huangfeng class missile boat tied up near the missile loading dock. The laser reflected back to its designator and gave the gunner the "go" to launch the missile. The gunner launched the Hellfire missile just as the rounds from the ZPU-4 began to impact the Apache. Several hits of HE-I and AP-I destroyed the forward section of the Apache which then crashed to the ground. No longer following a laser the Hellfire missile went wide of its target, crashed and exploded into the bay. The other Apache helicopters saw what happened to the first and took a defensive posture. Two Apaches backed off and flew to the North around the now burning command center as two others climbed to an altitude of five hundred feet to find the target. With no targets in range the ZPU-4 sat silent. Some of the crewman even lay on the ground, pretending to be dead, as they could hear the Apaches rotors now approaching. The third Apache passed above the now destroyed maintenance building and transferred into a hover, turning slightly left to right and back to the left, surveying the situation and looking for the deadly culprit who killed the first Apache. As the pilot dipped the Apache and started into forward flight the ZPU-4 crews sprang to life and swung the ZPU-4 ahead of the Apache. The gunner of the third Apache already sensed that something was amiss, the "dead" crew laying next to a gun that wasn't destroyed, and was ready for them. As the gun crew of the ZPU-4 started to fire the gunner on the Apache already had the big Hughes 230A-1 30mm chain gun cued up and was pressing the trigger. The 30mm rounds flew at the ZPU-4 like so many angry bee's. The mix of high explosive and armor-piercing cannon rounds shredded and destroyed the gun and all organic material around it.

Passing by the destroyed ZPU-4, the crew of the Apache observed the destruction that the 30mm cannon delivered. Nothing living remained or even resembled what it once was. Turning to the west across the bay, the gunner lined up and fired his remaining missiles at the *Huangfeng* missile boats tied up in front of the loading docks. Crew members from the boats were running down the pier, some even jumping into the water to escape the inevitable destruction of the Hellfire missiles. The Apache helicopters that flew to the north found another active 57mm gun on the north side of the base and quickly silenced it with a Hellfire missile. The Apaches worked in tandem with each other, one designating the target from a covered position while the other launched a Hellfire and quickly took evasive action. With the surface-to-air missile threat defeated the Apaches could concentrate on the task at hand, destroying the missile boats and patrol craft. Flying over the destroyed maintenance hanger two of the last Apaches designated the two Taechong II patrol boats, one of which was already burning from the strafing pass by Anthony Nelson's F/A-18. Two Hellfire missiles hit the first patrol boat, which turned it into an inferno. No one seemed to be on-board as another volley of Hellfires hit the second patrol boat tied to the pier. Two more Hellfires were sent at the patrol boats, which already were an inferno when the Apaches flew over them at three hundred feet. On the other side of the pier across from the patrol boats lay *Hanchon* and *Hungman* class landing craft. The gunners wasted no time in raking the hulls with 30mm cannon and setting them ablaze. One of the major targets that the pilots and gunners of the Apaches had been briefed about was the presence of a *Najin* class patrol frigate. The North Korean-produced frigates numbered only two, one on the east coast, which was sunk yesterday, and the one here on the west coast.

Built in the 1960's, the *Najin* class frigates were a source of national pride by the North Koreans and were employed as fleet flagships.

The pilot of the sixth Apache sighted the *Najin* as he finished engaging the last SO-1 class patrol boat in the middle of the bay. He told his gunner to line up the *Najin* as he swung to the left, the helicopter seeming to pivot on its nose. At a distance of twelve hundred meters the Apache started firing one Hellfire after another, keeping as low as he could coming across the bay at forty knots. The first Hellfire hit amidships, striking below the forward funnel and exploding its tandem anti-armor warhead. The tandem anti-armor warhead of the AGM-114F Hellfire had been proven years earlier that it could be effective against small naval surface warships and with that the decision was made for the U.S. Army to be tasked with a naval strike mission. In fact the AH-64A Apaches assigned to the Korean peninsula were the only Apaches in the world to have a direct over-water mission. The second, third and fourth missiles hit the forward superstructure turning the bridge and interior into a flaming cauldron. The sixth Apache launched its last missile which impacted the hull aft of the stern 57mm gun mount. The frigate exploded as ammunition from the 100mm and 57mm guns went off. The Apache, now closer raked the hull with its 30mm cannon as it passed overhead.

The loss of the first Apache weighed on everyone mind as they turned for base, their stubby wing pylon racks empty. Despite the loss of one Apache and two "Super Hornets" from ground-fire the mission was considered a success. The F/A-18 pilot that was shot down by the SA-2 earlier had been recovered by the rescue helicopters. Receiving only minor injuries on bail-out the pilot was very lucky. The Flagship *Najin* was a total loss, sinking into the mud next to its pier. Several other missile and patrol boats littered the bay as well as the two cargo tankers that Anthony and his wingman were directly responsible for sinking.

The JDAM's that they dropped hit and capsized both tankers, setting them ablaze. One tanker broke apart and sank with two minutes. Nearby, the whole tank farm was now ablaze as secondary explosions caught the rest of the fuel storage tanks on fire. The Apaches had proved once again, just as in Desert Storm, that they could be effective in combat.

Anthony nursed his crippled jet away from the target area. The mission had gone as planned but the intelligence on the ground defenses had been inaccurate. That was normal as North Korea had made it extremely hard to get on-site intelligence of its military capability. The leader, Kim Lu Doc, had made it extremely hard for any outsider to visit North Korea and even the western press were scrutinized and followed at every step. The military kept tabs on everyone and directed were they could go and what they could see. Even the North Korea people, some loyal to the state, had their restrictions. Anthony couldn't fathom living under such conditions. The people were directed to work for government programs putting in long hours for little pay, some living under terrible conditions. He thought that someday the people would get tired of it, just as in the Soviet Union years ago, and rise up against their dictatorship-type of rule.

Anthony's concentration was broken as the Master Caution light on his panel lit up and sounded a warning. He reset it and checked his gauges. He was losing hydraulic pressure, probable because of a leak in the system. He pulled back on the yoke to climb to a safer altitude. At six thousand feet he leveled off, the controls beginning to be very difficult to move. He surveyed the ground below, mostly mountains and valleys. It would be tough to crash land, so he decided that when the time came he would bail out. The rescue choppers wouldn't be far behind and they had to take this route on the way back so they could pick him up. He had heard that they had picked up a pilot of a downed F/A-18 over the radio but wasn't sure who it was. He had hoped it was his wingman. Anthony was about twenty miles north of the North Korean city of *Kaesong* when his engine fire light came on as well as a whole lot of warning lights. He tried the extinguish the fire in the right engine but to no avail. Smoke began to enter the cockpit as Anthony pulled his legs close up to the seat. He reached up overhead and pulled the ejection handles down, starting the ejection sequence. The canopy blew off and the seat rocketed upwards as Anthony felt the cold blast of air on his body at over two hundred miles per hour. The seat continued upwards and turned as his damaged "Super Hornet" continued on without him. Anthony fell unconscious for what he thought was a long time but came to, looking up at the canopy above him. He looked around and could not see his aircraft but spied black smoke coming from the other side of a hill. He took a mental note of his position as seconds later he heard several *swippf, pluckt, swippf, pluckt* noises pass close to him. He looked up again at his canopy which had several holes in it. He was being shot at. He grabbed the control line handles and pulled, increasing the speed of his descent.

TWELVE

DECEPTION

THE PRESIDENT LANDED AT ANDREWS AIR Force Base at 1800 hours on the evening of August 21th. The Presidential helicopter, Marine One, was standing by and took him directly to the White House where he was reunited with his wife and family. It had been a long ordeal and one he would likely not forget. For the second time in less than fifty years the United States had been at the brink of nuclear war. If not for the technology of the United States many hundreds of thousands of Americans would have lost their lives in a flash of white blinding light. President Jackson had the courage and perseverance to stand-up to his staff and ordered them *not* to retaliate with nuclear weapons. The world, he thought, would be better off without them. As he sat alone in the oval office he thought of the new technology that had been presented to him. The directed-energy weapons that had been developed the last twenty years were a fast and effective way to deal with a potential threat. They had been used to neutralize a threat to the United States at no risk to military or civilian personnel. There probably would be those in the future that would say the weapons were unfair or inhumane but then again so was war and the people it affected. President Jackson decided that if he could use them to avert a war or potential threat he would do so. For right now anyway, the general public need not know about them.

The President awoke in his own bed in the White House at 0812 on the morning of August 22nd. The world had already started a new day and there was much more to do. The President went to his bath, shaved and showered and put on a clean suit that someone, most likely his first lady, had laid out. His wife said that a head of state should always look his best even when he's not. The President left his room and walked to the head of the stairs. He stopped for a second, checking himself in the mirror before he descended the stairs. This morning was no different. The White House staff was busy going here and there about their various tasks. The President walked to his private office and met Janice Lang who was busy re-copying some paperwork. "Good Morning, Mr. President" Janice said as the President walked in. "Good Morning, Janice. I hope you slept well?" the President replied. "A lot better than the last few nights, sir" she added. The President nodded as he picked up the morning briefs. "I see we lost some more pilots over there" the President said, regrettably. "Three confirmed dead but one still missing" Janice reported. "Mr. President we have the press conference you requested scheduled for twelve o'clock noon" Janice Lang said. "Thank you, Janice" replied the President as he opened the door to his Oval Office and entered. He sat down behind his desk and read the report from Admiral Grayson. The attack on the North Korean naval base at Nampo destroyed ninety percent of the shore facilities and destroyed or damaged all the naval vessels present. One U.S. Army Apache helicopter was shot down by heavy ground fire as were three

U.S. Navy F/A-18 "Super Hornets". One navy pilot was confirmed dead, as was the crew of two of the Apache. One Navy pilot was still missing, his aircraft going down twenty-five miles north of Kaesong, according to an U.S. Navy AWACS aircraft. The President sat back in his chair and wondered if the pilot's lives could have been spared if the he had ordered *Thor II* to destroy the base and naval vessels. It was the same question that he would address to Admiral Grayson.

Janice walked into the room as the President was finishing his brief on the Joint Strike Fighter attack on the railyard at Sepori. The President was pleased that several more ballistic missiles were destroyed but had concern about were they were coming from. Admiral Grayson arrived after Janice and had a briefcase full of material to be hashed out. "Good Morning Mr. President" Admiral Grayson said. "Good Morning, Jack" the President replied. Janice sat in front of the President while Admiral Grayson took the seat next to her. "We have a lot to discuss, Mr. President, not all of it pleasant" the Admiral explained. "By all means Jack, continue" The President said. "Mr. President I received the latest photos on the reconnaissance missions from Groom Lake" the Admiral said, carefully looking at Janice. The Admiral handed the photos to the President while keeping the numbered index sheet in front of him. "We have destroyed a large amount of mobile ballistic missile's and launchers the last few days. Our intelligence shows a large percentage of them are coming from the north, near Chongju. The one's we have discovered on the railways are no problem, we can take them out with air strikes. We have discovered that in the last eight hours the North Koreans are moving them by trailer truck" the Admiral reported. "In addition to that, if you'll look at picture number seven, Mr. President, it seems we now have proof that the Chinese are shipping missiles to the North

Koreans" the Admiral added. The President looked over his glasses at the Admiral and then at the pictures spread before him on his desk. The pictures shown a cargo vessel with missiles poorly camouflaged on the deck. The President took off his glasses as his phone buzzed. He picked it up and was told that the Chinese President was on the line. "Very well, No wait. Tell him I'm not available and Miss Lang can talk to him shortly. Keep him waiting but don't let him hang-up" the President explained looking at Janice Lang. The President hung up and explained to Janice that he need more time. She agreed and left the room to talk to the Chinese Premier. Once the door shut to the Oval Office the President began. "Jack, the attack on Nampo, could it have been accomplished by *Thor II* ?" the President asked. "Yes Mr. President. That is one of the missions it was designed to do" the Admiral said. "Mr. President, we have used *Thor II* for a lot lately. The energy the weapon uses is in direct proportion to the type of target we attack. At last report *Thor II* has sixty-seven percent fuel remaining. The hardened missile sites took the most energy. If we use it now against targets that could be destroyed by air attacks or cruise missiles the nation could be vulnerable during another missile attack. *Thor II* will be at eighty-five percent power by 1800 hours tonight. We can use it safely against the missiles or other hard targets at that time" Admiral Grayson explained. The President was glad that Jack was honest with him. He didn't always see eye to eye with him but they had one thing in common, protection of the United States and her people.

The President and Admiral Grayson continued to discuss the action against North Korea. Admiral Grayson has said that WNN had reported from Panmunjom that at 8:00 AM today that North Korean soldiers had put down a rebellion by several groups of North Korean civilians.

The civilians that attempted to protest against the war between North Korea, South Korea, Japan and the United States. Several civilians had been killed while others had been arrested. It was clear to President Jackson that a regime change was on the horizon. By now the news of the nuclear blast in *P'oha-ri* had reached every person in North Korea. They could blame it on only one person, President Kim Lu Doc.

Janice came in a few minutes later and said the Chinese President was getting impatient. The President told he would take it as Janice sat down. President Jackson picked up the phone and pushed a button. "President Ming, Good Morning" the American President said. "Good Morning to you, Mr. President. I am sorry to disturb you as you must have plenty to do considering the circumstances" the Chinese President replied. "Not at all, I'm never too busy to talk to a friend of the United States, what can I do for you?" President Jackson said as he winked at Janice. Janice Lang held her hand up to her mouth as is holding in a laugh. "Mr. President, this is a very delicate problem but one I think I should make you aware of. I have received many report of objects flying over our country" the Chinese President explained. "I see, what kind of objects are they?" President Jackson inquired. "I do not know, nor does any of my Generals" the Chinese President replied. "Where do the objects come from? Have you intercepted any of them?" President Jackson asked. "No we have not been able to for they are too fast and are far too high. We have not yet determined their origin. I hoped that you had some knowledge of them" the Chinese President said. "No, I have no knowledge of this but I will consult with my staff and check with our other agencies. I will let you know if we come up with something" President Jackson said, swinging back in forth in his chair and looking at the ceiling, trying to sound like he was interested. "Where exactly have the reports come from?" President Jackson inquired. "As I said before Mr. President this is of a delicate nature. They have been observed over some of our more sensitive areas" the Chinese President explained. "I think I understand, Mr. President. I will look into the matter fully. Since I have you on the phone Mr. President I must inform you that I am going to impose a fifty-mile exclusion zone around North Korea until our business with them is concluded" the American president said. "I see. That is most unfortunate. We have several humanitarian shipments on the way to North Korea. They must be allowed to pass" the Chinese President insisted. "I'm afraid I can't allow it right now. Besides it may only be for a short time. As you probable know, the Aircraft Carrier *Kitty Hawk* and her Strike Group are approaching the area to the west of the Korean peninsula to enforce the exclusion zone. I trust you will not interfere with the operation" President Jackson explained. "No, of course not Mr. President if that is your wish" said President Ming. "I would appreciate it Mr. President. We are all on edge here but I believe this business with North Korea will soon come to an end" President Jackson explained. "I have heard that your naval forces in the Yellow Sea are larger than we expected, you now have an operational aircraft carrier, Mr. President?" the American President asked. "Well, yes we have an aircraft carrier but it is still conducting training cruises" President Ming explained. "I see, then the training is coming along well if what my Admirals tell me is true" President Jackson said, looking at Admiral Grayson. "Things are proceeding as we have expected" the Chinese President said. "Very good then. I thank you for calling, President Ming. If I find out anything on the objects you described earlier I will call you" President Jackson said. "Thank you, Mr. President. I bid you a good day," the Chinese President said.

The President hung up and looked at Admiral Grayson. "He's a very polite individual. Too bad he's incredibly deceptive," the President said. The Admiral reminded the President of the press conference at the Pentagon at Noon. It was 10:37 as Marine One landed behind the White House. The President, Admiral Grayson and several Secret Service agents boarded the helicopter as two F-16 fighter jets screamed overhead, ready to escort the helicopter to the Pentagon. The helicopter landed at the Pentagon where more Secret Service and some Marine Corps Officers met the President. Once inside the President made the usual rounds to say hello before adjourning to the Admiral's Office. Once in the office the President settled into his favorite chair. One of the Admirals aides's, a Marine Colonel, came in after knocking once and handed the Admiral a computer printout. "Mr. President, I'm afraid we have more bad news. The last over-flight over China by the ATAV's shows what appear to be ballistic missiles on railcars headed to North Korea" the Admiral said, regrettable. "That's disturbing. When will the missiles get to North Korea?" the President asked. "Most likely by tomorrow morning, if our intelligence is correct" the Admiral replied. "Well, we can't go stomping all over China, we'd have this escalate into a World War" the President said. "I agree Mr. President," the Admiral said, sitting down behind his chair. "The bridges over the Yalu River are they intact?" asked the President. "Yes, Mr. President" replied the Admiral. "Well, we can't hit the trains in China but we sure as hell can slow them down. Blow up the bridges over the Yalu, Admiral" ordered the President. "Do we have any targets in Pyongyang that we need to hit" the President asked. "Yes we do. Until now we have sparred the quarters of Kim Lu Doc and his staff. We have heard nothing from them through electronic surveillance for two days. They may have went underground" The Admiral said as he picked up the phone and dialed the secure line to General Howard's office. He ordered an all-out attack on all the bridges across the Yalu River and the remaining targets of opportunity in and around the capital city of Pyongyang.

It was nearing the deadline for the press conference. The first one that President Jackson would give since the war began. There would be a lot of reporters from every network and newspaper imaginable. The President wasn't worried, for he had all his facts together, a great military staff to back up technical questions and he was very articulate and comfortable in front of a camera, the one thing that a successful president must be. The news conference started right on time at twelve o'clock noon. A Pentagon spokesman introduced the President as the other members of the Staff stood by, just out of camera. The President walked up to the podium and put down his notes.

"Good Morning, please be seated" the President said looking around the room. He began, looking directly into camera. "I'd like to take a few minutes to dispel some information about the operation against North Korea. The United States, South Korea or her allies are not interested in the conquest of North Korea. The actions of the preceding few days has been initiated by North Korea who launched nuclear ballistic missiles at the United States, Guam, Japan and South Korea. The United States Military dealt with that attack effectively and decisively. No nuclear missiles detonated on United States soil or that of our allies. The United States Congress, in an emergency session, declared war on North Korea for the unprovoked attack on the United States and her allies. The United States Military is conducting on-going operations to remove the threat of nuclear missiles and neutralize the threat imposed by the North Korean military"the President explained. The President paused for a moment, turning his notes, then began again. "I'd like to extend my thanks to every member of the military for their patriotism and duty to our great country. The men and women of the Army, Air Force, Navy and Marines have shown unbridled courage throughout this entire ordeal. Sadly, the war we have entered has not been without losses. As the press has already made you aware, we have lost the U.S.S. *McClusky*, a guided missile frigate, in the Sea of Japan to elements of the North Korean Air Force. The *McClusky* was part of the *Reagan* Strike Group, which was targeted by bombers from the North Korean Air Force. Many members on the *McClusky* were lost and the families of those lost have my deepest and sincere condolences". The President paused again for a second or two, cleared his throat and began again. "As of today we have lost an additional three pilots with one listed missing. The names of the pilots are being withheld until we can locate the next of kin. I am told that in an operation of this magnitude that it is inevitable to sustain some kind of losses. The United States has and always will pay for it's freedom with the blood of its citizens" the President added. The President shifted gears and tried to get everyone thinking about North Korea and the end of hostilities. "Since the attack on our country and that of our allies we have heard nothing from President Kim Lu Doc or members of the North Korean government. The fact that the North Koreans are continuing to attack South Korea has shown us that they are determined to continue what they have started. In response to this I have ordered an exclusion zone of all aircraft and shipping traffic extending fifty miles from the borders of North Korea until further notice. All shipping traffic entering this zone will be intercepted by the US Navy and turned away. All airborne traffic will be intercepted and turned away also. The exclusion zone will go into effect and be enforced immediately. The actions of the last few days have cost both sides in lives and material. To halt all further aggression by the United States and her allies I call on the leaders and people of North Korea to cease hostilities by laying down their arms and walking away from their weapons of war. Those that do so will not be harmed in any way and will be guaranteed fair and humane treatment under the Geneva Convention. The United States has renounced the use of nuclear weapons in this war and will continue to negotiate with

271

other countries to sign the Non-Proliferation of Nuclear Weapons treaties of the past. Those countries who do not agree to curb their efforts concerning nuclear weapons programs will be considered a threat to the United States and her allies and will be dealt with in an appropriate manner" the President explained. The President concluded his speech and motioned for the members of the military staff to approach. "I like at this time to open the press conference to questions from the members of the press" the President explained. The President stepped back to confer with Admiral Grayson and then faced the podium. "First question, yes" the President said pointing to the blonde woman in the second row who had her hand up. She stood up and addressed the President. "Candace Wells, United Press International. Mr. President, one of the major stories of the last few days has been the reports of nuclear explosions in North Korea and the Sea of Japan. You said earlier "The United States Military dealt with that attack effectively and decisively". Can you confirm the reports we are getting about the nuclear detonations?" the reporter asked. The President took a deep breath before he answered the question. "The reports of the nuclear detonations in North Korea and the Sea of Japan are factual" the President replied. "The facts are that they were armed warheads from the ballistic missiles that the North Koreans launched at the United States and her allies. The US Military intercepted the missiles in what is termed as the boost phase. One warhead came down in the Sea of Japan while one impacted and detonated on the coast of North Korea" the President explained. Immediately there was a commotion in room as reporters began conferring with each other. The reporter who asked the first question continued. "Mr. President, can you tell us how powerful the detonation was and have any casualties been reported from the area?" The President shifted back and conferred with Admiral Grayson and then back to the podium. "I am told that the size of the nuclear detonation was recorded as between sixty and seventy kilotons. We have received no reports from the area since the detonation. I would also like to add that I am deeply saddened by this event. Our retaliation on North Korea is and will be conventional in nature" the President explained. Another reporter had his hand up. The President hoped the question would be more directed towards the US military. The President pointed at the reporter as he stood up. "Thank you, Mr. President. John Sitarski, NBC News. Are there any plans to mount a rescue mission for the survivors of the detonation on the coast of North Korea" the reporter asked. "The US military is still engaged in offensive operations with North Korea. There are no reports of survivors in the area but once we do receive updated intelligence I do not discount a humanitarian mission to the area" the President replied. The President continued taking questions from the reporters for the next few minutes. The last few questions delved into sensitive areas that the President wished weren't addressed. The last reporter, Jacob Travis from WNN, asked the last few questions. The President motioned to Jacob who stood up. "Thank you Mr. President. Jacob Travis, World Network News. Mr. President, you have stated before that the United States will continue operations in North Korea with conventional weapons. We have reports from inside North Korea that the attacks on the North Korean missile silos and some of the airbases seem to have come from unconventional weapons, would you care to comment on that?" the reporter asked. The President wasn't caught off guard but couldn't fathom what sources the reporter could be referring to. "I'm not sure of your sources but the majority of the attacks have been accomplished by aircraft from the US Army, Navy and Air Force. Other attacks that have supported the aircraft strikes were by cruise missile strikes by US naval forces in the region" the President reported. The reporter clearly not satisfied with the Presidents answer, asked one follow up question. "Mr. President, do you deny the

United States has developed directed-energy weapons which are now in use by the US military" the reporter asked. The President smiled and looked across the room. "Jacob, as you may not be aware, we have directed-energy weapons in the region right now. In fact, these weapons defeated the first ballistic missile attack by the North Koreans. I believe, not so many days ago, Admiral Grayson already addressed that issue by referring the press to the Lockheed-Martin website. The design, testing and deployment of the AL-1A Airborne Laser has been pretty straightforward. So, in answer to your question, No, I do not deny the we have developed directed-energy weapons which are now in use by the US military" the President replied, smiling. The pressroom erupted in some quiet laughter from the reporter's peers. It was Travis' own fault. He was new and had only two other press conferences under his belt. Travis sat down, clearly humiliated. If he had phrased the question differently the President would have had a tougher time. While the existence of the Airborne Laser had been publicized in recent years, *Thor II* and the ATAV's have been hidden for years in the budgets of the Department of Agriculture and the Central Intelligence Agency. Billions of dollars have been appropriated each year and listed as "Special Programs" on each department's line item budget. Not only have the funding for the projects been hidden but the projects themselves have been highly classified and hidden away from the general public, the main reason for Groom Lake's existence. If such projects were ever discovered they could be compromised by an unfriendly administration. Indeed such programs in the past were canceled or severely cut, the B-1A bomber of the late 1970's being a prime example.

The press conference ended without incident. The President returned to the White House with his secret service escort while Admiral Grayson and General Howard returned to the Admiral' office. The Admiral entered and sat behind his desk, opened a drawer and offered the General a cigar while he sat down. "I really thought Ron was going to blow it, Admiral" General Howard said, lighting his cigar "I know. I had concerns myself. We're lucky the present administration is aligned with us, but then again, if we were compromised our present programs would still continue, regardless. Since the early sixties we realized we couldn't get anything done if we changed horses in mid-stream. A lot of forethought and funding has gone into these programs and we can't allow them to be canceled by an unsympathetic administration" the Admiral said, leaning back and puffing on his cigar. "I've been in the Air Force for twenty-seven years and have only realized the last ten that it doesn't really matter who we vote for" General Howard replied. "Well, not in these terms but it's better to have a President who is on our side. I don't know about you, but Ron has my vote this November" the Admiral said. "Oh, sure. I didn't mean to imply I didn't vote, Admiral. Considering who's running against him we all would be better off with President Jackson. I just don't trust a candidate that wasn't in our special group" the General explained. "I agree. This election will be a great victory as far as we're concerned" Admiral Grayson replied. The two men continued talking for the next hour, secure in the fact that their careers were locked in for the next four years.

Captain Billings was in the Control Room when the radio officer advised him of a message. "Conn, Radio. We're getting traffic on the ELF" the radio officer reported. The Captain picked up the mike and replied in the affirmative. Cruising at seven knots one hundred feet below the surface the Extremely Low Frequency radio picked up the satellite message from COMSUBPAC. The Ensign from the radio room went to the Control Room immediately and handed the Captain the message, who read it at once. The Captain ordered the Officer-of-the-

Deck to make his depth sixty feet and reduce speed to four knots. The OOD relayed the commands to his enlisted crew and the submarine began to rise. The Executive Officer, "Teddy" Brown, came to the control room to consult with the Captain. "Teddy, looks like we're going to have company" the Captain said, handing the message to his XO. Commander Brown read the message.

> TO USS TOPEKA FROM COMSUBPAC. PREPARE AND RECEIVE SEAL TEAM SIX AT YOUR LOCATION. PROCEED AT BEST SPEED TO NK COAST SW OF P'OHA-RI AFTER SEAL TEAM ARRIVES. SEAL TEAM WILL DISEMBARK NLT 2400 HRS TO RECON   P'OHA-RI. RETURN TO BASE AFTER SEAL TEAM DISEMBARKS. SEAL TEAM SIX WILL BE RECOVERED BY USS PASADENA. END OF MESSAGE.

The Captain didn't envy the SEAL teams. They went in alone and had to get out alone. This mission they probably had been ordered to check for survivors from the nuclear detonation and check the area for contamination and damage. The area still had to be "hot" so the team would have to arrive with tons of radiation protective equipment. The Captain ordered the mast raised and peered through it to the south. He looked at his watch, which said 1730 hours. They better hurry if they want dinner, he thought. He studied several seagulls on the horizon before he spied the MH-60 come into view. Once the helicopter reached two miles the Captain ordered all forward motion stopped and for the OOD to surface the ship. The Topeka's low-pressure blower and trim tanks blew copious amounts of water from the ballast tanks allowing the submarine to come to her surfaced waterline. The Captain ordered the aft compartments to prepare for personnel. Several seamen in life vests emerged from the forward escape trunk aft of the sail onto the wet deck. Hooking up several safety lines the crewman waited for the approaching helicopter to transfer into a hover. Several safety lines, three per side, came down from the helicopter. Before the last rope hit the deck the SEAL team members and their equipment were sliding down the safety lines to the submarines deck. The submarine crewmembers helped the team fit their gear through the forward escape trunk hatch and then climbed down inside the submarine. With the SEAL team aboard, the MH-60 helicopter sped away to land on the JMSDF *Takanami* to refuel.

Once the Captain received word that the SEAL team was aboard and the ship was secure he ordered the OOD to submerge the ship, dive to eight hundred feet and increase speed to twenty knots. Minutes later, satisfied with the dive, the Captain then ordered a new course straight towards P'oha-ri. They had to hurry if they wanted to get there at midnight. The Captain left the bridge and went to the messroom one deck below the Control Room to greet his guests. The messroom was quickly converted to accommodate the SEAL team and their equipment. The tables were strewn with equipment, weapons and maps when the Captain arrived. The SEAL team leader, Lt. Commander Randall Lowe, saw the Captain enter and quickly called his team to attention. "At ease guys, you must be exhausted" the Captain said. "Thank you, sir. We all could use a little sleep" replied Commander Lowe. "Captain, I'd like to introduce my team. I'm Lieutenant Commander Randall Lowe, this is Lieutenant Chase McGovern, Lieutenant William Bickford, Lieutenant Jaeger Fursthower, and Lieutenant Duncan Lepore" Commander Lowe said introducing each member to the Captain. The Captain shook each man's hand firmly. "We'll be near your drop off point in less than six hours, Commander. You have exclusive use of the messroom until then, order anything you like, sleep when you like. No one will disturb you. If you need anything else just ask one of the Ensigns on the boat" the Captain explained. "Thank you Sir, we appreciate the lift and your hospitality" replied Commander Lowe. "Before I leave you Commander I'd like to get a better idea where exactly you need to go" the Captain said. "No problem" Commander Lowe said as he stepped to one of the mess tables. The table was covered with topographical maps of North Korea, China and even Russia to the north. The Captain saw dozens of maps that showed the wind and sea currents in the area as well as tide and weather information from the NOAA for the next week. "Captain, here is P'oha-ri and I'd like to be dropped off here, six miles west of it and about eight miles off shore" said Commander Lowe. "We can get you closer if you like, looks like the depth there is in the low hundreds" replied the Captain. "I know, but we've been advised that the NK Army may have units in the area. I don't want to arouse their suspicions if we can help it. That's not what we're here for" Commander Lowe explained. "If I may ask Commander, what exactly is your mission?" the Captain inquired. "Well, not getting too specific, We have been ordered to go ashore and assess damage from the nuclear detonation and if possible get any and all accounts of the damage from the indigenous population" replied Commander Lowe. "I see Commander. I'll tell you, I don't envy your task" the Captain said. "We'll be ashore by 0130 hours. En-route to shore we'll be monitoring the air for radiation. Once we find it we'll have to complete the rest of our mission in these NBC suits we brought along" Commander Lowe explained, showing the Captain the protective suits. The Captain was familiar with the Nuclear, Biological and Chemical suits that the SEAL team was issued. He had worn them many times during survival training and knew they became hot and uncomfortable in a short time. With the suit on and the mask in place you could drink fluid through straw but in a nuclear environment all you would be doing is sweating. "If we're lucky enough to find any survivors we are to interview them about the accounts before and after the detonation" Commander Lowe explained. "You speak Korean then?" the Captain asked. "No sir, I don't. Our linguist on this mission is Lieutenant Jaeger Fursthower. He is fluent in German, Korean and Chinese" Commander Lowe explained as Lieutenant Fursthower approached the Captain. Lieutenant Fursthower was a very tall, square-jawed man probably of European descent. "Captain, I am pleased to be in your presence. Your reputation precedes you" replied Lieutenant Fursthower who then proceeded to repeat himself in German, Korean and then Chinese. As he finished the greeting in Chinese, the Lieutenant bowed deeply to the Captain, showing his total respect towards the Commanding Officer. "I'm impressed, Lieutenant. Where did you study your languages?" the Captain asked. "I learned the language of my ancestors in my fathers home. It was necessary so that I could communicate with my fathers parents" the Lieutenant said with a slight German accent. "My father was married to a Chinese woman after my mother died when I was young and she is credited with igniting my desire to learn language. She had helped me to understand not only the language but the culture as well. I have completed most of my studies in college at Berkeley in Southern California" Lieutenant Fursthower explained. "I'm very impressed, Lieutenant. I hope you continue you passion if you decide to leave the Navy. The State Department could use a good man like you" the Captain said. The Lieutenant thanked the Captain for his kind words. After a few minutes of talking and some subtle joking around, the Captain excused himself to let the team get some rest.

On his way to the Control room the Captain stopped by the officers wardroom and told the officers present that the SEAL team was going to lights out in five minutes and to not have them disturbed. All the officers acknowledged and the Captain left and returned to the Control room. The OOD announced the Captains arrival on the bridge as the sonar officer broke over the 1MC. "Conn, sonar. We have contact on bearing 027 at about 53,000 yards" replied the sonar officer. The Captain nodded to the OOD as he picked up the 1MC mike. "Conn, aye" replied the Captain. He was amazed that the sonaroom picked up the contact. These kids were good. The *Topeka* was at eight hundred feet going twenty knots and they detected a contact at over twenty-five miles. All in all he didn't want them to get sloppy. "Sonar, conn. This is the Captain. Do you have a type and class or do I need to come forward?" the Captain asked sarcastically, looking at his Executive Officer. Lieutenant Commander "Teddy" Brown just smirked and turned away, not letting the crew see his reaction. "No sir, not yet but we are working the contact" insisted the sonar officer. "Conn, aye. Wake me when you do!" the Captain replied, shooting a glance at his XO who seemed to be holding back a laugh. Minutes later the excited Ensign came on. "Conn, sonar. The contact has been classified as a *Hainan* patrol boat. It is making eighteen knots on heading 180" the Ensign reported. "Conn, aye. Good work" the Captain acknowledged. The sonar crew had done a great job. Now it was the Captain's job to get them past the patrol boat and to the North Korean coast. He could easily engage the *Hainan* and blow it out of the water but that would alert any other North Korean units nearby and would compromise the SEAL team mission. Besides, he didn't even know what country the *Hainan* belonged to. Both the Chinese and North Korean governments had *Hainan* patrol boats in their navies. It probably was North Korean but without being classified as hostile the Captain decided to stealthily pass it by.

THIRTEEN

BATTLE OF KANSONG

SERGEANT VIC WHEELER HAD BEEN IN South Korea for nearly seven months. His unit, the 1ˢᵗ Armored Division, had been deployed for training with the ROK units when the war broke out. As a tank commander of an Abrams M1 main battle tank, Sergeant Wheeler had gotten used to these deployments the last few years since being pulled out of Germany. The fact that the US had moved from a garrison force to a rotational force in 2005, and not the declining political atmosphere of northern Europe, was cited as the criteria for the move from Germany. When hostilities began on August 18ᵗʰ his unit began to move towards the East Coast of Korea to block any armored thrust by the North Korean Army. Sergeant Wheeler had been in the US Army for seven years. It had been a hard life, but had its rewards. He was scheduled to be up for re-enlistment next fall and right now he couldn't decide what to do. All he knew was he had a girl waiting for him on his return to the US, a girl that didn't want to be married to a soldier.

Sergeant Wheeler had ten other tanks in his company, all M1A1 Abrams with the 120mm main cannon. He and his crew had become proficient with the Abrams, not only in the weapon trainers but in the California desert as well. The training in California was realistic in that the Army had "acquired" several Soviet armored tanks and vehicles to use in dissimilar combat training. The crews that "opposed" them during training were seasoned veterans of the US Army, some with combat experience during the first Gulf War. Sergeant Wheeler had learned to respect the capabilities of the newer Soviet tanks, particularly the T-62. With a 115mm main gun and firing the same type of ammunition as other tanks, the T-62 was a formidable opponent even without a seasoned crew. One hit from the high-velocity 115mm main gun loaded with armor-piercing ammunition would spell disaster for most tanks, even the Abrams if it was in the right place.

The fastest way from Camp Casey was to go east on the road from Seoul to Kansong. If the highway was left undefended then the whole North Korean Army could proceed directly to Pusan in eight hours. By proceeding to Kansong first, Sergeant Wheeler hoped to engage the North Koreans close to the DMZ where the AH-64 Apaches could support the armored units. The Apaches', or any air support for that matter, was a welcome sight when engaging a large opposing force. The road to Kansong was dirty and dusty, which is why Sergeant Wheeler decided to remain buttoned up in the tank. He could see most of the outside from his position and the driver could see the road to navigate. Once arriving at Kansong the Company Commander received word that the US Navy had lost one of it's guided missile frigates off the coast of South Korea by North Korean Air Force Bombers. He also heard that AH-64 Apaches from Camp Lewis had engaged several North Korean armored columns. A thought went through Sergeant Wheeler's head that maybe they were in the wrong place, after all there were three major approaches that the North Koreans were expected to use to drive into the Republic of Korea. The Kaesong-Munsan approach near the west coast, the Chorwon Valley north east of Seoul and the East Coast approach where Sergeant Wheeler's armored column was located. It was surmised that the North Koreans wanted to capture the port of Pusan, as they had done several years ago in the 1950's. Pusan was one of South Korea's deep-water ports and vital to the security and economy of the Republic of Korea.

Once the column had reached Kansong it was obvious that no enemy units had came through. The residents of the city talked to the ROK soldiers in the column, which rode in the Bradley fighting vehicles. The arrival of the US-ROK armored column came as no surprise to officials of the city. They had seen the armored columns many times as they practiced during their deployments in previous months. Sergeant Wheeler observed the conversation between the ROK soldiers and the city officials. At times it became heated and when it was done the city officials seemed to leave with a panicked look on their face. The same kind of look most people had when told that the North Koreans had launched a nuclear attack on South Korea. The M1A1 was capable of fighting in a nuclear and chemical environment but only for short periods. Sergeant Wheeler had trained for such tasks but hoped, as everyone did, that it would never come. Crews were also required to wear the NBC suits while inside their armored fighting vehicles, even though the vehicles were supposed to protect them from radiation and chemicals.

Encumbered by the suits, the efficiency of the crews dropped, sometimes to unacceptable levels. The Unit Commander's however accepted this, knowing full well that the efficiency of the enemy crews would be far below that of their own. Sergeant Wheeler talked to his Company Commander from his vehicle. The Commander told him that the people of the city were unaware of the hostilities that started earlier. The ROK Officer in charge told them to find a safe haven as the North Koreans may be coming. Within minutes the tempo of the city changed as people came out of no where. Some fled down the same road that the US-ROK column had come while most of the others went south towards Kangnung. Still some others, mostly elderly, stayed put. They had seen this before. The North Koreans had invaded the south years ago and had been pushed back to where they were today. They weren't afraid, some even had relatives in the north, which they hadn't seen in over forty years.

Two OH-58D observation helicopters loaded with rocket ordnance approached and raced ahead over Sergeant Wheeler column, headed due north. Minutes later a flight of AH-64 Apache' flew past, heavily loaded with ordnance. The area north of Kansong was a great place for a tank battle. Close to the coast, with little place to hide, the North Koreans would have to fight vigorously if they intended to survive. Sergeant Wheeler wasn't worried. With the *Reagan* offshore and the Apaches located at Camp Stanley, they would have superiority in the air as well as ground support. Still, Wheeler kept thinking that they might be in the wrong place. He kept himself and his crew busy, doing targeting drills while they traveled up the coast. The crew reacted quickly, rotating the turret to each target in seconds. Wheeler was satisfied with his impromptu training session. He was doing a check of the laser range finder when he heard the Company Commander say something unintelligible over the radio. Adjusting his headset he heard the Commander say that the OH-58D's had made contact with "a large force". The crew was silent as they strained to hear more information. Wheeler reached for his handbook of radio frequencies. Maybe he could hear for himself first hand. He found the frequency quite by accident and listened.

The crews of the two OH-58D's had indeed found a large force. Less than ten miles from them were no less than twenty-four main battle tanks, twenty armored personnel carriers with anti-tank missiles and several, towed AAA guns. At the front of the column were eight World War II-vintage, Soviet T-34/85 medium tanks along with four Type 85 ATGM carriers. The first priority of the OH-58D's was to advise the Apaches of the AAA threat, which was quickly dispatched by several Hellfire missiles. The Anti-Tank Guided Missile carriers were next. The ATGM carriers were a great threat to the M1A1 Abrams. The missiles could reach farther than the Abrams could shoot therefore they had to be destroyed quickly, which they were. The ATGM carriers were essentially thin-skinned armored personnel carriers with missile rails mount on top. The Apache' 30mm chain gun made short work of them, exploding its gas tanks along with some missiles and turning the vehicles into rolling, flaming hulks. The small, light OH-58D's kept the units in the rear area busy with 2.75 inch rocket fire, destroying several BTR-60 personnel carriers and command vehicles, while the Apache's concentrated on the main attack force.

The Apache's used their 30mm guns with ruthless efficiency, shooting at targets on each side as the helicopters swooped in, the gunners sluing the guns left and right with their helmet-mounted cuing systems. Half a dozen or more BTR-60 armored personnel carriers were torched along with four T-34/85 medium tanks. The remaining BTR-60's were wasting no time in firing their 14.5mm machine guns at the approaching Apache helicopters. Several rounds hit one Apache but nothing happened. The Apache responded by firing a Hellfire at the BTR-60, which exploded spectacularly. The pilot banked the helicopter over to the right as two other BTR-60's got the range and opened fire. One shot low while the rounds from the other found their target. Seventeen rounds of 14.5mm slugs tore into the tail boom ripping apart ring frames and stringers. One round found the bevel drive intermediate gearbox, destroying it. The Apache pilot got a tail rotor warning immediately and tried to right the banking helicopter. With the tail rotor thrust quickly diminishing the pilot struggled to bring the Apache down safely now only sixty feet above the ground. The spinning Apache became an inviting target as more 14.5mm rounds from the BTR's and 12.7mm rounds from the medium tanks found their way to the helicopter, destroying the 30mm gun, the turret sensors and gunner.

The pilot, realizing this was the end, chopped his power and let the Apache settle to the ground, fifty feet below. The Apache helicopter hit hard and rolled on its port side, collapsing its wing pylon as the main rotors chewed into the ground and disintegrated, sending up dirt and rock. The engine caught on fire as broken fuel lines sprayed onto hot engine surfaces. As the flames spread, several BTR-60's made their way to the helicopter to check for signs of life. The one closest to the downed Apache exploded the apparent victim of a Hellfire missile. Several North Korean soldiers were seen running and on fire trying to escape their own demise. The pilot of the downed Apache, Captain Jim Doran, awoke to a burning aircraft and helicopters flying overhead. He unbuckled his harness and tried to pull himself out but realized his legs didn't work. With two good arms he climbed out of his burning and crippled helicopter. Once on the ground Captain Doran looked back at his gunner. Several large holes were evident in the forward canopy, as was the lifeless torso of his gunner. The forward section of the helicopter had borne the brunt of the anti-aircraft fire, killing one of his best friends. Captain Doran tried crawling away but every second seemed an eternity next to the burning helicopter. When he thought it was about over, a force seemed to pick him up as he lapsed into unconsciousness.

The BTR-60 driver drove right up next to the burning Apache as he saw the pilot attempt to crawl out. The vehicle commander ordered two soldiers out of the vehicle to recover the prisoner while the gunner engaged the remaining helicopters. The Apaches seeing that one of their own was alive backed off out of range and advised that he would be taken aboard one the remaining BTR-60 at the front of the column. No one wanted to think about what would happen to him. All thoughts were on the remaining enemy battle tanks below. With Captain Doran's Apache shot down the remaining flight was at a disadvantage. Doran's Apache carried at least six live Hellfire missiles. The flight leader of the remaining Apaches ordered the gunners to shoot at only the T-62 tanks and try to thin out as many as possible. As each pilot maneuvered his AH-64 above the North Korean armored column, the gunners designated one then another T-62 tank with a laser. Each Hellfire homed in on the laser beacon, penetrated and exploded into the turret of the tank. Stored ammunition burned and exploded, sending tracers across the landscape. The Apache flight, minus one, with its stores depleted, headed for base to refuel and rearm. The Apache flight did a splendid job. Of the sixteen T-62 medium tanks only five remained.

As the Apaches flew overhead Sergeant Wheeler switched his frequency back and heard his Company Commander call for air support from the Navy, Air Force or who ever was listening. In an ever-increasing tone the Commander pleaded with the airborne combat controller who was safe and high above the carnage below. The North Korean column had been held up, fighting for its life, as the US-ROK column advanced towards them. In a good position, Sergeant Wheeler sighted the first tank, a T-34/85 come rolling over a slight rise at close to forty miles per hour. The Abrams gunner already had the gun on target when the laser rangefinder read 1820 meters. Sergeant Wheeler ordered the weapon fired and the tank lurched, sending the armor-piercing round down range. The round struck the turret of the tank from over a mile away, shearing it completely off. The body of the tank continued on and slowed, the fuel tanks finally catching fire and exploding. Not dwelling on success, the crew targeted the next T-34/85 tank, which was quickly closing in to its effective range of nine hundred meters. At 1237 meters the next T-34/85 tank exploded, the armor piercing saboted round destroying the tank and all those inside. Seconds after the round impacted the turret blew up from the stored ammunition inside. The Abrams to Sergeant Wheeler's right scored two kills on T-34's and one on a T-55 that had fired and missed his vehicle. The T-55's were now well within range and closely followed by the larger T-62's. All at once things seemed to go bad. Three Abrams were hit and hit hard. Sergeant Wheeler could see two Abrams burning and one not moving, its main gun destroyed, from his position. He ordered a left turn and full speed as the main gun swivelled to right to engage the enemy tanks while running at full speed. Sergeant Wheeler called out a T-62 to the gunner and fired the laser rangefinder. It read 1753 meters. The gun fired and the saboted round caught the T-62 square, penetrating into the frontal armor and driving into the engine compartment.

The T-62 exploded and soon was a hot cauldron of fire. The Abrams driver shifted position slightly and continued the charge at the front of the North Korean line as a T-55, which was disabled, fired at the passing Abrams. The round grazed the Abrams turret and exploded, sending the turret crew to the floor of the tank. Finding that everyone was okay the crew jumped back into action and swung the main gun back to the disabled T-55 and sent a 120mm HEAP round into it at point blank range. The T-55 exploded and jumped about a foot, before another explosion sent the turret spinning off. The T-62's had the Abrams in range but what was worse they had the Bradley vehicles in range also. Three of the Bradley's commenced a short run across the plains at top speed but couldn't outrun the stabilized 115mm main guns of the T-62's. The high-explosive rounds blew large gaping holes in the thin-skinned Bradley's killing several squads of ROK soldiers. Two more

Abrams were hit and burning as Sergeant Wheeler had the last T-55 in his sights. The big 120mm gun of the Abrams fired a HEAT round into the side of the unsuspecting North Korean medium tank. The T-55 opened up like a soup can as the turret exploded. Sergeant Wheeler heard someone report that two other Abrams were hit and on fire along with another Bradley. Down to four Abrams Wheeler remembered thinking at least things were even now. The Abrams lurched one way then another, the driver trying to throw off the aim of the North Koreans. Wheeler sighted a T-62 running straight away and tried for a kill. As the 120mm gun of the Abrams gun settled on target, the T-62 erupted in fire and shrapnel. Dust enshrouded the destroyed North Korean tank as Wheeler heard the familiar "WWHHHAAAA"sound above his tank turret. He ordered the driver to continue evasive driving while peering through his cupola periscope. Out of his periscope he saw two other T-62's go up in flames as dark shadows soon passed over them. Years of training in the desert of southern California had seasoned the tank crews of Charlie Company. Sergeant Wheeler was intimately familiar with the sound of an angry 30mm GAU-8 cannon when the Air Force A-10's flew over firing at the mock enemy forces.

The four A-10's from Osan AB arrived right on time. Armed with their 30mm cannon and a light load of Maverick missiles, the pilots extracted victory from the hands of the North Koreans. The A-10 flight leader was advised by the airborne combat controller not to engage any BTR-60 vehicles as a friendly was taken prisoner and was inside. The lead A-10 pilot complied and flew back and forth over the battlefield looking for more targets. The remaining Abrams and Bradley's regrouped and pressed North to try to locate the BTR-60 that had taken the Apache pilot prisoner. The A-10's located the last of the North Korean armored vehicles, all parked together and at least twenty soldiers waving white flags. The North Koreans wisely had enough, besides this war wasn't of their making. The Senior Officer approached the front of the group as a Bradley vehicle came close by, covered by several other Bradley's and three Abrams main battle tanks. The North Koreans were rounded up by the ROK soldiers, searched and stripped of their weapons. The ROK soldiers were professionals in every respect, for they had to be, given the alternative. Searching the BTR-60 vehicles the ROK soldiers found an unconscious US Army Officer. When the soldier found him he yelled for the Officer-in-Charge, who came running along with several other soldiers and a stretcher. Captain Jim Doran had numerous injuries including a broken back, two broken legs and a collapsed lung. He was in critical condition when the rescue helicopter arrived. The MEDEVAC-configured UH-60 landed and went to idle while the combat medical technician stabilized the injured Captain. Quickly loaded on the UH-60, the Captain was evacuated to the hospital at Seoul.

The Battle of Kansong was won by the joint US-ROK units but at a terrible cost. Six Abrams main battle tanks were destroyed along with twenty-four of their seasoned crewmembers. The Charlie Company Commander and its crew were killed when a 115mm round from a T-62 tank hit his Bradley fighting vehicle. Three other Bradley's were similarly destroyed with a loss of thirty-two ROK soldiers. Sergeant Wheeler, the ranking Non-Commissioned Officer, had taken temporary charge of Charlie Company. Charlie Company was told to transfer the prisoners to the ROK who would then transport them to Seoul. Sergeant Wheeler and what remained of his company were to proceed back to Kansong to rearm, rest and await reinforcements. The Air Force and Navy seemed to have a handle on things, at least for the time being. It was the start of a long costly war. Today was the deciding factor for Vic Wheeler. Next year he had planned to become a civilian again.

The SEAL team commander awoke at 2207 hours, his watch alarm vibrating on his wrist. The rest of his team was still sleeping for they hadn't had rest since twenty-seven hours earlier in Pearl. SEAL Team Six was hurried from the US West Coast to North Korea with a very important mission in mind. The nuclear detonation at P'oha-ri was of concern to the US government and other agencies, including the CIA. The United States wished to get first hand knowledge on the damage the North Korean nuclear weapon delivered so it could be presented to the United Nations Security Council. First hand accounts from the North Koreans was what the US was looking for, that was if the SEAL team could find any survivors. The interviews would be recorded by scrambled satellite transmission and downloaded by *Thor II* directly to the CIA.

The other nations of the world chastised the United States when it decided to go it alone in Iraq in 2003. Now the world would be shown how ineffective the United Nations sanctions really were. North Korea had been building up their nuclear program for years through at least three US Presidential administrations. North Korean President Kim Lu Doc had continued his father's work despite pressure from the six-party coalition and other nearby nations. The United States did not allow his work to go unnoticed however, publicizing his build up in the media. Nor did the United States just sit back and let his work proceed without going unchecked. The *Thor II* program was a great breakthrough for the United States, even though some sensitive information was leaked to high-level officials in Russia. Considering Russia's long-time relationship with North Korea it was a good bet that President Kim Lu Doc knew also, which didn't seem to deter his clandestine nuclear activities.

Several more *Thor II* satellites were in production and scheduled to be launched one per year until full global coverage was achieved. The present satellite, orbiting the Northern Hemisphere, was launched so it would give unlimited strategic capability over North Korea, China and Russia where the most serious threat from nuclear ballistic missiles were located. By re-tasking and re-positioning the satellite it could also reach targets near the equator such as Iran and the Middle East, but these countries were considered to be a lesser threat, considering Iran was five years or more from fielding a missile threat against the United States.

Commander Lowe got up and started waking his team members. "Equipment check in twenty minutes" he ordered, the lights going on when he spoke. The men milled about checking the equipment, while the smell of steak, eggs and pastries filled the air. Besides the dry sleeping accommodation's Lowe and his team always looked forward to meals on the Navy's attack submarines. Completing the equipment check the men went to the galley and grabbed trays for what would probably be their last warm, fresh meal in a while. The Officers returned to the mess room and sat on the floor, facing each other in a circle. Mealtime was an important time to the members of the team where each man talked and joked about everything but the mission. Personal bonds were strengthened, while each man learned something else new about his team member's.

The Executive Officer, Lt. Commander "Teddy" Brown, entered the room while the team was eating. "Please stay seated guys, don't get up" Teddy said. "Thank you, Commander" replied Commander Lowe. "I just wanted to let you know we are near the drop off point. When ever your ready, let me know and we can come shallow" replied the Commander Brown. Commander Lowe stood up, looking at his watch and told the Executive Officer of the *Topeka* that they would like to shove off by 2355 hours. The XO left the SEAL team and went to the control room to make the necessary preparations. The Officers of the SEAL team dressed, gathered their equipment and headed for the Aft Escape Hatch where they entered the submarine. Each man carried about eighty pounds of equipment plus his weapon and ammunition. The team carried a small inflatable boat with motor that would carry them to the shore of North Korea. Once ashore, the team would be on their own. The speaker by the Aft Escape Hatch crackled and the OOD announced the submarine was coming shallow. When the keel of the submarine was at thirty feet the OOD announced it was safe to embark. Lieutenant Fursthower, the largest of the team, climbed the ladder after one of the submarine rescue specialists, who opened the main hatch to the outside. The team proceeded up the ladder and pulled their inflatable boat to the wet deck of the submarine. While the equipment was still coming up the boat was inflated and the motor installed. The SEAL team stored its equipment in the boat as the submarine crewman got a thumb's up from the SEAL team leader. The crewman gave him a sharp salute that was returned and he disappeared into the submarine, closing and locking the hatch. From the control room the Captain had a clear view of the SEAL team from his search periscope. He ordered the OOD to submerge the boat slowly. The submarine hull dropped away from the SEAL team until they were floating upon the Sea of Japan. The Captain followed the SEAL team for the first hundred yards in the periscope until they were clear before he ordered the OOD to make his depth two hundred feet and plot a course to Pearl harbor. "Good luck, guys" the Captain said, as he ordered the periscope lowered and stowed. Indeed, the SEAL team would need every bit of luck available.

The SEAL team approached the coast of North Korea, now about two miles distant according to the night vision goggles, the internal laser rangefinder counting down the yards from the landing zone. The 10-horsepower Honda Marine motor silently propelled them forward while each SEAL team member huddled low in the boat, their weapons at the ready. Commander Lowe looked down the coast to his right where the city of P'oha-ri was to be found, about eight miles away. The area was still "hot" and would be for many years to come. He was doubtful the team would find any one living, and if they did they wouldn't be alive for long. The beach loomed up ahead. The team powered the boat right up though the surf and jumped out, hoisting the boat over their shoulders and continuing up the beach toward the natural cover. Lowe looked at his watch. They had hit the beach at 0053 hours on August 19th. The rest of the team stowed the boat while Commander Lowe and Lt. McGovern reconnoitered the area around the landing. The tide was beginning to come in which was good, it would hide any tell tale signs of activity on the beach. Returning to the team Commander Lowe was informed than the area had minimal traces of radiation. That was as Lowe expected, as most of the fallout from the explosion went southeast. Lowe and McGovern found a small cave about a half a click away during the reconnoiter that could store most of the gear from the elements. The electronic gear was vital to their mission and had to be protected. The rain was coming down in sheets by the time the team reached the cave. It was typical, Lowe had been rained on at some point in every mission he had been on in the last six years.

The light rain made life miserable but it gave one comfort, it gave the team cover as they approached the city. Commander Lowe was navigating by his GPS when Lieutenant Lepore advised him of rising radiation levels. The team backed off to a safe distance and put on their NBC suits. The suits were covered with night camouflage to throw off infrared sensors and the enemy's night vision. Once again the team advanced to the high ground west of the city. From about six miles away at his raised advantage point Lowe looked through his night vision goggles to see most of the city in ruins, some structures still on fire or smoldering. He could see no sign of life in or around the city. The coastal town, probably unaware, went about their business that fateful morning. Predominantly a fishing village, P'oha-ri had dozens of fishing boats which were used to provide sustenance to the residents and the surrounding area. The first indication the people must have had was the bright, blinding flash of the nuclear detonation.

Commander Lowe scanned down to the coast and saw several destroyed fishing vessels. According to the intelligence gathered from the reconnaissance flights ground zero was North of the city near the base of where the mountainous terrain started. Photos had shown that there were small settlements on the south and north side of the mountains and another one close to where Lowe's team was now. After checking the map Commander Lowe motioned to his team to head out north. The team had gone about eight hundred yards when they came across the first structure. Partially collapsed and smoldering, the structure was poorly constructed. Lowe switched the goggles to the infrared mode and got two reading's which were close to the structure, one which was moving. Through hand signals Lowe ordered his team to fan out and approach the contact. This was the first real contact and it was unknown whether it was hostile or not. It had been less than two days since the detonation so whoever remained most likely was a civilian, however Lowe did not discount the fact that it may be a North Korean national loyal to the DPRK. The North Korean military was being kept very busy and probably couldn't get here to investigate the damage. That was fine with Lowe, they would be here only forty-eight hours and then be picked up by the USS *Pasadena*. He needed to complete his mission and then retreat back to the landing zone, out of the radiation zone.

While Lepore and Fursthower covered their advance, Lowe, McGovern and Bickford advanced towards the contact. As Lowe drew closer he pulled the silenced MP-5 closer to his shoulder. He could make out the figure of a man in the darkness through the rain not less than ten yards ahead of him. An older man, about sixty years of age, he stopped and turned towards Bickford who crouched and froze, his weapon at the ready. McGovern, who was to the left of Lowe continued towards the man slowly and approached within twelve feet. The man, who must have sensed someone, spoke out loud as he raised his hand up to his waist with his palm down. McGovern could see the man clearer now, his face a deep scarlet red which seemed to be on fire. The man was wearing no shirt, or at least did not appear as such at first. The left side of his torso appeared to be burned horrible and the skin hung off his left arm loosely. He did not act as if he was in a pain and took a few steps away from McGovern. He was unarmed so Lowe ordered Fursthower to make contact. Fursthower approached and slung his MP-5 over his shoulder. The North Korean man stopped, turned again and spoke. Fursthower approached the man and spoke in Korean. He told the man that he would not be harmed. The man asked for help while holding Fursthower as tight as he could. Fursthower realized the man was blind, most likely from the light of the detonation. The man sat down at Fursthower's feet and began to cry. McGovern and Bickford went to the structure where the man seemed to have come from. Inside they found an older woman, probably the man's wife, in worse shape than the old man. She had burns over about eighty percent of her body and seemed to have difficulty breathing. McGovern slung his MP-5 and gave a quick assessment of her condition. Several cuts were on her arms and legs, a few of which appeared to be infected. She was coherent but didn't move as he kneeled next to her. She tried to raise her hand but couldn't, McGovern taking her hand in his gloved hand. The woman seemed to have her vision but was very weak. Judging from her wounds, McGovern was glad he was protected in his suit, the canister mask filtering out any airborne contaminants.

Jaeger Fursthower talked to the old man as he took the recorder out of his backpack. He checked the battery and started the recorder. He asked the old man if he would allow him to record their conversation. The old man agreed, not knowing why anyone would care to hear what he had to say. Fursthower asked the man's name and told him to tell him what happened the morning of the detonation. The man acknowledged he understood and began. The old man said he awoke at dawn, feeling good about the day ahead. He was a fisherman by trade and had two sons and a daughter by his second wife. The Communist Chinese, during the Korean War, had killed his first wife in 1954. He left his home area of Hungnam and retreated up the coast and settled at P'oha-ri in 1958. He said the North Korea government became increasingly hostile to fisherman in the late 1950's, sometimes taxing the local fisherman out of existence. The small city of P'oha-ri was far away from the large cities and quite a ways from the main highway to Chongjin, twenty miles inland. The city of P'oha-ri was an ancient city, one that had been ignored by many armies and even the North Korean government. The old man continued explaining that he owned three fishing vessels, which were operated by his sons. He proudly explained that he had the largest vessel in the harbor, an eighty-seven foot trawler, which was captained by his oldest son. His young daughter ran the fish market near the harbor, selling mostly to the local population. They all lived within half a mile from each other, typical of the older Korean populace. The old man started his day with his walk to the fish market where his daughter fed him his first meal of the day. Finishing his meal he made his way to the slip where his large trawler was tied up. The crew was loading up for a three-day fishing trip and he was looking forward to going also. His oldest son greeted him at the dock and welcomed him aboard. After loading the supplies the engines were started and the trawler backed out of the slip and headed to sea. The old man was proud to pilot the trawler out to sea. It was close to nine-thirty in the morning when the old man said that he, his son and the crew heard several loud explosions boom in the sky above. They dismissed it as North Korean fighters going supersonic but his son disagreed saying the sound was entirely different. Taking control of the trawler the old mans son turned the trawler back into the harbor, while ordering the crew below. At that second a loud, screaming sound came rocketing across the sky towards the harbor. Not understanding his motive at the time, his son pushed his dad off the bridge to the deck below. Following his dad below the son left the control of the bridge and pushed his dad into the sea. Seconds before he went into the water a bright white flash blinded the old man. He remembers being in the water as his son helped him swim underwater for several yards. They surfaced, gasping for breath and found only superheated air, which burned their lungs when they drew a breath. Diving again the father and son swam until they could no longer stand it. Surfacing again the two found their world had changed dramatically. The air was a little cooler now but his son described a dark mushroom cloud that hung above P'oha-ri, and continued to rise. The trawler in which they both shared many excursions was on fire and sinking. The buildings near the harbor were destroyed and on fire as well as many of the vessels in the harbor. From what his son could see, an explosion flattened the majority of the city. The son helped his father swim to the shore over a mile away. Tired and in agonizing pain his son vomited several times as he lay on the shore. They rested for several minutes before his son helped his dad find the trail to his home. The old man's son explained what had probably happened. He said that apparently a nuclear missile, either Chinese or North Korean, had fallen and detonated on the city. They had heard in recent years of the North Korean missile tests and hoped that war would not come again. His son explained that they probably would be dead within a week since they appeared both to have radiation burns. His son hugged his dad and said he would try to find his sister and would return with her by tomorrow. The old man said he walked the trail for seven hours, walking over badly burned corpses, both animal and human, which littered the trail to the northern most villages. He came across a few people who were dying and badly burned, their clothes fused through their skin. Some, who couldn't walk, crawled along the trail until they could no longer move. When he approached close to his home he felt his way the last three hundred yards on his hands and knees. He found his wife lying in the yard, bleeding from her mouth and nose. He helped her to the house and tried to make her as comfortable as possible. The old man drew a ragged breath as he began to weep. He knew she was probable outside, working in the garden when the explosion came. Her body was wet from urination and warm to the touch as he helped her inside their home. He told Jaeger that she was breathing better yesterday than today and knew she probably wouldn't make it through the night. The old man cursed war and everything that came with it as he continued sobbing, his head in his hands.

The old man's son didn't return by the morning and probably wouldn't. The team settled into the home, invited by the old man who was grateful to the care the men were providing to his wife. Lieutenant Lepore took the first watch followed by Bickford. At daybreak the team was awake but stayed undercover and for most of the day took turns helping the old man and his wife while measuring the radiation levels. The old man had taken five hundred REM's while his wife was in the high seven hundreds. At one point in the afternoon a small patrol boat was observed about six miles offshore, headed north towards Najin. Commander Lowe identified it as a *Hainan* patrol boat. The North Koreans must now be as interested in P'oha'ri as the United States. Lowe knew they wouldn't come closer for fear of contaminating their vessel. He zoomed in on the vessel with his 400mm Ziess binoculars. The patrol vessel was void of anyone topside and appeared to be making twelve knots. Lowe followed the vessel until it went out of sight. He noted the time in his log at 1437 hours and passed it on to everyone to keep an eye out for more patrol craft. If more were noted then it may mean the mission would have to be tweaked. The team had to motor out to at least six miles to be picked up by the *Pasadena*. They didn't need to be intercepted by a patrol boat when waiting for the submarine.

At nightfall the team left the old man and his wife to reconnoiter the perimeter of the blast. Commander Lowe decided, after conferring with Lepore, to not continue on to ground zero in search of survivors. The sensors indicated no movement in that area and Lowe didn't see any reason to put the team in more danger. Lowe ordered Fursthower and Bickford to reconnoiter around the hill behind old mans home where satellite photos had shown a settlement. Lowe reasoned that the settlement might have been shielded just enough so that survivors remained. Fursthower and Bickford headed out at 2035 hours and would return not later than 0400 hours. Commander Lowe, McGovern and Lepore left them and proceeded to an area close to where the old man said he swam ashore with his son. The team made the journey in forty-seven minutes, stopping every ten minutes to check radiation readings. Lowe was an experienced tracker who honed his skills on

Whitetail deer in the northeastern woods of the United States. He found the place where the old man left his dad and the team took up the trail. The team advanced quickly since they were well inside the radiation zone. The bodies of corpses littered the street, some villagers dying in the doors of their homes. The members of the team checked the corpse of each middle-aged man in an effort to find the old mans oldest son. Commander Lowe found him, described to a tee by his father, his identity confirmed by the two shark's teeth on a short necklace. Lowe removed the necklace and ordered his team to quickly retreat to the safe zone. Once in the safe zone the team made their way to the hidden cave near the landing zone. Checking the boat and other supplies the team returned to the old man's house at 0123 hours with the satellite transmitter and radio.

When they reached the house the old man was sleeping on his side with his wife next to him. Lowe stored the satellite transmitter and radio in the other room, which was drier and then checked on the old man. He was sleeping, breathing with a raspy tone. His wife however was not breathing at all and had died during the last few hours. Lowe decided not to wake the old man, partly because he couldn't communicate with him and secondly he needed his rest. Commander Lowe sat down and rested in his NBC suit. The sweat trickled down his back and made him itch. The first twelve hours in the suits were okay but now he was getting funky. When this mission was over he would be ready for a long hot shower. McGovern took up watch at the doorway with the night vision goggles while Lowe and Lepore rested. Both of them were hungry but dared not eat for fear of contamination. At 0337 hours McGovern signaled that he had a contact in sight. Zooming in he saw the unmistakable silhouette of Fursthower followed by Bickford. He signaled all clear and Lowe and Lepore set their MP-5's down at their side. Both men came in on the run thinking they were late. Fursthower explained that several contacts were made during the night and he had a few more testimonials recorded. Lowe commended both men and told them to relax. "How long will it take to upload the recording to the satellite?" Lowe asked Fursthower. " I have a little over three hours recorded so it should only take a few minutes give or take ten seconds" Jaeger explained while he sat down. McGovern signaled another contact as Lowe grabbed his MP-5 and went to the door. "Commander, I have a patrol boat offshore about three miles" said McGovern. Lowe checked the time. It was 0358 hours, a little more than twelve hours since the patrol boat passed earlier. Lowe noted it in his book. McGovern passed the night vision binoculars to Commander Lowe. Lowe saw the *Hainan* class patrol boat. It looked like the same one but he couldn't be sure, in any case it wasn't a good thing even if it wasn't the same one. Lowe told the rest of the team they might have to change their pick up time. If one of the patrol boats appeared again at between two and three tomorrow afternoon then it was a sure thing that they would probably be there when the team was waiting for the submarine. The worst case scenario was the submarine wouldn't approach the pick-up point. Lowe wanted to make the pick-up at 2200 hours tonight. He went to the other room and got the satellite transmitter. The transmitter scrambled the signal so that anyone listening couldn't understand the transmission. However if someone *was* listening they would know that *someone* was transmitting. Lowe set up the satellite antennae and proceeded to type his message.

TO FLEETOPSCOM, FROM JOHNNY REB. PICKUP AREA POSSIBLY COMPROMISED BY NKA NAVY UNITS. REQUEST PICKUP EARLIEST AT 2200 HOURS AUGUST 21 ON SAME LOCATION. MISSION COMPLETED. END OF MESSAGE.

Lowe completed his message and hit the "SEND" key. It took ten seconds and a reply came back "MESSAGE RECEIVED, STANDBY". Commander Lowe knew the message went straight to the Pentagon. Right now, in some office, the SEAL Operations Commander was fighting for his team to get picked up earlier than the scheduled pick up time. The safety of the teams was of the utmost importance. The screen came to life not two minutes later.

TO JOHNNY REB FROM FLEET OPS COM. REQUEST DENIED. PICKUP WILL BE AS SCHEDULED. NKA NAVY WILL BE DEALT WITH. MONITOR ENEMY UNITS IN YOUR AREA. ADVISE IF MISSION COMPROMISED. END OF MESSAGE.

Damn, thought Lowe. That was the first time they ever denied one of his requests. It was the first one given during wartime though. The navy must be having a tough time of it somewhere else. Commander Lowe ordered Fursthower to upload the recordings, while he went to check on the old man. He noticed he rolled on his back and had his hand at his wife's side. He also noticed he wasn't breathing and blood was coming from his nose and mouth. He checked his pulse and saw that he had expired, finally succumbing to the high dose of radiation he received during the detonation.

The men took turns standing watch during the day while others slept. Fursthower was on watch at 1545 hours when he alerted his team leader of a contact. Commander Lowe awoke and went to the window and carefully peered out. Not one but two *Hainan* patrol boats were less than a mile offshore and headed closer to where the team had their gear stowed in the cave. If that wasn't bad enough a *Taechong* II class patrol boat was escorting a *Hanchon* medium landing craft about two miles offshore. Lowe wasn't certain where they were headed until they both turned and came towards the shore. Lowe quickly went to the satellite terminal and frantically typed a message.

TO FLEET OPSCOM. FROM JOHNNY REB. URGENT MESSAGE. NKA MARINE UNITS LANDING ON OUR POSITION. TEAM COMPROMISED. REQUEST IMMEDIATE AIR SUPPORT OUR LOCATION. WILL EVADE TO THE SOUTH. END OF MESSAGE.

Commander Lowe shutdown the terminal, folded up the antennae and stowed the transmitter in his backpack. He ordered his team to evade and to rendezvous to a point south fifteen miles away, near the beach. The men went out the back off the house, two at a time followed by Lowe. The hillside gave a good view of the enemy but poor cover. Staying low and moving slowly, the team made it two miles to the south before the NKA soldiers detected some thing moving on the ridge above them. It took about fifty-five minutes for two squads to advance up towards the SEAL team. Not intended to go into combat with a larger force, the SEAL teams carried only the basic weaponry. Each man had a silenced MP-5 with 200 rounds of ammunition, a .45 caliber pistol with twenty rounds of ammo, two throwing knives, and a SEAL team survival knife. The team also carried one M-14 7.62 caliber battle rifle with sixty rounds for engaging targets at long-range and an M-79 grenade launcher with a bandoleer of twenty high-explosive rounds. Fursthower, the largest of the team, naturally carried the M-14 while McGovern carried the M-79 grenade launcher. "Commander, they are getting closer" said McGovern as he took out his grenade launcher. " I know, don't shoot that thing Chase or we'll have 100mm shells dropping all over us. They don't know who we are yet or they would be shooting already" explained Lowe. The SEAL team kept moving inland around the ridge out of range of the *Taechong* patrol boats 100mm gun. When the team reached the end of the ridge Lowe ordered McGovern and Fursthower to climb up to the next ridge above them. He told them not to fire on the North Koreans unless they got inside of 100 yards. Lowe, Lepore and Bickford continued on and set up below the ridge but in plain sight of McGovern and Fursthower. Lowe clicked the sight on his MP-5 to 200 meters. When the MP-5 fired at targets at that range it wouldn't be heard and the muzzle flash would be suppressed by the silencer. Lowe waited for the North Koreans to come. When they appeared over the ridge they were just walking, not paying any attention to anything in particular. Lowe fired three quick shots and two NKA soldiers fell. The other soldiers close by erupted in laughter, thinking the men fell down, and not knowing exactly what happened. Lepore and Bickford shot two rounds apiece for three more kills. Now the North Koreans started firing blindly in all directions, not knowing where their enemy was. Lowe had the range on them and continued firing single shots for single kills. Six more NKA soldiers went down while the others pulled back out of range. Knowing full well that an enemy was ahead of them the North Koreans radioed back for support. In about a minute the 100mm shells came screaming in over head and landed a mile behind Lowe's team. The shells sounded like a freight train as they rushed over head. After six rounds the firing stopped and the voices of excited North Koreans could be heard from over the ridge. This time the soldiers approached in a crouch, covering each other in teams as they advanced. They got to one hundred and fifty meters when Lowe, Lepore and Bickford opened up on them again. Switching to three-round burst fire, the SEAL team downed all but seven soldiers who escaped over the top of the hill out of range. The last soldier screaming to his buddies while trying to recover another soldier, was the last to fall, hit in the chest by two heavy 9mm bullets.

Fursthower and McGovern watched from their raised position as the other members of the team engaged the North Korean soldiers. They counted at least forty NKA soldiers killed while the remaining seven withdrew to the beach. Several soldiers must have been wounded as they lagged behind and had to be carried. Lowe signaled to Fursthower to remain as Lowe, Lepore and Bickford withdrew to the south. From Fursthower's position they could see the beach where the landing craft was and the patrol boats but had only a partially view of the city. The North Korean soldiers reached the beach in about an hour. Several other soldiers were visible now emerging from the landing craft followed by a Type-62 light tank. McGovern contacted Lowe by radio and advised him of the armor on the beach. Out of sight by the North Korean's Lowe and his two team members increased the speed of their retreat. Not wanting Fursthower and McGovern to be caught alone, he ordered them to retreat, evade and rendezvous at the scheduled site to the south. The North Koreans had more resources than the SEAL team and time was on their side. It was close to 1900 hours when Lowe, Lepore and Bickford reached the beach area. Lepore reported that he detected no discernable levels of radiation in the air since they were about twelve miles south of P'oha-ri and that they would be fine without their suits. Each member took turns getting out of their suits while the others covered them. Lowe walked into the sea to wash away whatever contamination remained on his suit. He put the suit in the weighted bag and removed his hood and lastly his gloves, dropping them in the bag. The remaining team members followed his lead and removed their cumbersome NBC suits. It felt good once he was out of the suit. Lowe washed his face for the first time in two days with seawater. Lepore found an outcropping of rocks near the beach and stored the suits under a few rocks. It would be dark in another hour or so. Lowe hoped the rest of the team would arrive before 2200 hrs. If they had to the team would discard their weapons and equipment and swim out the six miles to the submarine. The SEAL team had inflatable vests that allow them to float for up to ten hours. Lowe looked up and down the beach and could see nothing, which was comforting. The engagement with the North Korean's was brief and one sided. They obviously weren't prepared for what they found and most likely didn't have combat experience. The appearance of armor on the beach was of great concern to Commander Lowe. The teams carried nothing that could counter it, not even McGovern's M-79 grenade launcher. Climbing up from the beach to higher ground, Lowe set up the satellite transmitter again. Lowe powered it up and read the last message that was returned before the firefight.

TO JOHNNY REB FROM FLEET OPS COM. MESSAGE RECEIVED. STANDBY...
CONTACT PASADENA AT 2300 HOURS AND ADVISE OF ENEMY UNITS IN YOUR AREA. COORDINATE WITH PASADENA ON PICKUP POINT. AIR ASSETS ON THE WAY. EVACUATE AREA OF YOUR PERSONNEL WITHIN TEN MILES OF P'OHA-RI AS OF 2100 HOURS.
GOOD LUCK.

Good, that was more like it. Lowe liked to be in charge and hated when he was second-guessed. His Admirals knew him well and knew that Lowe would complete any mission assigned to him but had to be flexible. Lowe was responsible for his team members and didn't care to be left hanging. Lowe wondered what the military had planned for P'oha-ri that he had to evacuate ten miles. Fursthower and McGovern had arrived at 2000 hours and reported that the North Korean tank was closing on them but stopped and returned to the beach once it got dark.

Fursthower and McGovern went to the sea to get out of their NBC suits while Lowe sent another message to the Fleet Command advising of their position and that all team members were safe and out of harms way. He also advised the Command of the armor on the beach. The message was received and Lowe was told to proceed with the previous plan. Now all the SEAL team could do was to remain undetected and wait until 2300 hours to contact the *Pasadena*. Commander Lowe was glad the mission was almost over. He looked forward to getting on the *Pasadena* and getting some good food and lot of rest.

FOURTEEN

DOWN AND DIRTY

NATHAN WALKED TO STEVENS QUARTERS FOR the scheduled morning briefing. The Marine Sergeant on duty came to attention and knocked on the door. Steven answered and the Sergeant opened the door. Nathan entered the room and the Marine Sergeant closed the door behind him. "Good Morning Nathan" Steven said as he picked up his coffee cup. "Good Morning Admiral, Captain" Nathan replied to Steven and Captain Winters who stood across the room. The Captain already was enjoying a cup of coffee and cutting into a danish on the counter across from Steven's desk. "Nathan, help yourself, the cinnamon danish is still warm" Steven said not looking up from his desk. Nathan went to the counter and pored a cup of coffee from the stainless decanter and cut a large piece of danish before sitting in the chair in front of Steven's desk. "Well from the reports I see the Air Force has had a real busy afternoon yesterday" Steven said. "How so Admiral?" Captain Winters asked before taking a sip of coffee. "Well, the CAP from the *Kitty Hawk* detected a large surface fleet about 100 miles to the west of Haeju. They investigated and found several patrol boats escorting about a dozen heavily-loaded landing craft of various sizes. They reported it to Taegu HQ and the ROKAF dispatched four F-15K's loaded with Harpoon-L missiles. Osan AB got about twelve A-10's airborne loaded with Maverick missiles and blew away whatever was left after the South Korean's departed. The F/A-18's from the *Kitty Hawk* provided air cover for the A-10's while they did their work. "Sir, I thought that Osan AB was damaged by the missile attack" Nathan asked. "It was Commander, but with the help from the locals and the ROK they repaired about another fifteen hundred feet more of their runway and the base will be fully operational by tonight" Steven reported. "By the way, Washington is very pleased that we have gained control of the airspace over North Korea" Steven added. Nathan was pleased also. It made his job easier. He had eighteen sorties a day over North Korea, some as far North as Anju. The *Kitty Hawk* would be a welcome addition on the West Coast, relieving some of the pilots on the *Reagan* and allowing Nathan to concentrate more patrols to the east near Najin. Steven went on to explain that the boys on the Kitty Hawk have been busy enforcing the Presidents exclusion zone around North Korea. "A flight of F/A-18's intercepted a Chinese Badger reconnaissance aircraft about one hundred fifty miles north west of Seoul" Steven said. "They turned it away with no problem" Steven added reading the report. "This shit is getting hairy" the Captain replied. " I certainly hope those guys on the *Kitty Hawk* keep their cool or we could be in a real war with the Chinese" the Captain added. "I'm sure they will be fine. I have the utmost confidence in Captain Brookfield" Steven told the Captain. Steven continued reading the report. "I see here that the USS *John S. McCain* intercepted and turned back a Chinese cargo vessel suspected of transporting ballistic missiles" Steven reported, looking up from the report at Nathan. Nathan looked at Steven and said nothing, waiting for him to change the subject. The Captain didn't say anything either.

Nathan wondered if he was privy to Steven's action in the Indian Ocean.

Admiral Alexander told Nathan and the Captain of the SEAL team mission to P'oha-ri a few days ago. "I received word from Fleet that the North Korean Navy is now taking particular interest in the area. There are no less than seven North Korean Navy patrol boats en route to the area at high speed. The SEAL team may have even been compromised at this point. Fleet has ordered us to clear the area so the *Pasadena* can pick up the SEAL team at 2400 hrs tonight" the Admiral explained. "I'll assemble a strike package immediately" Nathan replied picking up the phone on the Admirals desk. "Ops, this is Commander Buckman. How many F/A-18's do you have configured for naval strike?" Nathan asked. Nathan heard the Ensign inquire to his staff and then came back on the line. "Commander, we have a full squadron loaded with Harpoon, AMRAAM and Sidewinder-X and another six aircraft loaded with Mavericks, 500lb. SDB's and Sidewinder-X" the Ensign reported. "Good work, Ensign. I'll be there in five minutes. Alert the crews to report for mission briefing in twenty minutes" Nathan ordered. The Ensign replied and Nathan hung up the phone. "Your dismissed Commander, I'm sure you have a lot of work to do" Admiral Alexander said. "Yes sir, thank you" Nathan said as he picked up his hat and walked to the door. "Commander, keep me advised of the mission, I may have some more Intel for you later" Admiral Alexander replied. "Aye, aye Admiral" Nathan said as he left and closed the door. Captain Winters took a sip of coffee and looked at the Admiral. "Commander Buckman is a good man, I'm sure glad he's on this mission, Admiral" the Captain said. "So am I Captain" the Admiral replied. Steven looked back at his report and saw that a naval aviator from the *Reagan* had been picked up by Air Force CSAR in the area north of Kumchan. " I see that CSAR has pick up one of our boys, a Lieutenant Anthony Nelson. He's fine but a little dehydrated. He'll be recovering in Seoul for a few days. The Chief of Staff is on the way to pin a medal on him" Steven said continuing to read the report.

Nathan arrived at the briefing room about ten minutes later after quickly sketching out a strike plan. The Ensign he talked with earlier came over with the list of aircraft and pilots. "Lieutenant Wilson just got back from his third Bronco 1 CAP about an hour ago, Sir" the Ensign said. "I see" Nathan said motioning for Wilson to come forward. Lieutenant Wilson came up to Nathan. "Lieutenant, I see you've been flying for twelve hours here, with only two hours downtime" Nathan said. "Yes Commander, that is true but I don't feel the least bit tired. I'm able to complete the mission, sir" Wilson replied. "I'm sorry Lieutenant, I need fresh pilots on this mission. A SEAL team needs support up north and I need you to be sharp both going and coming back. Again, I'm sorry but I'm ordering you to stand down for this mission. Report to your quarters for crew rest" Nathan ordered. The young Lieutenant was miffed but complied with Nathan's orders. "Aye, aye Commander" he replied before leaving the briefing room. Nathan gave the Officers assembled the briefing himself. He advised them of the SEAL teams last known location and where the patrol boats would be. "Fleet Intel reports the patrol boats are headed south from Najin at eighteen knots. Although this isn't their top speed, it is well above cruising speed and indicates they may have been ordered to reinforce the units near P'oha-ri. The SEAL team indicated that NK Marine units were landing so were have to assume a large force is in the area and that they may have armor assets" Nathan reported. Nathan looked around at the Officers assembled. Most were combat veterans but a few Lieutenants were present also. "The strike package will have two flights of four aircraft followed closely by one flight with six aircraft. Lieutenant Lopez will lead Able flight while Lieutenant Olsen will lead Baker flight. Each of your tasks is to take out the North Korean Navy patrol boats and any support craft found in the vicinity. Coordinate your activities while en route. Nathan saw Admiral Alexander enter the briefing room from the rear and called the room to attention. "As you were, continue Commander" the Admiral replied. Steven Alexander went to the front of the room and motioned for the Ensign and spoke softly to him. The Ensign left the room and closed the briefing room door. Steven stood back but next to Nathan as he continued the briefing. "As I was saying, the last flight of "Super Hornets", Charlie flight, will be loaded for close-in surface attack and carry Mavericks and 500-lb Small Diameter Bombs. The flight will be composed of six aircraft and I will lead the flight" Nathan said. The room was silent as a few of lieutenants looked around while some exchanged some whispers. "Once Able and Baker flights launch their missiles they will assemble at angels eight and provide air cover for Charlie flight" Nathan ordered. "The first aircraft will launch one hour from now. Any questions gentleman?" Nathan asked. No one asked any questions but Steven moved closer to Nathan. "Did I hear you right Commander. You will be leading Charlie flight?" Steven whispered to Nathan. "Yes Admiral, we are short handed. Seven pilots are in crew rest and two are injured. The rest are scheduled for CAPs, alert duty and a follow-up strike mission on the Yalu river bridges this afternoon" Nathan explained. "I see. You don't have to fly this mission Commander. One aircraft is not going to make a difference" the Admiral pointed out. "Admiral, are you *ordering* me not to fly the mission?" Nathan asked cautiously. "No Commander, not at all. I just think your first responsibility is to the rest of the Air Group" the Admiral suggested. "If you feel you have to fly then go ahead but you must designate someone to serve in your place in the interim" the Admiral concluded. "Very well, Admiral" Nathan replied. Nathan thought about who was qualified to take over. The man for the job, Commander Aulicino, was dead. Nathan looked over the roster in his hands. The next most qualified person was Commander Rick "Swift" Gray. Nathan told Steven of his choice and called Commander Gray to inform him. The Admiral was right. A single aircraft wouldn't make a difference but Nathan hoped his presence and combat experience would help the flight make it home. He hadn't been reported killed, just missing but Lieutenant Nelson would be surely missed on this mission.

Anthony Nelson had loved flying ever since his fifteenth birthday. He had soloed his first sailplane at the age of sixteen over his native Nebraska. Coming down at thirty feet per second in a parachute while being shot at however was not his idea of flying. He saw muzzle flashes several thousand feet below him to the left. He pulled hard on the control handle and the square canopy twisted and sailed towards the right, descending at a rapid rate. He looked above and could count about a dozen holes in his canopy. Sailing out of range the shooting stopped. When he was at five hundred feet he released the control handles and the descent slowed, but only a little. The holes in the canopy above were letting a lot of air escape. Anthony aimed for a clearing and hoped for the best. He hit hard and rolled on his left side and came to rest tangled up in a scrub tree. He unbuckled his harness and crawled free. He did a quick check and he seemed to be in good shape with no injuries just minor cuts from the scrub tree. He unholstered his M-9 pistol checked it and chambered a round. Anthony had three more magazines of

9mm auto for a total of sixty-eight rounds of which he hoped not to use any. He checked his two-way radio. It was working, as was the GPS sending unit. With any luck the rescue helicopters would be there in about an hour. He approached the ridge in the direction of where the muzzle flashes came from. Creeping low, he crawled the rest of the way so he could see over the hill and not expose his position. He could see movement below but couldn't tell who they were. He did see however they were hurrying towards his position. He backed off from the ridge and ran as fast as he could parallel to the ridge. He needed to stay up high to maximize his radio reception and look for approaching rescue helicopters. The people shooting at him could be either North Korean soldiers or civilians. Either way it didn't matter. They were shooting at him and as such were considered hostile. Anthony ran about a mile before stopping to check the progress of his pursuers. Hiding in a tree he looked back through his binoculars to see the three men had reached his parachute. They seemed to be dressed in peasant clothing and armed with bolt action rifles but one of the men had a radio. Great, Anthony thought, they were radioing for help. He took out his radio and turned it on adjusting the volume low. Anthony called twice identifying himself by call number only. The frequency was pre-set to the CSAR channel. He received a reply from the controller on the other end who advised him to stay put and they would get there. Anthony called again and advised them that he was being pursed by armed civilians and had to keep moving. The controller acknowledged and advised him to stay near his location if possible. Anthony could see the men had split up. Two of the men stayed together while the one with the radio advanced towards Anthony's position. Anthony turned off his radio and jumped down from the tree. He didn't want a confrontation but he did want to see Nebraska again.

The older North Korean man with the radio approached close to Anthony position. He was about fifty years of age but his hard weathered skin made him look seventy. His radio crackled about twenty feet from Anthony and a voice came on and said something in Korean. The man gave a short reply and kept walking right past Anthony's camouflaged position. Anthony was content to let him pass until the man abruptly stopped, raised his head and checked the wind. Anthony was upwind from him now and no doubt the old man had detected something out of the ordinary. Not wanting to let him get the upper hand, Anthony burst from his position and charged the old man from about twelve feet. The old man whirled around quickly and tried to get his rifle off his shoulder but Anthony sacked him with a tackle that would have made his old high school coach proud. The old man hit the ground with Anthony on top of him, his rifle flung to the side by the force of the tackle. The old man was about one hundred and fifty pounds, most of it muscle. Both men rolled over and over trying to gain the upper hand until Anthony checked his progress and stayed on top. The old man, not quite ready to concede defeat, hit Anthony square across the face with his radio sending Anthony rolling to the side. Almost knocked unconscious, Anthony looked back at the old man who was already up on his feet getting his rifle. Without hesitation Anthony pulled his M-9 pistol and fired twice at the man at point blank range. The old man grabbed his chest as he fell backward, the reports of the pistol shots echoing off the nearby hills. The old man's radio came alive with radio chatter. Anthony crawled over to the old man who lay on the ground. Not knowing what they were saying he grabbed the radio and turned it off. The old man breathed his last breath looking at Anthony. The old man's chest stopped heaving while his blood kept pumping out of it. Anthony got dizzy and vomited next to old man, not knowing if it was a concussion or he was just repulsed by what he had just did. One thing he did know was he couldn't stay here. If they found him now they might not kill him outright, which would probable be the worst thing. Anthony searched the old man and found some old rifle cartridges. He picked up the old man's rifle and headed towards the highest hilltop. Anthony still had to get clear of the area but at least the rifle would even things up a bit.

Anthony reached the top of a hill after about four hours and looked around. The top of the hill had several rock outcroppings that provided shelter from the elements and he could see quite a ways in all directions. Anthony again called on his radio and contacted the controller. He advised the controller of his position and that he had been injured. The controller told him a rescue team was being formed but couldn't get there till the morning. Anthony acknowledged and shut down his radio to conserve the battery. It would be getting dark in a few hours so he wanted to check the area around the hill to make sure he was secure. After dark Anthony returned to his shelter convinced he was safe and with the hope that the Air Force would pluck him from the hilltop in the morning. Anthony found a soft piece of earth between the rocks and settled in for the night. As he lay back and stretched out his stomach growled. He hadn't eaten since before the morning mission. He checked his survival pouch and ate a high-energy bar for dinner. The emergency water he left until he really needed it. The old man hit him pretty hard with the radio and opened up a deep gash running from just behind his left eye to his earlobe. It had stopped bleeding earlier but the side of his face was still stinging. He opened the first aid kit and wiped the area with an antiseptic pad to clean it up. It stung like hell and Anthony realized he should have left it alone. Storing his first aid kit Anthony settled back for some rest despite the pain on his cheek.

Anthony awoke abruptly at 0418 on the morning of August 19th. He heard the unmistakable sounds of high-altitude jet engines. Less than a minute later he heard muffled explosions in the distance, some which he could feel through the ground. Something big was happening and he hoped it *wouldn't* come his way. He reached for his radio and turned it on. He identified himself and asked the controller why the early wake up call. The controller advised him of big things happening in his area and to stay put on his hill. The controller cut the transmission short and Anthony turned off his radio. After a half hour the bombing and explosions stopped and he settled back down to sleep. At 0627 Anthony awoke. He stood up and stretched. It was damp last night and he got a cramp in his calf that sent him to the ground. Cursing himself for getting up too fast he rubbed the cramp away and looked around. Smoke rose in the distance from several locations. Anthony figured it was probably not more than five miles away. He figured he could make it in about four hours, his curiosity getting the best of him. He gathered his rifle and gear and headed out towards the smoke. After about an hour of carefully climbing down the hill he realized he was approaching a road. He could see the road coming from around the next hill but it disappeared from view, hidden by the scrub trees lining the lower hillside. Not knowing what was on the road he decided to climb back up higher and parallel the road till he could see better. It proved to be a wise move, as not less than ten minutes later a convoy of large trucks appeared from around the other hillside. In a concealed position Anthony took out his binoculars and watched the convoy approach. Seven vehicles with tanker trailers, No, wait. Not tanker trailers but ballistic missiles. Anthony knew he had to call this in. He reached for his radio and turned it on. He told the controller he went for his morning stroll and discovered a convoy of missiles. "Really big, freakin' missiles" as Anthony put it. He had gotten the controllers attention. It was a sure bet that this is what the Air Force and Navy had been kept busy looking for the last few nights. The controller told him to turn on his locator beacon and try to get clear as fast as he could. Anthony did what the controller said and hightailed it back up to his hilltop retreat. From his hilltop he could see the top of the convoy which had stopped between the hills for a while. Almost out of breath he called the controller for an update. He told him that the convoy had stopped and was north west of his position about two clicks. The controller came back and told him he was too close and to proceed to the south at least four clicks. "Shit, I might as well go back to where I came down" Anthony said aloud. Anthony called the controller back and acknowledged the order and started out to his south.

After an hour or so the Air Force came screaming overhead with their F-16's dropping 1000 lb. bombs. The earth shook and seemed to move from under Anthony's feet. He thought if he lived through this it would make a good book but then who the hell would believe it. The F-16's left but several explosions continued. The top of the hill where Anthony's retreat had been seemed to be on fire, which it was. The exploded rocket-fuel from the missiles no doubt scorching the earth of North Korea. Some A-10's appeared overhead a few minutes later and Anthony could hear their 30mm cannons firing even from two miles away. Who ever was left there was getting the shit kicked out of them. Anthony cautiously advanced to the position where he had the encounter with the old man. Searching the area, the old mans body was missing. Drag marks from a makeshift litter had shown that two men, probably the ones he was with, had removed the body. Anthony remained on the alert all through the day and into the night. He made it to his landing spot at 2200 hours and saw the canopy cut up with several large pieces missing. It made a good ground cloth in a pinch and the North Koreans must have thought so also. Convinced that he was alone on the hill he grabbed what was left of the canopy and bundled it up on the ground. Laying down he grabbed his radio and turned it on. He had to know when he could get out of here. The controller thanked him for his part in the last action. Anthony asked for a pick up in the morning and the controller said if he could stay in one place for the night he would be picked up at 0700 hours tomorrow, if the area was deemed safe. Anthony agreed and signed off. Resting his head back on the canopy drop cloth, he fell asleep, exhausted.

Nathan was in the pilot's dressing room when Admiral Alexander entered. "As you were, men" Steven said. Nathan stood up zipping his flight suit. "Did you come to wish me good luck, Admiral?" Nathan asked smiling. "No Commander, not exactly" Steven replied. "You left the morning briefing kind of abruptly and there are some facts you might want to know before you leave" Steven replied. Steven read from the papers in his hand. "Air Force Reconnaissance reports that seven bridges have been destroyed over the Yalu by aircraft from the *Reagan* Strike Group. Two bridges remain intact, one at Manpojin and the other at Chunggang-up. The report also goes on to say that an F/A-18 pilot from the USS *Reagan* was plucked from a hilltop in North Korea. It says Lieutenant Anthony Nelson was recovered alive at 0700 hrs today. He is reported being flown to Seoul for medical treatment for dehydration and minor injuries" Steven reported. Nathan and the other Officers exclaimed their approval with cheers and whistles. "That's the best news I heard in four days, Admiral" Nathan said. "I thought so Commander. By the way, good luck on your mission, I'll watch the launch from the bridge" Steven told Nathan. "Thank you, Admiral.

I'll see you this afternoon" Nathan replied as the Admiral walked away. Steven turned back and nodded in the affirmative while leaving the room. Steven made his way to the bridge. The Captain was on the bridge as someone called out "Admirals on the bridge". The Captain gave Steven the use of his chair. From here Steven could see a significant portion of the flight deck. The hustle and bustle of the flight deck was mesmerizing. Steven had long ago turned down duty on aircraft carriers to go into submarines and follow in his father's footsteps. There were times when he wasn't sure he did the right thing. The aircraft elevators came to life lifting the heavily-laden F/A-18's up to the flight deck. The flights with the Harpoon missiles were launched first quickly followed by Nathan's flight of six aircraft with Maverick missiles and 500 lb. bomb's. The Mavericks were a favorite of the navy pilots since they could be used to attack virtually anything. The Air Force pilots used them to great effect in the second Iraqi war blowing up everything from tanks to radar stations. This mission they would be used to attack the North Korea patrol boats and any ground forces that were threatening the SEAL team. The missiles had a range of thirteen miles and could be fired as close as one mile from its intended target. With their lightning speed and sixty-pound warhead they were devastating to anything in their path.

Steven watched as Nathan's aircraft was lifted up from the hanger deck and taxied into launch position. The launch personnel were all around Nathan's aircraft pulling safety pins and doing last minute checks. Even in wartime proper procedures were followed, but at a quicker pace. The aircraft was ready as Steven saw Nathan return the crewman's salute and set his head back against his headrest. The aircraft went to full power as the powerful new magnetic catapult shot forward carrying the F/-18 with it. Steven watched for a few seconds as Nathan's jet powered forward and began to fly. He climbed slightly to the right and then brought it back to the left and began climbing at a steeper angle to form up with the rest of the Strike Group flying over the *Reagan*. Steven stayed till the last jet was airborne and watched the Strike Group head off to the north. "Captain, I have some work to do in my quarters. Keep me advised of the missions progress" Steven ordered. "Aye, aye sir" the Captain said as Steven stood up from his chair. Steven continued to leave the bridge and heard someone say "Admiral's off the bridge" as he left.

Nathan was pleased with his launch. He had done it last month many times off of California so he could keep qualified for flying status. This time however his F/A-18 was heavier than before as it carried four Maverick missiles. He formed up just aft of Able and Baker flights and waited for the rest of his flight to form up on him. He checked the status of all his weapons and everything was normal. The SEAL team up north needed every straight shooter they could get and Nathan was determined to let them get their moneys worth. The rest of Nathan's flight was already airborne so Nathan gave the mission go ahead for Able and Baker flight. The Harpoon equipped "Super Hornets" would fly five minutes ahead of Nathan and hit the North Korean patrol boats hard with a decisive first strike. Whatever was left would be hit by Nathan's flight in addition to any grounds units.

Nathan approached the coast of North Korea. He hadn't been this close to North Korea since six years ago when he was flying off the *Kitty Hawk* during an exercise with the Japanese. It almost became an international incident when four North Korean MiG-21's intercepted a flight of Japanese F-15's and US Navy F-14D fighters acting as "aggressors". The Japanese drove off the MiG's and chased them to within twenty miles of their coast, while Nathan and his flight loitered in the area for them to return. The F-15's returned low on fuel and had to be refueled by KC-10's from Sapporo AB. It was one of about a dozen confrontations a year that ended without incident. The Japanese were lucky that the North Koreans didn't get more aggressive. The President of North Korea, Kim Lu Doc, had for years convinced his people that the west was determined to invade their country and the military exercises that South Korea, Japan and the US held were just a prelude to the inevitable. The North Korean Army and most of the civilian population believed what they had been told all these years and prepared for the worst. Nathan thought now that the war had began it made no difference who started it, just that people on all sides were dying. Nathan heard from the controller on board the JMSDF Early Warning Aircraft that was assigned to this sector. The controller had a clear view of Nathan's flight and what lay ahead. The controller advised Nathan that at least six large patrol boats were close to P'oha-ri and another four were offshore west of the harbor. This was where Nathan had been told the SEAL team went ashore and he hoped that they hadn't been discovered or worse, captured. Nathan proceeded according to his plan hoping that no SEAL team member had been taken prisoner and was aboard a patrol boat. "Charlie leader to Able and Baker lead" Nathan said into his mike. The lead pilot of each flight acknowledged and Nathan ordered them to proceed with the attack. Each of the pilots had experience attacking surface vessels and that was the reasoning that Nathan had selected them.

Nathan and his flight were about seven minutes from the coast. Nathan listened through his headset. "Baker leader to Able leader I'll take the boats to the west" Able Leader, Lieutenant Commander Cole, copied the transmission and ordered his flight to take the boats to the east of P'oha-ri. Cole was the first to launch his missiles, first one then the other. The Harpoon missiles dropped clear of the "Super Hornet", started their turbojet engines and headed down to cruise altitude. Other aircraft in the flight followed suit, their missiles heading down to cruise altitude on different bearings. Their aircraft now free of the extra weight the F/A-18's climbed to eight thousand feet to provide air cover for Charlie flight. The leader of Baker flight, Lieutenant Commander Cutler, launched his missiles at the lead boat west of P'oha-ri. The other Officers in his flight fired their missiles at each of the remaining five boats. Cutler's flight climbed slowly to the right out of the path of Charlie flight, which was fast approaching the shore. The Harpoon's fired from Lieutenant Commander Cole's aircraft approached the first patrol boat, a *Taechong* II. The crews on the *Taechong* were scanning the skies for the "Super Hornets" to come within range of their anti-aircraft guns. Not one crewman on the one hundred ninety-six foot *Taechong* knew what hit them. The first Harpoon hit amidships and blew a sixty-foot hole in the boat. The second missile, which was three seconds behind the first, arched high into the sky and slammed down into the bridge and exploded, destroying the rest of the ship. The crew on the second *Taechong* saw what happened to the first and sprang to life. The gun crews scanned the sea and opened fire on the closest Harpoon. Getting the range quickly, a Harpoon missile exploded at four hundred yards off its port bow. The second Harpoon managed to approach much closer amidst the hail of 57mm and 100mm gunfire, popped up and slammed down amidships of the *Taechong* II patrol boat, exploding deep inside the hull. The other Harpoon missiles from the F/A-18's in Able flight also hit their mark, destroying their targets.

News of the attack spread quickly to the other boats in the patrol boat flotilla. Gun crews manned their inadequate anti-aircraft guns and waited for the missiles to approach within range. The closest two boats began firing all at once at the approaching Harpoon missile. The 100mm guns from both boats fired as fast as they could at their maximum elevation but couldn't hit the Harpoon. The faster firing 57mm gun on the *Taechong* hit the first Harpoon directed at it as it came within range. The crew cheered as the missile exploded and trained their gun on the remaining Harpoon. The Harpoon missile, following its preplanned evasive flight plan, executed a sharp S-turn, popped up to five hundred feet and bored in on the *Taechong* from a seventy-five degree angle. The gunners couldn't follow the missile and had no hope as it hit the boat, exploding forward of the forecastle. The boat slowed immediately and turned to the starboard, its engines stopped. The two smaller SO-1 class boats in the flotilla had no chance at all, each being destroyed by the Harpoon missiles allocated to them. The second boat behind the damaged *Taechong* detected two more missiles but had no luck at all in downing them. Both of the Harpoon missiles struck the boat within seconds of each other, literally blowing it completely out of the water.

Nathan's flight was now within visual range of the patrol boats. Several were sinking and Commander Cole gave him his assessment from his position at eight thousand feet. Six patrol boats were destroyed and three severely damaged, while one was still operational along with a Hanchon class landing craft on the beach to the west of the city. He also located a sizable enemy ground force with armor three clicks west of the landing craft and another enemy concentration a half a click north of the landing craft. Nathan acknowledged and ordered the flight to break into two-ship formations. Nathan and his wingman would go after the ground force to the west while he ordered Lieutenants Dorsey and Calhoun to attack the remaining patrol boats. Nathan's number three and four man, Lieutenants Paulino and Moore were ordered to attack and sink the *Hanchon* landing craft. Nathan and his wingman, Lieutenant Sidris, pulled up slightly and turned, headed for his target. Dropping down to two thousand feet a mile from the beach he could see the remains of the patrol boats. The Harpoon missiles did their job very well. All the patrol boats were either sinking or on fire. Nathan could see more boats burning in the distance also. Flying over the beach Nathan could see the muzzle flashes from the automatic rifles of the North Koreans ahead of him. Still out of range he selected the ground attack mode on his flight control stick. The armor on the beach turned out to be a T-76 light tank, which would prove to be no problem. Nathan cued up the video sight on one of his Mavericks and launched it at the T-76. The missile screamed past the North Korean soldiers and impacted the tank, sending some of the soldiers to the ground. The T-76 practically turned inside out and exploded sending shrapnel in all directions. The explosion killed everyone within ten yards of the tank. Nathan's wingman lined up a pair of 500-lb SDB's and dropped them near a group of soldiers that had set up a light machine gun. The bombs hit twenty feet on each side of the RP-46 light machine gun destroying it and its crew. Those soldiers that weren't thrown to the ground kept firing their weapons as the "Super Hornets" roared overhead at four hundred knots. Coming around Nathan looked back and saw the confusion on the ground. In his headset he heard that Paulino and Moore had succeeded in destroying the landing craft. Lieutenant's Dorsey and Calhoun, who were about seven clicks to the east, had destroyed another *Hainan* patrol boat but Dorsey had taken some good hits from a 57mm weapon. He had to jettison two of his Maverick missiles into the sea in order to maintain his altitude. Calhoun reported he had taken a few 57mm shells, which destroyed his number two engine. Nathan ordered them back to the *Reagan* while he and flew over to deal with the last patrol boat. The last *Hainan* patrol boat was making close to thirty knots when Nathan saw it. He settled the crosshairs on the bridge and launched his second Maverick missile. The missile flew right through the bridge windows and exploded, killing the entire bridge crew. Nathan fired again, this time targeting the 57mm gun mount forward of the bridge. The missile hit just under the mount penetrating and exploding under the turret. The secondary explosions blew the forward part of the boat away and it began to settle by the bow. Nathan flew by at two thousand feet and noticed some activity on the aft deck. Despite the boat sinking the gun crews manning the 25mm and 57mm aft gun mounts were still firing their weapons. Climbing and rolling away to the right Nathan turned the "Super Hornet" in a tight circle and brought the nose of the fighter around. Nathan settled the crosshairs for his next missile just forward of the aft 57mm gun mount and let another Maverick loose. Nathan figured the gun magazine would be forward of the mount and his assumption was confirmed as the Maverick missile bored in and exploded under the deck. A thunderous secondary explosion consumed the aft portion of the boat as it broke in two, the forward section of the hull turning on its side and sinking.

With the destruction of the last patrol boat Nathan ordered the remaining pilots to continue engaging the remaining resistance from the North Korean soldiers. When they were each on their last missile

Nathan heard the AWACS controller on the JMSDF aircraft call him. "Hawk 27 to Charlie flight, you have two fast movers bearing 012 from your position, confirm?" Nathan called his cover flight to confirm. "Charlie Leader to Able leader, can you confirm that?" Nathan asked. Commander Cole confirmed it and said things were in motion. Commander Cutler locked up one of the contacts and called "Fox 1". Seconds later Cutler's wingman also called "Fox 1". Nathan could see the AMRAAM's go screaming north as he looked up towards the cover flight. Both of the MiG's were at twenty-seven miles when the AMRAAM's were launched and exploded five miles later, scattering their debris over the unpopulated North Korean county side. Commander Cole called "Splash 1" confirming the "kill" and "Splash 2" seconds later confirming the downing of the second MiG. The whole intercept was done by radar and the missiles were launched from beyond visual range. They were in a real shooting war now and the US Navy meant business. If the MiG's were allowed to approach within visual range they could bring their weapons to bear and more American lives would be lost. Nathan, for one, was glad that wouldn't happen. Nathan made a few more passes over the area and found no resistance from the NKA soldiers below. Climbing up to seven thousand feet Nathan flew out to sea and quickly caught up with the injured "Super Hornet". Looking over the aircraft he could see hydraulic fluid but was convinced it wasn't that much of a problem. The pilot, Lieutenant JG Samuel Dorsey, indicated his controls were stiff but still manageable. Nathan flew at his three o'clock and slightly aft and told him if it gets worse to eject and he would stay with him until CSAR came and picked him up. "Can't do that Sir, their having steaks tonight and I don't want to miss it!" Dorsey replied. Nathan chuckled to himself. That's the kind of Officers he liked to lead.

Nathan and Lieutenant Dorsey approached the *Reagan* and settled into the downwind leg of the approach. Nathan sent Dorsey's wingman on ahead as he had a fuel management problem and couldn't loiter with Dorsey while he made his way back to the *Reagan*. Dorsey retarded his throttle on his number one engine and let his airspeed bleed off before lowering his gear and flaps. Nathan observed the main gear of Lieutenant Dorsey's jet come down but it didn't appear to lock. "Lieutenant, how's your gear look?" Nathan asked. "It indicates down and locked, Commander" Dorsey reported. "Okay, nice and easy Lieutenant. I'll follow you in" Nathan said as he lowered his gear and flaps to stay with Lieutenant Dorsey. The wounded F/A-18 came down the glide slope towards the *Reagan's* aft deck. Normally a pilot would aim for the "three wire" on the arresting gear and catch it as the aircraft hit the deck, it engines going to full power in case the aircraft missed all the arresting gear cables. Dorsey's aircraft drifted to the right but he corrected it and brought it back into the "slot". As Dorsey flew low over the fantail he hit the number "two wire" and slammed down hard on the deck. The aircraft was stopped but its right main landing gear tire blew. Nathan flew overhead at five hundred feet as the deck crews were already making their way to the aircraft in an attempt to clear it from the flight deck. Nathan circled overheard for five minutes before receiving clearance to land. He came in and hit the "three wire" for a text-book landing before taxiing over to the forward aircraft elevator. The elevator quickly dropped away from the flight deck while Nathan unbuckled his harness and prepared to get out. Once the elevator stopped he climbed down to the deck and walked to the pilots briefing room. He was informed the SEAL team was picked up early and was headed for Okinawa. Nathan checked with the Operations Manager and decided against a follow up mission to P'oha-ri. Nathan's new priority was to prepare some combat air patrols near Najin, where the MiG aircraft seem to have come from. Military Intelligence had said that the major airfields were destroyed so Nathan was concerned about this new emerging air threat. If the North Koreans could launch fighter aircraft then they could also launch bomber aircraft. The *Reagan* was now only one hundred twenty miles off the coast. Days ago when the North Korean's launched a bomber attack against the carrier, the *Reagan* was one hundred and fifty miles off the east coast of South Korea. Nathan knew he had to find where the enemy aircraft were coming from. He had already seen what the Chinese-made cruise missiles could do to lightly armed warships.

Nathan cleaned up and changed into a clean uniform and headed up to CIC. The Captain was in CIC and Nathan talked about the new threat against the *Reagan*. "I can check with Admiral Alexander and see if he can find any information on the location of where the aircraft are coming from" Nathan told the Captain. "Good Commander, Maybe in the meantime the Admiral can authorize a TLAM strike on the facilities in and around Najin. I have reconnaissance photos showing several cargo vessels and patrol boats being readied for sea" the Captain replied. Before he left CIC Nathan ordered one squadron of F/A-18's be loaded and readied for long-range air patrols. Nathan walked to Steven Alexander's quarters and was let in by the Marine Sergeant on duty. Steven was at his desk typing on his laptop as Nathan entered. "Hello Commander!" Steven said. "Good afternoon, Admiral" Nathan said as the Sergeant closed the door behind him. "Nathan, How did your mission go?" Steven asked. "It was successful but not without incident. Lieutenant Dorsey took some AAA fire from a NKN patrol boat and had to return to the *Reagan*. He landed okay but the aircraft needs some major repairs and a new engine" Nathan explained. "Was the pilot injured?" Steven asked. "No, he was okay but he had a rough landing.

The rest of the mission was successful. We destroyed many patrol boats and the SEAL team was extracted early" Nathan reported.

Nathan discussed the MiG threat that was encountered on the mission with Steven. The latest intelligence showed that no operational airfields existed in the north around Najin. Steven quickly drafted a message to Air Force Headquarters requesting latest intelligence on NKAF airfields in and around Najin, North Korea. Nathan had the report from a few days ago that said that all the airfields in the north had been destroyed above the fortieth parallel. Nathan called the CIC and asked them to contact the AWACS covering the mission and ask where and when the MiG's were detected. Five minutes later the CIC controller called back with the information. The MiG's were detected near south of Kyongsong, North Korea at two thousand feet. Nathan went to wall behind him where a operations map of North and South Korea had been posted. He located the *Reagan's* present position and the North Korean cities of Najin and Kyongsong. "Steven, could you come see this?" Nathan asked. Steven rose from his desk and approached the map on the wall. "The AWACS first detected the MiG's here, south of Kyongsong. That's a lot closer to P'oha-ri than Najin. If the MiG's came from Najin or even Chongjin then they should have been detected sooner and on a different bearing" Nathan explained to Steven. Steven looked closely at the map while studying Nathan's calculations. "I tend to agree, Commander" Steven said. "I'm going to request the Air Force look at this one a little closer, from Chongjin to the south of Kyongsong. If something is there then we can hit it" Steven said as he sat back down at his desk. "Then I can take that as we may be undertaking a strike mission Admiral?" Nathan asked cautiously. Steven looked up at Nathan as he was typing and said "You may start planning a mission Commander, however we have no confirmed target as of yet". Nathan acknowledged his Admiral and excused himself from the room. He had a lot of work ahead if he was to put together a strike mission. The North Koreans had put lot of things underground, airfields being one of them. Nathan thought that if it was a deep target that the Air Force would have to take it out with their SPECOR bombs. Anything short of that then Nathan would order it destroyed by strike aircraft from the *Reagan*.

Steven finished his request to the Chairman of the Joint Chiefs. Having been his father's son certainly had its advantages. He could feel free to communicate with the Joint Chiefs without ridicule from his Commanders appointed over him. Admiral Grayson received the request in minutes through his staff and had sent Steven Alexander a reply. The Air Force had a recon bomber already warming up at *Reagan* AB. The ATAV's were fast becoming an essential part of the war. Steven wasn't complaining. He had seen it coming many years ago when he heard of such a project being thrown around at the Pentagon. The Admirals argued that updated Super Carriers could provide for the needs of the United States into the next century while the Generals argued that the Super Carriers were financially excessive and could be found and sunk by any third world country with the new-generation of surface cruise missiles. What was needed, and fast, was a new Land-Based Strategic Bomber force that could traverse great distances quickly and at ultra-high altitudes. It was also clear that what was needed was an aircraft that could operate worldwide, but from bases *inside* the continental United States. Since the 1960's the US government had spent huge amounts of money, sometimes close to forty percent of the defense budgets, on developing and building tactical aircraft wings for the Air Force and aircraft carriers for the Navy Air Wings. As the years went on, the world political climate deteriorated and the United States found that overseas basing of tactical fighters was impractical if not downright frustrating. It became most apparent during the early 1980's when the United States was involved with Libya in the Mediterranean. In the planning phase, the French government refused to let the USAF F-111's based at RAF Upper Heyford in the United Kingdom use French airspace on their mission to bomb Libya. This required the F-111 aircrews to endure a mission, which lasted three times longer than was normal. Some said it also contributed to the loss of some of the aircraft during the mission. There were other occurrences but the most recent was in 2003 when it was unclear which aircraft the Turkish government would allow the United States to fly from bases in that country when the US invaded Iraq to remove Saddam Hussein from power. The second Iraq war was the first time the ATAV's dropped weapons in combat. They launched twenty-three sorties from *Reagan* AB and another eighteen from the RAF base at Machrihanish, Scotland. Each sortie had a 98.8 % success rate and was recovered at its launching base less than five hours later.

The Reagan Administration perpetuated every ideal that a military man could think of. Protection of the United States, her People, at home as well as abroad and the men and women in uniform. President Reagan made Americans feel good about themselves again. He was a no-nonsense President, one that was needed for a long time. It was his administration that helped bring back a strong military, which fielded some of the weapon systems that Steven had seen today. The *Thor II* project was the direct descendant of Reagan's Strategic Defense Initiative or so called "Star Wars" program, dubbed so by the media. The ATAV's were developed from data in both the Stealth and NASA programs, which were allotted additional funding during President Reagan's second term in office.

Nathan went to the CIC and talked to the Officer on duty, Commander Rick Gray. The Combat Air Patrol sorties for the AL-1A's were cut back because the *Kitty Hawk* had taken on some of the missions near the DMZ. This allowed the *Reagan* Air Wing to concentrate on more sorties on finding mobile missile launchers. A three day tally of one hundred seventeen launchers confirmed destroyed was achieved by the *Reagan* Air Wing. Nathan learned that seven launchers with missiles had been destroyed by the Air Force with help from a downed Navy pilot from the *Reagan*. The pilot reported that the missiles were close to his position when he was awaiting rescue. The Air Force F-16's and A-10's came in and destroyed everything in the valley. Nathan asked about the status of the pilot, Lieutenant Anthony Nelson. "He is being released tomorrow and should arrive here in the afternoon with the mail on the COD aircraft" Commander Gray reported. "Good. We need everyone we can get. We may be hitting some targets up north in the morning. I'd like your input on the planning" Nathan told Commander Gray. "That's fine Nathan, whatever I can do to help. I can meet you in the briefing room after 2100 hours" the Commander said. Nathan agreed and then after checking the status of the Air Wing he left to get something to eat. Nathan arrived at the mess room and grabbed a quick salad, some fruit and an iced tea. He always said the Navy had the best iced tea. When he finished, he went to his quarters to gather some information on the upcoming attack up north. While sitting at his desk Nathan called Steven's quarters. "Hi Steven, this Nathan" Nathan announced. "Hi Nathan. Have you started planning a mission yet?" Steven asked. "Not yet, but I will be meeting Commander Gray at 2100 hours to work things out" Nathan explained. "That's good Commander. Could you come to my quarters, Nathan? I have something you have to see" Steven asked. "Sure, do you need me right now?" Nathan asked. "

Uh, yes Commander. As soon as you can get here" Steven replied as if pre-occupied. Nathan hung up the phone and made his way briskly to Steven's quarters. The Marine Sergeant on duty opened the door to Steven's quarters without knocking, already aware that Commander Buckman was on his way. Nathan entered the room and made his way to Steven's side. Steven had his laptop computer on his desk and he seemed to be viewing something in real-time. "Here Nathan, sit here for the best view" Steven told Nathan. Nathan sat in the Admiral's seat, a plush comfy leather chair with arm rests. The screen of the large laptop was over seventeen inches and seemed to have two sections to it. The larger screen seemed to be of a satellite view of the earth below but from a lower altitude than most satellites. The second screen near the bottom had text typed by someone, most likely Steven. The last line of the text message read " ALTITUDE 187, SPEED 6.8, ZOOM AT 40%". "So, where are we now?" Nathan asked, not recognizing any of the topography. Steven pointed out the numbers on top of the main screen which all but the first few seemed to be spinning by. Nathan recognized them as Latitude and Longitude coordinates along with the present time, 2037 hours. "I see we're making good time" Nathan replied as the numbers approached those that he recognized. "Your looking at real-time video from aircraft 93-017, the Air Force' Advanced Tactical Aerospace Vehicle or ATAV for short" Steven explained. Steven leaned in and typed "ADJUST ZOOM TO ZERO IN 10% INCREMENTS". The reply came back "ROGER". In seconds the screen adjusted back so the earth surface could be recognized. Nathan could see the outline of Sakhalin Island in the lower left and ahead was the coast of Hokkaido Island, the northern most island of Japan. "Excuse me again, Nathan" Steven said as he leaned in to type. Nathan rolled the chair back a bit so Steven could type. "ADJUST ZOOM BACK TO MISSION STATUS" he typed and back came the usual reply confirming it. The picture on the

335

screen adjusted slowly at first and then reverted back to a forty-percent zoom. The image altered slightly as the aircraft rolled to the right on its new course. The message screen blinked another message from the crew. "COMMENCING RECON MISSION; TARGET AREA IN SEVEN MINUTES". Nathan leaned forward his arms folded in front of him on Steven's desk. "This is amazing" he said out loud. Steven pulled up a chair so he could see the show also. "Yes it is Commander, and the best part is its interactive" Steven said. The screen in front of him focused down about ten degrees on both sides of the aircraft, which gave a resolution footprint about one hundred miles wide. Since Steven was looking for aircraft and airfields he typed " ENERGIZE INFRARED SCANNERS". The pilot typed back "ROGER" on his keypad. The screen changed slightly to a gray scale image dotted by areas of orange and red near the populated areas. Steven noted the progress of the mission on his notebook where he had the coordinates written of the areas in question. The city of Ch'ongjin, North Korea loomed up ahead. Several areas shown up as orange but nothing out of the ordinary, according to Steven. As the aircraft approached Kyongsong, North Korea several orange dots in a row were discovered to the west of the city about six miles. Steven adjusted the picture and zoomed down to three miles above the objects. A closer inspection revealed that red blotches, indicating jet engine exhausts surrounded the dots. Nathan recognized the outline of the aircraft, as did Steven. They were MIG-29's. Nathan counted seven of them with another three emerging from a covered bunker near a large building or a factory. Steven hit the lock key and froze the picture and with it the coordinates. Steven typed "THIS IS YOUR TARGET; CONFIRM". The reply came from the pilot "TARGET CONFIRMED; AIRFIELD AT 41 DEGREES 33' 39" NORTH, 129 DEGREES 37' 44" EAST". Steven hit the lock key again and the picture went back to real-time in full screen. Nathan watched as the message screen blinked messages continually to other aircrews. He knew then that aircraft 92-017 was obviously not alone.

Major Samuel Cox copied the coordinates into his fire-control computer. His Flight Commander, Colonel Bill Collins, took off from Groom Lake and was fifteen minutes behind aircraft 92-017 in his own aircraft, ATAV 92-012. Major Cox had been monitoring the reconnaissance video and messages from the aircraft in front of him. When Admiral Alexander designated the target Major Cox immediately started programming in the coordinates for the four MK 5 Mod 2 SPECOR weapons. Two weapons would target the center of the runway about three hundred feet apart rendering it useless. The third weapon would take out the large building structure identified as an aircraft factory producing copies of the Soviet MiG-29. The forth and last weapon was targeted for the small fuel depot south of the factory. The two other aircraft behind him would target other areas on the airfield and the factory to make sure the facility was leveled.

The reconnaissance aircraft 92-012 was far away and turning as the first bombs from Colonel Collins aircraft began to drop. Prior to the bomb drop Colonel Collins pulled the throttles back and the aircraft slowed to around 2000 mph at 150,000 ft. The bomb bay opened and seven seconds later four SPECOR weapons were falling earthward. The first SPECOR hit within two feet of its aim point eight hundred feet down the runway. The weapon penetrated twenty feet into the ground before it exploded, sending up concrete and huge amounts of earth. Two MiG's had previously taken off and two others were already racing down the runway when the first weapon hit and were unaffected by the blast. Two other MiG-29's, that were well into their takeoff roll, were consumed by the dirt, concrete and other debris of the explosion and rolled off the runway and exploded, killing both pilots. The second SPECOR weapon hit eight hundred and ten feet from the first, three seconds later. The first MiG that missed the first explosion also missed the second but his wingman was not as lucky. The explosion took off his right wing and the aircraft consumed itself in a huge fireball. The aircraft stopped burning seconds later as concrete and earth fell on the MiG, snuffing out the flames. The third SPECOR hit the factory in the center near the production line, penetrating the four floors before exploding. The explosion blew out the concrete walls of the factory and collapsed the steel girder frame. Fires broke out in many places around the dying factory and explosions followed for many minutes afterward. The forth weapon destroyed the tank farm to the south of the factory. The fuel tanks that weren't destroyed outright by the initial explosion ruptured from the heat from the burning jet fuel. The fires soon burned out of control sending plumes of black smoke over the factory and runway.

Nathan sat back in his chair in awe. He had never in his life witnessed such a detailed attack in real-time video. It was true he saw video clips from gun cameras and recon pods but nothing compared to this. As if the first four SPECOR weapons weren't enough, a second ATAV dropped sixteen 2000lb JDAM bombs in a pattern to complete the destruction of the complex and runway. The attack was ordered by Admiral Alexander who witnessed it and confirmed the destruction of the airfield in real-time all from his personal quarters on the *Reagan*. Nathan also saw the destruction of the airfield and the launch of the three MiG's. No doubt they would be looking for the *Reagan*. Nathan rose and went to the map on the wall. He found the present position of the *Reagan* and the location of the now destroyed airfield not less than one hundred miles away. He picked up the phone on the desk, dialed the CIC and told them to launch the alert aircraft and intercept hostile aircraft on bearing 325. The Officer in Charge of CIC acknowledged and soon the familiar sound of F/A-18's in full afterburner were heard launching from the *Reagan's* forward catapults. The pilots of the F/A-18's were airborne in less than four minutes from the order to go. Each aircraft carried a full complement of missiles and fuel tanks for an extended long-range air to air mission. The pilots climbed to eight thousand feet and contacted the Japanese AWACS on station. The 767 AWACS confirmed to the pilots a flight of three aircraft in close formation climbing but leveling off at twenty thousand feet on bearing 345. The aircraft had reached a speed of six hundred knots and were still accelerating towards the 767 AWACS a mere two hundred miles away.

The flight leader of the F/A-18's called the *Reagan* to confirm the identity of the targets. Nathan walked into the CIC as the controller received the call. "Commander Buckman, the Flight Commander is requesting confirmation" the controller asked Nathan. Nathan motioned for the headset, adjusted it and keyed the mike. "Flight this is Big Dog. Targets have been VID as hostile. You are cleared to arm and fire" Nathan ordered. The Flight Commander acknowledged and proceeded to acquire the targets. He wasn't sure how Nathan VID the target but if he said he did then that was good enough for him. The radar down link from the 767 AWACS was crystal clear and in milliseconds had sent the calculations to the AMRAAM missile' radar seeker. The first MiG was locked up and two seconds later the Flight Commander announced "Fox 1" into his helmet mounted microphone. His wingman, who locked up the second MiG, also announced "Fox 1" and sent his AMRAAM streaking across the night sky. The AMRAAM's were launched from outside their operating range but ran on an intercept course towards the MiG's. When the missiles approached sixty miles the seeker heads acquired the MiG's and homed in at over two thousand miles per hour. The first MiG blew up and exploded as the AMRAAM struck it just aft of the wing in it's number two engine. The second MiG took evasive action and dived down to eight thousand feet and away from the approaching F/A-18's. The second AMRAAM missile acquired the third and last MiG and dove on it from twenty-two thousand feet. The missile hit the MiG directly behind the cockpit, exploding and blowing the aircraft in two. The second MiG was making more than seventeen hundred kilometers an hour going away and too fast for the F/A-18 "Super Hornets" to intercept. Reluctantly the flight turned to the south to try to provide the 767 AWACS with air cover.

The pilot of the second MiG-29 knew that he had come close to death. His mission orders were to avoid contact with any American fighter aircraft but to approach and shoot down the radar-equipped surveillance aircraft at all cost. He turned to the south and climbed to fifty thousand feet. If the American fighters wanted him they would have to work for it. He pushed hit throttles to maximum and accelerated towards the Japanese AWACS. The pilot turned on his radar and got a good return on the 767 AWACS. He could fire his two PL-12 long - range air-to-air missiles in less than two minutes.

On board the *Reagan*, Nathan was elated with the destruction of the two MiG's but it soon turned to dismay when the 767 AWACS reported that the last MiG was pressing home its attack at supersonic speed. Nathan and Captain Winters observed the updated data on the MiG while it approached the 767 AWACS. "Captain, the Alert fighters can't intercept it in time" Nathan said. "Well, I'm not gonna just sit here on my ass" the Captain said rolling his unlit cigar in his mouth. The Captain walked over to a technicians console and put on a headset.

"This is Top Dog calling USS *Lassen*, Command" the Captain barked in the microphone. A technician in the *Lassen'* CIC answered and told the Captain to standby. The Captain became agitated. "Hurry up damn it this is a war!" the Captain exclaimed. The Commander of the *Lassen* came on the line and Captain Winters quickly advised him of the situation. "Make this one a quick shot Bobby, knock the bastard down" replied Captain Winters. Captain Robert Wilson had been the Commanding Officer of the USS *Lassen*, an Arleigh Burke Destroyer, for the last three years. He had sailed with Captain Winters on several occasions and both had a great deal of respect for each other. The *Lassen* was sailing twelve miles directly ahead of the *Reagan* looking for hostile targets on, below and above the surface. The *Lassen* had been tracking the contacts for ten minutes and had witnessed the destruction of two of them by the *Reagan's* alert aircraft. The *Lassen'* SPY-1D radar had locked on the last MiG while a SM-3 Extended Range missile was selected for launch. Once confirmation was received from the *Reagan* the fire-control team went into action. The information was downloaded into the missile and then a technician launched the missile. The SM-3 ER burst from the forward vertical launch system hidden below the deck. The missile arced high up into the night sky like a flare that had gone wild and headed down range. The SM-3 ER missile achieved its maximum speed of twenty nine hundred miles per hour while less than forty miles from the MiG. The missile reached the top of its ballistic trajectory and then started its dive on the unsuspecting MiG.

The MiG was flying at fifty thousand feet and was close to Mach 1.5 when the pilot first got a hint of something wrong. His rear radar-warning receiver showed an imminent threat so he banked slightly to the left. The threat warning disappeared and the pilot resumed his course towards the 767 AWACS. As he leveled out his aircraft on his original course he got the same warning but it was too late. The SM-3 ER missile hit the aircraft directly between the engines and exploded. The aircraft folded in two and began to spin out of control. Traveling over thirteen hundred miles per hour the induced spin was powerful enough to break apart the rest of the aircraft, the forward fuselage breaking free and falling to the sea below. The pilot had no chance, trapped by the centrifugal force of the spin in the now disintegrating aircraft.

Watching the events unfold in the CIC, Nathan was relieved by the destruction of the three MiG-29's. He would be very happy when this was all over. Captain Winters advised Nathan that the Air Force was sending a large B-1B strike force against the North Korean navy base at Najin. There were thirty bombers scheduled to drop their 2000-lb. JDAM's at 0400 hours on August 22, less than seven hours from now. Nathan was tasked with protecting the bombers to and from the target against any enemy fighters and also to find and destroy any active surface-to-air missile sites. Nathan selected two squadrons from his flight roster. The first squadron would consist of F-35 Joint Strike Fighters and would precede the bombers with HARM's and Maverick missiles. The second squadron of F/A-18E "Super Hornets" would escort the bombers to and from the target. Nathan learned that the bombers would approach at twenty-seven thousand feet directly from the east. After the bomb release the bombers would accelerate and turn due south and fly out to sea and back to Okinawa. Nathan decided to have the F/A-18's intercept the bombers about thirty miles out to sea and fly in with them after the area was clear of SAM sites. The "Super Hornets" would fly above the bombers at thirty thousand feet with their attack radar linked to the 767 AWACS patrolling off the coast about one hundred miles. If the AWACS did detect anything the "Super Hornets" could attack it without putting their radar in active mode.

It was almost 2300 hrs when Nathan finished coordinating the combined effort with the Air Force. Technology certainly made things easier this time around. Nathan could remember not too long ago when the Navy and the Air Force just did their own thing, not coordinating with anyone. Nathan liked how things were now, as they should have been all these years. After all each service had the same goal, to protect the United States and her interests abroad. Nathan picked up his notebook and conferred with a flight controller before leaving the CIC to go to his quarters. With any luck he could get a few hours sleep before the morning briefing. Nathan got to his quarters and found his mail delivered for the last few days. His bed was made and lavatory was cleaned. Being a senior officer did have its privileges. He could remember when things were different. Nathan took off his shirt, shoes and trousers and lay down on his bunk. He started looking over his mail and saw two letters from his wife. It had been three days, intense days, since he had caught up on his mail. He opened the first one and read it quickly. It was dated August 13, 2008, before all hell broke loose in the Sea of Japan, Nathan thought. "The hotel is really great and everyone is really nice. The kids were excited the first two days but then I got into a routine, which makes things easier. Breakfast before eight o'clock then up to the room to watch a movie, which always leads to a nap. After the nap the kids would want to go for a walk or a swim in the pool. The pool was nice as it gave me a chance to get caught up on the letters. After a swim the kids were ready for lunch so we would either eat at the hotel or I would take them into town to sample the local cuisine. After lunch we would go sight seeing on the many tours the hotel provided. After the excursion into town the kids were always really tired so we either went to the pool or back to the room. Some younger couples arrived at the hotel three days after we did. I got to know them really quick and we set up a schedule to take turns with the kids. I get my afternoons free the next two days. I'm scheduled for a massage and facial and the next day I'm getting a spray-on tan. I know how you like me in an over all tan!" Nathan thought back to when they were first dating. She always got a real tan just from being at the beach or at home. He would give anything to see her just for five minutes. Lying on his bunk Nathan fell asleep in his T-shirt and boxer shorts, her letter, still in hand.

FIFTEEN

THE BEGINNING

NATHAN AWOKE IN HIS DORM ROOM. It was Saturday and since it was a holiday weekend, there was no training. His roommate, Ensign Aulicino had slept in also. He had gotten in later than Nathan did and there was no telling what he got into. Nathan got up and went to the bathroom. After he showered he cleaned the bathroom, which needed some attention. He heard Aulicino stir and looked out as he rolled out of his bed and onto the bare floor. He swore as he rolled on his back, seemingly with a hangover. Nathan walked over to his desk not bothering to ask how he was. "Morning Jimmy, out late?" Nathan laughed. "Go to hell" Jimmy replied, looking up at Nathan from the floor. "So what are we doing this weekend, Jimmy. We have three days, wanna go somewhere?" Nathan asked. "Yeah, I suppose we should. God, I wish I could get laid" Jimmy said holding his head. "I take it the brunette you were with didn't exactly work out last night?" Nathan asked paging through his phone book at the desk. "No, she didn't. What a little tease" Jimmy replied. "I'll take that as she out drank you!" Nathan said. "I don't know, all I know is that we were having a good time, drinking and dancing and she and her girlfriends left abruptly. The barmaid said they left out the backdoor at 1:30 AM" Jimmy said. "I see" Nathan said reaching for the phone. "Your not even listening to me are you?" Jimmy asked. "Not really" Nathan confessed laughing at Jimmy, who was still on the floor. Nathan dialed the number, which rang twice before someone answered. "Hello" they answered. "Yes ma'am. This is Nathan Buckman calling for Jennifer Kelly" Nathan said. "Thank you, I'll ring her room" the woman said. The phone rang three times before someone answered. "Hello" the voice said. "Hi Jennifer, this is Nathan" he said. "Hi Nathan, how are you?" she asked enthusiastically. "I'm great. I'm off for the next few days. Are you busy?" Nathan asked. "Well, Amy is coming up from West Palm and is going to meet Steven in Orlando. She asked me if I would like to go and I said yes" Jennifer said. "Well that's good. I talked to Steven last night. I planned on meeting him in Orlando also. I guess you've been tricked young lady" Nathan confessed laughingly. "Your such a shit" Jennifer said laughing with Nathan. "I confess though, it would be good to see you, I've missed you" Jennifer confided. Nathan missed her too, but didn't want to seem too eager. "Me too. So I guess the plan is we're staying at a place called the Grand Kissimmee Hotel and Resort" Nathan said. "Oh good, you'll love that. Have you ever been there?" Jennifer asked. "No. Actually this will be my first time in Orlando" Nathan replied. "So how are we going?" Jennifer asked. "I'm gonna pick you up and carry you there on my shoulders" Nathan joked. "Good, I always like to travel first class" Jennifer laughed. "I'll leave here in about an hour and come pick you up" Nathan told Jennifer. Jimmy kicked Nathan's chair and motioned to himself. "Yeah, Jennifer do you have any girlfriends you know that can come along at short notice?" Nathan asked. There was a pause on the other end. "So, I'm not enough for you Nathan?" Jennifer replied playfully. "No, No. That's not it. I have a friend also that would like to come along" Nathan confessed. "Sure, I'll ask around but I can't promise anything" Jennifer said. "Good. Thanks Jennifer. I'll pick you up at your dormitory in about three hours" Nathan replied. "Good, then I'll see you then sweetie, bye" Jennifer said. "Bye Jennifer" Nathan said. He hung up the phone and looked at Aulicino who had fallen asleep on the floor. He looked around on the desk and spied a large book "Aeronautical Principles". Yeah, that ought to do it. About eight hundred pages. Nathan grabbed the book, walked over to his roommate and dropped the book, square on his stomach. Jimmy awoke clutching his stomach, trying to suck in air. "Oh, you bastard" Jimmy replied when he caught his breath. "Me, what about you. I set you up for the weekend and your ass falls back asleep. And you wonder why you can't get a woman. Get on your feet Ensign. You have exactly thirty minutes until my car pulls out of its parking spot. If your not in it its gonna be another lonely weekend" Nathan said laughing at Jimmy. Jimmy made his way to the bathroom while Nathan started to pack his bag. Socks, swim wear, and cologne. Lets see what else. He had a good suit he just bought and probable it would be a good idea to bring in case they went to a formal dinner. Some casual wear and shoes, toiletries, yeah that should about do it.

Nathan brought his bags out to the car he rented for the weekend. A brand new Jeep Grand Cherokee, just like the one Jennifer owned. Jimmy came out running, dropping half of his stuff on the way. Nathan took a deep breath. It's gonna be a long weekend he thought. They both loaded the car and left the base. It was 9:00 AM. when they got to Interstate 10 and headed east. With luck they would pick up Jennifer and the mystery guest at around Noon. Jimmy slept most of the way which, was just as well, except for his snoring. Nathan put on the headset to his Walkman and the rest of the trip went smoothly. Nathan arrived in Tallahassee at half past Noon. He found Florida State

University with no problem and pulled into the area where Jennifer told him to park. He saw several guys and girls hanging about. He nudged Jimmy. "Wake up sleeping beauty, we're here" Nathan said loudly. Jimmy rolled upright from his position against the door and passed some gas. "Jimmy, roll the window down, Damn!" Nathan exclaimed. Jimmy got out and stretched while Nathan shut off the car. They attracted particular attention from a group of girls sitting in front of the dormitory. One girl who had to be close to six feet tall approached Nathan. "Hi, you must be Nathan" she said. "Yes, I am" Nathan said extending his hand. "I'm Sondra. I'm the lookout" she said laughingly. Nathan laughed also. "Jennifer should be down in a few minutes. One of the other girls left to go get her" Sondra said. "So are you joining us this weekend, Sondra?" Nathan asked cautiously. "I'm afraid I can't. My boyfriend is coming into town" Sondra replied. "Oh, that's too bad. Well, I'm sure you will both have a great weekend. It was nice meeting you Sondra" Nathan said as he saw Jennifer exit the dormitory with her friend. Both girls had two suitcases and what appeared to be make-up cases. Sondra said goodbye but went to help Jennifer with the suitcases. Nathan unlocked the trunk lid while Jimmy followed Sondra to help the girls. Nathan rearranged Jimmy's luggage and could hear the introductions as the girls approached. Jennifer set her make-up case down and ran to give Nathan a big hug and a kiss that was returned. "Boy I really missed you, Nathan. I can't believe it has been a month already" Jennifer said holding Nathan. "I missed you too" Nathan said kissing the top of her head. Jennifer let go and turned to introduce Nathan to her friend. "Nathan this is Cindy Welsh, Cindy this is Nathan" Jennifer said. Nathan said hello to Cindy and shook her hand. Cindy was about five-foot eight and had really blonde hair, even lighter that Jennifer's. She seemed quiet but that was normal since she just met her blind date for a long weekend. They all loaded into the car and started the trip to Orlando. Not far from Tallahassee on Interstate 10 Nathan turned down Interstate 4 towards Orlando. Since Jennifer had been there before Nathan decided to ask her directions. "So how do you get to the Grand Kissimmee Hotel and Resort" Nathan asked Jennifer, who was sitting next to him in the front seat. "Actually its close to Orlando. Don't worry, I'll guide you the whole way" Jennifer replied. Nathan felt her hand on his arm. She had warm hands. Nathan looked in the rear-view mirror. Jimmy and Cindy were getting along very well. They were engaged in a lively conversation about flying, both one of their passions.

They arrived in Orlando three hours later and found the hotel with no problem, thanks to Jennifer. Nathan was impressed when he saw it and was glad that he brought some extra money. Situated on a lake it was an impressive site. It was several stories high with a red roof. A raised monorail train came into the hotel and was available to whisk visitors to any part of the amusement park. Nathan started to get the luggage out but Jennifer stopped him and said the porters would get it and then they would park the car. They all walked inside the lobby and Nathan was overwhelmed. The ceiling seemed to go on forever but in reality went up over six stories. Nathan and the girls checked in and found there were two rooms available, one for the girls and one for Nathan and Jimmy. Nathan asked if Steven Alexander and Miss Kelly had checked in. The woman behind the desk confirmed that they checked in last night and had reserved the rooms for Nathan and his party. Nathan thanked her and joined Jennifer in the lounge area by the piano. "So what do you think, Nathan?" Jennifer asked. "This is fantastic" Nathan replied. Nathan saw that Jimmy and Cindy had hit it off to a good start as they both went outside to check out the pool. "I see Steven got separate rooms for us" Jennifer said inquisitively. "Yeah, I see he did" Nathan said looking around the magnificent lobby. He was wondering how that would go over. Jennifer knew that Nathan had a girlfriend in California but up till this point it hadn't deterred her. Whatever happened this weekend, Nathan hoped to still be friends with Jennifer and Steven and Amy also. "Would you like to see what the rooms look like?" Jennifer asked. "Sure, were on the fifth floor" Nathan said. "I guess Jimmy and Cindy can catch up later, they each have their own key" Nathan explained. Nathan and Jennifer rode up the elevator to the fifth floor and found each of their rooms, one on one side and the other down a ways and across the hall. They went in Jennifer's room first. It was a very spacious room. Jennifer pulled back the blinds revealing a view of the lake. "Nathan would you like this room instead?" Jennifer asked. "No that's ok. This is your room. You take it." Nathan said walking close to Jennifer. He put his arm around Jennifer. "It's very romantic, I mean the lake view, don't you think Nathan?" Jennifer asked. Before Nathan could answer a knock came at the door. Nathan went to door and the porter wheeled the luggage cart in and past Nathan. "Hi, just put them on the bed that's fine" Jennifer told the porter. Nathan reached for five dollars in his pocket and gave it to the porter and thanked him as he left. "You girls are staying for a week right?" Nathan said laughing looking at the girl's luggage. "Nathan, you know girl's have to have more stuff than guys" Jennifer shot back. Just then Cindy and Jimmy arrived at the door. The door swung open and Cindy apologized for barging in. "Nathan, can I talk to you" Jimmy said motioning Nathan out in the hall. "Excuse me girls" Nathan said stepping in the hall and closing the door. "What's up Jimmy?" Nathan asked. "Nathan I was wondering, could we sort of switch rooms? I mean, can you bunk in here with Jennifer?" Jimmy asked. So things were progressing faster than Nathan had realized.

Nathan hadn't planned on this. It was true he liked Jennifer a lot but didn't want to be put in this position. The rooms had two queen-size beds so it probably wouldn't become a problem. "I'll have to check with Jennifer first" Nathan said as he knocked on the door. The door opened and Cindy walked out with her make-up case and her upright luggage on wheels. "Thanks Nathan" Cindy said as Nathan held the door for her. "I'll get my stuff in a little bit" Nathan told Jimmy. Nathan walked in his new room and closed the door. "Hi roomy" Jennifer laughed looking at Nathan as she unpacked her suitcase. Nathan laughed also and went over and collapsed on the other bed. He was tired from the trip and all the driving. "Oh man" Nathan said lying on the bed. "Don't sound so happy" Jennifer said. "No, it's not that" Nathan replied. "Well, what then?" Jennifer asked, coming over to face Nathan as she sat on her bed. Nathan sat up facing her directly. "I just want to have a nice weekend with no problems" Nathan confessed. " I see. Nathan why did you come here this weekend?" Jennifer asked. "Like I said Jennifer, I just wanted to have a nice weekend with my friends and no problems" Nathan confided. "Then lets do just that. Nathan are you still seeing that other girl in California?" Jennifer asked. Nathan hoped the subject wouldn't come up. "Well, yes I am" Nathan confessed. "Does she know you are here with me?" Jennifer added. " No, no she doesn't" Nathan said as he looked at the floor. "Don't look at the floor, look at me" Jennifer said. "You truly just want me as a friend Nathan?" Jennifer asked looking squarely at Nathan. "Right now I do and I know I don't ever want to lose you as a friend" Nathan said. Jennifer smiled and had shifted her position on the bed, lying on her side with her head on the pillow. "I'm glad you are honest with me. That's the best way to keep me as a friend. And I don't really care if you have a girlfriend" Jennifer said. Nathan was glad to hear that. Jennifer was, pound for pound, more confident that Jill in many areas. "What do want to do before dinner?" Jennifer asked Nathan. "I'd really like to walk around and take this all in and then maybe get a massage" Nathan replied. "Would you like some company or would you like to be alone?" Jennifer asked. "If I wanted to be alone I would have stayed in Pensacola. I came here to spend time with you" Nathan told her. Jennifer smiled and then got up and kissed Nathan on the cheek. Jennifer called the front desk and arranged the massages.

Nathan went to Jimmy's room and knocked and was met by Jimmy. "Hi, Jimmy. How's it going?" Nathan asked. "It's going real good. I glad I came this weekend. Cindy is so different than anyone I have ever met" Jimmy explained. "That's good Jimmy. Cindy is a friend of Jennifer's so please don't do anything embarrassing, okay?" Nathan replied. "No, not at all. Nathan, I want you to know for the record that switching rooms was *her* idea" Jimmy said. "Really?" Nathan replied. He wondered if the whole thing was set up in advance by Jennifer and Cindy. Cindy didn't seem the kind that would mess around on the first date let alone on a weekend, but Nathan could be wrong. He decided to avoid trying to analyze it further. Nathan gathered his bag and toiletry kit and told Jimmy to give his room a call about 7:00 o'clock to see where to meet them for dinner. Nathan made his way back to the room and began to unpack. He heard Jennifer in the bathroom freshening up and noticed a clean top and capri pants lying on her bed. Nathan wasn't prepared when she walked out, wrapped in her towel. "Oops, I didn't think you would be back so soon" Jennifer apologized. Nathan was embarrassed and intrigued all at once. "Jennifer, I'll leave so you can get dressed" Nathan said. "Nathan, don't be silly. I trust you. Just stay, I'll just be a minute she said, bending over to retrieve her top and pants on the bed. Jennifer went into the bathroom but left the door open. "Where would you like to eat tonight?" Jennifer asked from inside the bathroom. Nathan put his toiletry case on the nightstand and turned around to answer her. "I'm not sure" Nathan said as he saw her drop her towel in the mirror on the large dresser across from the bathroom. Damn, Nathan thought. This is going to be harder than he thought. "Uh, yeah, where do you recommend Jennifer" he asked trying not to stammer. "We can try the restaurant in the hotel. Look and see if the menu is in the nightstand" she said. Nathan looked and found the menu. The prices were reasonable considering where they were. Jennifer finished dressing and came out of the bathroom with her hair done up on her head. She looked really beautiful. Nathan had a hard time remembering that they were just going to be friends. "Do you have to use the bathroom?" Jennifer asked. "Yes I do, just for a second" Nathan replied. He went in taking his toiletry case with him. He had to urinate since he hadn't stopped on the trip. Nathan looked at the bathroom. Very nicely decorated with soaps, lotions and other toiletries.. The tub and shower was really big with clear see-through sliding doors. That ought to make bathroom time really interesting Nathan thought. He shaved, brushed his teeth and put on more cologne. There wasn't much room for his bag considering all of Jennifer's things so he put his bag underneath the sink. He walked out of the bathroom and Jennifer was lying on her bed talking on the phone. "Okay Amy, we'll see you about seven-thirty in the lobby" Jennifer said as she hung up. "That was Amy. We are meeting her and Steven for dinner at 7:30. We have to hurry if we're gonna make our massages" she said. "Good, lets go" Nathan said. They went to the Spa and checked in and were led by an attendant to the dressing rooms. Nathan stayed outside while Jennifer slipped into the hotel robe. When she was finished he went in and slipped out of his trousers, boxers and shirt. He went to the massage room where Jennifer was waiting along with two female masseuses. Jennifer hopped up on the table, slipped out of her robe and lay on her tummy while the woman masseuses covered her bottom with a towel. Nathan was facing her and pretended not to look. "Okay Nathan, your turn" Jennifer laughed. Nathan grabbed a towel and put it around himself while he dropped his robe. He sat up on the table and then turned to face Jennifer while lying on his stomach. Both the masseuses started at the same time and seemed very skilled at their craft. Nathan even felt the kink that was in his leg seem to fade, the first time since his leg was broken in the bull ring. Jennifer reached out with both hands to hold Nathan's. She smiled as he held her hands. Now, after just a few months of meeting each other, they both seemed to be on the same page.

After the massage they cleaned up, dressed and waited in the lobby for Steven and Amy. Steven appeared first with Amy in tow. She wore a nice white blouse with a red skirt and heels. He hadn't seen her in about three months. Her hair was still a shimmering red but now was accented by blonde highlights. She looked fantastic and was almost Nathan's height as she threw her arms around Nathan and gave him a hug and a kiss. "Hi, Nathan. How have you been?" she asked. "I've been very well, and you." Nathan replied. "Oh you know, living the American dream" she laughed while giving her sister a hug. Nathan shook hands with his friend, Lieutenant Commander Steven Alexander, who now was technically his superior. "Hello Ensign Buckman, how are you?" Steven asked. "Good Steven, and you" Nathan asked. "I'm doing very well, Thank you. Congratulations Nathan. I heard you graduated third in your class. I'm sorry I couldn't be there" Steven said apologetically. "That's ok, It was pretty uneventful" Nathan said. Truthfully Nathan had wished that Steven had been there. Others had their families and friends. The only person that was there for Nathan was Jennifer. She drove over three hours for an hour ceremony, had dinner and drove back three hours to Tallahassee. Jennifer was fast becoming a good friend, one he could count on.

They were seated immediately and served shrimp appetizers and champagne. Since Jennifer couldn't eat shrimp she opted for some fruit. Steven made a toast to Nathan congratulating him on his graduation and even some other couples nearby joined in when prompted by Steven. They all congratulated Nathan in turn. They ordered dinner and talked for hours. Steven and Nathan talked about the Navy and Nathan's course of study while Jennifer and Amy talked about girl stuff and the upcoming Thanksgiving holiday. "Jennifer, invite Nathan to Thanksgiving dinner at mom's. I already asked her and she said one more won't make a difference" Amy explained as she leaned over to Jennifer. "I'm not sure. I'll see how the weekend goes" Jennifer said. "Sweetie, us girls have to leave for a while" Amy said to Steven when she stood up with Jennifer. Both Steven and Nathan stood up for the girls while they left then seated themselves again. "I know he's crazy about you Jennifer" Amy said as they walked to the ladies room. "He may be Amy but there's still someone else in the picture. I'm not settling for number two" Jennifer said. "Is he still dating the girl in California?" asked Amy. "I think involved is a better word. He's in Pensacola but his heart is in LA" Jennifer replied. "If he just wants to be friends that's okay. He's a great guy. I wouldn't mind it turning into something else though" she added.

The girls returned to the table just in time for dessert. Steven announced that dinner was on him. It was his way of welcoming Nathan to the Navy. Nathan was overcome a little and thanked Steven, Amy and Jennifer for being such good friends and supporting him. Nathan felt Jennifer's hand on his arm. She leaned over and he met her halfway with a kiss on the lips. Jennifer started with some tears but Steven broke in. "Now we don't have time for that people" he said as he poured more Champagne into the girl's glasses. Jennifer wiped her tears with a tissue and put it in her purse. Nathan had another glass of Champagne along with Jennifer and Steven while Amy declined. "One of us has to stay sober to find the room" She said sharply. The night was getting late and after a long day everyone decided to call it a night. They all said goodnight and promised to meet at breakfast tomorrow morning at 9:00. Nathan had the start of a headache and needed some air so he asked Jennifer to join him. "We can go outside and down the walkway. I want to show you something" Jennifer told Nathan. Nathan walked outside with Jennifer holding onto his arm and down the walk near the lake. Nathan felt good, the night air clearing his head. Passing some trees, Jennifer walked towards a clearing. "We have to be quiet but I want to show you this" Jennifer whispered to Nathan as she pulled him through the trees. They walked to a gazebo in the middle of the lawn. From the gazebo Nathan could see the amusement park across the lake. "This is where they are going to build the chapel. I first heard about it a couple of years ago. I thought this would be a great place to be married, don't you think" Jennifer asked as she held Nathan around the waist. Whether it was the Champagne, the night air or just her, Nathan held Jennifer closer and tighter. Jennifer stopped talking and returned Nathan's embrace, burying her head next to his chest. She looked up at Nathan and spoke. "It's getting late and we're gonna have a big day tomorrow. Do you want to go back and get some sleep?" Jennifer asked. "Yes. I think that would be a good idea" Nathan replied, bending down to kiss her.

Nathan woke up at seven the next morning. The sunlight shown in from the window just enough so Nathan didn't have to turn on the lights. Nathan was in his own bed and still wearing his boxer shorts. He had a headache, which he attributed to too much Champagne the night before. Jennifer kept up with him and seemed to have no ill effects until they came up in the elevator. He rolled over and saw that she was lying on her bed facing away, dressed only in her red thong. Nathan got up and carefully covered her with a sheet as he went to the bathroom. He looked at her as he passed to the bathroom and saw that she was still fast asleep. He remembered only walking home from lakeside and getting in to bed, which was just as well. If something had taken place the previous night with Jennifer he could not remember. If indeed something had happened then Nathan hoped that his friendship with her was still intact. After shaving he started the water and stepped inside to take a long, hot shower. After a few minutes the door to the bathroom opened and Jennifer walked in to use the toilet. She sat there holding her head in her hands and didn't say anything. Nathan knew she had to hear him in the shower so he turned his back to her to give her as much privacy as he could. She finished, washed her hands and face and dried them before returning to her bed. Nathan continued with his shower and when he was finished he came out of the bathroom dressed in his dress shorts and polo shirt. Jennifer was still in bed but had the sheet overtop of her head. Nathan finished by putting his socks and sneakers on. After hanging up his towel and storing his toiletry bag Nathan went to gently wake Jennifer. She woke and spoke softly to Nathan while still under the sheet. "I feel so terrible" she said rolling over and peeking out at Nathan. He could see her face and her cheeks were pretty red. "It's probably the champagne. How many glasses did you have?" Nathan asked. "I'm not sure" Jennifer said softly. Nathan gathered his wallet and sunglasses. "Are you up now or do you want to go back to sleep?" Nathan asked.

"No, I need to get up" Jennifer said. "Good. I'm gonna go downstairs for a coffee and I'll be back in forty-five minutes. That should give you enough time to get ready for breakfast. Do you want me to bring you back a coffee?" Nathan asked. "Thank you Nathan. I would appreciate that" Jennifer said as she got up to go shower. Nathan said goodbye to her as he opened the door. She walked into the bathroom, holding her arms across her chest.

After closing the door, Nathan walked to the elevator. He got off at the lobby and went to the restaurant and grabbed a quick cup of coffee and a paper. He found a secluded chair on the second floor near the gift shop and sat down. After thumbing through the headlines he started thinking about California and Jill. It had been about three months since he had seen her and two weeks since he had talked to her directly. He told Jill at that time that he couldn't fly back for Thanksgiving because his training schedule would resume the day after. With his training schedule and her work schedule communication was becoming exceedingly difficult. She had left some really personal messages on his machine, which no doubt Jimmy had heard also. Nathan returned every single call of hers but had missed her every time. He hoped it was by accident but truthfully he wasn't sure. According to Jill she was busy with work and her girl friends and had just missed his calls. She also had said months earlier that she couldn't make his graduation in time, which was on a Friday morning because her boss needed her on Fridays. Nathan was disappointed and that was when he started to turn to Jennifer. She knew that Nathan was alone in Florida and had no living relatives except his aunt who was too old to make the trip. Jennifer jumped at the chance to attend Nathan's graduation and they had kept in touch through the last few weeks. Nathan had grown very fond of Jennifer and it was real easy to be around her. She was younger than Nathan, by three years, and at only five-feet tall more than a foot shorter than him. Still though at one hundred and eight pounds she was very powerful for her size. Nathan liked seeing her in the tops she usually wore which showed off her powerful arms. He enjoyed kidding with her that she lifted cars to keep in shape, referring to her biceps.

Nathan finished his coffee and went down to the restaurant to get a coffee for Jennifer. He returned to the room about five minutes later that expected. He knocked and entered the room with his electronic key. Jennifer was sitting on her bed, dressed in a short skirt and pink shirt, and watching television. She looked really pretty and Nathan told her so as he handed her the coffee. "I don't feel pretty. I feel like shit" she said as she took a sip of hot coffee. "How's the coffee?" Nathan asked sitting next to her on the bed. Jennifer's thigh touched Nathan's as he sat close to her. "It tastes good. Thank you" she said as she kissed Nathan on the cheek. "Your very welcome, sweetie" Nathan said which was out of character. He always referred to her as Jennifer. She looked at him and giggled. "That the first time you called me sweetie" Jennifer said smiling at Nathan. "Yeah, I think your right" Nathan said as he pretended to watch the television. Jennifer was intensely more interesting than anything on TV. "Nathan, do you remember anything about last night?" Jennifer asked cautiously. " I remember that I was really tired and drank too much" He said laying back and grabbing a pillow. He adjusted the pillow so he could watch TV. "I don't remember anything either. I mean I remember coming up in the elevator but I can't remember anything after that" Jennifer said as she looked out the window. She took another sip of coffee before setting it down on the nightstand. She rolled over to look at Nathan. She didn't say anything at first, she just looked deeply into Nathan's eyes. "I don't remember anything in the room. I mean I don't know if anything happened between you and ..." Nathan stopped her. "Jennifer, nothing happened. I was kissing you in the elevator and you passed out. I carried you into the room and put you on your bed. I didn't undress you, I just set you down on your pillow. We both drank a lot of Champagne last night. I do care for you very much, though" Nathan said as he stroked her long blonde hair. Jennifer smiled at Nathan as a tear appeared. Nathan wiped it away as quickly as it appeared. "If something were to happen like that I would want everything to be perfect" Nathan said holding Jennifer and rubbing her back. "You're a good friend, Nathan" Jennifer said lying close to Nathan. They held each other for a while until the phone rang. Jennifer rolled over to answer it. Her skirt rode up, revealing one of Jennifer's perfectly tanned thigh's. "Hello. Hi Amy. Oh sure, we're up" Jennifer said, looking at the clock. Nathan could hear Amy through the phone from where he was laying. "Sure, we'll see you in fifteen minutes" Jennifer said as she said good bye and hung-up. "What's the plan" Nathan asked. "Breakfast then off to tour the park" Jennifer said.

The breakfast buffet at the hotel was impressive. Nathan knew he ate too much but everything was so good. He saw that Jennifer ate quite a bit also. Nathan sat back and finished his coffee. "So where are we off to after breakfast?" Nathan asked Steven. "Well, we thought about touring a special section of the amusement park first" Steven replied. "Nathan, I think you'll like it. They have these areas designed from countries all around the world like Japan, Germany and Mexico. I'll bet you like Mexican food, don't you?" Amy asked. "Yes I do, very much" Nathan replied. He thought about what food he was brought up on in Texas. His aunt was a great cook and Nathan loved her steak fajitas, tortilla soup and enchiladas. "I think it sounds like a good idea" Nathan said sipping the last of his coffee. "Good, let's finish up here and head out then" Steven said. Nathan and Steven argued over the bill as Jennifer got up with Amy and went to the ladies room. "Jennifer, you drank a lot of Champagne last night. Are you okay? I've never seen you drink so much" Amy said. "Amy, I'm fine" Jennifer said from the bathroom stall. She rested her head on her hands, her head still pounding. She still felt like shit but wasn't going to let Amy have the satisfaction of knowing it. "How did last night go?" Amy asked, while combing her long red hair in the mirror. "It was okay. We went for a walk then we came back and went to sleep. We were both really tired" Jennifer replied. She finished and opened the stall door and went to the sink to wash up. "You mean he didn't try anything?" Amy asked. "No Amy, he's a gentleman and we are just friends!" Jennifer replied in an exasperated tone. The girls finished in the ladies room and rejoined Nathan and Steven. Steven had the entire breakfast billed to his room but Nathan insisted that he pay cash for Jennifer and his part. The four of them made their way up to the monorail train platform. One train had left minutes earlier and another was approaching the platform. The train stopped and the four of them got on. Once all the other passengers were seated the train pulled away and proceeded ahead. Nathan got a good view of the hotel from the train. The lake was bigger than he thought and he could see many personal watercraft sprinting about. Nathan planned to try his hand at one tomorrow morning.

The monorail stopped and they all got off. While walking towards the gate Nathan saw Jimmy and Cindy. Nathan called to him and Jimmy stopped to wait for the group. "Good morning Nathan, Jennifer" Jimmy said. Nathan nodded as Jennifer spoke. "Good morning Jimmy" Jennifer said as she hugged Cindy. "Jimmy, this is my sister Amy and her boyfriend Steven Alexander. Everyone made the usual greetings and then went through the gates and entered the park. "What shall we do first?" Jennifer asked. "Nathan what you like to do?" Amy asked. "I'm not sure. Why don't you take me on a tour since you both have been here before" Nathan said. "That sounds like a good plan" Steven said. "Okay, lets go" Jennifer said as they set out into the park. The girls naturally walked ahead and talked about where to go while the men stayed back a few paces. "So how is your training going in Pensacola?" Steven asked. "Its going real well, We start flying in the T-2C Buckeyes next month. When we get back we have two cross-country flights we must prepare for and pass the evaluations" Nathan said. "I can't wait until we get into the jets, the T-6A's are just too slow for me" Jimmy said. "Your just saying that because I out flew you on the last evaluation" Nathan mused. Steven laughed while Jimmy was clearly embarrassed but came back real quick. "That's only because I had a poor wingman" Jimmy replied. The last evaluation Nathan and Jimmy were evaluated on their basic combat skills in the T-6A's. Nathan and his wingman, working together, successfully "downed" both Jimmy and his wingman over the Gulf of Mexico. "Well, I hope you both do well. We need all the good pilots we can get" Steven said.

The trip through the amusement park was very interesting. Amy treated everyone to lunch at the Mexican restaurant in the "Mexico" section of the park. It was good food and Nathan liked the setting near a canal, which doubled as a ride attraction. Nathan was walking with Steven and Jimmy when Jennifer stopped to adjust her shoe. Jimmy whispered to Nathan if he got lucky with "that" yet. Nathan was caught a little off guard but he knew with Jimmy, anything was open ground. Nathan didn't know if he would pursue a relationship with Jennifer or not but he decided to stop Jimmy right now. "Jimmy, that's very inappropriate" Nathan said angrily as he walked away from Jimmy. He caught up with the girls and found out that they wanted to go into town and do some shopping. Rather that tag long Nathan decided to go back to the room. Steven also retired to his room and said he had some calls to make. Jimmy set off with the girls and decided to go into town with them. They all rode the monorail back to the hotel and said their good byes and then left in Nathan's Jeep. Steven walked into the hotel with Nathan. "Nathan, I overheard what Jimmy said to you back there. You really care for Jennifer, don't you?" Steven said. Yes, I do Steven, and I think I always will" Nathan said.

Nathan passed his cross-county flight evaluation the week before Thanksgiving. He was so excited he called Jill without hesitation when he got back to his room. After the phone rang several times he got the answering machine and left a message and hung-up. He picked up the phone again and dialed another number. He had to talk to someone and share the news. The phone rang and a girl answered. "Yes, I'd like to talk to Jennifer Kelly. This is Nathan Buckman" Nathan said. "Hi Nathan, this is Cindy" she explained. "Hi, how are you?" Nathan said. "Very well and you" Cindy asked. "I've been good. Is Jennifer available?" Nathan asked again, careful not to be rude. "Sure, I'll put you through to her room" Cindy explained. Jennifer's room phone rang twice and then she answered. "Hi Jennifer, its Nathan." He said. "Hi Nathan, how are you sweetie?" Jennifer asked enthusiastically. "I'm great. I just passed my cross-country evaluation" Nathan explained. "That's great Nathan. I'm so proud of you. I know you said you were worried about it last week in Orlando but remember, I told you that you would have no problem with it" she explained. Jennifer did have a knack for instilling confidence in him and that was very attractive to Nathan. "Yes, you did Jennifer and I want you to know how much I appreciate your confidence in me" Nathan said. "That's sweet, Nathan. I'll always believe in you" Jennifer explained. "Hey, since you passed your evaluation why don't we celebrate" Jennifer continued. "What did you have in mind?" Nathan asked. "When do you get out of school next week?" Jennifer asked. "Well, the instructors said we won't be flying next week because of maintenance so that means we'll be in the class room or doing self study. I imagine I'll be done by two o'clock on Wednesday" Nathan replied. "That's good. I can come pick you up and we can go to my Mom's house for Thanksgiving" Jennifer explained. "That's an awful long ways Jennifer. Its about six hours one way and I have to be back to school on Friday morning" Nathan replied. "Its okay, I'll have you back by then" Jennifer promised. "Nathan, *please* come home with me and have Thanksgiving. It will be our first Thanksgiving together" she said. Nathan knew that they both were growing closer in their relationship. "Jennifer, I'd love to come home with you. I'll rent a car and meet you at your dorm" Nathan replied. He could feel her beaming on the other end of the phone. "Okay, I'll call my mom and let her know. By the way, Amy and Steven will be there also" Jennifer replied. Nathan told her that was fine. He would enjoy seeing Steven again. Nathan would be done with his initial flight training by Christmas and wanted to talk to Steven alone and get his thoughts on where he should go with his career.

Jennifer and Nathan arrived at Jennifer's Mom's house in West Palm Beach at about nine o'clock Wednesday night. While unloading the suitcases from the back of the Jeep Nathan told Jennifer the good news. "Guess what?" Nathan said to her. "What?" Jennifer said looking up at Nathan with her arms around his waist. "Well, the Captain told us at noon time today that we had no training scheduled for Friday so you may have to put up with me for a few more days" Nathan explained. "That's great, sweetie" Jennifer said jumping into his arms and kissing him. Nathan held her up and kissed her back but more passionately than he ever did before. He lowered her slowly to the ground as the porch light came on. Nathan could see a little better now and could see Jennifer was smiling at him. She grabbed some luggage and started to the front door as Nathan grabbed his own and closed the trunk on her jeep. Jennifer introduced Nathan to her Mom, Janet Kelly. Amy and Steven came out from the family room and greeted them also. "It's so nice to finally meet you Nathan. I've heard a lot about you" Janet said to Nathan. "Yes Ma'am. It's nice to meet you also. I thank you for inviting me on such short notice" Nathan replied. "Not at all. Steven could you put Jennifer's bags in her room? Nathan I hope you don't mind sleeping in Amy's room?" Janet said. Nathan looked at Jennifer's mom and then smiled at Amy. "Oh no, your not sleeping with me, your just using my room!" Amy said laughing at Nathan. Janet started laughing with Amy and then Steven joined in. "No, that's fine. I don't care where I sleep" Nathan replied. Jennifer gave Steven a hug as Amy did the same to Nathan and then showed him to her room. Amy took Nathan on a quick tour of the house. It was a big house with a fireplace in the family room and a pool and patio. The patio had a wet bar and a built-in barbecue grill. The front of the house had a large living room with an attached dining area. The table was already set with five places. This was as far south in Florida as Nathan had been. They walked outside and around the pool. "I'm glad you could be here Nathan" Amy said. "So am I. I was telling Jennifer that I didn't have to be back until Sunday" Nathan explained. "That's great. We can show you around then. Maybe we can go to South Beach down near Miami, would you like that?" Amy asked. "Sure, that would be great" Nathan replied. Where ever he went would be okay as long as Jennifer was by his side.

Nathan awoke Thanksgiving Day in Amy's bed at about 8:00 o'clock in the morning. The window was cranked open a little and a cool South Florida breeze entered the room. Amy's room was by the pool and Nathan heard the pool pump kick on and also heard someone moving about outside. He raised up to see Jennifer cleaning the pool with a pool skimmer. Nathan put on his bathrobe and went to the cabana bath down the hall to shower and shave. The door to the pool patio was unlocked so Nathan left it that way as he entered the shower. Nathan started showering and after a few minutes Jennifer came in from outside. "Nathan?" Jennifer asked cautiously. "Yes Jennifer, its me" Nathan replied. "Good Morning. Would you like some coffee?" she asked. "Sure. I'll come out for it though. I'm almost done" Nathan replied. "Okay. I'll be waiting for you" Jennifer said. Nathan finished showering and began shaving. After a good close shave he toweled off again and donned his robe before going back to Amy's room. Once back in the room he got out a new pair of Levi's and a clean shirt and put them on. After hanging up his robe he went to find Jennifer who was in the kitchen talking with her mom. "Good Morning" Nathan said. "Good Morning Nathan" Jennifer said. "Good Morning Nathan. How did you sleep?" Jennifer's mom asked. "Very well. Thank you Mrs. Kelly" Nathan replied. "Nathan what can I get you for breakfast?" Jennifer's mom asked. "Oh, I don't know. Just coffee I guess" Nathan replied. He really was hungry but didn't want to show it. "Jennifer was going to have some scrambled eggs, would you care for some?" Mrs. Kelly asked. "Yes, that sounds good, thank you" Nathan said. "Here's your coffee Nathan. Come sit with me" Jennifer said. Nathan sat at the breakfast table near the kitchen. It was nice setting overlooking the pool from inside. Jennifer came around Nathan and kissed him on the cheek before sitting down next to him. He looked at her and smiled which she readily returned. "Mom, Nathan told me last night that he doesn't have to leave until Sunday, Is that okay?" Jennifer asked. "Oh sure. Nathan, you can stay as long as you want" Janet said as she was putting the sausage in the microwave. "I'm sure this is a nice break for you" Janet said. "Yes Ma'am. The Navy has quite an intensive training program" Nathan replied. Jennifer's mom served up quite a breakfast for Nathan and Jennifer. Scrambled eggs, sausage, toast and a cinnamon coffee cake that Jennifer's mom had made earlier in the week. She even had fresh squeezed orange juice from her neighbors orange tree's across the street. Janet continued prepping things in the kitchen for the Thanksgiving feast in the afternoon as Jennifer and Nathan ate breakfast. Nathan loved the eggs. And the orange juice and the coffee cake. Nathan had one more cup of coffee before finishing. "So what did you want to do today Nathan?" Jennifer asked. I'm not sure. We don't have to do anything if you don't want" Nathan replied. "We could go for a walk after breakfast, would you like that?" Jennifer asked. "Sure, that would be great" Nathan said.

Nathan helped Jennifer clear the breakfast dishes and he even wiped the table. Nathan asked Jennifer's mom if she would like to go with them for a walk, but she declined. "Oh thank you Nathan, that's sweet but I have enough to keep me busy here. You two go and have a good time" Janet Kelly said. Nathan grabbed his wallet and then he and Jennifer started out on their walk. They walked around the circle in their development and then down towards the newer homes in the plat. "I'd like to own a home like this someday" Jennifer said pointing to a large house on the corner lot not far from her mom's. Nathan agreed with her, not letting on that he could have put a down payment on one with the bonus he earned from Lockheed-Martin last year. "I'd like to design my own house and have it built someday" Nathan said. "That's really cool.

What would you design?" Jennifer asked. "I think one like your mom's but with an office area and a recreation room for entertaining" Nathan replied. "Wow, that's a big house" Jennifer exclaimed. They walked for about an hour and then came back to the house just as Steven and Amy drove in. "Morning Nathan" Steven said as he got out of the car. "Good Morning, Steven" Nathan replied. "We had some errands to run for Amy's mom" Steven said as he opened the back of Amy's Blazer. "Here, let me help you" Nathan offered. Nathan and Steven carried the bags into the house as the girls walked ahead. "Oh just set them down on the floor. I'll take care of them" Janet said. "Steven, thank you for going to get these" Janet said handing Steven some money. "No Janet, I'll cover it. It was my pleasure" Steven replied. "Thank you Steven, that's very sweet" Janet replied. The girls disappeared for a moment and then appeared later wearing only their swimsuits. "Nathan, Steven. Go change, we're gonna play volleyball" Amy said. Steven went to the back bedroom and changed and Nathan went to Amy's room and found his swim trunks. He changed and met both girls out at the pool. He helped Jennifer set up the net across the small pool and tossed the ball over the net to her. "That's quite the little swimsuit Jennifer" Nathan said referring to her pink bikini. The suit was bright pink but when soaked with water seemed to become transparent. "You think so. When I go to the beach I wear even less" Jennifer confessed. "I'd pay good money to see that" Nathan joked. Jennifer jumped up and spiked the volleyball at Nathan, who dodged the ball. Nathan dove and swam under the net and grabbed Jennifer's tanned legs as he stood up with her balanced high on his shoulder. She was laughing as Nathan held her high above the net. "How many points do I get if I throw you over?" Nathan said. Jennifer caressed the back of his head. "You'll get more points if you don't" Jennifer said laughing. Nathan let her down slowly and Jennifer kissed him as he did. "Hey, none of that in the pool!" Amy screamed, laughing from her chaise lounge. Steven joined them and they enjoyed a few sets of volleyball before lying in the sun for a few hours. "When are we going to South Beach?" Amy asked. "Well, we can't go tomorrow, that's shopping day" Jennifer said. Jennifer stood up and adjusted her swimsuit before sitting down on the end of Nathan's chaise lounge. "Friday after Thanksgiving is when we traditionally go shopping with our mom" Jennifer told Nathan. "God Bless you. I'd hate to be in the stores on that day" Nathan replied. "You and me both" Steven said. "What are *you* guys gonna do tomorrow?" Amy asked. "Nathan, we could go fishing or maybe scuba diving, you know, guy stuff" Steven said. "That sounds like a plan" Nathan replied. "Let's go to South Beach on Saturday since that's really our last day here, agreed" Jennifer asked. Everyone agreed. Nathan had heard stories of South Beach. Some areas of the beach allowed nudity and almost everywhere it was very liberal in what people were allowed to wear.

Jennifer and Amy went to shower and clean up first, which left Nathan and Steven alone. "Hey Steven, I have something we could do tomorrow" Nathan said. "What would that be?" Steven asked. "It's a surprise, but I'll bet you'll love it" Nathan said. "Well, okay Ensign. You have peaked my interest" Steven replied. "Don't say anything to the girls, okay" Nathan said. "Okay" Steven replied thinking what Nathan had up his sleeve. Nathan went to clean up in the cabana bath before dinner while Steven used the master bath. The table was already set and the girls helped their mom serve dinner. Jennifer's mom had plenty of food and at least one of everyone's favorite on the table. It was a sure bet that they would have enough food for tomorrow also. Janet served dessert later after everyone relaxed in the family room. She had baked two pies, her famous "mile high apple pie" and a pumpkin pie. One of Steven's favorite was Janet's apple pie with her special cinnamon ice cream. Steven ate his pie and ice cream in the family room and Amy ended up on his lap, talking about homes. Nathan could see that Steven was the happiest when Amy was close to him. He knew he had found his soul mate. Nathan had two pieces of pie, one of each and some more cinnamon ice cream. He took his dish to the sink and thanked Janet for inviting him and told her how good the pie and ice cream was. Janet told him the "secret" of the cinnamon ice cream and Nathan swore never to reveal it. The girls helped their mom clean up and then went to the local video store to get some movies for the night.

Lying on the couch next to Steven, Nathan began a conversation about the Navy. "Steven, once I get qualified for carrier duty what are my options?" Nathan asked. Steven thought for second or two before he spoke. "Well, once you are assigned to an Air Wing there will be more time to decide what you want to do. For now I would continue to practice my flying and combat tactics in case we ever get involved in another Iraq. Even if we never do, the possibility exists you may encounter aircraft from hostile nations while on deployment" Steven replied. "Once you get up in rank and get more experience you may consider being a instructor pilot or even a squadron commander. If you progress quickly in your career you could easily become an Air Wing commander on board an aircraft carrier. He is basically the third in command and consults with the Captain of the ship on all air operations" Steven added. Nathan and Steven continued talking about the Navy and its role in the present political climate. "The Navy has always had the mission of projecting power, Nathan" Steven explained. "Ever since the Great White Fleet sailed around the world in the early twentieth century, the nations around the world knew the U.S Navy could be ordered to go anywhere there was a potential political situation. There is nothing else in the world that can diffuse a potential problem than having a U.S. Carrier Strike Group a hundred miles or so offshore of an aggressor" Steven explained.

The girls returned with the movies and Amy wasted no time in putting one in. Nathan sat up on the couch as Jennifer came over and sat close to him. Amy sat in Steven's lap and got comfortable. The movie was some sort of mystery-adventure that really didn't hold Nathan's attention but he was polite and watched the movie anyway. Jennifer was snuggled up next to him as close as she could get when the movie ended. She got up to use the bathroom while Amy took out the movie. "Nathan, would you and Jennifer like to watch another?" Amy asked. "I'm not sure. I'll see what Jennifer wants to do" Nathan replied. Jennifer returned and looked at the clock. "Amy, its 9:30, I think I'm going to bed. I want to get a good night sleep before we go shopping tomorrow" Jennifer said. Nathan agreed and said goodnight to Steven and Amy while walking towards the hallway with Jennifer. "I'll just be a minute Jennifer" Nathan said as he stepped into the bathroom. Nathan brushed his teeth, washed up and used the toilet before returning to Amy's room where he slept. Jennifer was waiting in the room, dressed only in her kimono. Nathan walked in and closed the door to the hallway so he could have some privacy. Jennifer stood up and walked over to Nathan who was taking off his shirt. "Thank you for spending Thanksgiving with me" Jennifer told Nathan. "Thank you for inviting me. I had great time and your mom is such a great cook. I've never seen so much food" Nathan said holding Jennifer close. Jennifer looked up at Steven and looked deep in his eyes. Jennifer held Nathan around his neck as be bent down and kissed her. She returned his kiss. Nathan caressed her long silky blonde hair as he pulled her closer. He kissed her again before he spoke. "Jennifer, I really like being here with you" Nathan said. "I like you too, Nathan. I want you to know you're the sweetest man I have ever met and I'll always be your friend and be there when you need me" Jennifer said with a slight inflection in her voice. Nathan looked at her and detected tears forming as she said good night and turned to open the door. She told him to sleep well and she would see him in the morning.

Nathan awoke at seven the next morning and decided he had to run a few miles before breakfast. Jennifer was awake in the family room and decided to join him. Since she grew up in the area she showed Nathan where she went to high school. They had ran together for about three miles talking, laughing and flirting with each other before heading back to the house. The last half mile Jennifer pulled ahead and urged Nathan to "catch up" or be left behind. Laughing, Nathan closed to just behind Jennifer and kept pace with her till they reached the house. "How come you couldn't pass me?" Jennifer asked. "Oh, maybe because I liked the view I was getting" Nathan said walking around the driveway trying to catch his breath. Jennifer laughed and threw Nathan a towel that she retrieved from her car. After cooling down they both went inside to clean up and eat breakfast. Jennifer's mom had another big breakfast and plenty of coffee waiting for them when they both returned to the kitchen. "Nathan, do you run lot?" Jennifer's mom asked. "Yes ma'am. About five miles a day" Nathan replied as he sat down to pancakes and sausage. Nathan was hungry after his run. Jennifer sat next to him and ate fruit and yogurt while Nathan started eating. "Jennifer, is Amy up yet?" Janet asked. "Yes, she is about ready" Jennifer said as Steven came out to the kitchen. Steven said good morning to everyone as he sat across from Nathan. Janet served up another plate of pancakes and sausage for Steven and asked Nathan if he wanted more. "No thank you. I'll just have some of Jennifer's fruit" Nathan said as he looked at Jennifer. "Here, you can finish this, sweetie. I have to get ready to go shopping" Jennifer explained as she stood up and kissed Nathan on the cheek. "The pancakes are great Janet" Steven said. "Thank you, Steven. It's good to cook for people who appreciate it" Janet replied. Amy came out and said good morning to everyone and kissed Nathan on the cheek. She walked over to Steven and kissed him on the lips, citing she saved the best for last. "You taste like maple syrup" she said laughing and wiping her mouth with Steven's napkin. "I wonder why" Steven said holding her around her small waist. "You know Nathan, these girls are going shopping for the better part of the day. They ought to make shopping an Olympic event for these girls" Steven said joking with Nathan. Jennifer walked out dressed in jeans and a light floral print top. Her hair was done up on her head, showing the graceful lines of her neck. "Morning Amy" Jennifer said. "Good morning, Jen. Is mom ready to go yet?" Jennifer asked holding Nathan's shoulder. Nathan put his arm around her waist and caressed her back. Janet came out from her bedroom and asked if Nathan or Steven needed anything else. "Not at all Janet, You girls go and have a good day. Nathan and I will clean up before we leave" Steven said. "Oh, thank you Steven. You guys are the best" Janet said kissing Steven and then Nathan on the cheek. The girls left and Steven and Nathan cleaned up the dishes, wiped the table and swept the breakfast room floor. They both sat in the family room and finished the rest of the coffee while Nathan retrieved the yellow pages from the coffee table. He looked up a number and then dialed.

Nathan confirmed the information he looked into before and then told Steven. "So are you game? It will be quite an experience. One you can tell your grandchildren" Nathan said laughing. Steven agreed and they both got ready to leave. Nathan got in Jennifer's Jeep which she left for him and proceeded to get on I-95 South and head towards Lantana airport. Arriving at the airport Nathan spied four of the T-6 Texan trainers parked on the tarmac near a building with "TOP GUN" painted across one side of it. "So Nathan, the instructors here are certified, right?" Steven asked cautiously. "Yes, Steven. I checked it all out. The school is certified also" Nathan explained. Nathan parked and they both went inside the office to register. After signing waivers and paying the fee Nathan and Steven were taken by each instructor and dressed in a flight suit. The instructors then led them to a room designed to look like a World War II era briefing room, complete with charts and pictures. After a twenty-minute session on air-to-air combat tactics, which bored the hell out of Nathan, the instructors led the students to their respective aircraft. Each aircraft was identical except for the number markings. The instructors led each student around the aircraft showing them how to do a pre-flight check of their "warbird". Nathan checked the oil on the big 300hp engine while the instructor inspected the nose gear. "I see your familiar with this type" the instructor said. Nathan just nodded and resumed his pre-flight check, vaguely listening to his instructor who was walking ahead of him. With the pre-flight checks done each "student pilot" climbed in the cockpit and received a short briefing on the control and engine systems. The instructor's, satisfied with the student's progress, then climbed into the seat behind his "student" and started the engine. With both aircraft's engines running the instructors then taxied to the end of the runway and awaited clearance by the tower. The aircraft received clearance and the instructors advanced the throttles to maximum and then released the brakes. Nathan's instructor waited the usual five seconds and then released his aircraft's brakes. The T-6 Texan accelerated down the runway and lifted off after about a quarter mile. The aircraft turned to the east and climbed to about three thousand feet and headed for the coast. It was a crisp, clear November day. A good day for combat flying, Nathan thought.

After flying for about a half hour both of the aircraft headed in opposite directions for ten minutes to allow their "students" a chance to get used to flying the aircraft. Steven steered his plane to the right and then the left, sliding out of one of his turns. Nathan took over the controls of his aircraft with authority at the instructor's request. Nathan rolled left then right and then recovered to straight and level. He put the aircraft in a steep dive and then rolled out and headed back in the opposite direction looking for Steven. "You're a fighter pilot" Nathan's instructor said. "Naval Aviator" Nathan corrected the instructor. "Sit back and enjoy the ride" Nathan added, smiling while dropping the visor on his helmet. "Blue Combat, ready" Nathan's instructor said into the radio. The reply came back. "Red Combat, ready" said the red instructor in Steven's T-6 Texan. "Game on" replied Nathan's instructor adjusting his seat harness. Nathan scanned the skies for the "enemy". He spied Steven's aircraft ahead and low at about five miles. Putting his aircraft in a slight dive towards Steven to reduce his frontal area, Nathan called out the sighting to his instructor seated behind him. "Damn, son. You got a great pair of eyes" the instructor replied. Nathan continued in a descent until he could see the aircraft in his "gunsight". Steven must have detected Nathan's aircraft as he banked and pulled hard to his right losing precious airspeed. Nathan pulled to the left and kept him in sight as Steven brought the aircraft back to the left in front of Nathan. A little out of range, Nathan decided to gain some airspeed and then make the "kill". Steven had his speed back but continued turning to the right no doubt to look for Nathan. Nathan pressed the trigger on his yoke and he heard the recorded sound of machine guns enter the cockpit. The on-board computers recorded "hits" from the low powered lasers and, depending on the severity of the hits, the computer activated smoke from under the aircraft. Steven continued turning and Nathan followed in a slight bank all the while pressing his trigger. Steven's aircraft started trailing smoke and Nathan was declared the winner of sortie one. With the computers reset the game began again, this time with Steven climbing to five thousand feet and spotting Nathan below him. Following his instructors advise, Steven performed a split-S and descended toward Nathan from his five o'clock. Nathan caught Steven in his rear-view mirror and powered his engine up to 90 percent, pulled back and went vertical rolling out and under Steven. Throttling back, Nathan let Steven get ahead and then pulled up to three-thousand feet, lined up and "fired". The bottom of Steven's aircraft burst forth with smoke. Again, Nathan was named the victor. The next sortie Steven was determined to win. He enlisted the help of his instructor again and got a crash course in advanced tactics. "Stay fast. Remember speed is life. Let him work for this one, don't let it be a shutout!" the instructor explained. Steven advanced his throttle to ninety percent and climbed back up to six thousand feet. Both pilots called "game on" and the hunt commenced. Nathan had trouble finding Steven this time. When he did see him it was too late. Steven flew at Nathan and pressed home his attack at five thousand feet. Approaching at his nine o'clock Steven pressed and held the trigger while banking towards Nathan. He kept Nathan in his "gunsight" until his instructor told him to break off. This time it was Nathan's aircraft that trailed heavy smoke. He was at a lower flight level and wasn't fast enough to evade. It hurt his pride but he was glad his friend was the one who made the "kill".

Nathan landed first followed by Steven. Nathan taxied the T-6 Texan over to his spot followed by Steven's instructor. The aircraft shut down and both pilots and instructors climbed out and walked together to the briefing room. After talking to the instructors about the "mission" a woman entered and each handed Nathan and Steven a packet with brochures and a video disc in it. Nathan and Steven thanked both instructors and the staff for a good time and went to the car. "Well, I'll have to hand it too you Nathan. I had a great time, thank you" Steven said. "Don't mention it Steven. Wait till the girls see the video tonight!" Nathan said laughing. Nathan found the interstate and drove north on I-95 back to the house. "I see Jennifer's really taken a likening to you Nathan" Steven said. "Yes, I've noticed that. We are becoming really close friends" Nathan replied, wishing the conversation didn't come up. "Have you heard from Jill lately? How is she doing?" Steven asked boldly. Steven was his closest friend and Nathan thought he deserved the truth. "Steven, the truth is I haven't talked to Jill directly in over three weeks. Except for phone messages I have had no contact with her. I don't understand what is going on. She didn't come here for my graduation from Officer Training School because she said her boss couldn't let her go" Nathan explained angrily. "That is possible, Nathan. I know the company has been extremely busy lately. But, I suspect you don't believe her?" Steven asked cautiously. "I really don't know. All I do know is Jennifer has been there for me when I need her. She is the most confident, beautiful woman I have ever been involved with" Nathan replied. "Nathan, let me ask just one question. If Jill called you tomorrow and wanted to be with you, would you choose her? Steven asked. "Yes, I would. I mean I haven't broken it off with..." Nathan stopped in mid-sentence. "Nathan, forgive me for asking but if you haven't broken it off with Jill is that fair to Jennifer?" Steven asked. Nathan thought for a moment and reflected on what Steven had just said. Jennifer was a outstanding person and deserved better. He was glad things didn't progress any further in Orlando and last night which would have complicated matters and make it that much worse. They all planned on going to South Beach tomorrow and Nathan had to get some serious alone time with Jennifer and explain things.

Nathan and Steven arrived back at the house at three o'clock after some lunch and shopping of their own. Steven asked to stop at the Gardens Mall and do some quick Christmas shopping for Amy, Jennifer and Janet. Nathan had been in a lot of malls but really liked the Gardens

Mall. After going to several jewelry stores Steven found what he needed and was ready to leave. Nathan drove back to the house and arrived minutes before the girls and their mom. "Did you guys have a good day?" Amy asked hugging and kissing Steven. Steven lifted Amy as he hugged her and then set her down. "Yes, we had a fantastic day and managed to do some shopping of our own" Steven replied. Steven and Nathan started unloading the girls packages from the car and managed to make it in two trips. "So did you do some Christmas shopping?" Nathan asked Jennifer. "Yes, I did and I also picked up some little items for me" Jennifer said with a smile. "What little things?" Nathan asked now intrigued. "You'll have to wait for tomorrow on the beach to see them" Jennifer replied, now flirting with Nathan. Nathan knew the flirting was contagious so he had to curb it. His main thoughts now were to keep Jennifer as a friend. Janet put her packages away in the room and set to heating up the leftovers from yesterday.

The house was soon smelling of turkey, potatoes and stuffing as the girls set the table for their mom. They all sat and had dinner and the girls discussed where they shopped and who they saw on Worth Avenue. "I'm pretty sure it was Al Pacino, Amy" Janet said. "Did you see how he turned and then got into the limo? He didn't really *want* to be recognized" Janet added. "So what did you guys do today?" Jennifer asked. "Well, we had a most interesting day. Interestingly enough that we had to have a video made of it" Nathan said. "A video" the girls all said in unison. "Oohh, this I have to see" Amy replied. With everyone done with dinner they cleared the table and sat down in the family room with their dessert and coffee for the show. Nathan went to retrieve his video disc and put in the CD player. "Don't worry, this is rated PG for all audiences" Nathan explained as he pushed play. The CD started and the TOP GUN logo came on followed by the address of the school and instructors names. With a short introduction the CD went right to the flight line showing Nathan and Steven doing the pre-flight with their instructors. "Oh boy. Nathan I bet you could show those guys a thing or two" Amy said laughing. Jennifer moved close to Nathan and got comfortable as she held his hand. The video progressed to the flying footage and approximated a gun camera eye view for the audience. Nathan got a round of applause as he scored the first "kill". The room quickly changed as the girls rooted for Steven to make the next kill. Nathan made the next "kill" and got a thumbs down by Amy while she cheered Steven to victory. The last sequence was of Steven's approach and "kill" of Nathan's aircraft. The girls gave Steven a standing ovation while Amy kissed him. Jennifer said that Nathan deserved a consolation prize and kissed him on the cheek. "Really though Jennifer, he shot me down two out of three so he was declared the overall winner" Steven explained. "Okay, then he deserves a victory kiss" Jennifer said, sitting on Nathan's lap facing him. Jennifer kissed Nathan on the lips and hugged him close. "You're *my* Top Gun" Jennifer whispered in his ear. She moved and sat next to Nathan while they ate their desserts. "That must have been really exciting. Where did you find that place Nathan?" Janet asked. I came across it while on the Internet. Since I was down here I wanted Steven to try it also" Nathan replied. After dessert and more conversation about Nathan and Steven's adventure everyone turned in for the night. Nathan, Jennifer, Steven and Amy had a big day planned tomorrow.

Nathan awoke the next day at about seven o'clock. It seemed he was the only one awake so he shaved and showered and then returned to his room to dress. As he walked out of the bathroom in his robe he saw Jennifer sitting on the couch in the family room. She was dressed in her running shorts and sports bra and was enjoying a cold drink of water. Nathan quickly dressed into casual shorts and a Polo shirt and went to join Jennifer. "Good Morning Jennifer" Nathan said. "Good Morning Nathan. How did you sleep?" Jennifer asked as she took a sip of water. "I slept very well, thank you, and you?" Nathan replied. "I woke up about six and couldn't sleep any more so I decided to go for a run. I think I did close to about five miles" Jennifer said finally catching her breath. "That's good. I did that pretty much everyday when I was in OTS" Nathan explained. "Are you looking forward to going to South Beach today?" Jennifer asked. "Yes, I am. I have heard about it but never actually went there" Nathan said enthusiastically. "There is gonna be a lot of people there, some of them are Europeans who aren't used to wearing much when they are at the beach. I hope that won't bother you" Jennifer said in a playful manner. "Oh no, not at all" Nathan quickly replied. "I'm looking forward to it and truthfully I'm kind of curious what you will be wearing" Nathan added. Jennifer laughed as she was getting up. "Well, you'll just have to remain curious till we get to the beach, because I'm not gonna be modeling it for you now" Jennifer laughed. Jennifer said goodbye as she went to shower and clean up. Nathan heard Janet's bedroom door open and she walked out a short time later. Nathan was occupied with a magazine when she greeted him in the family room. "Good morning Nathan" Janet said as she was setting the breakfast table. "Good morning Janet, how did you sleep?" Nathan asked. "Oh very well, thank you" Janet replied. "Do you like egg omelets?" she added. "Yes I do" Nathan replied. "What would you like in it" Janet asked. "Well, just about anything you have would be fine, thank you" Nathan replied. "Good, that's one omelet with everything coming up" Janet said while starting the coffee maker.

Nathan continued reading his magazine while Janet was busy in the kitchen preparing breakfast. Jennifer came out of the bathroom in her robe and sat next to Nathan at the breakfast table. "Good Morning Jennifer" Janet said as she brought two cups of coffee to the table "Good Morning, Mom" Jennifer said. Nathan and Jennifer both thanked Janet for the coffee as they each took a sip. "So when would you like to leave for the beach?" Nathan asked Jennifer. "As soon as Amy and Steven wake up and get going. I'd like to be there by at least noon. After that it gets *really* crowded" she emphasized. Janet served Nathan and Jennifer breakfast just as Steven and Amy made their way to the breakfast table. Everyone exchanged good mornings as Steven seated Amy in her chair and then sat down next to her. "Steven, Amy, Jennifer. What kind of omelets do you want?" Janet asked. Jennifer asked for one with tomato and cheese while Steven and Amy wanted one with the works. Janet started the omelets as Steven got up and helped himself to pouring two cups of coffee. "So we're off to the beach today, right gang?" Steven said. "Yeah, I can't wait" Amy said. " I need some sun so bad" she added. "You girls make sure you bring your sun tan lotion today. Its supposed to reach in the high 80's with lots of sun" Janet warned. "We will mom. I'm all packed, I just have to slip into my swim suit and shorts and I'm ready" Jennifer said nudging Nathan with her bare foot under the table. Nathan looked at her and she winked playfully at him. Nathan wondered what she would be wearing at the beach. Everyone got their omelets at the same time and Janet pulled up a chair to join them. Steven talked of his past Thanksgivings and how fun they were and how he was glad to share this one with Amy, her family and his best friend. Janet and Amy thanked him both while Amy held his hand under the table. Steven grabbed his orange juice glass and made a toast to friendship and many more holidays. "Janet, Amy and I were talking and next Thanksgiving I'd like us all to meet at my house, if that's okay"

Steven said. "Wow, sure that would be great. I haven't been to California in years" Janet said. Nathan peered at Jennifer who was finishing her omelet and saw she was wearing a small pair of diamond earrings. "I'd take those earrings out before we went to the beach" Nathan told her. "Yeah, gee I almost forgot they were in. Thanks sweetie" Jennifer said.

Everyone finished breakfast and seemed to want to get ready to go so Nathan started clearing the table while Jennifer and Amy went to change into beach wear. Janet thanked Nathan and told him how much she would miss his help when he was gone. Nathan thanked her for everything and told her how much he enjoyed himself. The girls naturally took more time than Nathan and Steven getting ready so Nathan packed up Jennifer's Jeep with towels, some beach chairs, food and water from Janet and Nathan's bag. With everyone ready they all said good bye to Janet, who hugged them all and loaded into the Jeep. Nathan drove with Jennifer sitting next to him in the front seat while Amy and Steven stretched out in the backseat together. The trip went quickly as everyone was talking and in a good mood. Nathan had never seen South Beach before. They parked in a lot across the street and walked to the beach. Nathan carried the cooler and his bag while Steven carried the beach chairs and Amy's and Jennifer's bags. After walking for a while on the beach they found a spot that everyone was comfortable with and set up the blanket. Steven set up the beach chairs and umbrella while Nathan put the cooler down and wrapped a blanket around it to keep it cool. It was a very warm day considering it was November and Nathan even started to sweat from carrying the cooler from the car. He sat down and took off his beach shoes while Steven and Amy dropped their shorts and took off their shirts. Steven wore conservative boxer-style swim trunks while Amy sported a new, neon green thong bikini and top. Steven was a lucky man. Amy raced Steven to the water and Steven caught up with her just as she made it to the surf, scooping her up in his arms. Steven walked her in the surf where they both got wet as Amy screamed. Floating in about waist-high water Steven and Amy embraced each other, kissed and began talking to each other.

"What did you think of Amy's new suit?" Jennifer asked Nathan. Nathan looked around at the other bathers, some of which had only half of their thong bathing suits on. "It's very nice. The green neon really makes her red hair stand out" Nathan replied. "Don't you think it's a little too revealing?" Jennifer asked inquisitively. "No, not at all. If she's comfortable wearing it then it's fine" Nathan replied. Jennifer stood up and unbuttoned the top of her shorts. "I'm really glad you feel that way" she said looking at Nathan and smiling. Jennifer took off her shirt and revealed a black bikini top with spaghetti straps that tied loosely in back. The small material that supported her breasts barely covered them. "Very nice" Nathan commented. "Should I keep going" Jennifer asked. "By all means, continue" Nathan replied. Jennifer turned slightly away from Nathan as she undid the rest of her shorts and let them fall to the blanket revealing a very small black thong. The front material barely covered her and the rear thong string seemed virtually to disappear. Jennifer turned around for Nathan to take it all in and then sat down next to him. "Very nice, Jennifer. That was worth waiting for" Nathan said. "That was the surprise, I got it yesterday while we were shopping" Jennifer explained. "I like it very much" Nathan said. Jennifer sat up and hugged Nathan, pressing her breasts against his bare chest. She kissed him on the cheek and then sat down closer to him. "Did we bring any beer in that cooler" Jennifer asked Nathan. "Sure, do you want a Corona?" Nathan asked. "Yes, please" Jennifer said. Nathan pulled two bottles of Corona from the cooler and sealed it back up. He opened one bottle and handed it to Jennifer then he opened his. The beer tasted good on a hot day like today. Jennifer sat back in her beach chair, her loose top revealing even more. Nathan didn't care if she didn't. By the looks of it most of the women on the beach were topless or very close to it. Nathan watched Steven and Amy frolicking in the water. They both seemed to be enjoying each others company.

After liberally applying more suntan lotion to her stomach and thighs, Jennifer broke her silence. Nathan noticed she was almost finished with her first beer and seemed to have something on her mind. "Nathan, what is going to happen with us? I mean, when you go back to Pensacola?" Jennifer asked. Nathan knew what she meant and decided to try his best. "Well Jennifer, I want you to know I really care for you a lot. As you know I have someone back in California who I have been intimate with and have started a relationship. Right now at this point I haven't heard from her in over a month except for messages on a machine. I really don't know where the relationship stands" Nathan explained. "Okay. You said that she doesn't know you're here. Are you going to tell her?" Nathan didn't really know if he should tell Jill knowing she would probably be a basket case but he told Jennifer he would. "When I get back to Pensacola I will make it my mission to find out what is happening. If it's over between her and I then it's over" Nathan said reluctantly. "Nathan, I'm sorry. This must be very hard for you. I said before that I'll always be your friend and be there when you need me. I mean that Nathan" Jennifer explained turning to face Nathan. Nathan reached out for her hand and held onto it. Jennifer was a wonderful woman, friend and someone he could really trust. Nathan and Jennifer looked out over the Atlantic together, still holding hands. A part of Nathan wished he could continue the relationship with Jennifer but deep down he knew that it was Jill that first touched his heart, very deeply. Jill deserved another chance and Nathan deserved an explanation.

SIXTEEN

CAPITULATION

NATHAN RECEIVED THE REPORT FROM CIC that the raid on Najin was successful at 0557 hours on the morning of August 22. Eight more SA-2 surface-to-air missile sites had been destroyed as well as over ninety-seven percent of the facilities at the Naval Base at Najin. Only a few operational patrol boats remained in the harbor and most of them had no fuel in their tanks. They would be easy pickings for a subsequent raid by the F/A-18's on the *Reagan*. Nathan had four long-range combat air patrols scheduled for the day. One he was particularly concerned about, near Chongjin. No aircraft had been detected but the JMSDF AWACS off the coast detected radar emissions consistent with fighter aircraft. Chinese fighter aircraft to be more specific. The Joint Strike Fighters landed on the *Reagan*, first followed by the weary F/A-18 pilots. Just as the last F/A-18 from the raid on Najin landed, two "Super Hornets" took off at 0635hrs on the first combat-air-patrol mission of the day. Once airborne the F/A-18 flight leader reported a contact "low and slow" approaching the *Reagan* at her six o'clock. The controllers confirmed the contact as a Grumman C-2 Greyhound.

The aircraft was used in the Carrier On-board Delivery role and this particular one carried Lieutenant Nelson and the crew's mail. Nathan was looking forward to seeing the Lieutenant. His actions since being shot down had been discussed in every compartment of the *Reagan*, if not the whole Strike Group.

The Grumman C-2 hit the three-wire and slammed to a stop on the flight deck. Raising its arresting gear, the aircraft taxied near to the island to unload its cargo. While the enlisted deck crewmembers help unload the mail, Lieutenant Nelson climbed down the crew ladder followed by Admiral Jack Grayson, the Chairman of the Joint Chief of Staff. Both of the men were greeted by the Captain of the *Reagan*, Bruce Winters, who escorted them both to the bridge. "Admirals on the Bridge" an Officer announced as the men filed into the bridge. The C-2 aircraft that had delivered the Admiral minutes before was being positioned on the number two catapult. Within a few seconds the calculations were computed to gently move the aircraft down the ramp to achieve its takeoff speed. If the C-2 aircraft were launched at the speed of an F/A-18 or even an F-35 it would surely suffer structural failure and result in the loss of the aircraft along with its crew. "We're about ready to launch the C-2, Admiral" Captain Winters said. "Good, send that back breaking son of bitch off the deck" the Admiral replied laughing. The Captain watched as the deck crew cleared it for launch and stood clear. Slowly at first, the C-2 accelerated down the deck until it was clear of the catapults and over the bow of the *Reagan*. The C-2 started flying immediately and circled back to the west from where it came. "So Captain, where can I make this presentation" Admiral Grayson asked. "We can do it in the conference room Admiral or if you prefer we can use the recreation room and televise it to the rest of the ship. We could be ready in about two hours" the Captain said. "Good, the recreation room it is. In the meantime I'll need to talk with Admiral Alexander. Lieutenant Nelson, I'll see you in two hours" the Admiral said. "Yes sir, I'll be there" Lieutenant Nelson replied.

The Captain ordered a Marine Sergeant to the bridge to escort Admiral Grayson to Steven Alexander's quarters. The Gunnery Sergeant arrived minutes later and cleared the passageways as the Admiral followed close behind, shaking hands with the crew as he went. The Sergeant on watch at Admiral Alexander's quarters knocked on the door and then opened it. The Gunnery Sergeant escorting the Admiral stood aside at attention as Admiral Grayson walked past and enter Steven Alexander's quarters. "Steven, how are you doing son?" the Admiral asked. "Quite well, Admiral. And you?" Steven asked, shaking the Admiral's hand. "Well, good despite this bad back, and that C-2 flight didn't help it any" the Admiral explained. "But I'd go through it all again in order to decorate that young Lieutenant" the Admiral added.

Steven invited the Admiral to sit down and both started discussing the plans for the next few days. "Steven, since the start of this action *Thor II* has tore the heart out of the North Korean military. Our main concern since the second day was if China and Russia would stick their nose into this. They both have the idea we have them outgunned and their right. Without their nuclear ballistic missiles they have lost their bargaining chip. I can tell you here and now Steven, that pleases me to no end" the Admiral explained. "*Thor II* is a great advantage as well as the ATAV's but someday soon the technology will be available to other countries. It has been said that military secrets are the most fleeting of all, Admiral" Steven said. "That is true Steven, but I hope not in my lifetime anyway" the Admiral replied. Steven turned the conversation to current events.

"Admiral, we have just received confirmation that the naval base at Najin was all but destroyed by our latest air raid. Only a few patrol boats remain and those have little or no fuel and a small contingent of crewmembers" Steven reported. "That's good news Steven. I have more good news. You may hear some reports on WNN soon that the North Korean leadership has defected to China. We believe it to be true with our sources in Beijing and elsewhere" The Admiral said. "We can't confirm that President Kim Lu Doc was among them but certain high ranking officials have been positively identified passing into China near Tantung" the Admiral explained.

Steven thought for a second or two before addressing the Admiral again. He didn't want to be misunderstood. "Admiral, we have received small resistance the last few days, I assume we should continue our operations?" Steven asked. It was true; the last few days the North Koreans had put up minimal resistance and without much success on their part. Steven had though for days that only local commanders were running the show since there was no coordinated efforts in any area. The North Korean Navy was mostly non-existent on the East Coast and pretty much decimated on the West Coast thanks to the pressure from the ROK Air Force F-15's and the Air Group on the *Kitty Hawk*. "Steven, I think we need to keep up the pressure and keep flying missions. I'd hate to have some missiles pop-up and hit Japan or elsewhere just because we relaxed our guard" The Admiral explained. "I understand Admiral. I am told that the F-22's from Tyndall AFB arrived in theatre last night and are forward-based at Taegu" Steven replied. "That's correct. As of 1200 hours today they will take over the escort missions for the AL-1A's. That will free up more of your "Super Hornets" for combat air patrols, strike missions and the like" the Admiral said. Steven made some notes on his desk while the Admiral shifted in his chair. "By the way Steven how is Commander Buckman doing?" the Admiral asked. "He's doing a bang up job here, Admiral. He personally led a strike mission to lend assistance during the extraction of the SEAL team up near P'oha-ri. The strike force destroyed many NKAN patrol boats without the loss of any of our aircraft" Steven explained. "That's fantastic, I guess I should have brought more citations" the Admiral said as he lit one of his cigars. "Admiral, we'll continue the pressure for the next few days as ordered but what are the long-term plans?" Steven asked. The Admiral puffed on his cigar for a few moments before answering. "Well Steven, for now the President doesn't want a repeat of Iraq in 2003. We don't give a damn what happens to North Korea as long as they don't have any weapons of mass destruction" the Admiral said. "The President is determined that we not make the same mistakes in our history. He promised the Chinese and Russian Presidents that we would not use nuclear weapons. We haven't. He promised them we would not invade North Korea and we won't. It would be too costly. Iraq almost put us in the poor house for Christ sake!" the Admiral bellowed.

It was true; Iraq had strained everyone's budgets to the breaking point. Steven was glad that President Jackson had made some sound decisions. He had friends that had died in Iraq back in 2003 and again in 2004 while the US attempted to stabilize the country. Now that Iraq had a semi-stable government that was fairly secure the United States had turned to deal with North Korea, its most immediate threat. It was unfortunate for North Korea that they took the first steps and started the conflict. Those that followed the leadership blindly for the past fifty years would come to know that their leaders were wrong. The United States had no interest in North Korea except that of peace. The phone beeped on Steven's desk. He answered it and said thank you as he hung up. "Admiral, they are ready for us in the recreation room whenever you are" Steven replied. "Good, lets go. Lets not keep that young Lieutenant waiting" the Admiral said standing up and grabbing his briefcase. The Marine Sergeants escorted the two Admirals to the recreation room, which was transformed into a miniature television studio. In attendance were Lieutenant Nelson, Captain Winters and Nathan along with some junior officers involved in the broadcast of the ceremony. "Attention on deck" the Marine Sergeant spoke aloud as he stepped aside and led Admiral Grayson and Steven enter the room. "Thank you, as you were everyone," Admiral Grayson said. The Admiral made his way across the room to Captain Winters and Nathan. "Good Morning again, Captain" Admiral Grayson said. "Good Morning, Admiral. Is there anything I can get you?" Captain Winters asked. "No not right now, but when we finish this important business I could use a strong cup of coffee and a big breakfast" the Admiral said. "I think we can accommodate you Admiral" Captain Winters replied. The Admiral looked at Nathan standing to the right of the Captain. "Nathan, It's good to see you again. From what Admiral Alexander tells me I should be decorating you also" Admiral Grayson said. "Not at all Admiral, I just do my job the best way I can" Nathan replied. "Nonsense son, your too modest. I'll have something for you soon but this day is Lieutenant Nelson's" the Admiral said quietly while shaking Nathan's hand. "Thank you Admiral" Nathan replied. The young Ensign in charge of the broadcast signaled to Nathan that everything was ready. The Ensign was visible nervous and seemed to be perspiring. "Admiral, I believe we are ready, if we could take our places we can begin" Nathan replied. Nathan stood next to Captain Winters who in turn shadowed Admiral Alexander. In the center behind Admiral Grayson stood Lieutenant Nelson. Admiral Grayson stood behind the small podium and took out the Medal and papers that accompanied it. The Navy Commendation Medal was approved for Lieutenant Nelson after the word reached the Pentagon about his role in summoning an air strike on the mobile ballistic missile battery convoy in North Korea, after his aircraft was shot down. Admiral Grayson started the presentation, which lasted only a few brief minutes but was broadcast to the entire ship. Cheers could be heard in the ship for several seconds after the Admiral pinned the medal on Lieutenant Nelson.

After the Ensign signaled that they were off the air Admiral Grayson invited Lieutenant Anthony Nelson to join him and the rest of the senior staff for breakfast. Anthony quickly accepted. The naval officers were treated to a short history of the old Navy when Admiral Grayson first enlisted and some not-so-declassified stories of Steven's father's exploits in the submarine service. "Steven, one of the funniest things your dad ever did was in the North Pacific in '76. You see, he had his ass chased all over the North Pacific near the Kamchatka peninsula by this Russian Alfa. After about two days of dodging the Alfa and trying to tap that damn cable, the Alfa developed a malfunction and had to surface. Your dad thought it was playing possum but surfaced right next to it anyway. He said the look on the crew's face was priceless. Your dad asked the Captain if they were okay and if they needed assistance. The Captain of the Alfa said the boat developed a battery fire and had to ventilate. With some indecent hand gestures the Captain of the Alfa bid your dad a good day and then your dad went right ahead with his mission and tapped that cable" the Admiral said laughing heartily. "I'll tell you Steven, you dad has some brass balls to be sure" Admiral Grayson continued. Nathan looked at Steven Alexander and smiled. Nathan hadn't heard this story from Steven but then again maybe Steven hadn't heard it either. "Admiral, if you will excuse me I need to go to CIC" Nathan said. Admiral Grayson looked around and after seeing everyone was finished with their coffee spoke to the officers. "Not at all Nathan. Steven, Captain, and the rest of you fine officers I thank you for indulging an old Admiral but I know we must all return to our duties, for there is a war on. God bless you all for the work you do" Admiral Grayson said. The rest of the officers said their good byes and filed out and went back to work.

Steven Alexander entered CIC followed by Nathan. The technician on duty informed Nathan that the AWACS had pinpointed the source of the radar emissions. "Sir, the emissions seem to be coming from Chinese fighter aircraft based near Yenchi" the technician reported. "Do we know of what class the fighter aircraft are?" asked Nathan. "Yes sir. According to their radar signature they seem to be J-11's, the Chinese equivalent of the Soviet SU-27" the technician replied. Nathan explained to Steven that the J-11's were a *copy* of the SU-27 manufactured by the Chinese without license. "They are the basic airframe of the SU-27 minus the radar. The Chinese developed their own attack radar for the J-11, which was vastly inferior to the Soviets. It's on a par with the older F-4E models" Nathan explained. "However inferior I'd don't want a confrontation with them, Is that clear Commander?" Steven ordered. Nathan acknowledged. He didn't want to be here any longer than necessary. The senior technician advised Nathan that Admiral Grayson's aircraft was about to launch. Nathan acknowledged and watched the video monitor of the waist catapult. The C-2 Greyhound aircraft launched and gained altitude as the four-ship escort of F/A-18's followed. They would escort the Admiral all the way to Kyoto, Japan where the Admiral would get a hop to Hickam AFB and then home to Andrews AFB. Nathan wondered what he and Steven had discussed in his quarters earlier. "Did Admiral Grayson leave any additional orders, Admiral?" Nathan asked. "Actually, he did Commander. We will be discontinuing our AL-1A escort mission as of 1200 hrs today. The Air

Force has sent reinforcements and will be taking over that mission, Commander" Steven replied. "Other than that it is business as usual. Continue your combat air patrols over North Korea and report any unusual activity" Steven ordered. Steven left the CIC and returned to his quarters. He knew there wasn't much left to do. The only thing that was left to do had to be done by diplomats.

Jack Grayson arrived at Andrews AFB thirty-two hours after taking off from the *Reagan*. He was exhausted and only got about six hours of sleep. The E-4B waiting for him at Hickam AFB had the most comfortable quarters of any aircraft, including Air Force One. Once on the ground he went to the Pentagon to get an update from his staff and then on to the White House to brief the President. Wendell Cuomo, the Director of the CIA, was also at the Pentagon and had some interesting information that the President would find useful. Jack took the helicopter flight to the White House and entered. After saying hello to everyone he was greeted by Janice Lang and escorted to the Oval Office. "Admiral, President Jackson is on the phone with the Chinese President. I think something big is about to break" Janice said. "You look so tired Admiral is there something I can get you?" she added. "A pillow, maybe?" Jack said as he entered the Oval Office. The President acknowledged the Admiral's presence with a friendly wave and motioned for Janice and him to sit. Janice sat next to the Admiral and waited for the President to finish. "Thank you Mr. President, I appreciate your cooperation in this whole matter. I am extremely grateful that this business is coming to a close" President Jackson said. "That is correct Mr. President, the blockade around North Korea will be lifted as of Noon tomorrow, however only humanitarian shipments will be allowed to unload" the President added. The President looked at his

Chief of Staff and motioned for coffee but the Admiral declined. "No, Mr. President, the United States is not restricting shipments, that would be the United Nations. We are just there to enforce the sanctions. Our aircraft will continue to operate over North Korea and support the ROK and other agencies in the recovery effort" President Jackson replied. "Thank you again Mr. President, good day" President Jackson said as he hung up the phone. "Jack, good to have you back" the President said as he stood up and shook the Admiral's hand over the desk. The Admiral winced a little as he leaned forward to shake the President's hand. His back wasn't what it was before all this started nine days ago. "Well, I have some good news. I just talked with Dao Pac Ming and told me that the North Korean government has capitulated. I also talked with none other than Kim Lu Doc who was sitting right in front of him" President Jackson explained. "So the bastard made it," the Admiral said. "I was just briefed by Wendell Cuomo, your CIA Director, who told me that the North Korean President had three unsuccessful attempts on his life in the past two days. Even one of his General's tried to kill him for Christ sake" the Admiral reported. Janice Lang looked surprised as she made some notes on her pad "Well, he's safe, for right now anyway. But he doesn't have a country, he's in exile" the President said. The Admiral shifted his weight in the chair before addressing the President. "Mr. President, the F-22's are now conducting operations over North Korea and we have cut back the AL-1A's to those operating near the DMZ only. *Thor II* can handle any other threat and is at full power status" the Admiral reported. "Excellent. Then we're in good shape then?" the President asked. "Yes sir. The F-16 and F-15 replacements have arrived from stateside and our units in Japan are on stand-by alert. Also, the carrier *Abraham Lincoln* has relieved the *Ronald Reagan* Strike Group in the Sea of Japan this afternoon" the Admiral added. "Those men did a hell of a job, Admiral" the President said. "Yes sir, they did." the

Admiral added. "Janice, I told the Chinese President that the ROK and the UN will be taking control of the relief efforts. The US military will not set one boot on North Korean soil. Make sure *that* is reported to the press" the President said. "Mr. President, Director Cuomo also advised me that a North Korean scientist was taken into custody by his undercover agents. The individual wished to defect and could provide valuable information. He was found wandering around after the attack on the Yongbyon research center" Admiral Grayson explained. "Very well. Let's keep that quiet, but keep him happy and comfortable" the President ordered. "Mr. President, if you have nothing else I need to get some press releases out" Janice said "Oh sure Janice, go ahead" the President said as he stood up. Janice stood up to leave and Jack Grayson got up also. Janice left the Oval Office while Jack sat back down with a groan. "I need to sleep for a few days Ron" the Admiral said. "You certainly earned it Jack. Why don't you go home and rest? I'll get in touch with you if I need you" President Jackson said. "Thank you Mr. President. I believe I will do just that" Admiral Grayson replied getting up from his chair. Jack Grayson said good bye to the White House staff and then boarded the helicopter for Andrews AFB. The helicopter hadn't gotten halfway to Andrews when the Admiral slipped fast asleep in his plush chair.

Nathan sensed that the war must have been winding down. They hadn't anything to shoot at in two days. The patrols over North Korea produced nothing but boredom. Several mishaps almost took place and the Captain was livid. He promised every naval officer if they were involved in an incident and it was deemed their fault that they would never fly off the *Reagan* again. He told them so in a most colorful way. Nathan's duties consisted mainly of checking on the pilots and the status of the aircraft and their missions. Everybody was getting restless. They either wanted some action or they wanted to sail for home. Nathan also looked forward to sailing home and embracing his wife and kids again. Walking past one of the recreation rooms on the way to the bridge Nathan heard crewmembers exclaim loudly with jubilation. One of the young Lieutenant's from one of the "Super Hornet" squadron's was near the door saw Nathan. "Commander, did you hear? We're going home, the war is over. They just reported it on WNN!" he exclaimed as Nathan walked into the recreation room. "Attention on deck" someone yelled. The room fell silent as all the officers came to attention. Now Nathan had the floor. "Lieutenant, does WNN govern *where* this ship sails?" Nathan asked sarcastically. "No Commander, It does not" the Lieutenant reported, now regretting his outburst. "Lieutenant, *who* governs where this ship sails?" Nathan asked the Lieutenant. "Sir, the President of the United States and the National Command Authority govern where this ship sails" the Lieutenant replied while still at attention. "That is correct Lieutenant. When they and only they decide we will sail home you will informed by the Captain of the ship. Until then I suggest you all check the duty roster and get back to work. Dismissed. Not one crewman moved and it was not until Nathan detected the odor of a cigar that he realized why. Captain Bruce Winters was about two steps behind Nathan, obviously enjoying Nathan's speech. "You heard him, dismissed. Get your asses back to work!" the Captain bellowed chewing on his cigar. The recreation room cleared in seconds. "Quite the speech Commander" Captain Winters said. "The Admiral phoned and wants us in his quarters. Would you accompany me there?" the Captain asked. "Yes Sir" Nathan replied as he walked to Steven's quarters. The Marine Sergeant on duty outside the Admiral's quarters came to attention as he opened the door and let the Captain and Nathan in. "Come on in Captain, Commander. Have a seat" Steven said. "You probably both have heard the rumors already, so I'll make it brief. The Pentagon has just contacted me. The USS *Abraham Lincoln* Strike Group will relieve us on-station as of 1400 hours today. We are ordered back to North Island after a scheduled crew rest of forty-eight hours in Pearl" Steven said. "Thank Christ" the Captain said. "Amen to that" Nathan added. "I agree. Its been a demanding nine days. Captain, you may announce the orders to the crew at your discretion" Steven said. "Very well Admiral" the Captain replied. "Commander, you may cease over flights of North Korea at 1200 hours today and recover the E-2C's. Gentleman, we are going home" replied Steven.

During the next hour the men exchanged stories from their youth and about their careers. All three complimented each other on the job they did and the Captain requested that Commander Buckman be assigned to the *Reagan* permanently. The Captain excused himself after a while and went to the bridge. Nathan and Steven settled down into talk of career, home and family. "So do you think you would like this assignment again?" Steven asked Nathan. "It has been pretty rewarding, but I'd like to do more flying" Nathan replied. "You're a great fighter pilot, Nathan. I think you should pass that ability and knowledge on to our younger pilots" Steven said. "Do you mean an assignment with the Top Gun school?" Nathan asked. "If that's what you want Nathan, by all means, put in for it. You will definitely get your fill of flying" Steven replied. "Well, its something to think about" Nathan said. Its true Nathan would get his fill of flying and he would be home almost every night, sleeping next to his wife and seeing his kids in the morning. Nathan had been fortunate this deployment. He had been gone from home for only six weeks and it would be another three weeks or so before he got back to North Island. Most deployments in peacetime were four to six months. He had done them before but now the kids were getting older and he actually wanted to be home at night. "When we get to Pearl I'm going to get a hop and fly to San Diego where Amy is waiting for me" Steven replied. "Let's get together when you get back" Steven added. "Sounds like a plan. Chicken and Corn on the cob?" Nathan asked. "Sure, and you buy the beer Commander" Steven replied amused at Nathan's comment. "It will be good to see Jill. I haven't seen her and your kids in about three months. I'm sure Amy and Jill have a lot to catch up on" Steven said.

Nathan thought about Amy and Jill. They had become good friends even though Nathan had become involved with Amy's sister, Jennifer, years ago. Nathan thought about Jennifer from time to time and was glad that he was still considered a friend. Nathan and Jill had a rocky start to their relationship. After Nathan's initial carrier air wing pre-deployment training he got to spend some quality time with Jill. She flew to Pensacola and stayed in a beach house near the base. It was there that they re-committed themselves to each other and Nathan confessed that he thought that Jill wasn't interested in him anymore. Jill had gone through some hard times when Nathan left. She had become pregnant with Nathan's child soon after he left for Pensacola and lost it six weeks later. That was the real reason she couldn't make his graduation. Jill's friend was instrumental in her recovery and stayed with her many nights after Jill came home from the hospital. Nathan told her to never keep anything from him no matter what but she confessed she didn't want it to interfere with his training. Nathan held Jill during the whole night when she told him, though her tears, that she still wanted to have his children. The doctors told her that she would be fine and the miscarriage did not do any permanent damage. Nathan told her that night that he wanted no other woman to bear his children.

Steven Alexander was at the wedding as one of Nathan's bridegrooms and Amy filled in as a bridesmaid. Nathan's best man was Jimmy Aulicino who had gotten married the month before to Cindy Welsh. Jill and Nathan's wedding took place in San Diego in June of '93. Nathan had a lot of his friends attend from Lockheed-Martin and other agencies. Steven's Dad, Robert Alexander, then the Chairman of the Joint Chief of Staff, also attended the wedding. He very generously gave the couple a wedding gift of a week's vacation in Maui, all expenses paid. It was at the reception that Nathan got to talk to Steven's father and learned that the relationship between he and Robert Alexander had started even before Nathan graduated from college. Robert Alexander had heard of Nathan's work from a family friend that was a professor at University of Texas at Austin. At the time a Vice Admiral, Robert Alexander worked at the Defense Advanced Research Projects Agency (DARPA) and had Nathan investigated by the FBI before passing his name on to Lockheed-Martin as a potential engineer in the classified Airborne Laser Project. His ideas and the work he had already accomplished impressed the engineers at Lockheed-Martin and the company hired Nathan right out of college. Robert knew his son Steven would run into Nathan at Lockheed-Martin but didn't realize the two would develop such a close friendship. Unknown to Nathan at the time, his request for Officer Training School went right to the top and was approved by none other that Admiral Robert Alexander, the new Chairman of the Joint Chief of Staff.

Nathan looked up at Steven after making some notes. "Well, I hope that the world will be a safer place now" Nathan said. "I can't see why it wouldn't be Nathan. Even though we may develop weapons and defenses of awesome power it still falls to mankind to develop the wisdom to manage them responsibly" Steven replied. Nathan agreed with Steven. "Speaking of management I must check in at CIC. I still have a few missions flying" Nathan said. Nathan said good bye to Steven and left his quarters and headed for CIC. He checked in at CIC and ordered the rest of the days missions to stand down except for the inner perimeter air patrols. After everything was in order Nathan left and went to join the Captain on the bridge. The last F/A-18E "Super Hornet" from the mission over North Korea was in the landing pattern and Nathan watched the recovery with the Captain. "Seems like a lot brighter day, doesn't it Commander?" the Captain said. Nathan looked out over the flight deck to the Sea of Japan and beyond. "Yes, Captain. I do believe it is" Nathan replied. The Captain swivelled in his chair, looked at his watch and then spoke. "Come to new heading 180 degrees. Plot a course to Pearl Harbor and make revolutions for twenty-five knots" the Captain ordered. The commands were repeated by several other officers, along with the helmsman. The bridge crew went about the business of performing their tasks as before but Nathan noticed that each of the men had a smile on his face. Indeed, Nathan thought, it was beginning to be a brighter day.

GLOSSARY

AAA - Anti-Aircraft Artillery. Also referred to as "Triple A".

AEGIS - Advanced radar tracking and missile fire-control system found on modern U.S Navy cruisers and destroyers. Named for the shield of Zeus in Greek mythology.

AEW- Airborne Early Warning. General refers to the U.S. E-3 AWACS or the JMSDF Boeing 767. May also include other platforms such as E-2C Hawkeye and the IL-76 Mainstay.

Active Sonar - A type of Sonar that sends out high-frequency sound waves from an on-board array. The sound waves travel to the target and bounce back to the sensing unit. This type of Sonar is very accurate and gives the exact position of the target but also gives away the exact bearing of the detecting unit to the enemy. Active Sonar emits a very loud "pinging " noise in the water that can be heard by other units with Passive Sonar. The newest US Navy Active Sonars remedy this problem by focusing the sound waves in a tight cone, much like a flashlight beam, where the only vessel that can hear the Active Sonar is the intended target.

ADCAP - The U.S. Navy's premier torpedo, the Mark 48 ADCAP (Advanced Capability). The ADCAP has a speed of 60 knots and a range of 45 miles.

AGM-88 HARM - Second generation High speed Anti-Radiation Missile. A Mach 2 + missile, It is equipped with a 146-lb blast-fragmentation warhead and is fired at a distance of 35 to 60 miles depending on launch aircraft altitude.

AGM-65 Maverick - Family of air-to-surface missiles manufactured by Hughes-Raytheon. Made in several versions with different warhead and guidance systems. It is carried by U.S. Navy F/A-18's, P-3C and F-35 Joint Strike Fighters.

AGM-84 Harpoon/SLAM - Short range (60-180 nautical miles) U.S. Navy cruise missile. The basis for many follow-on designs.

AGM-154 JSOW - Joint Stand-Off Weapon. Utilizes a low-cost 1000-lb. Bomb fitted with INS/GPS guidance. It has a stand-off range of 25-30 miles depending on launch altitude.

AIM-9 Sidewinder - The standard U.S. Infra-red heat-seeking air-to-air missile. Latest version (AIM-9X) has an all-aspect tracking system with pilot being able to lock onto targets behind his own aircraft

AIM-120 AMRAAM - The premier U.S. air-to-air missile, the AIM-120 Advanced Medium Range Air to Air Missile. The AMRAAM Mod 3 has a speed of Mach 3.4 and has a range in excess of 80 miles.

AARGM "Quick Bolt" - Follow-on to the successful HARM, the Advanced Anti-Radiation Guided Missile has programmable microprocessors allowing it attack multiple targets in any weather. The AARGM also has a programmable in-flight loiter mode. Able to strike targets at over 2200 mph.

ASW - Anti-Submarine Warfare.

Baffles - The area directly astern of a surface ship or submarine in which passive sonar is ineffective. Passive sonar detection cannot be made because of the noise generated by the platform's own machinery and propulsion systems.

BMEWS- Ballistic Missile Early Warning System.

BSY-1 - A U.S. Navy advanced integrated sonar and fire-control system on Los Angeles class attack submarines.

BVR - Beyond Visual Range.

CAP - Combat Air Patrol

Cavitation - The formation of air bubbles on a rotating propellor as it increases its speed of rotation. Cavitation is source of very loud, undesirable noise for submarines.

CENTCOM - U.S. Central Command

CIA - Central Intelligence Agency

CINCPACFLT - Commander in Chief, Pacific Fleet

CIWS - Close-In Weapon System. Refers to many small caliber (20mm, 25mm and 30mm) defensive weapon systems located on board modern warships.

COB - Chief-Of-the-Boat. The Senior Non-Commissioned Officer on board U. S. Navy submarines.

COD - Carrier On-board Delivery mission. Usually refers to The C-2 Greyhound aircraft.

Convergence Zone (CZ) - an occurrence where sound waves are turned or "bounced" back to the surface or receiving platform. This happens roughly every thirty nautical miles. Multiple CZ contacts are possible if conditions are right.

CONUS - Continental United States.

CO - Commanding Officer. The person in charge of a ship, aircraft or group. May be addressed as "Captain" while their actual rank is another grade.

CSAR - Combat Search And Rescue. Made up of primarily rescue helicopters but may include other types aircraft to search and support the rescue in hostile territory.

DIA - Defense Intelligence Agency

DMZ - De-Militarized Zone.

ESM - Electronic Support Measures. Usually a passive radar warning receiver able to detect enemy radar emissions from aircraft and surface ships.

E-2C Hawkeye - The U.S. Navy's carrier borne AWACS platform. Also in use by many other countries.

ELF - Extremely Low Frequency radio band.

ET-80 - A Russian- manufactured 53 cm wire-guided active-passive homing torpedo.

EXCAP - a fictitious next generation follow-on of US Navy torpedoes. The Mark 70 EXCAP (Extreme Capability) is a heavy dual-speed, dual-capability, wire-guided torpedo that has a maximum speed of 98 knots and a range of fifty to seventy miles, depending on speed. The EXCAP is a 26.5 inch torpedo with a launch weight of 3500lbs. and is equipped with a warhead packed with 1800 lbs of PBXN-103 explosive.

F/A-18 "Hornet"- The premier U.S. Navy fighter aircraft. Designed to replace the A-7, F-4 and A-6 attack aircraft. Current versions are "E" and "F" models referred to as the "Super Hornet". New versions include the E/A-18 "Growler" designed to replace the aging EA-6B "Prowler" Electronic Warfare aircraft.

FLIR- Forward Looking Infra-Red

Floating Wire - Also called trailing wire. A receiving antennae that can be streamed underwater at shallow depths to receive message without the need for the submarine to surface.

GBU - Glide Bomb Unit. Special units fitted to general purpose bombs to make them more accurate.

GBU-29/30/31/32 JDAM - Family of "Smart" weapons developed for the entire arsenal of U.S Military Aircraft, the Joint Direct Attack Munition uses the more sophisticated GPS guidance units.

Geosynchronous - Also called "Geostationary", a satellite in this orbit, about 22,230 miles, will take a whole day (24 hours) to circle the earth. The earth travels at the same speed so the satellite appears to fixed or "locked" into the same point over the earth.

GPS - Global Positioning System

H-5 Harbin - Chinese variant of the Russian Il-28 "Beagle" attack aircraft
H-6 Xian - Chinese variant of the Russian TU-16 "Badger" bomber.
Hainan - Chinese fast attack craft. Displacement of 392 tons. Length 192 ft. Top speed 30 + knots. May carry YJ-1 missile, ASW rocket launchers and mines.

Han - A front-line Chinese-manufactured nuclear attack submarine
HEAT - High-Explosive Anti-Tank.
HEI - High Explosive-Incendiary.
HEAP - High-Explosive Armor-Piercing.
HY-2 - Chinese anti-ship cruise missile with a 165-kg warhead and a range of over fifty nautical miles.

ICBM - Inter-Continental Ballistic Missile

IRBM - Intermediate Range Ballistic Missile

J-7 - Chinese variant of the MiG-21 fighter/Interceptor.

Kuznetsov Class - Largest class of Russian aircraft carrier to-date. The two ships, Kuznetsov and Varyag, were completed before the break-up of the Soviet Union in 1991. Length: 918 feet. Beam: 121 feet. Displacement: 58,500 tons. Carries up to 30 aircraft internally or up to 54 aircraft in hanger deck and stored on flight deck. Additional armament includes 12 - SS-N-19 "Shipwreck" anti-ship missiles, 8 - SS-N-11 surface-to-air missile launchers, and 6 - 30 mm CIWS cannon mounts. Varyag sold to the Chinese as a "training" carrier to explore the use of carrier-based aviation.

Los Angeles Class (SSN 688) - The US Navy's premier attack submarine.

LRIP - Low Rate Initial Production. A phase in production of a new weapon system where the "bugs"are worked out of manufacturing techniques, tooling and documentation before shifting to Full Rate Production (FRP).

Luda I/II/III - Chinese destroyer built in several variants. With a length of 433 feet and a displacement of 3,670 tons, these destroyers are a serious threat to smaller combatants and submarines. Heavily armed with Guns, HY-2 anti-ship missiles, ASW rocket launchers, depth charges and mines. Type II carries two helicopters.

Luhu - New, advanced Chinese destroyer. With a length of 468 feet and a displacement of 4,200 tons, these destroyers are a serious threat to smaller combatants and submarines. Heavily armed with Guns, YJ-1 anti-ship missiles, ASW rocket launchers, depth charges and mines. Also carries two helicopters.

MAD - Magnetic Anomaly Detector

1MC - Shipboard announcing system on board U.S. Navy submarines.

Ming - Chinese diesel-electric attack submarine. Having a length of 249 feet and a displacement of 2,113 tons the Ming is classified as a coastal defense submarine. Has eight 53 cm torpedo tubes.

MiG - Russian acronym for Mikoyan-Gurevich Design Bureau. The MiG company designed some of the greatest designs in the world such as MiG-29 and MiG-31.

Mk-41 - Vertical missile launch system used on several U.S. Navy warships.

Mk-46 - U.S Navy lightweight ASW torpedo carried by helicopters, aircraft and surface ships. Exported to other U.S. friendly countries.

Mk-50 - U.S Navy advanced lightweight dual-purpose torpedo carried by helicopters, aircraft and surface ships. replaces and supplements the Mk-46 torpedo. Not presently exported.

Nautical Mile - equal to 6,079 ft. or 2,026 yards.

NBC - Nuclear, Biological and Chemical

Nimitz Class (CVN-68) - Standard US Navy aircraft carrier, continually updated and improved since the original design.

NKA - North Korean Army

Oliver Hazard Perry Class (FFG-7) - Low-cost, mass-produced guide missile frigate for the US Navy. Most ships have been regulated to training and patrol duties in home waters.

OOD - Officer of the Deck. Term for Officer in charge on the bridge of US Navy ships.

Patriot Missile- A long-range high-altitude surface-to-air missile (SAM) system capable of downing aircraft and ballistic missiles that are in the terminal stage.

P-3 Orion - A long-range US Navy Anti-Submarine Warfare aircraft. In service with many US friendly counties.

RC-135V Rivet Joint - Specially configured C-135 used for surveillance of ballistic missile tests.

ROE - Rules of Engagement. Determines how a unit or force may conduct operations to a known contact or opposing force.

RWR - Radar Warning Reciever.

Romeo - Soviet class of diesel-electric submarine built to 1950's design.

SAET-60 - An older class of Russian torpedo, still effective but susceptible to modern countermeasures

SAM - Surface-to-Air Missile. Describes any missile shot at aircraft from the ground.

SCUD - Older type of short-range Soviet ballistic missile built in the 1960's. Designed for a nuclear warhead and equipped with a rudimentary guidance system, it is considered outdated and inaccurate with conventional munitions.

SEAD - Suppression of Enemy Air Defenses.

SEAL - SEa, Air and Land. The U.S. Navy's Special Forces contingent.

Seawolf (SSN-21) Class - The US Navy's super stealthy attack submarine built in the late 90's. Larger than the Los Angeles class and outrageously expensive, only two examples have been built before production ceased. The Seawolf class carries more weapons than any other US Navy SSN.

SET-53 - Russian torpedo widely exported to other countries.

Seventh Fleet - A large U.S. Navy group based at Pearl Harbor, Hawaii, in the Pacific Ocean. The Seventh Fleet conducts naval operations in the Pacific Ocean and as far west as the Indian Ocean.

SH-60 Seahawk - The standard US Navy multi-purpose helicopter. Expanded into many variants.

SM-1/SM-2 - The U.S. Navy's Standard Missile for Air Defense. Subsequent versions are being developed for Anti-Ballistic Missile Defense.

Snapshot - A term in submarine language meaning to launch a torpedo down a bearing of a known threat.

Snorkel - A term coined in the first World War where German diesel-electric submarines would surface to periscope depth and raise a device known as a "Schnorkel". This would allow the diesel engines to take in air while the submarines were near the surface and in turn charged the batteries for the electric drive. Modern submarine manufacturers have developed an AIP or "Air Independent Propulsion" system to free diesel-electric submarines from having to surface as often.

SSK - A diesel-electric powered attack submarine. An affordable alternative to the nuclear powered submarine. Extremely quiet although considered very slow.

SSN - A nuclear powered attack submarine. Top-of-the-line in attack submarines, for those countries able to afford and maintain them.

SU-27 - Modern Russian tactical aircraft with many variants. Similar to US Navy's F/A-18E.

TB-16 - A standard U.S. Navy Nuclear Attack Submarine towed array.

TB-23 - First U.S Navy "thin line" array found on SSN.

TERCOM - TERrain-COntour Matching. A guidance system found on the Tomahawk Land Attack Cruise missiles.

Tomahawk - US family of cruise missiles designed and built in the late 1970's. The missiles have many variants depending on launch platform and mission requirements.

Top Gun - The US Navy's advanced fighter weapons school.

Type 18 - A multi-function search periscope found on US Navy SSN's.

V-22 Osprey - STOL / VTOL aircraft developed for US Marine Corp in late '90's.

VHF - Acronym for Very High Frequency radio band.

VLF - Acronym for Very Low Frequency radio band.

VLS - Acronym for Vertical Launch System which is installed on some US Navy submarines and surface warships.

Wild Weasel - A term coined during the Vietnam era when the US Military configured aircraft specifically to seek out and attack enemy SAM and AAA defenses. Known in the US Navy as "Suppression of Enemy Air Defense" or SEAD missions.

XO - Executive Officer. The Officer that is the second in command of a vessel.

Ying Ji (YJ-1 and YJ-2)- Chinese cruise missiles.

Z-9 Harbin - Ship-borne multi-role helicopter found on most Chinese warships.

BIBLIOGRAPHY

MAGAZINES

Aviation Week and Space Technology   McGraw Hill Publications
Air and Space Smithsonian   Smithsonian Institute
Combat Aircraft   Ian Allan Publishing
Proceedings   United States Naval Institute
U.S. News and World Report   U.S. News and World Report
World Airpower Journal   Aerospace Publishing Limited, Airtime
Publishing, Inc.

BOOKS

Clancy, Tom   Carrier - A guided tour of an Aircraft Carrier   A Berkley Book - 1999

Clancy, Tom   SSN - Strategies of Submarine Warfare   A Berkley Book - 1996

Clancy, Tom   Submarine - A guided tour inside a nuclear warship   Berkley Publishing Group   1993

Gunston, Bill   Spick, Mike   Modern Air Combat   Salamander Books, Ltd.   1983

Gunston, Bill   Spick, Mike   Modern Fighting Helicopters   Crescent Books   1986

Gunston, Bill   Modern Helicopters   Prentiss Hall Press   1990

Gunston, Bill   Rockets and Missiles   Crescent Books   1979

Hogg, Ian V.   The Illustrated Encyclopedia of Ammunition   Quarto Publishing Limited 1985

Hutchinson, Robert   Jane's Warship Recognition Guide   Harper Collins Publishers 2002

Hutchinson, Robert Jane's Tanks and Armored Fighting Vehicles Recognition Guide Harper Collins Publishers 2002

Hutchinson, Robert Jane's Aircraft Recognition Guide Harper Collins Publishers 2002

Kaufman, Yogi Stillwell, Paul Sharks of Steel Naval Institute Press 1993

Miller, David Miller, Chris Modern Naval Combat Crescent Books 1986

Miller, David Foss, Christopher F. Modern Land Combat Salamander Books, Ltd. 1987

Polmar, Norman The Naval Institute Guide to The Soviet Navy, Fifth Edition United States Naval Institute 1991

Richardson, Doug Modern Spyplanes Prentiss Hall Press 1990

Schwab, Capt. Ernest Louis (USN-Ret) Undersea Warriors - Submarines of the World Publications Int., Ltd 1991

GAMES

"Harpoon 97 Classic"   Interactive Magic 1996
"Jane's Naval Warfare Collection"   Sonalysts 1997

PAMPHLETS, HANDBOOKS

Department of Defense North Korea Handbook PC-2600-6421-94 1993

INTERNET SITES

Federation of American Scientist (FAS)
McDonnell Douglas
Lockheed-Martin
Jane's International
Central Intelligence Agency (CIA)

ABOUT THE AUTHOR

The author was born and grew up in a small town outside of Albany, N.Y. and developed a fascination with jet aircraft, naval warships and the military at an early age. After graduating high school the author embarked on a career in the U.S. Air Force conducting maintenance on all types of aircraft, while traveling throughout the United States. While working in different military commands and with government contractors during his career the author has gained a unique knowledge of modern aircraft and weapon systems. A firm supporter of the military, the author is also a member of the U.S. Naval Institute. He presently lives in South Florida.

Printed in the United States
71758LV00004B/86

9 781425 991531